ONE CHRISTMAS NIGHT

JULES BENNETT

MOST ELIGIBLE COWBOY

STACEY KENNEDY

MILLS & BOON

First Published in Great Britain 2022
by Mills & Boon, an imprint of HarperCollins*Publishers* Ltd
1 London Bridge Street, London, SE1 9GF

www.harpercollins.co.uk

HarperCollins*Publishers*
1st Floor, Watermarque Building,
Ringsend Road, Dublin 4, Ireland

Special thanks and acknowledgement are given to Jules Bennett for her contribution to the *Texas Cattleman's Club: Ranchers and Rivals* series.

ISBN: 978-0-263-30391-9

1122

ONE CHRISTMAS NIGHT

JULES BENNETT

Michael, I could dedicate all the books to you and that would still not be enough to express my love.
Yours Forever, Jules.

One

This could not be happening. Of all the slaps of reality, this one hit the hardest.

Morgan Grandin gripped the edge of her vanity top in the bathroom of her boutique, the Rancher's Daughter. Out of all the Grandin clan, she was the only one who never wanted to be part of that ranch life, so she'd paid homage by giving her boutique an appropriate name.

And if her family didn't like the fact she wasn't part of the family business, they certainly wouldn't like this next chapter of her life.

Morgan stared down at two blue lines. This was certainly not the way she'd planned on starting her Monday morning...or her own family. She'd always been the odd woman out as far as the Grandins went, but this would definitely make her even more of a standout.

From the moment she saw those two lines, she wanted this baby. But she had to look forward and formulate a plan that would suit her and her child's needs. What a mess she'd gotten herself into.

After washing her hands and drying them, Morgan glanced at herself in the gold-framed mirror. Well, she didn't look any different. Shouldn't she look…motherly?

She turned to the side, staring at her flat stomach. Both amazed and terrified, she imagined the little life growing inside of her.

How could she make this work being a business owner and a single mother? She wasn't married. She was also unlike her siblings, who had all found love and were living their own happily-ever-afters.

No, Morgan had opted for a drunken fling with the one man who drove her absolutely crazy—both in bed and out.

On a groan, she smoothed her red hair over her shoulder. All of this information couldn't be processed at once. She still had a store to maintain and customers to assist. This wasn't just some hobby she had, this store was her dream. She'd have to keep her little secret until she could get a grasp on her new reality.

For now, she couldn't even bring herself to tell her siblings…and she sure as hell couldn't tell Ryan Carter until she gathered her composure and her thoughts.

One night. They had one night and now their entire lives were changed. The dynamics within her own family would change, too. Everything would be different from this moment forward.

While her siblings were falling in love, Morgan opted for a one-night stand with her enemy.

Before that night, she couldn't even stand Ryan—how in the world could she raise a child with him? They'd never agree on anything from choosing the name to choosing a school.

How could they be so completely different, yet be so perfectly in sync in the bedroom? That night had been nothing short of magical and memorable. Every touch, every kiss, was all she had thought of for the past month.

Oh, they'd both agreed that night would never happen again and they weren't to speak of it. She'd been on board with that because who would believe she hooked up with Ryan Carter? The entire town had seen them either bickering or snubbing each other.

And while part of her regretted that night, the other part ached for round two. Ryan had been the most attentive lover and the only man to ever make her want to sneak around for more.

At this point, though, she had to be smart about any decision she made. She wasn't just thinking for herself anymore.

Morgan pulled in a deep breath and stepped from the bathroom of her boutique. She couldn't hide in here forever. Reality wouldn't change simply because she didn't want to face it. She took pride in her shop and that wouldn't stop or slow down now.

But who would run the place when she was off having a baby? Or if the baby got sick? She had a young college girl, Kylie, who worked here as she took online classes that one day would launch her career in fashion design. Morgan knew without a doubt that she could depend on her, but this store was everything to Morgan. While she could definitely afford to take time off, or even not work altogether, Morgan wanted to work. She loved being hands-on and socializing with the women of the town. She couldn't just unload this place onto someone else.

Morgan made her way to the front of her store and forced the worries to the back of her mind.

One day at a time. That was all she could do right now.

She flicked the lock on the double doors and propped them open, letting in much-needed sunshine. She inhaled the crisp winter air as she set her sidewalk sign out in front of her shop. The cool rush actually felt good on her heated skin. She hadn't realized just how worked up she'd gotten, but her nerves and emotions were all over the place.

Thankfully, though, she wasn't sick…yet. Good grief, when would that happen? So far, her cycle was off and she was emotional for no reason and she was only a month into this pregnancy.

Morgan turned and hit something hard. No, not something…someone.

Firm hands gripped her arms in an attempt to steady her and she reached out, encountering a very solid chest. She knew that chest. No amount of alcohol during their heated night could make her forget exploring such excellent muscle tone.

"You okay?"

Ryan's low voice caressed her, sending her nerve endings tingling. She could not, *would not*, be attracted to him. Their bickering had gone on for so long, that had to trump their one night of passion. The only time they seemed to get along was when their clothes came off and too much champagne was involved. Clearly neither of those things were happening again.

Vic always said how Ryan was a grumpy bastard who never said much, but he always had plenty to say when arguing with her.

"I'm fine. Just fine." Morgan stepped back and dropped her hands. "Everything's fine."

Shut up.

"Good to hear." Ryan smirked, his blue eyes shone bright with amusement. "You've been avoiding me."

"Have I?" she asked with a shrug. "Don't take it personal. I thought we agreed not to see each other again."

And if there was no pregnancy, she could hold tight to that promise. The sexual tension between them had bubbled for too long. What she'd always thought of as annoyance had clearly been attraction.

The night of the Halloween Masquerade Ball at the Texas Cattleman's Club and all the flowing champagne had been a powerful combination forcing them together—not to mention Morgan had overheard her brother discussing how Ryan was attracted to her.

The end result had been the most intense, memorable night of pleasure in her life.

But now she had to face the consequences. *They* would have to face the consequences. What label could they put on each other now? Enemies? That seemed a bit harsh, all things considering. As much as he deserved to know, now wasn't the time.

"Royal isn't that big of a town," Ryan told her, oblivious to her inner turmoil. "I always saw you around, but over the last month, you've been scarce."

She pointed toward the open doors of her shop. "I've been right here, so you weren't looking too hard."

Ryan's piercing stare sent a shiver through her. That stare had hit her so many times over the years. More often than not, she'd been irritated by those bright eyes beneath his Stetson, yet other instances she'd had a stirring of something she couldn't describe…or maybe she just didn't want to. She'd pushed aside any unwanted attraction because Ryan Carter could not be the man for her. The idea was simply absurd.

Yet she'd overheard her brother Vic and his best friend, Jayden, discussing Ryan at the party. In fact, they'd specifically mentioned Ryan's attraction to her, which had taken her off guard. He'd never shown her that attraction, unless his grumblings counted as flirting.

Morgan certainly wouldn't deny Ryan's sex appeal, but he drove her crazy. All of that arrogance and how he was so damn opinionated really grated on her nerves. They argued about everything from how they ordered their coffee to life on the ranch. She could almost guarantee whatever her viewpoint was, his would be the opposite.

But the man knew when to shut up and exactly what to do in the bedroom…which nearly overrode his negative qualities.

She never would have made a move if her brother hadn't planted that proverbial bug in her ear. She should never listen to gossip or eavesdrop. Look where that got her.

Ryan tipped his black hat and looped his thumbs through his belt loops. That was another thing about him. The man was consistently boring with his wardrobe. Jeans, black T-shirt, cowboy boots, hat. Simple and plain. No suits for this cowboy and he made no apologies that he didn't do fussy. He might own a twelve-thousand-acre ranch, but you'd never know by looking at him that he had so much wealth and power.

The yawn of silence agitated her, as did those piercing blue eyes.

"Why are you staring at me?" she asked. "Don't you have somewhere to be?"

"What if I came here to see you?"

A knot formed in her belly. "Did you?"

He shook his head. "I was actually meeting someone at the coffee shop, but had to park down the street."

Royal did have a bustling downtown area and she was lucky enough to have the Rancher's Daughter boutique right in the heart of it all. Of course, that also meant running into everyone whether she wanted to see them or not. And right now, she wasn't ready to deal with Ryan or her hormones.

Aside from the fact she now carried his child, Morgan hadn't mentally recovered from their night together. Every delicious moment seemed to be on repeat in her mind. Even when Ryan hadn't been with her, he'd never been far.

And now, she would be bound to him forever.

Ryan couldn't figure out why Morgan seemed so standoffish. She'd jerked away from him immediately when she'd seen who had caught her before she fell.

And now she would not look him in the eye. Interesting.

Maybe that spark between them hadn't diminished, even though they'd agreed on only the one night.

Had she thought of him since the Masquerade Ball? He hadn't seen her at the Texas Cattleman's Club since then and had started to wonder if he should text or call. He'd never been a clingy guy and never, ever begged for a woman's attention…but damn if he couldn't get that night out of his head.

Shouldn't he have gone back to being irritated at her by now? They were at odds every single day before their intimate encounter and he had no idea why he couldn't slide back into that mindset. He loved going toe-to-toe on any subject just to see how feisty her temper could get when he won the argument.

But he'd been exposed to a completely different side of Morgan and now he couldn't get that vulnerable, sexy woman out of his mind.

They'd not only agreed to the one night, afterward they'd both agreed it was a mistake. They weren't right for each other and neither of them was looking to get into a relationship. Life on his ranch was busy and that was where he devoted his time. It was the only commitment he wanted at this point in his life. Besides, one drunken night didn't lead to a permanent commitment.

Still, he wouldn't mind a little fling with the sexy shop owner, but she looked like she'd rather be anywhere else than chatting with him right now.

Was she having that much regret over what they did? Granted, the night hadn't been planned and a little too much champagne had been involved, but considering they'd been together a month ago and he still thought about it every single day…that was simply too much to ignore.

Yet, getting caught up in that short period of time would only prove to be a disaster. He had to get his head on straight and forget how perfectly they went together… because this was reality.

"I need to go back inside."

She pulled her green cardigan tighter around her body and scurried away, leaving Ryan more confused than ever. Morgan wasn't a shy or timid woman, she didn't play games, and she most certainly never ran away. What the hell was up? She hadn't argued with him or used that quick wit and sharp tongue like her typical go-to… which baffled the hell out of him. Who was this version of Morgan?

Ryan glanced inside the open doors and watched for a second as she took a few accessories from one display and put them on another. She seemed focused on work and going about her life, which is precisely what he should be doing instead of acting like great sex had changed his entire world.

Ryan checked his watch and pulled in a deep breath as

he started on down the sidewalk toward the coffee shop. He didn't have the time to devote to something that happened weeks ago and he needed to clear his head space and concentrate on his ranch. With everything going on in this town from the weddings to the babies to the secrets, Ryan would do well to remember that he could get wrapped up in any of those disasters if he wasn't careful. That was why he avoided town as often as he could.

While he wanted to ultimately have a family of his own to leave his legacy to, he certainly was in no hurry. When the right woman came along, he'd know.

So for now, he'd best keep his head down and his attention on the ranch. Nothing else mattered.

Two

Why were maternity clothes so insanely hideous? How could she incorporate a new line when she literally hated each article of clothing she'd been looking at? No woman gaining weight and losing her waistline wanted to wear the equivalent of a tent.

Morgan shut down her laptop, refusing to entertain anymore ugly clothes. She'd never carried maternity clothing in her store before, but with her wakeup call from earlier this morning, this should be an avenue to consider. Not to mention with half the town getting married and having children, branching out didn't seem like a bad idea.

Granted, she didn't need to take on more work to gain another demographic of customers. The Rancher's Daughter had already well surpassed last year's profit and the year wasn't over yet.

It would take some time to figure out what to bring in,

but perhaps she could launch her maternity section after the holidays. And, who knew, maybe later she could add an adorable baby line?

An image of little cowboy boots and gingham dresses popped into her head. Morgan glanced around the store and mentally reconfigured everything. Redecorating and looking forward to future sales and new customers was much easier than facing reality.

When she'd turned and plowed right into Ryan earlier, she'd panicked. She hadn't seen him since their night together and she'd had no idea what to say. Leading with "I'm pregnant" seemed harsh, though he would have to find out at some point.

What was the protocol for telling your one-night stand and sworn enemy that you were now bonded for life and he had eight months to get ready?

Morgan couldn't dodge him forever. Although Ryan likely assumed she was insane, the way she refused to look at him and practically ran back into the safety of her store. She'd just been caught off guard, that was all. She just needed a day or so to process everything, not to mention she should make a doctor's appointment to make sure that test wasn't a false positive. But she'd taken both in the box and had the same results.

And then there was that whole missed period thing.

Yeah. There was no denying what had happened and the sooner she faced those facts, the better. She honestly didn't know who to tell first. Her family? Would they be disappointed or shocked or both? They already had so much going on with her sister's upcoming nuptials and the whole scandal with Heath Thurston wreaking havoc on the Grandins and the Lattimores. That man had caused an absolute nightmare requesting the largest estates in all of Royal to be dug up while he searched for his supposed inherited oil.

Morgan hated that her sister would be marrying Heath's twin brother, but there was no way to prevent love…or so Morgan assumed. She'd never been in love, and right now, finding love was the least of her worries.

She had to talk to Ryan privately, and out on the sidewalk in the middle of town hadn't been the place. Should she call or just go straight to see him? How would he respond to this life-altering news? Maybe he didn't want to be a father. What if he decided he wanted nothing to do with their child? How could she handle being a single mother?

All of these unknowns would surely drive her mad if she didn't get some control over her thoughts. She needed a plan. That was how she had such a successful business—she planned every last detail. Carrying that over into her now unsteady life would surely help matters…she hoped.

There were many people in her life she trusted and could confide in, but they were each so busy with their own lives, did they have the time to listen to her crisis? Her brother Vic would do anything for her, but she really would rather have a woman's perspective right now.

Of course Zanai would lend an ear and no doubt offer sound advice, but her best friend had just fallen in love, as well. Her world right now was perfect and Morgan didn't want to put a kink in that.

Morgan brought the new gold cocktail dresses from the back to put in the front window. Kylie had taken the day off, which was just as well. Morgan needed to stay busy and keep her mind on something else so she didn't have a total breakdown. Morgan planned on taking a couple days off this week, which would be perfect for her to mentally decompress and figure out her next steps.

She adjusted the shoulder on the mannequin just as the front door chimed. With a smile on her face, she turned to greet her customer, but spotted a welcome and familiar face.

"Hey, babe."

Her sister Chelsea came bouncing in with a wide grin. Of course the woman was overjoyed with life. She was marrying her true love, Nolan, in just a few weeks. A Christmas wedding was nothing short of fairy-tale material and Morgan couldn't be happier for her.

She really didn't want to ruin Chelsea's plans or their big day with a surprise pregnancy announcement. Maybe after Chelsea returned from her honeymoon would be better timing.

Morgan was just glad their family had come together over the past month after Vic decided to share the ranch. Now the siblings were one unit again instead of divided.

"What's up?" Morgan asked, stepping down from the window display. "Are you visiting or shopping?"

Chelsea immediately pointed to the new dress in the window and gasped. "You didn't tell me this was coming in. Gold will be fantastic for my rehearsal dinner."

Morgan moved to the rack of new arrivals and located her sister's size.

"Go try it on." She held the garment out to Chelsea. "I'll get your picture and put it up on my social media. You'll make the perfect model."

Chelsea rolled her eyes. "I don't know about that, and my hair is a mess."

"You're gorgeous all the time, now go." Morgan shooed her sister away. "I'll bring you this adorable strappy heel that also just arrived and you can complete the look."

Morgan went to the back and unboxed the new shoes, grabbing her sister's size. Just for fun, she also decided to get some accessories. If Morgan suggested anything to Chelsea, her sister would buy it. Might as well start padding that baby fund.

"I have everything ready for you," Morgan stated through the dressing room door.

"I actually stopped in to see if the things you ordered for my honeymoon had come in yet," her sister called back.

Oh, right. Morgan had every intention of looking that up…but her morning had taken a drastic turn.

"I'll get on that while you change."

Morgan maneuvered her way around the fat, circular ottoman and adjusted the folded plaid throws she had on display for the new home accent line she'd started carrying. Her cell vibrated in the pocket of her cardigan as she reached the counter. The moment she pulled out her phone, she recognized the number of a frequent customer and town busybody.

"Good afternoon, Sylvia."

"Oh, Morgan. Darling, I need to find the perfect dress for a Christmas party and I'm afraid I waited too long. Please tell me you have something in my size that will wow everyone and nobody else will be wearing."

Morgan tried to make every customer feel beautiful and special whether she was looking for a casual, stay-at-home outfit or a blingy, sparkly dress for a high-society event. She often ordered one dress so there were unique styles and no clones in this small town. If Morgan didn't have what a customer requested, she'd find a way to get it.

"I'm sure I can gather some things for you," Morgan promised. "Would you like to stop in and try on, or did you want an appointment after hours? Kylie will be taking appointments on Thursday for some one-on-one shopping."

In her midsixties, Sylvia Stewart always chose personal shopping, wanting to feel even more special, like she was the only customer. She also loved the chance to catch up on all the gossip she missed while traveling since retiring as Augustus Lattimore's secretary. Right now, Morgan really hoped Sylvia would choose her usual, because Kylie was an absolute pro at dealing with overdramatic shoppers.

"Why don't you pull them and send me some pictures," Sylvia suggested. "I'll let you know if I want to try one on or have you look for something to order."

Relieved, Morgan disconnected the call and immediately went to pull some dresses.

"What do you think?"

Morgan turned to see her sister standing at the opening of the dressing room. Chelsea stared down at the wrap style and adjusted her top.

"Do I look okay?" she asked. "I love it, but I always think things look better on other people than me."

Morgan rolled her eyes. "Oh, stop. You're stunning. I just need to know if you're thinking of getting it, because Sylvia called and needs me to put together some things for her."

Chelsea narrowed her eyes. "Don't you dare sell me the same dress you sell that woman."

"That's why I'm asking."

Morgan laughed as she took a few options behind the counter and hung them in the closet area for her VIP customers.

"Did you get a chance to check on my order?" Chelsea asked as she put on the earrings Morgan had left for her to try.

"I'm doing that now." Morgan went to her laptop as Chelsea came up beside her. "I got a shipping confirmation for the clothes, but the shoes were on an entirely different order. Let's see where things are."

But the moment the screen came to life, Morgan's breath caught in her throat at the same time Chelsea gasped.

"Maternity clothes?" Chelsea asked. "You're going to carry maternity now? You've never mentioned that before. How exciting and great for the town with all the marriages and babies popping up!"

Morgan chewed the inside of her cheek, thinking of a proper way to respond. She couldn't to lie to her sister, but at the same time Morgan still had to process everything and she hadn't even talked to Ryan yet.

"Just thinking for now," Morgan replied honestly.

She quickly closed out of that tab, but the next one betrayed her.

"'What to expect in the first trimester'?" Chelsea read aloud.

Her attention immediately went from the screen to Morgan, and now Morgan had no way of hiding the truth.

"Are you pregnant?" her sister whispered.

"I just found out this morning," Morgan confessed. Some of that heavy weight instantly lifted from her shoulders. "Nobody knows, so please don't say anything."

Her sister's eyes widened. "Did you plan this?"

Morgan jerked back. "Planned? No, of course not! I'm just as shocked as you are. Well, probably more so."

Chelsea continued to stare for another moment and rubbed her forehead. "Can I ask who the father is? Do you know?"

Morgan sighed. "Of course I know, Chels. I don't just sleep around."

"I didn't mean that the way it sounded."

"How else could it sound?" Morgan fired back.

Chelsea reached for Morgan's hand and squeezed. "I'm sorry. I'm caught so off guard, I don't even know what to ask."

"I'm well aware of who the father is, considering I've had no social life for months and, bam, one time and here we are." Morgan pulled in a shaky breath and tried to not freak out, because speaking about all of this aloud made the entire situation sink in. "I haven't told him yet. You're the only person who knows."

Chelsea tipped her head. "It's Ryan, isn't it?"

"What makes you say that?"

"Are you kidding? The whole town saw the way you two were kissing at the masquerade party at the clubhouse before you snuck out. When two people are typically arguing and at odds, then they do a complete one-eighty, it draws attention." Chelsea shrugged and quirked a perfectly arched brow. "I'm just doing the math and coming up with the fact that was a month ago."

Wonderful. The moment people discovered she was pregnant, they'd immediately know also. That party had been amazing. Morgan had loved her mask she had special ordered with all the beading, feathers and bling. Every member of the TCC had been in attendance, but her friend Zanai really stole the show with her special makeover before the event. She'd always been a beautiful woman, but just needed a boost of confidence. The Masquerade Ball had been the perfect opportunity for Zanai to show her true self, which gave her the edge she needed to win the heart of Jayden Lattimore.

The night had been absolutely magical with the dancing and laughter…and Ryan.

She couldn't ignore the fact she still thought about him, about what they'd shared. But an intimate fling wasn't exactly the solid base needed for parenting skills… and that didn't even factor in all of the fiery arguments they'd had in the past.

"When are you going to tell him?" Chelsea went on, obviously drawing her own conclusion without Morgan confirming.

She shifted back to the laptop and closed out the telling tab. As she worked on finding the whereabouts of her sister's order, Morgan shook her head.

"I honestly don't know," she admitted. "We're not in a relationship, so I don't want him to think I'm expecting something from him. I mean, I can clearly financially handle a child."

"I've no doubt, but Ryan is going to want to be in the baby's life."

Morgan opened her mouth, but before she could say anything else, the door on the shop chimed as another customer came through.

"Not a word to anybody," Morgan murmured. "I'll keep you posted, but for now it's just us. Not even Layla. Got it?"

Morgan wanted to tell her other sister, Vic, her parents and grandma in person. She just needed the time to process everything herself before she took it to the entire family.

Chelsea nodded. "I'll take this dress with the shoes and accessories you picked out for me."

As she slipped back to the dressing room, Morgan went to assist her customer and wondered just how long this secret would remain so hush-hush.

Three

The sign in the window said Closed, but she was still in there. Ryan had seen her sporty little car parked in the usual spot.

Morgan's behavior this morning had plagued him the entire day. He'd been riding the fence lines and trying to focus on what his ranch foreman had been saying, but all Ryan could think about was how the Morgan from this morning was quite different from the Morgan he'd always known.

Sex wouldn't have made her so agitated and leery. The last time he'd seen her, they'd agreed they wouldn't mention having sex ever again, but did that mean they were never speaking at all? He'd almost rather go back to their verbal sparring matches than to have silence. He wasn't a chatty guy unless he was arguing with Morgan. He realized now that every single time they'd quarreled, she'd been damn sexy.

Who knew anger could be so arousing? Maybe the line between irritation and passion was narrower than he'd ever thought.

Ryan never backed down from a challenge and he demanded honesty from those around him. He'd learned early on in life that people treated you the way you allowed them to.

He wouldn't let Morgan hide whatever it was that bothered her. If she just didn't want to talk, fine, but he had a sinking feeling there was something else going on.

Had he done something? He thought they'd both had a pleasurable night and were in agreement when they parted ways, but now...

Their one-night stand came on the coattails of years of frustrations and arguments. He had no clue what the next steps should be, but he needed to figure that out in the next few seconds.

Ryan spotted Morgan through the double glass doors and tapped his knuckles on the frame. When she spun around and caught his gaze, she simply stared for a moment. Time seemed to stop and he wondered if she was going to ignore him or let him in. He waited maybe only a few seconds, but it seemed much longer as those striking blue eyes stared back.

Damn. He could get lost in those baby blues, but he'd vowed long ago to never lose himself in a woman again.

After being jilted and finding time to heal properly, he knew this version was stronger than ever before. No matter the relationship, whether friendship or intimacy, he demanded honesty and he had to remain in control. That was the only way he could keep his heart guarded.

Sure, Ryan could have texted Morgan, but he wanted her to look him in the eye because she'd refused earlier. He wanted to read her body language and if he had done something, then he would apologize in person to show respect.

And, fine. He wanted to see her. So what? Maybe he needed to see if they would revert back to arguing or if something else had sparked between them.

Morgan was a striking, intriguing woman he couldn't get out of his damn mind. For the past month he'd replayed that night over and over.

Vic and Jayden had put that stupid thought in his head about Morgan being attracted to him at the Masquerade Ball. Maybe she had been, but if she still was, she was clearly confused and reacting completely out of character. He had to see for himself now that no alcohol was involved and time had lapsed.

Finally, Morgan made her way toward him and flicked the lock. She eased the door open as she narrowed her eyes. Ah, yes. There she was. That spitfire he found way too damn appealing.

"We're closed."

"Clearly. We need to talk."

Her eyes widened a fraction. Was that fear? Hesitation?

Something was definitely up with her and he wasn't leaving until he figured out what happened to make such a bold, strong woman react so out of character.

"I was just getting ready to leave."

Again, she wouldn't meet his gaze up close. Ryan certainly didn't want to make her uncomfortable, but he did want to know if he'd offended her or hurt her in some way. Morgan never backed down from anything, especially an opportunity to tell him exactly what was on her mind.

Ryan slid his finger beneath her chin and tipped her head up so she had nowhere else to look. Her sharp intake of breath didn't stem from fear...no, that was desire looking back at him.

There was his answer. He didn't know why that revelation made him so happy.

"Are you letting me in or are we going to talk like this for the town to see?" he asked.

Her eyes darted over his shoulder, then back to him. She took a step back and eased the door wider, gesturing him inside.

Ryan glanced around at the stylish decor that combined modern metals with rustic Southern charm. There seemed to be so much inventory, yet everything had a neat, orderly vibe.

He turned to face her as she locked the door once again.

"I've never actually been in here," he admitted. "You've got an impressive place. No wonder it's so successful."

Morgan remained by the door and nodded. "Thank you. I never really wanted to be part of the ranch and this was always a dream of mine, much to my family's dismay."

"They have to be proud of your accomplishments."

"I suppose they are now that they see this isn't a hobby and I work as hard as they do. I just prefer people and fashion to cattle and spurs."

Ryan waited for her to move or speak or anything to break this tension that seemed to surround them. Being alone with her, having her so close physically but so far mentally, confused him. She was the sexiest woman he'd ever seen and there was no way to deny the pull that still tugged at him. Even after an entire month with no contact, he was just as mesmerized and turned on as ever.

"Do you want to tell me what has you so spooked?" he finally asked, breaking the ice.

"Spooked?"

Ryan shrugged and hooked his thumbs through his belt loops as he widened his stance. He figured he wasn't going anywhere for a while. They would either argue or tear each other's clothes off…he just had to wait and see which one.

"Something about me or what happened between us has you afraid," he clarified. "Did I do something or offend you in any way? Other than our usual bickering, that is."

"Offend me? No, of course not. You might annoy the hell out of me, but you'd never purposely hurt me."

Relief hit him and he realized he'd been holding his breath. He never wanted to hurt or disrespect any woman…despite what he'd been through in his past.

Morgan demanded respect and that was what she deserved.

"I know we said that night shouldn't have happened," he started. "But it did and ignoring it seems to be making things more awkward. I can't even get you to bicker with me anymore. I miss winning every argument."

Morgan didn't even crack a smile at his lame joke. Instead, she chewed on her bottom lip as her eyes darted down to her boots. He couldn't help but notice that instant difference between them. His well-worn boots likely had dirt on the bottoms from the ranch and were definitely not a fashion statement. Her boots looked like she'd just taken them off the display and paired them with her knee-length dress.

Everything about her screamed polish and poise. She lived her life making beautiful things happen while he… well, he kept the ranch running with worn jeans that were twenty years old. He really didn't care about buying new things when the old worked perfectly fine.

"We can't go back and erase what happened." She shifted her attention from the floor to him as she took a step forward. "We just drank too much alcohol."

"I knew exactly what I was doing."

He never let his mind get that clouded from anything. He'd gotten through some of the most difficult times in his life by remaining in control. He wouldn't have such a successful ranch if he let his emotions get the best of him.

"Having a few drinks isn't what made me sleep with you," he added. "I wanted you. Plain and simple."

Her eyes widened, and her mouth dropped to a perfect O. He couldn't tear his eyes away from those lips, painted a pale pink today. He also liked when they were red and he'd kissed the hell out of them. Maybe smearing her lipstick should become a new hobby in lieu of fighting with her.

Just the thought of all the things they'd done had him wondering why they'd agreed it shouldn't happen again? The way she looked at him, the way she'd responded to his touch...

"I'm pregnant."

Ryan jerked at the bomb she'd set off right between them. He must have misunderstood or something, but there was no way...

One look at her face and he knew this was no joke. He was going to be a father.

Okay, so she hadn't meant to blurt that news out there like that, but she hated secrets and she couldn't keep the baby from him any longer. Now that her sister knew, Morgan only felt it right to tell Ryan. She had planned on calling him and setting up some time to meet tomorrow, but when he'd tapped on her door moments ago, she knew the time had come.

And he'd only stopped by to clear the air. He probably regretted that now.

"Pregnant?" he asked.

Morgan nodded. "I only found out this morning, so I'm still in shock myself."

"But we were careful."

"I thought we were, too. I wanted to tell you, but I didn't know how or when. I guess there's no perfect time or place to change someone's life, but you need to know that I don't expect you to provide for me or the baby. Of course that's your right, but I am successful with a family that will support me and—"

"We'll get married."

Morgan froze and stared at Ryan as he removed his black Stetson and raked his hand through his hair. He tapped the brim of the hat against his thigh as he held her gaze, clearly waiting for her reply.

"I'm sorry," she snorted. "Was that a proposal?"

"It was a statement."

Anger bubbled within her, and Morgan crossed her arms over her chest and attempted to remain calm.

"First of all, your delivery needs a ton of work. Second, there's no way in hell I'm marrying you just because I'm pregnant. That's the most ridiculous thing I've ever heard."

Ryan's lips thinned. "It's not ridiculous. I always planned on having a family with children I could pass the ranch to in the future. And despite what you might think, I won't be part of my child's life just whenever I feel like it. I will be hands-on and that includes being supportive of you, too."

"I can take care of myself," she insisted. Wasn't he listening?

"I'm aware that you can, but you don't have to and you *shouldn't* have to." He held up his hand just as she opened her mouth. "And I'm not only talking financial. This will be emotional, as well. We're going to have to work as a team from here on out despite what either of us wants."

He set his hat back on top his head and continued to stare at her as if waiting for her to say something about that preposterous proposal. Over her dead body would she marry a man simply because they slept together and she carried his baby. That was not only archaic, that was a recipe for disaster. Why would she settle for a loveless marriage that would likely end up in divorce?

"I will be perfectly fine," she reiterated. "I'm glad to hear you want to be part of our baby's life, but that doesn't mean you need to be a permanent fixture in mine."

Ryan took a step, then another, until he closed the distance between them. In an instant, his familiar, masculine scent enveloped her and those blue eyes captivated her. She couldn't move, couldn't think.

"Maybe I want you with me," he murmured. "Maybe I want to protect you. Maybe I want to make sure you're safe, that our baby is safe."

He reached out and trailed a fingertip along her jawline, causing a whole host of shivers to race through her. Damn her hormones for betraying her.

"Are you going to tell me that you'd rather ignore the chemistry between us and skip to coparenting and maybe friends?" His thumb grazed her bottom lip. "Can you be just my friend after what we shared?"

That heated night full of passion and fulfilled fantasies had been well beyond friendly. Was it any wonder she kept scrolling through those memories? She had to keep reliving it because it had seemed like a dream. No intimacy had ever been that intense, that…memorable.

And now he was tempting her with more nights.

But marriage? She wasn't about to fall into that trap. They'd barely gotten along in the past—why did he think living together and playing house would solve things?

Her sister Layla recently married Josh, and her other siblings would be heading down the aisle soon, Chelsea to marry Nolan and Vic to marry Aubrey.

Morgan was clearly the only one being logical. Love and happily-ever-after seemed fine in theory, but in reality, did that even exist anymore?

Just look at her uncle Daniel, who'd had a fling for a few months with a young woman named Cynthia. He never knew she had been pregnant with his daughter when he headed back to Paris. When baby Ashley was three, Cynthia married Ladd Thurston and later had twins Heath and Nolan. No one ever said a word about Cynthia and Ashley's past. The web of lies and deceit was woven so tightly in this town, Morgan had to watch every single step she made so she didn't get tangled up in it.

Yet here she stood, fighting every emotion she had against temptation with her own secret pregnancy.

"I'm sure there's a space between friends and lovers we can settle into," she explained, trying to ignore the tingling from his touch. "We'll be parenting together, that's all. I'm not wearing your ring or taking your name."

Ryan dropped his hand, but remained right in her personal space. Damn that man and his potency. Why did she have to be attracted to him physically? If she wasn't pregnant, maybe they could revisit that evening.

But she was pregnant, and the fun times and careless ways were over. Now they had to focus and do what was best for the child, and that sure as hell didn't include a wedding. Maybe they needed to get back to arguing. At least she could ensure her clothes would stay on.

"I don't have to buy you a ring, and feel free keep your name if you want."

He stared at her like he'd just come up with the most logical solution. Morgan took in a deep breath once again and attempted to make sense of how her day had been a total roller-coaster ride from the moment she awoke.

Morgan shook her head and moved toward her check-out counter. She needed a barrier between them to gather her thoughts and get a grasp on common sense.

"I'm not marrying you," she repeated as she shut down her laptop and tidied up her space. "And if you were not being so territorial, you'd see this is a bad idea."

She moved her favorite gold pen, lining it up with the computer. Then she shifted it to the top, then the other side. Finally, she plopped it into her glass holder with the others.

"Are you going to keep fidgeting with that pen instead of looking at me?" he asked.

Morgan sighed and glanced up. She hadn't heard him move, but once again he stood so close. Too close. Close enough to touch, to kiss.

She seriously needed to get ahold of her hormones because she couldn't be selfish and take what she wanted. Having a physical relationship with Ryan at this point would only be confusing and likely make him think she wanted that marriage.

"I don't need to look at you," she countered. "I've already given you my answer. I'm not getting married, now or ever."

Ryan's blond brows rose and his tanned forehead wrinkled as he had the audacity to smirk. "Is that right? You're the only one from your family not married or engaged."

"And? What's that supposed to mean? Just because that's what they want to do doesn't mean that's what I want to do." Morgan crossed her arms over her chest and tipped her chin up. "They also all want to live the farm life and that's also not for me, which is another reason we aren't getting married."

"I wouldn't ask you to run my ranch," he scoffed. "I'm asking you to move in, marry me, and build the next generation of Carters. I have no motives to steal you away from the life you've created for yourself here. I'm not asking you to grab your leather gloves and rope cattle. I'm asking you to join me in a legacy I've created and can pass to our child."

Good grief, this man was totally serious. The only thing that gave her pause was that he was hot, he rocked her world, and he was stable in his life. But that didn't mean she wanted to share that life with him. Ryan wasn't a bad catch…if she wanted to catch someone. He would make a great husband, just not her.

She had to get him to the point where he understood or at least thought she denied the request for his own good.

"Listen," she began again. "We're not getting married just because I'm pregnant. One day you might actually fall in love and want to spend forever with that person. I don't want to be the one to hold you back."

"When I have a family, we will all live on my ranch and be one unit."

Apparently they were at a stalemate because there was

no way in hell she was budging. She refused to marry, but even worse, to settle for a marriage out of some archaic obligation. They would be surrounded by resentment, and that was no way to raise a child.

"You think about it," Ryan added. "I don't need the answer right now."

"Are you listening to me? I gave you my answer."

He leaned in. His chest bumped hers as his mouth hovered a breath away from her own.

"You heard me as well, so here we are," he murmured. "Two people who are stubborn."

Another reason they couldn't marry. They couldn't stop arguing.

"I always get what I want," she volleyed back, more than ready to stand her ground.

In an instant, Ryan's arm snaked around her waist and pulled her body flush with his. Before she could even gasp, his mouth covered hers and that fire he'd ignited a month ago fanned to life once again. Morgan gripped his shoulders and couldn't help the way her body responded. No matter what her head said about common sense, she couldn't help the physical pull that swept aside all rational thoughts.

With his lips on hers and that strong hold, not to mention the hard planes of his body, Morgan was having a difficult time remembering why she'd turned down that oh-so-romantic proposal.

Ryan shifted, easing back just enough to brush his lips along hers. His hand settled over her stomach as he murmured, "Think about that marriage for our baby."

His abrupt release had her grabbing for the counter to steady herself. She watched as he walked toward the door, flicked the lock, and stepped outside—leaving her confused and sexually frustrated.

If he thought one heated kiss would sway her, he would have to try harder than that. Morgan refused to let her emotions guide her choices…that was how she got into this mess to begin with.

Four

Maybe he'd been too harsh, too demanding.

Ryan gripped his steering wheel as he headed back toward Yellow Rose Ranch. His plans today had been coffee with a contractor to discuss some remodeling of his guest house, riding the fence lines to check for weak or worn areas, then talking with his ranch foreman about moving a herd to another pasture. He got two of the three done.

Running into Morgan earlier had put a spin on the end of his day. Now he knew why she'd been so cryptic. While he did meet with the contractor and ride the fence line, he sure as hell didn't have the mental capacity or the energy to discuss moving cattle.

Tomorrow he'd have to go back to the contractor and discuss renovating some of his main house, as well. Adding in a nursery close to the main bedroom would have to take priority over renovating the guest cottage.

A baby. He was going to have a baby. Well, Morgan was having a baby. *Their* baby.

The idea that he had a chance now at the family he'd always wanted thrilled him. He was going to have a legacy, someone to pass all of his land and his estate down to, and a new generation of Carters.

He'd almost had that lifestyle once, but it had all been ripped from his hands. He'd thought himself in love, but he'd been young and naive with stars in his eyes. He was older now, wiser, and he sure as hell didn't believe in love. What did that have to do with marriage?

With Morgan so adamant against marriage, he had to think she didn't believe in love, either. Her mind worked similar to his in the manner of business. They were more alike in that way than he'd ever thought before, so now he had a leg up. He would have to use that angle to his advantage to get her to see his way.

Of course, using her attraction wouldn't hurt, either. She'd been damn near ready to climb up his body back at her boutique. Just thinking of how hot she made him had Ryan really wishing she'd just agreed to his proposal and come back to the ranch. What did she have to think about? She hadn't given his proposal any consideration before she threw out her automatic rejection.

Why wouldn't she want to marry him? He took offense to that, actually. Because she was Vic's sister, they'd known each other for several years. They were damn good together in bed and they were going to have a child together. Many marriages were built on much less.

Maybe she hadn't wanted a shotgun wedding and perhaps his delivery could have used a little finesse, but in his defense, he'd been caught off guard. A pregnancy was definitely not something he'd been expecting. Ryan merely thought she'd been acting cagey because she hadn't seen him since their night together. He thought she felt awkward, but apparently she'd known that morning and had been afraid to say anything.

He honestly had no idea how Morgan was handling the news. He hadn't asked and he also hadn't asked her how she was feeling. He'd gone straight into selfish mode because he'd instantly panicked and flashed back to seven years ago when his fiancée left him standing like a fool.

He'd vowed then to put himself and his ranch above anything and anyone else.

But that time period didn't give him the excuse or green light to be an ass. Morgan deserved better and he'd never win her over by being a bully. He had to rethink and regroup.

He'd won arguments with her before and all he'd had to do was think like her. She wanted to have the control, so all he had to do was make her believe she held the reins and he'd win once again. Because this would be their most important argument to date.

Ryan's cell chimed just as he pulled into his drive. He paused in front of the automatic gate beneath the arch that had the ranch logo and name on display.

He saw Jayden's name and tapped his screen. Ryan put the call on the speaker as the gate slowly slid open to give him access.

"Hey."

"Bad time?"

"No," Ryan replied.

"I just called to vent. You sure you're not busy?"

"Let me guess. Heath Thurston?"

"Damn straight," Jayden confirmed.

Ryan's best friend had always been a go-with-the-flow type of guy and never let anything rattle him. But this nonsense about Heath's claim of oil beneath the Lattimore and Grandin ranches had turned the entire town of Royal upside down and had everyone questioning everything they'd known.

Was it any wonder Jayden Lattimore was so upset? The idea of someone digging beneath a ranch that had sat for decades untouched wouldn't sit well with anyone.

"I'm just damn thankful the surveyor didn't find any oil beneath the estates," Jayden stated. "But Heath is still a pain in my ass."

Ryan pulled up next to the stables instead of going on back to the barn. He needed to unwind and a nice, long ride might do the trick.

"Heath was looking for what he thought was a serious payout with oil," Jayden went on. "Who knows what he'll do now that he is losing ground with his claims."

"He really needs to end this," Ryan grunted.

"Agreed. Nolan says Heath's heart is in the right place, but I don't see how. I'll never understand how those two can be twins and be polar opposites."

According to Jayden and Vic, Cynthia, the mother of Nolan and Heath, had oil rights deeded to her by the Grandins and Lattimores. Supposedly the oil sat beneath the two largest ranches in Royal—owned by the wealthiest families. Upon her death, the deed would have gone to her daughter Ashley, if she'd lived. Now it was with the Thurston boys, and Heath had been hell-bent on staking his claim since he'd found the papers in his mother's effects.

All that did was cause an uproar for the past several months. Having the Lattimores and the Grandins as enemies wasn't the smartest move, but Heath didn't seem to mind. Clearly he had his eyes on the prize—the oil.

Ryan killed his engine and rested his arm on his console. "How are things going with Zanai?"

"She's the best thing that's ever happened to me."

A stirring of something akin to jealousy coursed through him. Where the hell had that come from? Jayden and Zanai were in love. That wasn't an area Ryan ever wanted to venture into again. To open up and be exposed to such vulnerability seemed like a nightmare. Ryan was happy for his friend, though, and wouldn't say anything to degrade what he'd found.

"So, how is *your* love life?" Jayden asked. "Anything to report?"

No way would he be getting into this, especially now that Morgan carried his child.

And that was just another area he and Morgan need to discuss. When and how would they tell people? Time was not on their side and a baby clearly couldn't be hidden away forever. They couldn't even hide their secret a few months.

"Nothing to share," Ryan told his friend.

"Is that right? Well, I guess you'll tell me when you're ready."

Ryan didn't want to say anything more and give Jayden clues to what happened immediately following the Masquerade Ball.

"I'll let you go," Jayden told him. "I assume I'll see you at the Christmas party, right?"

"I wouldn't miss it."

Ryan disconnected the call.

The Christmas party at the Cattleman's Club was always the biggest event of the season. Now Ryan had to decide if he wanted to show up alone or if Morgan would be on his arm. If she went with him, everyone would know the status of their relationship had changed.

Clearly everything hinged on what Morgan decided she'd do as far as they were concerned. And that was where he came in. He owed her an apology for not asking about her health, he owed her an apology for assuming she'd just drop everything and be thankful for his proposal, and he needed to figure out how the hell to get her to marry him.

Damn it. Apologizing wasn't something he'd ever had to do with her. They'd run into each other at various events or restaurants, get into a quarrel, and go on about their way. Odd, but that was just their thing.

Apologizing would be a big move in this new path with their relationship.

Ryan stepped from his truck and headed toward the stable. He hadn't ridden Midnight in some time and his oldest, dearest horse was just what he needed to get a clearer picture of his future…and his potential bride.

Morgan scooted the raw edge table from the front of her store toward the middle. She had piles of clothes stacked all around the perimeter of the showroom and had rearranged twice already. She was tired, irritable, and she had a mess on her hands that needed to be put back together before she opened in the morning.

Right now she either wanted to call in Kylie for emergency help or sit in the middle of this pile of accessories and shoes and cry. She didn't even know which thing she'd be crying about, so maybe just a good blanket cry to get everything out would be best. Then she could be done and move on stronger than ever.

She really should have waited on Kylie to help her, but Morgan had needed to get some of her frustrations out. Her business she could control, so she'd always used this passion as her outlet.

Morgan stared at the table placement and hated this spot, too. She should just burn the thing and start from scratch. Maybe she needed to hire a designer to come in and have a nice renovation. Hell, while she was at it, she should change the name of the store. The Rancher's Daughter seemed so…simple.

Morgan blew out a sigh and rubbed her hands over her face. She couldn't very well change everything all at once. She was just irritated and scared as hell that her life was out of control right now. She was grasping at anything that was within her power to maneuver or change.

She hated feeling like she had no say-so in the path her life was heading down. But she couldn't go all crazy with every other part of her life, either. Now that Ryan knew the truth, she really should confide in Zanai. Her best friend would be supportive and just the shoulder Morgan needed to lean on right now.

Aside from the pregnancy, there was still a heavy dose of confusion. She couldn't keep up with going from bickering to ripping clothes off to pregnancy. No wonder she felt on the verge of a meltdown.

When Ryan left earlier, Morgan thought of little else other than that kiss. He'd purposely put that sexual thought in her head and he knew what he was doing. She wasn't going to lose control again…not with him.

Morgan's cell chimed and she turned, trying to remember where she'd set it in this disaster. The sound echoed again and she found the device beneath a stack of boot socks on her checkout counter. She really might need to call in Zanai or Kylie for reinforcements.

She answered her cell without looking at the caller.

"Hello," she greeted as she walked back toward the empty table.

"Are you busy?"

Ryan's low, sexy drawl stopped her.

"I'm still at the shop."

"At this hour?"

Morgan walked to her large, round ottoman where she'd shoved it near the dressing rooms and took a seat. She toed off her boots and figured she might as well get comfortable.

"I have a lot to do," she explained. "I don't just open and close. I have to restock, reorganize, change displays. Kylie is a great employee, but there's only so much she can do and at the end of the day, this business is my life."

"You need to hire more help," he suggested.

She had every intention of doing just that so she could alleviate some of the pressure and stress during her pregnancy, but he didn't need to know her plans.

"I'm not telling you how to run your ranch, so don't tell me how to run my store."

She crossed her legs up onto the ottoman and wiggled her toes. She would sit just a moment and then get back to straightening up her disaster.

"Did you call to give me business advice or did you need something?" she asked.

"I called to see if you wanted to come by the ranch tomorrow for dinner when you were done working."

Morgan jerked back as his question caught her off guard. "I'm not dating you, Ryan. I'm having your child."

"So we're working backwards. It's just dinner, Morgan. You have to eat and my chef will prepare something amazing."

"Ryan. I'm not coming to your ranch for dinner or as your wife and right now, I'm too tired for another argument. I need to work."

She disconnected the call and wondered if she sounded ungrateful or rude. She didn't mean to be either, but she didn't want to give him false hope, either. Other than really great sex and a baby, they had no common ground.

Couldn't he see that she only meant to save them both from heartache down the road?

Morgan shot off a quick text telling him she'd made a doctor's appointment if he'd like to join her next week. The baby was all they could have in common and she had no intention of shutting him out of that part of her life.

She set her phone on the ottoman and came to her feet. Stretching her arms and back, she pulled in a deep breath and glanced around to decide where to start. Things might not be perfect, but she had to get this store back in some type of order.

Her stomach growled as she headed toward her stack of V-neck tees. Ryan had mentioned dinner and she realized she hadn't eaten anything since lunch. Maybe she had a granola bar in her purse. She seriously needed to stay on top of consistent meals for the baby. Everything about her life would be geared toward her child from here on out.

She decided to leave the table right there for now and started folding and displaying her variety of tees. She could add the boot socks in a nice wire basket in the middle and put up some signage about her Christmas sale starting tomorrow.

After nearly an hour, that part was done. Now for the rest of the store.

Morgan turned to grab another stack of tees and jumped at the man looking through her front windows. No, not any man. Ryan.

Of course he decided to show up after hours…again.

Morgan stepped over her various piles and signs and around racks to make her way to the front door. She flicked the lock and had a déjà vu moment from a few hours earlier.

"I do have open hours, you know."

"I never asked how you were feeling," he said. "Earlier, I mean. I didn't check on you. I can admit when I was being a jerk."

Ryan smiled, and her heart skipped. Great. This was not what she needed right now. She barely had time for a bathroom break, let alone teen-level giddiness. Besides, she wasn't used to this unexpected wave of emotions. Before, Ryan only got her blood pressure up. Now he stirred her arousal.

He held up a bag and ushered his way inside. "I brought food."

The aroma wafting by as he moved inside had her stomach growling again and she totally forgave him for earlier. Morgan closed and locked the door then turned to face him. He'd stilled as he glanced around the chaotic area.

"You not only fight with me, you get into it with your clothes, too?"

"You're hilarious. I'm rearranging and it's gotten out of control." She crossed her arms over her chest and cocked her head. "How did you know I was hungry?"

Ryan shrugged. "I didn't know, but when you said you were still here, I assumed you hadn't gone out for food."

"You would assume right." She started to reach for the bag. "Thanks for bringing me something."

He handed over the food and propped his hands on his narrow hips. Nobody should look that good in a pair of jeans, worn boots and a plain black T-shirt, yet here he was conjuring up way too many unwelcome feelings. She shouldn't want him when she'd already had him, right?

Except that was the problem. She knew just how good they were together and her lips still tingled from their earlier encounter.

"Don't you have a worker who can help?" he asked.

Morgan nodded. "Kylie. She was off today and then texted about twenty minutes ago to say she has to take care of her grandmother for the next few days."

He glanced around once again as if trying to decide to run or stay. Honestly, she loved her job, loved being hands-on in the business she'd built from the ground up. Yes, there were times like this when exhaustion settled in, but that was just part of any job. Had she worked the ranch life like the rest of her family, that would be no different. At least she'd gone into her dream field, so most days didn't even seem like work.

"Where do you need me?" he asked.

Morgan blinked and clutched the paper bag at her side. "Excuse me?"

He glanced around again and laughed. "You obviously need help, so point me in the right direction. Be warned, though, I know nothing about fashion."

He knew enough to know not to mess with a good thing. Casual clothes were clearly his sexy staple and all she'd ever seen him in. Even at the masquerade party, he'd had on that same outfit, but he'd put a black blazer on to match his hat. No suit, no dress pants or dress shirt… just typical Ryan Carter attire. The man made no apologies for who or what he was—and maybe that was just another reason why he was so damn appealing.

Arguing and walking away was so much easier than trying to figure out this constant pull toward him.

"I don't need help," she told him.

Ryan slid his palm over his stubbled jawline and held her stare. "You're still going to try to be stubborn in the middle of this mess when it's nearly nine o'clock?"

Morgan didn't say anything. Instead, she took the sack to her counter and opened it to see what he'd brought her. A chicken sandwich and some fruit. Her stomach grumbled again.

"Thank you for this." She took a seat on her small stool and pulled out her meal. "Time got away from me and I didn't plan on being here this late."

"Did you plan on turning your store inside out?"

She shook her head as she grabbed a fresh strawberry. "I didn't plan on that, either."

Morgan attempted to eat without looking like something from *National Geographic*. She tore into that sandwich and had it gone in record time, though. She also tried not to keep staring at the man who was wandering around looking at clothes, hardware, tables and the rest of the disaster. It was the second time he'd been in her personal space like this and he just seemed so…imposing.

Having him here in her little world was much too intimate and she honestly didn't know if that excited or irritated her.

Those broad shoulders and rough boots were so out of place. Even in the haphazard area of her normally posh and polished boutique, Ryan Carter had a commanding presence.

"So, what are we moving around?" he asked, turning back to face her.

"We?"

He propped his hands on those narrow hips and she had to fight not to remember how easily she'd wrapped her legs around them.

Focus, Morgan.

"You can argue all you want about being independent, but I'm going to help you tonight. You might as well tell me where you want things or I'll do it myself." He picked up one of the mannequins from the floor and held it up. "What size is she? I'll find something for her to wear."

Morgan couldn't help but laugh. He looked so absurd, but he was dead serious. He wasn't going anywhere and she needed the reinforcements. Nothing wrong with admitting that on occasion.

"Fine. You can help, but you are not choosing outfits or everything would have on a plain T-shirt and jeans."

A corner of his mouth kicked up. "Nothing wrong with that, darlin'."

Ugh. Why did he have to be so Southern and sexy? And why did she have to be pregnant with his child? Of all the men in the area that she could have had a fling with, she'd opted for Ryan Carter.

Thanks, champagne.

Once she finished eating, she came around the counter and thought about how she really wanted things. Since she had an extra pair of hands, she might as well take advantage.

She just had to remember that was all she should be taking advantage of from this man.

Five

Ryan waited for Morgan to decide what she wanted done. He watched as she walked around muttering to herself. Something about Christmas dresses and a sale.

Just as she pivoted back toward him, Morgan's foot got tangled in a pile of denim and she fell forward. Ryan reached for her, just as she fell. She landed against his chest, her hands gripping onto his biceps as that mass of red hair curled all around them both.

He recalled another situation where all of that hair covered him, but this was not the time or the place to start replaying that moment. Unfortunately for him, he never could get control over when or where those delicious memories popped up.

"You okay?" he asked.

Ryan shifted so he could maneuver them both away from the piles on the floor. Morgan straightened herself. Shoving her hair from her face, she gave him a curt nod.

"Sorry about that."

Her eyes were everywhere but on him again. They'd created a child and she couldn't even look at him? She'd had no problem in the past going toe-to-toe with him, and this sudden change in Morgan confused the hell out of him.

"Morgan."

Her eyes darted up to his now and he closed that minuscule distance between them.

"We're not swiping at each other and we're not lovers. Let's find something in between. We can handle this situation together, but you've got to relax."

The noise she made could best be described as something between a snort and a laugh.

"Relaxing is what got me into this in the first place," she stated. "I just… I can't touch you. So, no more of those sneaky kisses. Got it?"

"Sneaky kisses?" Now he laughed. "Honey, you weren't complaining last month or earlier today. But if you want me to keep my lips to myself, I will. You'll have to tell me when you want that to happen again."

"I won't," she retorted.

He doubted she'd stick to that claim, but he'd let her have this small victory.

"Are you angry about our night together?" he asked. "Or are you angry that you can't get it out of your mind?"

Morgan's lips thinned, and her eyes narrowed. "I'm angry that you want to talk about it when we should both be moving on. Clearly, the only time we get along is when we're not talking, so we're going to have to figure out a way to communicate with our clothes on."

"That doesn't sound fun."

Morgan rolled her eyes. "I'm serious."

Yeah, he had been, too.

"I know we agreed that sex was a mistake, but I can't ever think a child is a mistake." He had to be completely honest. "And the more I think about our time together, the more I can admit it wasn't a mistake, either."

Morgan gasped. "Don't say that."

"I'll never lie to you and you need to know where I stand."

Those bright eyes of hers had a healthy mix of desire and irritation. There was such a narrow space between the two and she had an amazing talent of riding that line to keep him guessing.

He wanted her. Maybe he always had and he'd never stopped.

Unable to resist temptation, Ryan reached out and trailed his fingertip up her arm, then back down. He took her hand and lifted. Flattening her palm against his chest, Ryan kept his eyes locked on hers. He waited for any sign that she didn't approve; she had nothing but desire in her eyes.

"Your words and that look you're giving me don't match," he murmured. "Makes me think you're just saying you're not attracted when we both know that's a lie."

"I don't want to be," she corrected him.

And that whispered statement was all he needed to bank in his pocket of ammunition. Morgan's admission couldn't be taken back now and at least she was honest. That was one area they had in common, but commonalities weren't a high priority for him right now.

First, he wanted Morgan. Second, he wanted her to agree to his proposal and move into his estate. They could work out the rest later.

"Who are you fighting now? Me or yourself?" he asked as he hovered his lips near hers. "You're a grown woman with needs. We both want the same thing."

"Physically, yes," she agreed. "But everything else—"

"Doesn't matter. Not in this moment."

He rested his hands on her hips and shifted her around so his back was to the windows in case any passersby happened to look inside. She couldn't argue with him about the proposal and moving in if he kept that sweet mouth occupied. Guess he was going to go back on that promise of no more kissing.

Ryan stepped into her, lining up their hips perfectly and eliciting a soft moan from Morgan. She closed her eyes and sighed as her hands came up to cup his elbows.

"This can't work," she insisted. "We bicker all the time and sex isn't the solution. We have a child coming that we need to think about."

Oh, he'd thought of little else since he discovered he was going to be a father. But that had nothing to do with this ache he had inside for Morgan. If anything, that attraction burned hotter than ever before. Something primal and territorial had settled deep within him since learning the news.

Ryan feathered his lips over her jawline and to that sensitive spot just beneath her ear. She shivered against him as her grip on him tightened.

He walked her backwards with no clue where to go, but he sure as hell wanted out of the line of sight of the street. Even at this late hour, Royal always had busy restaurants and the last thing he and Morgan needed was more fodder for the gossip mill.

"Wh-what are we doing?" she whispered.

"Going somewhere private."

He glanced over her shoulder to the closed door that led to the back. Ryan had no clue what was in there, but he didn't care. They would be alone and that was all that mattered right now.

"Is this a good idea?" she asked, her eyes searching his.

Ryan reached around her and opened the door as he stared down at her. "If you want to stop, say so."

"But we shouldn't."

"Who made that rule? Because last I checked, we were adults." He took a few more steps until they'd crossed into the storage room, and the door closed behind him. "If you say no, we'll go right back out there and finish picking up. Just say the word."

Morgan closed her eyes once again and sighed. "Let's forget about reality. Just for tonight."

Ryan didn't realize he'd been holding his breath, but relief spiraled through him. Then he remembered her demand.

"I'm not allowed to kiss you," he reminded her. "I need your permission."

Her eyes flew open, then darted down to his mouth. In a flash, Morgan grabbed his face and rose up on her toes. She captured his lips and arched into him. Permission granted.

Finally. After a month of wondering if their fiery passion was just a onetime thing or if his fantasies lived up to the reality... Ryan was about to find out. The way Morgan came to life in his arms was a hell of an indicator that alcohol had nothing to do with their first heated encounter.

Ryan didn't ask again if she was sure. He'd asked already and she never said no. She also aggressively kissed him since they'd gotten back here. She'd made her answer clear.

So Ryan decided to take control.

His hands moved to the hem of her shirt and he lifted it up over her torso. Morgan stepped back enough for him to pull the material over her head and fling it to the side.

Soft red curls fell over her shoulders as those bright eyes met his. That familiar desire stared back at him, just like at the masquerade party, where all he'd been able to see was her eyes until they'd gotten back to his place and he'd stripped her bare.

Now he couldn't wait to have an encore performance.

She'd sworn she wouldn't do this...not again.

But how could she deny her wants? Who said this was wrong? Maybe they didn't have everything figured out in this weird relationship, but that didn't mean they couldn't be intimate. Morgan didn't even have the excuse of alcohol this time.

And it hadn't just been the champagne from the party. She'd overheard Vic and Jayden talking about how it was obvious Ryan was into her, which had shocked her. Morgan had just assumed she and Ryan were totally opposite and irritated each other.

Clearly, conversing wasn't their thing and they communicated much better in other ways.

Morgan didn't want to wait, or chat, or even think about this moment. She just wanted to live in it.

With quick work, she stripped down to absolutely nothing while Ryan watched with those hungry eyes that made her feel sexy and beautiful.

His heavy-lidded gaze landed on her stomach and before she realized what he was doing, Ryan reached out and placed both hands over her bare skin.

A tremble vibrated through her at his strength and warm touch. She couldn't get enough and could possibly start begging.

"You're the most beautiful woman," he told her. "You're even sexier now that I know you're carrying my child."

She reached for the button of his jeans and before she could finish, he took control. He unfastened everything and shoved them and his boxer briefs down to his knees, then maneuvered until he could kick them out of the way. He grabbed her once again, this time on her backside as he lifted her up.

Ryan spun them, pressing her back against the wall. The spiral rush of exhilaration aroused her even more.

She fit perfectly between the hard wall and Ryan's firm chest. He placed a hand by her head and kept the other on her hip as he joined their bodies. Morgan cried out as whole host of euphoric sensations overcame her. This fast, frantic passion was still so new to her and she wondered if that thrill would ever wear off...or if Ryan would always be so incredibly potent.

Morgan gripped his shoulders as his mouth covered hers. He seemed just as needy for all of the connections. Knowing she had this power over him, to make him lose control, turned her on even more.

His hips jerked faster against hers and Morgan couldn't take it anymore. She tore from the kiss and arched against him to pull even more pleasure from his body.

"That's it," he murmured, urging her on.

Just as her climax slammed into her, Ryan groaned and trembled. She clung to him with her eyes shut, wanting to hold on to this feeling of pure bliss.

But moments later, their bodies calmed and she still clung to him.

"Don't tell me you regret this," he muttered.

She shook her head. "No. I don't, but I'm not sure it's the smartest thing for us to be doing."

Ryan helped her stand on her own as he took a step back. He reached up to smooth her hair from her face, then grabbed his pants and pulled them on. He left them undone, as if he wasn't quite finished with her.

Once he gathered her clothes and handed them over, Morgan dressed. The silence became too much, but she really didn't know what to say.

"This might not be smart," Ryan finally stated after a moment. "But I can't get enough of you."

Yeah. That was where they seemed to fully agree. She couldn't get enough of him, either. But getting along intimately didn't exactly make for a solid foundation for anything at all and outside of sex, they bickered.

So now where did that leave them?

Six

Was there a protocol for doing the walk of shame into your own shop wearing the same clothes from the previous night?

Morgan had gotten home well after midnight, couldn't sleep, and had headed back to the store well before she was due to open. Even though Ryan had helped her get the showroom from war zone to presentable, there were still touches she wanted to do. Plus, she just wanted to look at it with fresh eyes.

As helpful as Ryan had been—in more ways than one—Morgan had been a bit distracted and her mind all muddled when they were working in here last night.

First things first, she wanted to change her clothes. She wanted something fresh and more in the holiday spirit. She'd gotten some new sweaters in and even though this was Texas, the weather had mood swings, resulting in chilly nights.

Once Morgan grabbed a new outfit and did a quick change, she went into her office and pulled her hair into a neat low bun and applied some lip gloss. As she stared in the arched floor-length mirror in her office, Morgan couldn't help but turn to the side and smooth her hands over her still flat stomach.

Surprisingly, she didn't feel bad like she'd heard other women talk about. Morning sickness hadn't hit and she hoped it stayed away. Her appetite had grown…and apparently not just for food. Who knew pregnancy pulled out so many hormones and emotions?

Morgan lifted the white sweater and eased down the waist of her taupe wide-leg pants. She still couldn't believe there was a little life in there. She'd never thought about being a mother or having a family of her own. In this town, marriages and babies seemed to be contagious lately.

Morgan flattened her hand over her belly and vowed that no matter what, she would put the baby first. Above all else, she valued family and even though she was terrified of being completely out of control with the unknown here, she also couldn't deny the excitement at the idea of a baby. Her baby.

Well, hers and Ryan's.

Morgan readjusted her clothes and tried to push Ryan to the back of her mind, but damn it, he just kept creeping right up to the front where he didn't belong. She had her life going just fine and all set the way she liked it. Then he had to come along with that sexy black masquerade mask where all that had been exposed was that kissable mouth and those bright eyes. The champagne fountain had flowed a little too freely and the next thing she knew, they were back at his ranch and in his bed. Maybe not her brightest moment, but she couldn't change the past.

And last night had been about taking what she wanted because she needed to be in control of something in her life right now when everything seemed to be chaos around her.

She should have regrets, but she didn't. Ryan was unlike any other lover she'd ever had. But great sex and a child on the way didn't make for a reason to marry. She didn't love him and he didn't love her.

Maybe she was the only one thinking clearly here because love didn't exist for everyone…and marriages didn't always last. She refused to put her child on a roller coaster of instability simply because Ryan wanted to build a family dynasty.

Thankfully, she had several months to lay groundwork and get a solid plan in place. She and Ryan would just have to sit down like the adults they were and come up with a course of action…one that didn't involve a loveless marriage.

Morgan busied herself accessorizing the mannequins in the window and adjusting the draped lights to give the party dresses the best glow. She loved this new line and knew the women in Royal would flock to grab them for the upcoming Christmas party at the TCC.

Just as she stepped away from the display, Sylvia Stewart stood waving on the other side of the window. Morgan smiled and waved back, though inwardly she cringed at starting her day with the town gossip. Morgan truly wished Kylie didn't have to care for her grandmother. She could really use her at the store right now.

Morgan went to the doors and flicked the lock and opened one side for Sylvia.

"I'm a little early," Sylvia stated as she stepped right on in.

"No problem at all. I was going to have these dresses sent to you this morning."

Sylvia waved a hand and shook her head. "I ran out to meet a friend for coffee and just thought I'd take a chance that you or Kylie was here."

"Come on in." Morgan gestured inside the store. "Would you like another cup of coffee or water?"

"Oh, no, dear." Sylvia did another glance around the newly decorated area. "I'm fine. I do love how you re-arranged the place. You really maximized the space."

"Thank you."

Morgan loved the new floor plan, as well. Ryan had played a huge part in helping with the heavy lifting... but Morgan would leave out that nugget of information.

"I had to make room for more stock," she added. "I'm always busier at Christmas so I just wanted a fresher look."

Morgan went behind the counter and opened the double doors to the closet area. She pulled the items for Sylvia and hung them on the raised stand next to the desk.

"Would you like to try them on here or take them and let me know what works for you?" Morgan asked.

Sylvia started toward the desk, but stopped and glanced down.

"Oh, what was that?" she muttered as she bent down. She came up holding something. "I hope I didn't break this. It was just there and I stepped on it."

Morgan focused on the item in her hands...and realized that was Ryan's watch. Wonderful. Had he lost that in their haste to get to the back room for sex or had it slipped off when they'd been moving furniture and displays?

"Oh, that must have fallen off a customer's husband,"

Morgan stated. "I'll set it back here and try to find the owner."

Sylvia turned the watch over and smiled as her eyes darted to Morgan. "Looks like the owner is Ryan Carter, unless someone else has the Yellow Rose Ranch logo on their watch."

But of course he had his own damn logo on his watch. A man with an ego that inflated would do something as trivial as that.

"He's not the husband of anyone," Sylvia added with a quirk of her silver brow. "Maybe he stopped by to see you? After the way the two of you were hanging all over each other at the Masquerade Ball, I would have assumed you'd be engaged by now with as fast as the couples in this town are moving."

Why get engaged when you could bypass that and go straight to family life?

Morgan certainly wasn't going to give Sylvia any more information or ammunition than necessary about Ryan.

"He actually did stop by yesterday," Morgan admitted. "I needed help moving some of these larger tables and that display stand with the boots. Ryan is good friends with my brother and Vic is always looking out for me. Ryan happened to be free to assist and his watch must have fallen off during the move."

Sylvia's knowing smile and quirked brows didn't budge as she handed over the watch. Morgan laid it on the desk and would text Ryan about it later. For now, she had to divert the nosiest woman in all of Royal.

"So, what did you decide about your dresses? Trying on here or taking them with you?"

"Oh, I think I'll just take them. What about accessories and shoes? It's Christmas and I do like to splurge on myself, especially for a party. Will you and Ryan be attending together?"

Morgan couldn't help but laugh. "Ryan and I are just friends, but I haven't even thought about a date yet."

"You two were pretty friendly about a month ago." Sylvia winked. "Don't worry. Some girls need their secrets and that cowboy would be a great secret to keep. I won't say a word."

Oh, maybe not *say* a word, but she sure as hell would send out texts.

Whatever. Morgan was well aware people had seen her and Ryan kissing at the ball and they'd seen them leave together, as well. So what?

As Morgan gathered up shoes, jewelry and a few clutch bags, Sylvia decided to keep chatting.

"Is Heath going to be at your sister's wedding?" she asked.

"I would assume so," Morgan replied, taking a delicate gold chain from a display. "He is the brother of Chelsea's fiancée."

"I would just think he wouldn't want to be at an event filled with Grandins and Lattimores."

Yeah, Heath Thurston probably wasn't thrilled, but Nolan was his twin and he wouldn't let him down.

Morgan was all for family ties. She just hoped no animosity spilled over into Chelsea's life once she and Nolan were married.

"I'm sure he'll be on his best behavior at the wedding," Morgan assured Sylvia.

She made a few trips to the desk with boxes of shoes and any accessory she could think of that would go with the chosen dresses.

"Let me bag all of this up for you and then I'll help

you to your car. I'll wrap the jewelry and place it inside
the shoe box that I believe will be the best pairing."

Sylvia beamed. "You are so good to me. I'll be sure
to let you know something by tomorrow. You still have
my credit information?"

Morgan nodded. "I do."

"Wonderful. And, for what it's worth, Ryan is quite a
catch. You two would be a lovely couple."

Great. Just what Morgan needed, the validation of
Sylvia. Morgan wondered just how long it would take
for word to get out that Ryan's watch was on the floor
of her boutique.

Seven

Ryan stepped out of the shower and wrapped a towel around his waist. He'd worked damn hard today on the ranch, but no amount of manual labor could remove last night from his head.

Several times throughout the day he'd wanted to text Morgan, but he didn't want to appear clingy. The last thing he'd ever want anyone to believe was that he was desperate. He wasn't. But he did have every intention of getting what he wanted. There was no way he'd ever let a chance at having a family pass him by for a second time. He had a legacy to protect and an estate he wanted to leave to his namesake.

Maybe that made him sound old-fashioned like Morgan claimed, but he didn't care. He wanted his child close and Morgan with him. Love didn't have to enter the equation. Not all marriages were based on such fairy-tale ideals. He wasn't looking for love and he knew she wasn't, either, so why couldn't they make this work?

He'd gone to her shop with every intention of talking her into marrying him, and they'd ended up naked again. Clearly they needed a chaperone because they couldn't even have a conversation without getting intimate these days.

Ryan padded through to his adjoining walk-in closet. One side was completely bare and he had no idea why he even used this bedroom. The massive closet seemed a bit over-the-top when it only housed a few boots, hats, tees and jeans.

The doorbell echoed up to the second floor and he stilled. He wasn't expecting anybody and he'd sent his chef home. Maybe a stable hand needed something, but they usually called or texted.

He could look at his cameras, but he'd answer the door regardless. Ryan hurriedly pulled on a pair of jeans and fastened them as he headed out of his room and down the steps leading to the foyer. He crossed the cool tile floor and reached the double doors as the doorbell chimed once again.

Ryan opened one side and Morgan jolted back, her hand going to her chest.

"Sorry. I didn't know if you heard the first bell."

Ryan rested his forearm on the edge of the door and leaned in as he took in her pretty little polished outfit. She'd put her hair up on top of her head and had minimal makeup, yet looked like the sexiest woman ever. Perhaps that was because he knew exactly how she looked beneath those wide-legged pants and fitted sweater.

"I just got out of the shower."

Her gaze traveled down his bare torso, then back up, and she attempted to square her shoulders and compose herself. Too late. That familiar hunger had already flashed in her eyes and revealed her true thoughts. Apparently they weren't done with that aspect of their relationship...good to know.

"Sorry about that." She cleared her throat and went on. "I thought I could swing by on my way home and drop off the watch."

"Watch?"

She pulled a watch with a leather band from her pocket and handed it over.

"You had it?" he asked, taking the piece. "I thought I lost it in the barn or out in the field."

Morgan pursed her lips. "I didn't exactly find it. Sylvia Stewart found it. On the floor of my shop. I'm sure the entire town now knows that you were in my boutique and since you're not married, everyone will think you were there to see me."

"I was there to see you," he defended himself, dropping his arm to his side. He took a step forward and pulled in a deep breath. "And I don't care what Sylvia or her gossip monger friends think. We're allowed to see each other or anything else we feel like doing."

Morgan offered a soft smile. "That may be, but I do have a reputation as a woman and as a small business owner."

"I understand that," he told her, taking another step forward. "Your reputation isn't tarnished simply because I lost my watch in your shop. What did you tell her?"

"A portion of the truth," she stated with a shrug. "That you stopped by to help me do the heavy lifting because she had noticed that I rearranged, so it was an easy way to skirt around the rest of the story."

The rest of the story. That made it sound like there was an ending to what they had going on, but Ryan knew they'd just gotten started. There wouldn't be an ending, not as long as they were parents together.

Which only reminded him of another thing.

"Why don't you come inside and we can talk."

Morgan stared for a minute, then let out a burst of sweet laughter. "You're kidding, right? You're half-dressed and if I come inside, we both know what will happen."

"You're damn good for my ego."

"Oh, please." She rolled her eyes and shook her head. "Your ego doesn't need inflating any more. I'm just stating a fact."

Yeah, he knew that, but he also knew they had to have some serious conversations.

"We need to talk," he informed her. "And it's dinnertime so stop stalling."

Her eyes darted away and he knew he had her.

"Come in, we'll eat in the kitchen, I'll even put a shirt on if the sight of my mere naked chest is too much for you."

"Wow. You really are full of yourself." She threw up her hands and motioned for him to go inside. "I'll come in, but we are just talking...and not about this marriage nonsense. We can discuss the baby."

Considering the baby went hand-in-hand with the "marriage nonsense," he would have to be careful how he wove those conversations together.

As much as he wanted her physically, that would have to wait. There had to be more to them than sex and he would have to prove to both of them that they could be more than just bedmates.

Morgan took a seat on the leather stool tucked beneath the large island in Ryan's kitchen. As promised, he'd put a shirt on and now stood at the stove preparing…she really didn't know what.

"I didn't know you could cook."

He flashed that sexy grin over his shoulder and she silently cursed the nerves that danced in her belly.

That was just hunger pains. Had to be. She wouldn't still get all giddy over a smile after all they'd done—would she?

"I can cook," he informed her. "You can't live on a ranch and not know how to prepare food. There are too many mouths to feed. But I do also have a chef that comes in four days a week. He is phenomenal and you'll weep when you try his homemade stew."

Her stomach growled at the thought of anything homemade. It wasn't often she had time to do much cooking or go out to a nice restaurant. Even though she'd grown up in a home with a chef, she was typically out late or working and never sat down with the rest of the family.

"Nelson also baked homemade rosemary bread this morning, so it's fresh," Ryan added. "Perfect timing."

"I didn't mean to actually come for dinner. I'm returning your watch."

"You could have called and I would have picked it up at the shop." He reached over and pulled out two large bowls. "But I assume you wanted to see the ranch again and I had invited you today anyway. Remember?"

Oh, she remembered.

Morgan rested her elbows on the granite and didn't reply. While the Yellow Rose Ranch was certainly impressive, she'd grown up on a ranch herself. With her siblings and their staff, there were definitely those mouths to feed like Ryan had mentioned. But she'd never learned to cook well or for a crowd. There were always people in and out of her home, but their live-in chef had taken care of all of those needs.

Morgan didn't hang too much with the ranch hands and once she was old enough to make her own decisions, she distanced herself from that lifestyle. Vic never understood. Neither did Chelsea, Layla, or the rest of the family. Morgan had always had a different vision than working on a ranch. She understood the legacy and the importance of it, but at the same time, that didn't mean she had to follow in the footsteps of her family simply because it was expected of her.

And she'd keep making her own decisions now, too.

Ryan's log-and-stone three-story house with porches all around was something to behold. It sat right in the center of Yellow Rose as if he wanted to see all of his land from anywhere inside. The man might be a working rancher, but he was still a billionaire and certainly lived like one.

She'd been around this lifestyle her entire life and wanted nothing to do with living on a ranch. But now her world would be tied to his forever.

Perhaps she could have just called and he would have come by her store to pick up his watch. Ryan had been right in saying they needed to talk, but she honestly had no clue where to start.

"Can I do something to help?"

"Just relax." He busied himself getting drinks and setting everything on the island. "Were you busy at the store today?"

Morgan reached for her tea and stared across the counter. Ryan stared back, legit waiting on her reply and she couldn't help but snort.

"Is that what we're doing now?" she asked. "Pretending this is a relationship?"

Ryan took a seat across from her and reached for his fork. "I'm not pretending anything. Just asking a question. I was busy riding more fence lines today and we have one mare that's about to deliver any day so we've been keeping an eye on her. One ranch hand didn't show up for work and decided halfway through the day to text that he wasn't coming back."

Morgan listened to him discuss his day and knew he worked hard. Her entire family were ranchers and the amount of work that went into running a successful operation could be exhausting.

There was something to be said about a hardworking man. They were loyal and very likely trustworthy. But she didn't know him well enough to fully trust. How could she? Before they'd fallen into bed together, all they managed to do was snipe at each other. How could she even consider a marriage of any kind if they didn't have a foundation of trust?

Ryan had always been Vic's friend, never hers. Until now. But were they friends? She had no idea what label to put on this unusual relationship.

Morgan pushed away the worry as she took her first bite of stew. The groan escaped her before she even realized. Then she took another and came to the conclusion Ryan's chef was a gift from heaven.

"Good, right?" he asked with a smile.

"I don't have the right adjective. I haven't even tried the bread yet."

"Nelson can turn a pile of ingredients into something magical and make it look so easy."

"He should open a restaurant if he can cook everything this good," she told him.

"He's not going anywhere," Ryan replied. "I overpay him for just that reason. I never want him to leave."

Morgan tore off a piece of the rosemary bread and dipped it into the stew. Oh my word, how could anyone be this masterful in the kitchen?

"Is Nelson's cooking reason enough for you to move in here and marry me?"

Morgan nearly choked on her bread. She reached for her tea and took a long drink, mostly to gather her thoughts.

"Well, you went a whole twenty minutes without bringing up your favorite topic." She took another drink, then set her glass back down. "I can visit, but I'm not living here or marrying you."

"I see no reason not to." He kept his head down and focused on his dinner like this was a done deal. "A child needs both parents and as I told you yesterday, I want to not only help the baby, I want to be there for you."

Morgan set her fork down and opened her mouth, but Ryan held his hand up.

"We've been through this, I know. Just hear me out."

Nothing would change her mind, but she would let him speak before she shot down his proposal once again. She'd been raised to be respectful, so she'd let Ryan say anything he wanted while she enjoyed the most delicious meal she'd had in a long time.

"I spent the entire day thinking of a solution," he started. "Being selfish or controlling is not my main goal here. My goal is to have my family all together and be one unit. I want my child to grow up on the ranch and learn what real work is."

"On that we can agree," she replied. "I don't want my child believing he or she would always get money simply because we have it. I want them to work for it."

"So marry me and we can build this life with the same vision."

Morgan sighed and sat back in her leather bar stool. "A life? What kind of life is being trapped in a loveless marriage? You think you'd never want to date again or maybe find a woman you actually want to spend your life with?"

Ryan pushed away from his side of the island and came around to stand next to her. He placed a hand on the back of her stool and turned her to face him fully. Morgan swallowed at the intensity of his gaze. Ryan was completely serious about this situation and her words were not cutting through his hard head.

"I tried love once," he explained through gritted teeth. "I still have the internal scars to prove it. I'm here for the family and the legacy, that's it. You and I have chemistry, so why shouldn't we try? Live here for one month. That's all I'm asking. I know you want to challenge me at every point, but just give this idea a try and then decide."

There was no desperation in his voice, but an underlying command. He wanted this to happen. He wanted her in his home and very likely in his bed.

"You think I'll change my mind after a month?" she finally asked. "My stance will be the same. Neither of us deserves to be trapped in a marriage."

"I'm not trying to trap you. I'm telling you this is for the best and once you stay here and see that, you'll agree."

Ryan rested his big, strong hands on her upper thighs. The man was wearing her down with his home and hearth vision and that sexy bedroom stare. She could do much worse than having Ryan Carter demand she move in and marry him. The attraction alone tempted her. The idea of spending all of her nights with Ryan heated her body and stirred her desires. Maybe she should consider being with the father of her child. They could learn to make a unit, a family.

Morgan chewed the inside of her cheek as she thought of how to answer. He didn't lay out a bad option for the both of them to try this arrangement for a month. Perhaps if she stayed, he'd see that playing house wasn't all that fun. If she left a towel on the floor or snored too loudly or cluttered his bathroom vanity with her beauty bottles, maybe then he'd be ready to coparent while living apart.

"One month," she agreed. "At the end of that month, you'll have to respect my decision to remain single and we can go back to our bickering like we're used to."

A corner of Ryan's mouth kicked up. "That won't happen, but challenge accepted."

He covered her lips with his and Morgan's belly quivered at the prospect of living with this potent, captivating man.

Without a doubt, the next month would prove to be memorable.

Eight

"You're doing what?"

Vic's voice boomed through the cell speaker and echoed in the boutique as Morgan continued to scroll through the new maternity line she'd been considering. She knew her older brother would be shocked at this news, but she couldn't exactly keep it from him.

"You heard me," she told him. "I'm moving in with Ryan."

"I get that, but what the hell for?"

Yeah, that was part of the story she really didn't want to share, but yet another aspect of her life she couldn't exactly hide for much longer.

"Well, that's something I'd like to discuss in person. Do you have time to run by the store? I don't open for another thirty minutes."

"Why do I have a feeling I'm not going to like this?" Vic asked.

Morgan clicked on an adorable A-line dress with pockets. "I don't know if you'll like it or not, but I'd rather not get into my personal affairs over the phone."

"I'm on my way."

He disconnected the call and Morgan went to unlock the front door. Vic was just down the street getting some supplies for the Grandin ranch when he called and Morgan had dropped the bomb. She didn't want him to hear about her living situation or pregnancy from anyone else and this would be news that would blast through town faster than a wildfire.

And as far as the baby news, she had to tell him. Out of all of her siblings, she had always been closest to Vic and she knew he would support her and be there for her no matter what. Besides, Chelsea already knew so this would only be fair.

Moments later, the chime on her door echoed and she glanced up to see her brother striding in. He adjusted his Stetson and made his way toward her desk.

"Spill it," he demanded. "What's going on with you and Ryan?"

"Well, good to see you, too." Morgan came to her feet and crossed to give him a kiss on the cheek. "Would you like to get some Christmas shopping done for your fiancée? I know exactly what Aubrey would love."

Vic propped his hands on his hips and glared at her. "Stop stalling and tell me what's going on."

She was stalling and he was about one more breath away from steam shooting out of his ears. Morgan clasped her hands in front of her and pulled in a deep breath.

"I'm pregnant."

Vic continued to stare and silence enveloped them. She waited for him to say something, anything, but he seriously just stared.

"You're joking," he finally stated.

Morgan snorted. "Is that really something I'd joke about?"

Vic shook his head and muttered something beneath his breath.

"What?" she asked. "Just say it."

"I can't believe you and Ryan are having a baby," Vic exclaimed. "When I... I never expected... I mean, you two were pretty into each other at the Masquerade Ball, but this is..." Vic seemed completely flustered.

"Yeah, that's pretty much how I felt, too. He wants me to marry him, but that's taking things a bit far. So we're trying to live together, basically to prove each other wrong."

Vic reached out and took her hands in his. "This is moving rather fast, don't you think?"

Morgan nodded. "Extremely, and that's why I'm not marrying him. We need to figure out the best course of action for the baby. But Vic, please don't say a word. We're not ready to tell people yet."

Her brother gave her hands a reassuring squeeze. "I won't say a word."

Morgan let out a sigh of relief and closed her eyes. "Thank you."

Vic pulled her into a tight embrace and she realized that was all she needed. Some comfort from her big brother. Just that simple gesture eased some of her worries. No matter what her future held, she knew Vic would always be there for her.

When she eased back, she couldn't help but laugh. "You know, this is partly your fault."

Vic cocked his head and adjusted his hat. "And how do you figure that?"

"Oh, I overheard you and Jayden talking about Ryan. I believe your exact words were, 'It's obvious he's into her.'"

Vic's smile reminded her of when they were younger and he'd get into mischief and then try to lie his way out of it.

"Well, maybe we embellished just a bit," Vic defended himself. "And none of this is on me. If you were eavesdropping, then that's totally on you."

"So you're saying you tricked me?" she scolded. "Are you serious right now?"

"What? We knew you were listening." He shrugged as if that conversation didn't change her life. "Everything will work out. You'll see."

Morgan tucked her hair behind her ears and moved behind her desk to take a seat. She couldn't go back in time and change anything, and being angry or irritated with Vic wouldn't get her anywhere, either. She had bigger issues and worries than her meddling brother.

"I know you share everything with Aubrey," she began. "But I'd appreciate it if you didn't say anything about the baby. We'll tell everyone, we just need some time. We're still processing and trying to figure out what we're doing."

Vic nodded. "Understandable, but when she finds out that I knew and didn't share, she'll be upset."

Morgan offered a smile. "Well, I'm sure she'll get over it and you deserve nothing less for planting that idea in my head. Besides, she'll forgive you and slide into the role of auntie very well."

Vic groaned. "Damn it, I didn't even think of the hit my credit card will take."

"Your credit card can handle it." Morgan crossed her legs and rested her arm on the desk. "I really appreciate you stopping in. I wanted to tell you, but I didn't know how or when. Then you called and the opportunity presented itself."

"I'm glad you told me. Just make sure you're doing what is best for you and the next little Grandin. No matter what Ryan wants, you have to look out for you first."

Morgan nodded in agreement. She knew at the end of the day, she would have to do what was best for her and her baby.

"I need to get going," he told her. "You promise you'll let me know if you need anything at all? No matter the time or anything. I'm here for you. Got it?"

Tears pricked her eyes as Morgan came to her feet and hugged him once again.

"Well, don't cry." He chuckled as he wrapped his arms around her once again.

"Damn pregnancy hormones," she muttered as she eased back. "Thanks for keeping my secret."

He tipped his hat and turned on his booted heel and left her boutique. Morgan patted her damp cheeks and went to the closest mirror to see if she looked a mess. She was a hideous crier. Red nose, red-rimmed eyes, splotchy skin. Must be her pale complexion that betrayed her when she showed emotion.

Morgan figured she was okay as she adjusted her long red hair over one shoulder. She did feel better now that Chelsea and Vic knew the truth. Next up was Layla, then Mom, Dad and Grandma. Luckily, Layla was busy with her new husband, and her parents and grandmother were visiting friends for the weekend. She wouldn't have to tell them for several more days.

First things first. She planned on taking a few of her things to Ryan's house later. He was meeting her at her family ranch after she closed so he could help her gather whatever she wanted to bring.

For the next month, she was going to play house with Ryan Carter and she only assumed they'd be sharing a bed. His bed.

"Looks like you're staying longer than a month."

Ryan stared at the suitcases and totes they had hauled over from her parents' house where she still lived. He would have offered for a few of his employees go gather her things and move her in, but he wanted to be discreet for Morgan's sake. He hadn't told a soul about their situation and until they discussed things further, he wanted to respect her privacy.

"No, this is it for a month," she informed him. "I have a lot of clothes, shoes and accessories. Plus there's the party at the TCC for Christmas and Chelsea's wedding. It looks like I packed my entire closet, but I swear I only brought necessities."

Five suitcases and four totes were necessary?

"Don't you own a store you could grab clothes from whenever you want?" he asked, turning to focus on her.

Morgan rolled her eyes. "I sell what I have to my loyal customers, that's the whole point. Of course I keep pieces, but I can't exactly go in every day and grab something new. That's not how a successful business is run. I would think you'd understand profit margin."

She glanced toward the wide staircase leading to the second floor and then glanced down to all of her belongings.

"Which room is yours?" she asked. "I assume upstairs."

"My room is upstairs," he confirmed as he took a step toward her. He lifted her chin and turned her to face him. "But you'll be in the room across the hall from me."

Morgan jerked back, her brows drew in, and she

blinked. "Excuse me? We're not sharing a room? I thought that was the whole point of me moving in here."

Ryan framed her face with his hands and held her in place. He wanted to be very clear and didn't want there to be any confusion.

"You're here because I want you to see how we could be as a family. But we shouldn't sleep together, Morgan. We've done everything backwards, and for the sake of our child, we need to see if we can live together."

Morgan continued to stare at him and he knew his statement had taken her by surprise. Honestly, his stance shocked him, too, but this would be best in the long run.

Damn if it wouldn't be difficult being so close to her and not being intimate.

"You're serious."

Ryan nodded. "The room is all ready for you and you have your own bath with a large soaker tub. I figured that room would be best so you can relax after working all day on your feet."

Morgan stared another minute before she took a step back. She didn't say another word as she went to one of her suitcases and extended the handle.

"I'll get these," he told her. "You shouldn't be lifting anything."

She completely ignored him and started for the steps. "I'm more than capable of taking the lighter ones."

"Then you can wheel them to the elevator." He gestured toward the hallway. "But I really can get everything if you want to go on up and check out your room."

"First thing you need to learn about me is that I don't sit by and watch other people do the work."

She wheeled the suitcase down the hall, then glanced around, and back to him.

"I have no clue where I'm going," she admitted.

"That would have been a more dramatic exit if you had." Ryan lifted two of the totes. "Follow me."

Making his way down the hall, he led Morgan to the elevator. Once they were upstairs, he started showing her around her room, hoping she'd get distracted enough that he could go back and get the rest of the load.

"This bathroom is even bigger than mine and I didn't think that was possible." She trailed her fingertips along the edge of the marble counters. "Oh, my. Now, this vanity really makes me have some envy."

She pulled the faux fur stool out and took a seat. She stared at her reflection in the mirror and then noticed the bouquet of fresh cyclamens.

"Did you have these brought in for me?" she asked, catching his reflection in the mirror as he stood behind her.

"I wanted you to feel like this room was for you," he admitted.

He wasn't about to tell her he'd had the stool delivered and the bedding completely changed out, and added a new white chaise so she could relax at the end of the day.

"The cabinet is stocked with towels and bubble bath. There's a variety because I didn't know what scent you'd like or if you were allergic to anything."

Morgan came to her feet and turned, but rested against the vanity. With her hands by her hips, fingertips curled around the edge of the counter, she tipped her head and looked both adorable and sexy. He had to take a mental step back and focus.

Yes, they were alone, but they also had to take charge of this situation and not allow their hormones to control them.

"You're seriously going to tell me that this big tub is all for me?" she asked, a corner of her mouth tipping up in a naughty grin. "That this big bed will only be for me and you'll stay across the hall in your bed? Am I understanding this correctly?"

Ryan nodded. "For this month that you agreed to, yes. If you want to stay after that and marry me, I'll have your stuff moved to my room so fast."

"You won't last a month with me under your roof with nobody and nothing around to stop us."

Why did that sound like a challenge?

And why did she sound like she was going to seduce him?

Damn. Maybe he underestimated his willpower around this sexy vixen. That look in her eye said she was hell-bent on proving him wrong.

Game on.

Nine

"What the hell is all of that?"

Morgan glanced up from her position on the steps and smiled at Ryan's scowl as he stood in the foyer looking up.

"It's decoration." She fluffed more of the fresh garland around the banister. "This place really needed to be more festive."

"I have a tree up in the living room. That's festive enough."

Aw, poor baby didn't like her putting her feminine touches in his domain. Too bad. She didn't like sleeping alone when the best lover she'd ever had slept mere steps away.

They'd rolled into day three of living together, and she really didn't know how much longer she could go without his touch.

"Yeah, I fixed your tree, too," she informed him.

"Those ornaments were pretty sparse. I added a few of my personal touches."

Ryan closed the door and continued to stare. Morgan came down another step and went about her decorating.

"Bad day on the ranch?" she asked. "You seem... cranky. Or perhaps it's sexual frustration."

"I'm fine."

Considering his declaration came through gritted teeth, she had to assume he was anything but.

"Nelson made meat loaf and mashed potatoes with fresh asparagus for dinner. If he keeps making such delicious things, I'm going to have to buy bigger clothes." Morgan stilled and then groaned. "I guess that's irrelevant at this point. I'm going to blow up like a whale anyway."

"You look fine now and you'll look fine no matter what size you are later."

An unexpected flutter filled her and she didn't want his compliments. She wanted in his bed for the duration of her stay and she wanted to figure out a solid plan for parenting. That was it. None of these extras that delved too far down into the barrel of emotions.

"Do you want to help with my idea for the exterior or should I ask TJ?"

Ryan sighed. "Leave my ranch foreman alone and the outside is just fine. I'll throw a wreath on the front door if that makes you feel any better."

Morgan finished adjusting the gold ribbon wrapped around the garland, then came down off the steps. She made her way to Ryan, got within inches, and crossed her arms over her chest.

"Have you always hated Christmas or are you trying to be difficult?"

"Neither." He took off his hat and hung it on the metal

hook near the front door. After raking his hand over his mussed hair, he propped his hands on his hips. "I just never understand why so much energy is spent on something that will be taken down in a short time. I celebrate the holiday and buy appropriate gifts, but I don't have the time to take for anything else."

Something was off with him and she couldn't put her finger on it. Even through all of their quarrels, he'd been a fairly easygoing guy. Ryan had always been cocky, a little arrogant and totally in control of his emotions. He made jokes at her expense and could seduce her with just one look.

This was a whole other side of Ryan and something in her wanted to figure out every aspect of him. When he had days like this, who did he typically talk to? His ranch foreman, his ranch hands, and his chef were all centered around business. Did he open up to Vic or Jayden?

"What happened?" she asked.

Ryan blinked and stared. "When?"

"Today. Something happened and you're upset."

Silence settled between them and she waited for him to say something. That intense stare he had gave no indication of what he was thinking or even feeling. Up until now, she'd been able to read him pretty well. But they'd also only had very intense relationships on each side of the spectrum. They were either arguing or passionate. They'd yet to find middle ground and that was precisely where they needed to land.

"It's nothing."

He started to turn and head toward the steps, but she grabbed his arm. Clearly caught off guard, Ryan glanced from her hand curled around his biceps to her face.

"Don't lie to me," she demanded. "If you don't want

to talk about it, say that, but don't say it's nothing when obviously you're upset."

"Fine. I don't want to talk about it."

He pulled from her grasp and continued up the steps, muttering about the garland the entire way. Morgan watched until he disappeared and even then she continued to stare at the top of the landing.

Whatever he was dealing with likely had to do with the ranch. She shouldn't be annoyed that he wouldn't talk to her. She'd been adamant from the start that she didn't want more with him than coparenting and intimacy. She couldn't ask him to be all in if she had no intention herself.

Still, she couldn't explain why, but she wanted to be that person he talked to. She didn't want him to just keep feelings bottled up. How would that help anything?

He needed space and she needed dinner. Once he cooled off, maybe he'd want to talk. She just wished she didn't care so much. This was only day three and she couldn't even imagine how she'd feel come day thirty.

Ryan stepped from his bathroom to the adjoining bedroom and stilled. There on his king-size, four-poster bed sat a tray with dinner, tea and a note written on the napkin.

I'm turning in early. Hope tomorrow is better.
M

He stared at the note and her delicate handwriting. He was having a baby with the woman and had never seen her writing until now. There were so many little things he just didn't know and he had no idea what all he was missing, but he did know he owed her an apology.

The day at the stables had been depressing and infuriating. Most days he loved his job. He loved the manual labor of running a ranch. But then there were days like today when losing an animal made him realize the fragility of everything around him.

And instead of being thankful that Morgan was comfortable enough here to make the place her home, he'd shut down and lashed out.

Why was he always apologizing to her?

Oh yeah. Because lately he'd been a jerk. He never intended for her to be the target of his frustrations, but she was there and he seriously needed to get a grasp on his control.

He hadn't been in the shower too long, so perhaps she hadn't gotten in bed yet. He would just tap on her door, apologize and thank her for dinner.

Guilt niggled at him because he'd invited her here so he could take care of her. Even though she claimed she didn't need his help, he'd wanted to prove to her that they would be a great team together.

Ryan pulled on a pair of boxers and rubbed his chest as he made his way out of his room and across the wide hallway. He listened for a moment, but didn't hear anything. He tapped the back of his knuckles on the door.

"Morgan."

Silence. He tapped again and the door eased open just a bit. He pushed it slightly and peered inside. All he saw was a book lying on the bedside table, her jewelry all displayed on the top of the dresser, and a floral robe draped over the bottom of the bed.

Then he heard it. Humming and water running.

Ryan turned his attention toward the bathroom and debated on leaving or following through. He'd come here for a reason and the apology couldn't wait. She deserved better.

He tapped on the bathroom door and the water and humming instantly ceased.

"Yeah?"

"Thank you for the dinner," he called through the closed door. "I'm sorry about earlier. It was just… I didn't have a great day and I didn't mean to take it out on you."

He waited for a reply, but the door eased open and Morgan stood before him wearing only a towel wrapped around her. She'd piled those red curls up on top of her head and her face was void of any makeup.

She looked like a damn fantasy come to life. Yeah, coming in here had been a mistake. He could have texted or called from across the hall and saved them from this face-to-face meeting. Between them, they only had two scraps of clothing for coverage.

If he slept with her now, she'd think that was all he wanted from her. And while everything in him needed Morgan in his bed, he also had to think long-term. If they didn't get some ground rules set, they'd never accomplish a joint union that served both of them and their child.

"You're entitled to bad days," she told him. "Don't worry about apologizing to me."

He never wanted to admit she was right, but in this instance, she was. Bad days were simply part of life and the fact that she understood churned a deeper emotion within him that he wasn't quite ready to face.

"Did you eat dinner?" he asked, turning away from any unwanted thoughts.

"I had some, but decided a relaxing bath sounded better."

He couldn't stop his eyes from traveling over all of that

creamy exposed skin. He clenched his fists at his sides when she eased the door open a bit farther.

"There's plenty of room in here for two," she offered.

Why had he refused this before? Oh, yeah. He was trying to be a gentleman and see if they could make this work if they removed sex from the equation.

That was the most idiotic plan he'd ever had in his life. No man would turn down such an invitation. But, again, she deserved better. She deserved a man who would treat her with respect and he wanted to show her that they should get married. And she wouldn't marry him if all they had was a physical connection.

So no matter how damn much he wanted her, he couldn't have her.

Ryan smoothed a wayward strand of hair from her forehead and trailed his fingertip down her jawline.

"You are too tempting," he murmured. "But I wasn't kidding about not sleeping together. We have to try at something solid that isn't based on the emotions of sex or fighting."

"All we have to do is whatever the hell we want," she retorted. "There's no reason for rules here, Ryan. We both want each other, so why are you doing this?"

He took a step back and crossed his arms over his chest. "Because our baby needs parents that can work together, who might actually have something in common other than chemistry. I want to show you that we can have it all if we try."

"So you don't care that you'll go back to your room and leave me alone and aching? I know you'll be just as miserable. Come in here with me. Let me help you forget about your bad day."

Oh, she could certainly make him forget a good many things. But he had to keep his eye on the main goal and that had to be his family. He had a heritage to protect and plans were already in place. He'd been close once to love and legacy. Then he realized love didn't matter, but family meant everything. He yearned to find that again and refused to ever give up. Now that he had a second chance, he would fight with everything in him to secure the future of Yellow Rose.

"When you decide to marry me, you'll be in my bed."

Ryan turned and left her room before he betrayed the vow he made to himself. He wanted the hell out of her and she knew it. She had a valid point that they were alone and nobody was there to stop them. He completely understood and agreed. But he needed her to see where he was coming from and until that moment came, Ryan would have to stand his ground.

Ten

Ryan had just stepped out the door to head to the stables when a familiar SUV pulled up to the house. He made his way to the drive that separated the house from the path to the main stable as Jayden stepped from his vehicle.

"Hey, man. What are you doing out this way?"

Jayden adjusted his sunglasses and stopped at the edge of the yard. "Had to run some errands for Zanai and was going by. Just thought I'd stop and see why I haven't heard from you in over a week."

Ryan really didn't know where to start with his friend, but he did know he shouldn't share everything. Not quite yet.

"I'm sorry," Ryan told him. "I meant to get back with you yesterday, but then we had a stillborn foal and the entire day went to hell."

"Hate to hear that. Is there anything you need?"

Ryan shook his head. "We're all good here."

"Well, the main reason I wanted to talk was to tell you Zanai and I are getting married."

Ryan smiled. "Congratulations. When is the day?"

"We're looking at spring. Zanai is in a hurry, but she wants better weather. I really don't care when we do it, so long as she knows she's mine forever."

Forever. That was what marriage was all about. Not love or feelings or all of those up and down emotions. Ryan wanted this family and he wanted his own forever. He longed for a stable, secure relationship for himself and his child. Those things were far more important than love.

"I'm there," Ryan assured him. "Can you stick around? Maybe come in and have a drink? This is worth celebrating."

Jayden shrugged. "If you have the time, but I don't want to intrude."

Ryan slapped his friend on the back and gestured toward the house. "Come on in. I've got a twenty-year bourbon I've been saving for a celebration."

"You don't want to save it for your own celebration?" Jayden asked as they reached the door.

"Don't worry, I have plenty of other bottles."

As soon as they stepped inside, Jayden started laughing.

"Since when did you become so festive?" he asked.

Jayden turned and his eyes landed right on a pair of cowgirl boots by the front door.

"And since when did you wear a tiny boot?"

Jayden's eyes came up to meet Ryan's and he realized his mistake. Ryan should have offered anything else other than coming inside.

"No wonder you couldn't return my calls or texts." Jayden rested his hands on his hips and raised his brows.

"Well, who is she? The same woman who caught your eye at the Masquerade Ball?"

No need to lie about the woman in his life, especially since most of the town saw him and Morgan leaving that party together. That didn't mean he had to go into the whole baby situation, though. Some things were still too fragile to discuss and Ryan still struggled to grasp that hard nugget of reality, as well.

"Yes, it's Morgan."

Jayden stared for another minute before a bark of laughter echoed in the foyer.

"I should have known. Man, you two work fast. We just had the Masquerade Ball a month ago. You went from dancing and kissing to living together? No wonder you didn't want to give me relationship advice when I asked you weeks ago."

Yeah, well, Ryan still was in no position to discuss relationships or dole out any advice on the topic.

"So, you're serious?" Jayden asked. "I never thought I'd see the day you finally settle down. After Margie—"

Ryan held up a hand. "She's long gone and I'm in a good place."

Physically, not emotionally…or sexually.

"Well, I'm glad you found a way to move on and Morgan is one beautiful woman. You two look good together."

Ryan motioned toward the front living area. "Come on in and have a seat. Let's talk about anything but relationships."

Jayden settled into a leather club chair as Ryan pulled out the bourbon and two Glencairn glasses from the mini bar in the corner of the room.

"Want to discuss Heath putting my family through the wringer or the fact that old survey says oil isn't there and yet he's still not backing down?"

"I'm not surprised." Ryan took the glasses and headed to take a seat across from Jayden. "He believes your families have something that belongs to him. And there's no dodging the guy. His brother is marrying Morgan's sister in a couple weeks. Those two have started mending whatever fences they've torn."

Ryan set the glasses on the round table between them and eased back in his seat. Everyone in town seemed shocked that Heath was persisting. Most people had assumed that once the old surveyor's report turned up in the investigation, Heath would give up. But instead he'd hired his own surveyor. Ryan honestly didn't want to get caught up in the chaos considering he had his own issues to deal with.

"Chelsea's wedding is going to be awkward as hell." Jayden picked up his glass and swirled the contents. He took a sip of his bourbon, then another. "Damn. That's good. I'm glad I stopped by."

Ryan laughed and tipped his glass up in a mock cheers. "You're always welcome here, my friend."

Jayden relaxed into his seat and rested his elbow on the arm. "So, let's get back to Morgan."

Ryan knew Jayden wouldn't let this topic go. But some things had to be kept private and everything going on between him and Morgan was best left between them.

"How about we discuss the bachelor party?" Ryan suggested. "Vic and I will make sure you have the bourbon you want."

Jayden nodded and just like that, the conversation shifted and the weight lifted from Ryan. He knew it was only a matter of time before everyone knew just how serious he and Morgan had become. They couldn't hide forever.

Morgan pulled into the drive and waited for the gate to slide open. She still wasn't used to coming here after work. She had never lived with a man outside of her own family before. This unique situation was certainly not one she'd ever planned on, but she'd told her parents the truth and they fully supported her decision to stay with Ryan.

Pregnant from a one-night stand, living with a man she barely knew, and trying to keep a secret from the town seemed like just the gossip she never wanted to be a part of. Yet here she was.

Part of Morgan thought she'd miss the home she grew up in, but she couldn't deny how much she loved her room and the little touches Ryan had added to make her feel special. Fresh flowers each day really went a long way to making her feel more at ease. She couldn't be bought into a marriage, but she wasn't going to turn down being wooed.

Wooed? Did that word seriously just roll through her mind? Clearly she needed more sleep or something. None of this was about romance. Even Ryan would agree to that. Neither of them cared about love or any other deeply binding emotion. She wasn't sure of his backstory or what made him so adamant on marriage, but whatever happened in his past had nothing to do with her or what was happening now.

As she approached the house, she stopped her car and just stared at the sight ahead of her. Then she laughed. This man was confusing the hell out of her with his opposing views on the holiday.

Morgan pulled on up and killed the engine. She grabbed her bag and stepped from the car.

"Now you decide to do exterior lights?" she called out.

Ryan glanced down from his position on the ladder. "You wanted lights. Here you go."

"I would have helped you had you waited until I got here."

She almost said *home*, but this wasn't her home. This was only a temporary arrangement.

"And I'm sure you have guys who would have done this," she added.

Ryan hooked the last bit of the strand in the fastener and started to climb down. He wiped his hands on his jeans as he took a step back to survey his work.

"I'm sure I do, but I'm also capable. I had to go into town and buy the damn things so I hope this is what you like."

Even in his growling, Morgan knew he'd done all of this because he cared. But how deep did that care run?

Yes, they were having a baby together, but she couldn't let that be the only reason she stayed with him. A child was no reason to declare your entire life to one person... who could very well be the wrong person. Caring and loving were two completely different things and one day, he might want to fall in love and do this marriage thing for real.

Morgan crossed the yard and stood beside Ryan. The twinkling white lights across the porches and banisters, combined with the garland and gorgeous wreaths on the windows and doors, brought a tear to her eye.

"It's magical," she murmured. "For someone who doesn't want to go all out, you did just that."

"Carmen at the supply store guided me," he confessed. "She's been here before so she told me exactly what I should do and I bought everything she said because I didn't want to screw this up."

And that statement right there tugged at Morgan's heart in a way she'd never known possible. He must have spent the entire day doing this for her after going through such a bad day on the ranch yesterday. He'd turned right around and put her wants ahead of his healing.

Morgan turned to face him and rested her hands on his shoulders.

"Thank you."

Ryan reached up, swiping a tear from her cheek. "Are those good tears? I never can tell when women cry."

"Definitely good tears." She wrapped her arms around him and held tight. "This was the best surprise. I don't know the last time anyone surprised me."

Ryan's strong arms came around her and Morgan closed her eyes, wanting to lock this moment in her core memory forever. Ryan was more than a wealthy rancher or good-time guy. He had a giving heart, which made his mood yesterday all the more concerning.

Not only that—to experience this side of Ryan really tugged at something internally for her. How could he be even more tempting than before? Seeing him go out of his way with such a sweet gesture only added another layer of temptation she didn't know if she could resist.

Morgan eased back and held his face in her hands. The coarse hair from his beard tickled her palms, but she was finding that she loved the tickling sensation.

"What happened yesterday?" she asked. "And don't blow me off."

Ryan's lips thinned and he reached out, curling his fingers around her wrists as if holding on for support.

"We lost our foal." He blew out a sigh and added, "We tried everything and I had our vet there, too. Nothing we did could save her."

Morgan knew that ache of losing an animal. Ranches were full of so many, but losing even one was a painful experience.

"I'm really sorry," she told him. "I know that doesn't change the situation. Even though I gave up ranch life, I still grew up on one and I understand what you're going through. I remember the first animal we lost when I was little."

Morgan turned her hands and held on to his between their bodies as she recalled the memory.

"Dad wanted all the kids in the barn to watch the birth because he was determined that we saw everything, good or bad, at the ranch. We had no idea the calf would be stillborn. Honestly, maybe that's what turned me off to that lifestyle. I was only eight, but I remember thinking I didn't like pain and I didn't like the darkness that seemed to overshadow us that day. I only wanted to see the good and the pretty of the world."

Ryan's soft smile had her heart doing a flip. "And here you are making the world, or at least Royal, beautiful."

Morgan's breath caught in her throat. She hadn't thought of her life that way. She just knew she loved fashion and she had a smart business sense about her. You couldn't grow up on a successful ranch and not be business savvy. But she'd never put all of that together until just this moment.

"Do these decorations make you want to marry me?" he asked.

Morgan tried not to cringe because even though he offered her a grin, she knew he wasn't entirely joking.

"Not even going all out on Christmas decorations will make me marry you," she informed him. "But you did earn yourself an invite into my bed."

Ryan released her and shook his head. "I'm pretty sure you would have let me in there no matter what."

"True," she agreed. "But now I'll let you have all the control. I could just…you know, lay there and let you have your way with me."

Ryan's eyes closed and he rested his forehead against hers. "You could tempt a saint, I swear."

"Is that a yes?" Morgan slid her arms around his waist. "You don't have to be noble on my account."

He chuckled and shifted to look her in the eye. "Oh, I'm not noble. I'm just planning for the future and what's best for this family. Say yes to marriage and I'll let *you* have control in the bedroom."

She didn't want control enough to give up her freedom or to be trapped. Morgan stepped away and adjusted her purse strap on her shoulder.

"I guess we'll both just have to stay in control outside of the bedroom."

Which was a shame when they were both so, so good inside.

Eleven

Ryan stared at the black-and-white image. He'd seen plenty of livestock ultrasounds, but he had no clue how the hell to decipher anything with Morgan's. The doctor assured them this little peanut shape was indeed their baby. A strong heartbeat and measuring right on target eased a worry he hadn't realized he'd been holding on to.

The first baby picture of his child. He really didn't know where to put it because nobody could see this. He'd have to keep it in his bedroom because anywhere else in the house he would run the risk of one of his staff seeing it.

He hated hiding the pregnancy like something to be ashamed of. Nothing about what he and Morgan shared should be labeled as shameful, but he also had to respect her wishes. She wanted to share the news at the right time. Her family knew but were sworn to secrecy. He hoped they could share an engagement announcement at the same time.

Ryan stepped from his truck and headed into the house. He knew exactly where he'd keep the ultrasound photo…right next to the ring he'd purchased the day after he had discovered the pregnancy.

He and Morgan had parted ways after the doctor's appointment this morning. He had paid a hefty sum for a private appointment at a discreet office two towns over with the doctor Morgan wanted. If they were keeping this under wraps for now, they couldn't exactly be seen together at the ob-gyn's office in Royal.

Ryan had been relieved to know the baby and Morgan both looked great and the summer due date would be here before he knew it. He needed to bring in a designer to work with Morgan on the nursery. No doubt she would want her touch on everything and he would give her nothing but the best.

She might see his move as over-the-top, but his child and the woman he planned on marrying would both have the best. And even though Morgan could buy anything she wanted, he still planned on keeping her satisfied, with no need to worry about a thing.

Maybe she would see that he wasn't trying to buy her. Moving in for this short time would show her just how genuine he truly was and how serious he took family matters. Having lost both of his parents when he'd been in his early twenties and then having a fiancée walk out on him days before their wedding, Ryan wanted to cling to the hope that this time he would have his own family. This time Yellow Rose would have a future with the next generation. He didn't start anything this grand just to grow old alone and sell to the highest bidder. Everything he did, he did with the intention of growth and legacy.

There were several things he needed to get done on

the ranch, but he also had a few things to do before Morgan returned home after work.

Home. He kept thinking of his place as her home, but she only occupied one little corner of his three-story house. Oddly enough, he wanted her to put her stamp on other areas. Maybe she'd leave her purse on the kitchen island or a blanket on the sofa where she'd been watching a movie.

Even seeing another set of dishes in the sink would make him so happy. He shouldn't be this excited, but damn it, he'd accomplished all he'd wanted as far as his career. Now it was time to focus on building his family and settling them here at Yellow Rose Ranch.

Once Ryan had the photo locked away in his bedroom, he changed into his work boots and headed down to the stables. He pulled his cell from his pocket and made a few calls to put his plan into motion. Everything had to be perfect.

He would win her over…and he'd win this challenge.

The day had been busy and long, which only led to the Rancher's Daughter being extremely profitable.

As much as Morgan loved her business and providing for her customers, everything in her body ached. She hadn't expected pregnancy to shrink her energy levels, but since she was brand-new at all of this, she was learning day by day.

Kylie had opened the store this morning, then left around one. Morgan seriously didn't think she could have gotten through the day without her, but she still needed to hire another employee. Sooner rather than later.

All Morgan wanted was to soak in a hot bath and to lie in bed and read. Kylie planned on opening again tomorrow, which meant Morgan could hopefully sleep in a little.

Or if she had her way, she'd be lying in bed with Ryan, but he still had a roadblock put up. She had every intention of wearing him down…but maybe tonight wasn't the time. Tired didn't even begin to describe her body. She should be thankful, though. She still didn't have any morning sickness.

Morgan stepped into the house and the aroma of garlic and yeast instantly filled her senses. She followed the smell into the kitchen where Ryan stood at the island dishing up dinner.

"I heard lasagna was your favorite."

Morgan stilled. How on earth had he heard that? Had Vic called and spoken to Ryan?

He turned from the island and faced her. His hands dropped to his sides and he closed the distance between them. Morgan held her breath as he reached out and tipped her chin up.

"You're working too much. Let Kylie take on more or hire someone else before you wear yourself down."

"I'm working like I always do."

His fingertips feathered across her jawline until he cupped her cheek. She resisted the urge to turn in to his comforting touch.

"You're a different person than you were six weeks ago," he reminded her. "The doctor said you'd get tired easily and to listen to your body."

Morgan laughed. "Right now my body is saying it just wants to relax in a bubble bath, but that dinner smells amazing."

"Go on upstairs and relax. Dinner isn't going anywhere."

She wrinkled her nose and glanced over his shoulder. "It looks like you went to a lot of trouble."

"Nelson did everything," he replied. "All I did was keep it warm. Go on. Eat when you're ready."

Morgan hesitated, but she really just wanted out of this bra and off her feet. She had no idea her breasts would be the first thing to change. Her bra was already getting a little too tight for her comfort. How would she be in another month? Another six months?

She also hadn't realized just how much she could change in a month. Never did she think she'd be living in Ryan Carter's home—even if temporarily. Then again, he'd changed so much, as well. Or maybe he'd been the same and she just now realized what a good heart he'd been hiding.

Either way, all of this confusion stirred a deeper emotion within her. She had to hold her ground, though. Everything had been moving so fast and her thoughts bounced between confusion and excitement.

Morgan made her way up to her room and as soon as she crossed the threshold and flicked the light on, she gasped.

There in the opposite corner right next to the double doors leading out onto her own private balcony stood a Christmas tree at least six feet tall, completely adorned with clear lights, white-and-gold ornaments that glistened in the light, and a gorgeous angel tree topper.

Morgan stood frozen, simply taking in the sight before her. If Ryan was trying to play some kind of game with her emotions, he was doing a damn good job. Tears pricked her eyes and she really wished these pregnancy hormones would calm down.

She closed the door behind her and stripped out of her

clothes. After running a warm bubble bath, she nearly cried as she sank into the bliss.

This was all she'd dreamed of all day long. Her own en suite bathroom was pretty grand, but she didn't have a large soaker tub like this. Her mother loved to redecorate, perhaps she could help. A complete bathroom overhaul wasn't a bad idea.

When her belly growled, Morgan figured she'd been in the tub long enough. The water had started to cool and she really did need to eat. Then she'd be ready to lie in bed and just relax. She'd likely fall asleep the moment her head hit the pillow even though it was still early in the evening.

Morgan grabbed the towel from the warming bar and dried off before wrapping herself up in the oversized terry cloth. Even these towels were amazing. How did a bachelor have all the right things that any woman would love?

No, not any woman. He wanted her. Not for love, but out of obligation and some sense of loyalty. If she wasn't pregnant, Morgan knew she wouldn't be here right now. And the idea of another woman in her place sent an instant burst of jealousy through her.

Why would she care who Ryan married or moved in after this month was up? She didn't want any part of a relationship her brother hatched by some silly trick. How could she trust such a connection that stemmed from a one-night stand?

Her siblings were all married or getting married to people they absolutely loved, and that was great for them, but Morgan was just fine being single or dating.

Honestly, though, she couldn't think of the last date she'd been on and once the baby came, she had a feeling her social life would only consist of mommy-and-me playdates.

Even then, Morgan didn't like the idea of another woman sharing Ryan's bed, learning his touch, knowing what made him irritated or sad or angry. Morgan had learned many of his character traits and for reasons she couldn't explain, she wanted to hold every bit of that information close to her chest and keep it all for herself.

She padded barefoot into the adjoining bedroom to grab her robe off the end of the bed. Again, she stopped. Now there was a tray of food on the table beside her bed. She moved closer and smiled at the hearty portion of lasagna, bread, salad and tea. On the perfectly folded napkin was an assortment of colorful vitamins.

The handwritten note simply said, *For you and the baby.*

She'd been taking her prenatal vitamins with each meal and clearly Ryan had been paying attention. How much had he taken in? Clearly her love for the holidays and the time she got off work he'd noticed.

She also couldn't help but wonder if he was caring for her to persuade her into marriage or if he would be doing all of this stuff anyway had she already agreed.

Regardless, she was thankful and she'd tell him just how much. Of course, she'd rather show him, but he was still being difficult.

Morgan slid on her robe and tightened the belt, wondering how she could spin all of this to her advantage. Perhaps she could start persuading him. She hadn't tried enough seducing because she'd been so tired lately, but each night she went to bed, knowing he was so close and aching for his touch.

Now that she'd had him, she didn't know how she'd

ever turn to anyone else. It would be impossible not to compare other lovers to Ryan.

Since her time was limited here and Ryan was still standing his ground, it was time for her to take charge and go after what she wanted. Isn't that what he was doing?

Ryan Carter had finally met his match...and his ultimate challenge.

Twelve

Ryan rounded the curve of the staircase and headed toward his room. As he started down the hallway, he stilled and his attention landed on Morgan's closed door.

Was she in there right now soaking in a hot bath with iridescent bubbles kissing her skin? She likely had that red hair piled on top of her head. Maybe a few wayward strands had fallen to lie against her neck.

When he'd brought her food up earlier it had taken every bit of his willpower not to go on into that bathroom and help make sure she was good and relaxed.

Ryan cursed beneath his breath. He could still go in there right now and take her. She'd more than shown him that she was willing, but how would that further his goal? He didn't want a temporary fix to any situation. He wanted Morgan forever to help him build the next generation and be one cohesive unit as a family.

Maybe she would come around. He had to keep looking ahead and whether Morgan believed him or not, this decision would be the best for her, too.

He only wished he didn't have to be so damn noble like she'd accused. He'd used every last bit of his self-control where she was concerned. Over the past few nights, he'd lain awake wondering what she was doing across the hall and wondering if she was over there thinking of him, too.

Usually ranch business kept him tossing and turning, but now the insomnia could only be attributed to the fiery beauty who'd turned his world upside down, yet still refused his proposal.

Ryan ignored the invisible tug toward her room and cursed himself once again as he headed to his. He had some emails to look over and some decisions to make regarding the sale of several head of cattle and he wanted to explore adding in more mares. There was a new ranch about an hour away that he hoped to do business with and build a solid relationship with the new owner.

A nice glass of bourbon and a night on the balcony doing some work should help take his mind off Morgan. Probably not, but he had to at least try and he still had this business to run.

Ryan stepped into his room and closed the door, immediately pulling his tee over his head. He toed off his boots and removed his socks. Decompressing and forcing himself to relax was the only way he was going to get through these next few weeks.

Ryan went to the dry bar in the living area of his room and poured three fingers of his favorite bourbon. He pulled his cell from his pocket and opened up the emails as he headed toward the double doors leading to his balcony. Maybe a little fresh air would calm him.

He loved the outdoors and he loved the vantage point that his room provided over the property. He could see the barns, the pond, and some of the acreage with his livestock dotting the horizon.

There was nothing he loved more than seeing what he'd created. Knowing now that he had an heir to pass his estate to warmed and settled something deep inside. He'd been given a second chance with the most unexpected woman. They would make a dynasty together, of that he was sure. He was pretty damn proud of what he had to offer to not only Morgan, but their baby.

He'd taken wise investments and the inheritance from his parents and turned everything into the Yellow Rose Ranch. No other name would have fit this place. His mother had a plethora of yellow roses in her gardens year after year and he always wanted to remember her. The homage only seemed fitting.

The moment he stepped onto his balcony, Ryan stilled.

"Thank you for the dinner and the Christmas tree."

Morgan sat on the sofa against the solid balcony wall with her bare legs stretched out along the cushions. Her hair was piled on top of her head as he'd imagined…and that damn robe splayed open giving him the best view he'd ever seen on this balcony. The only thing beneath the parted material was moonlit skin.

Damn. She was good at this.

"You're welcome."

Everything in him had to tear his gaze away from all of that exposed skin that he desperately wanted to touch. His grasp on this invisible string was about to snap and he didn't know how much longer it would hold.

"Did you not want to sit on your balcony?" he asked. "It has a nice view, too."

A slow grin spread across her face as her gaze dropped to his bare chest. "Not like this."

His body instantly stirred and the loose grip on his resolve was nearly gone.

"You're playing a dangerous game."

Morgan swung those long, lean legs over the side of the couch and came to her feet. She spread her robe even wider as she rested her hands on her hips.

"No, I'm taking what we both want."

And that was it. The gauntlet had been thrown down and he was damn well going to pick it up because there was only so much a man could take.

Ryan crossed to her in two strides.

Without a care or a second thought, he jerked that robe from her shoulders and let it fall to the floor behind her. Her eyes widened as did her smile, as if she knew she had won.

In his defense, though, he sure as hell hadn't lost.

"Finally," she murmured a second before he captured her lips.

Ryan couldn't touch her enough. He wanted his hands all over her. He gripped her backside and pulled her hips flush wish his, her breasts pressed against his bare chest. He was not a damn bit angry that he'd given in.

They both needed this and she was sexy as hell for taking charge.

"Were you coming out here to work?" she muttered against his mouth.

"Work doesn't exist for the moment." He framed her face with his hands and forced her attention on him. "Nothing else matters but right here, right now."

Her eyes remained fixed on his as her hands went to the buckle on his belt. Ryan sucked in a breath as she worked his jeans open and shoved them down, taking his boxer briefs with them.

"I hope your ranch hands are in the bunkhouse." She laughed.

"You ask now after you've already been sitting out here practically naked?"

She shrugged. "I was only worried about you, nothing else."

His heart clenched and he hated that unwanted sensation. He didn't want his heart involved. He'd tried that before and it had left him emotionally scarred.

This was sex. Just like the other two times with Morgan. There were no deeper feelings to explore.

"They're probably all in the bunkhouse," he assured her. "And it's well on the other side of the barns. Nobody can see what we're doing up here."

She poked a finger into his chest. "Then take a seat, cowboy."

Who was he to ignore a demand like that?

Ryan shifted around her and sank down onto the sofa. Morgan stared down at him. The gentle evening breeze picked up her stray tendrils and sent them dancing about her shoulders. Morgan's body seemed to radiate a shimmering beauty with the moonlight and soft glow spilling out from his bedroom.

She rested a knee on one side of his hips, then straddled him with her other. Delicate hands came to rest on his shoulders as she continued to keep her wide stare on him.

There was more than passion in those expressive eyes, there was determination. He could appreciate her drive and her desire. They were matched in so many ways, yet he couldn't look at this as more than a smart decision to further the future goals of his ranch.

Ryan gripped her hips as she joined their bodies and every thought in his head vanished. There was only now with this woman. Her short nails bit into his skin as she began to move. Her quick actions were a sure sign she'd had too much pent-up passion as he'd held her off as long as he could. He should have known he wouldn't be able to last the entire month without having her and he should have known Morgan would go after what she wanted.

Knowing she was this turned on, this aroused for him, only added to his pressing need for her. Ryan gripped her backside with one hand and thrust the other up into her hair, sending the knot tumbling down. Vibrant red strands fell around her shoulders as she dropped her head back and arched into his body.

Her hips jerked faster and watching her lose herself in the intensity of the moment was all he needed to let go. They'd been dancing around this moment for days and he couldn't hold back any longer.

Ryan pulled her mouth to his and captured her lips. He needed to feel all of her, to touch her any way and every way he could. Morgan's body calmed seconds before his and Ryan banded his arms around her waist. He nipped at her lips gently before easing back and staring up at her.

Those full, damp lips, her hair in a mass all around them, and those sexy heavy lids with her eyes locked onto his had Ryan already positive this was just the start of tonight's festivities.

"Thanks for the tree and dinner," she told him with a smile.

"You already told me that."

He smoothed the hair back from her face, wanting to see more of her and wondering if he'd ever get enough.

"I wanted to thank you properly," she amended.

Ryan ran his hands up and down that smooth skin on her back and down over her hips. She shivered beneath his touch, which only proved to him he held some power over her. She wasn't immune to his advances or uncaring. She wanted this, maybe from a different standpoint than him, but didn't they technically have the same goal in mind?

They both wanted stability for their child and they both had amazing chemistry. Why couldn't she see this was so much more than temporary or some challenge to see who could win? They both could.

Soon she would come to realize that this might not be the same type of relationship as so many in Royal had found with everlasting love, but he and Morgan had a pretty damn good possibility to be a dynamic couple. Love didn't have to factor in one bit.

When she trembled once again, Ryan gathered her close and came to his feet, with her still wrapped all around him.

"It's a little chilly out here." He kept his focus over her shoulder as he carefully carried her back into his room. "Maybe you can keep expressing your thanks in here where it's warmer and more comfortable."

Her lips grazed his neck. "I still have plenty of ways to show my appreciation."

Ryan's entire body heated up all over again at her sultry tone and promise. He hoped like hell this was just one of the many nights she would spend in his bed and wondered if they were just one step closer to putting that ring on her finger.

Thirteen

"I told Vic and Chelsea they could tell Aubrey and Nolan about the baby. And Layla could tell Josh."

Morgan waited for Ryan to say something, but he just tightened his hold around her as she leaned into his side. They'd gathered blankets and come back out to the balcony to enjoy the beautiful night sky. Ryan had lit the heater and they lay entangled on the sofa. Clothes were still strewn about, but she was in absolutely no hurry to pick them up.

She'd come home with every intention of going to bed early, but relaxing with Ryan trumped any book or a nap.

The clear sky gave them a spectacular unobstructed view of the stars and full moon. The magical night enveloped her, giving her a glimpse of too many possibilities. But she couldn't let her imagination get away from her. She couldn't allow herself to feel too much or to give her heart an opportunity to break. She had to focus on their child and not be selfish with looking for anything more than a stable foundation.

"I didn't know we were making an announcement yet."

Morgan pulled in a deep breath. "I didn't think it was fair to ask them to keep secrets from their partners."

His fingertips caressed a pattern up and down her bare arm as she lay against him. She couldn't see his face and she wondered what he was thinking.

"Vic was relieved and asked if he could tell Jayden. But I'd like us to tell Zanai and Jayden together, unless you don't want to?"

"It's fine," he told her. "It's funny, we wouldn't even be here if Vic and Jayden hadn't told me you were attracted to me."

Morgan's breath caught in her throat. A heavy dose of dread settled heavy in her belly.

She flattened her hand against his chest and eased herself up to turn and face him.

"What did you say?"

Ryan stared back, clearly unaware of the turmoil and anger that his words had set into motion.

"At the masquerade party," he clarified. "Vic and Jayden told me that you were attracted to me. I honestly had no idea before that. I thought we just annoyed and tolerated each other because the town is so small, it's impossible to avoid everyone."

How could she be so damn foolish? Her own brother and his best friend had clearly been laughing at her behind her back. And now Vic knew she was pregnant and temporarily living with Ryan. Oh, he must really be loving that.

Morgan came to her feet and untangled herself from the blanket. She'd known her brother filled her in about the little trick on her, but she had no idea they'd done the same to Ryan.

"I cannot believe this," she muttered as she grabbed the first article of clothing she could find.

"What's wrong?" Ryan asked.

She jerked on her robe and knotted the belt. "What's wrong? My brother and Jayden. That's what's wrong. You want to know what they told me?"

Ryan's jaw clenched, and his lips thinned. "Probably not."

"They told *me* that *you* had the hots for *me*." Morgan crossed her arms over her chest and tried to calm down, but she was furious. "What the hell game were they playing?"

Ryan stretched his arm along the back of the sofa and with no readable expression. How could he remain so calm when faced with this ugly truth? Morgan was ready to drive over to Vic's house and punch him in the face. How could she trust him? How could she trust any of this situation when all of it had been based on lies and deceit? And now an innocent baby and real feelings had been tossed into the mix.

"Maybe they were playing Cupid," Ryan offered.

Morgan narrowed her gaze. "I'm not amused and why would two grown men even care? This is ridiculous. Damn it."

Ryan shoved the blanket aside and came to his feet. When he reached for her, she wanted to back away, but none of this was his fault.

"I had no idea they did any of this," he told her, gently squeezing her shoulders. "I'm sure getting worked up isn't good for the baby or your sanity. I'll be angry enough for the both of us and talk to Jayden. What the hell had those two been thinking?"

"I just don't get it." She shook her head, trying to make sense of it all. "Vic surely couldn't care less who I end up with as long as I'm happy. I don't understand why he and Jayden said anything at all."

"Who knows? Maybe because they're both in committed relationships and happy and want the same for us."

It still sounded so odd for Vic to meddle like that. Though joking and pranks had always been his style. But hadn't this gone a bit too far? Granted, they'd likely had no idea she and Ryan would tumble into bed that same night.

"I hate being made to seem like a fool," she muttered.

Ryan framed her face and tipped her head up so she had nowhere to look but at him.

"You're not a fool," he corrected her. "And would you honestly take back what happened? We're having a child and you're living here now. I have zero regrets."

Another ribbon of frustration curled through her. She didn't want to give Ryan the wrong impression. She still had no intention of marriage.

"I don't regret the baby," she admitted. "And I'm only here temporarily. I can't—"

Ryan captured her lips and threaded his hands through her hair as he pulled her body flush with his. All thoughts vanished from her mind and she couldn't even remember the point she was trying to make.

When he touched her, he made all of her emotions rise higher than her thoughts. Making her feel more amazing than she ever had seemed to be one of Ryan Carter's many talents.

"Not tonight," he murmured against her lips as he rested his forehead against hers. "No more talking of the future tonight."

At some point they would have to talk, but right now,

she just wanted more of his touch. She slid the robe back off and let it slide silently to the floor.

Ryan lifted her and carried her back into his bedroom. She'd never had any intention of sleeping in here with him, but one night wouldn't hurt. She wanted this man and she wanted him to continue to show her just how much he needed her. Because deep down…she needed him, too.

"Why did you have to call us in here so early?" Vic asked.

Morgan had asked Vic, Chelsea and Layla to her store before she opened. She needed to talk to them privately and this was the only place that would ensure they wouldn't be overheard.

Morgan stared at her brother and sisters and tried to find the right words because the more she had thought about what Vic and Jayden did, the angrier she became. Her sisters likely didn't know any of this had taken place, but since they knew the rest of the secret, it was only right to have them here now.

Vic didn't look a bit relaxed as he stood beside the plush white high-back chair where Chelsea sat. He had his hands propped on his hips with an intense stare aimed directly at her.

"Is something wrong with the baby?" Layla asked.

Her sisters' worried looks had Morgan shaking her head.

"No. The baby is fine and I appreciate you all keeping that secret for now."

"Then what's the problem?" Vic asked.

Morgan rested her hip against the table that had a beautiful display of fluffy throws and fuzzy socks. Her cozy collection had been selling even better than expected for the holidays, which made that risk a success. She only hoped her new maternity line would be as successful.

"Well, dear brother, the problem is you meddling in my affairs." Morgan laced her fingers in front of her and never wavered her gaze. "How dare you. I trusted you to be there for me in everything in life, not push yourself into molding the outcome."

Layla held up her hands. "Hold up. Care to fill me in?"

"Go ahead," Morgan told Vic. "Let her know what you and Jayden did. I'm sure you found it hilarious at the time yet you look a little nervous now."

Vic adjusted his Stetson and blew out a sigh. "Morgan, we never meant to be deceitful and we sure as hell weren't laughing at you and Ryan."

Chelsea came to her feet. "Would someone tell me what the hell is going on here?"

"Our brother decided that I needed assistance in my social life," Morgan explained. "He and Jayden told me that Ryan was attracted to me, but they told Ryan I was attracted to him."

Morgan redirected her attention back to her brother. "How long before the Masquerade Ball did you two work on that scheme?"

"There was no scheme," Vic explained. "Jayden and I actually thought you and Ryan needed a nudge. You had danced around each other for months. All that bickering and griping at each other, it was clear you both were attracted."

"I can get my own dates," she countered. "Do you know how humiliating that was to discover?"

Vic took a step forward and reached for her hands. "I never, ever meant for you to be angry or upset and I sure as hell never thought you were a fool. I thought you liked Ryan and he liked you. It was that simple because neither of you were making a move."

When she looked away, Vic cocked his head to continue to hold her in his sights. "Are you angry with how things turned out? I mean, you're living with the man and having his baby."

"No, I'm not sorry how things turned out," she told Vic, then glanced to her sisters. "And it's temporary. Ryan is insisting I marry him and he wanted to play house for a month to convince me."

Chelsea and Layla both smiled and Morgan jerked her hands from her brother's. She didn't like those similar stares looking back at her. She didn't want them to intrude in her personal business. She just wanted...

Hell. She didn't even know anymore.

Perhaps that was the crux of the entire situation. What had started as a joke had turned her life upside down. Her feelings for Ryan grew stronger each day and she didn't like it. She wanted to be in control of her wants and needs, but she hadn't been in control of anything since that night.

Now Vic was smiling, which also grated on her last nerve.

"Stop looking at me like that when I'm trying to be upset," she scolded.

"We just love you and want you to be as happy as we are," Layla explained. "You deserve to find someone to spend your life with and you're already starting a family. It just makes sense."

Yeah, it made sense...if she wanted a relationship based on a meddling brother and a joke.

"I know you all mean well," she told them. "But what Ryan and I have and are doing is so far removed from what you guys have with the love you've found."

Chelsea offered a soft smile. "It doesn't have to be."

They didn't understand, and that was fine. Morgan knew what was and wasn't happening with her relationship with Ryan. She had everything crystal clear in her head. It was just those sweet gestures and their passionate night that had thrown her off. He was trying to sway her into marrying him, but why? When they had a good thing going like this, why muddle it with marriage?

She meant it when she said he might find someone later and actually want a marriage where love existed. She wouldn't want to go through a divorce and overturn the life they'd created for their child. Morgan had been blessed with a solid upbringing and she would settle for nothing less with her own baby.

"That's all I wanted to say," Morgan told her siblings. "I only called Chelsea and Layla in here because they knew about the baby and I wanted them to know how all this happened."

"No need to pull in the big guns," Vic said, laughing as he looked at the three sisters. "I'm truly sorry, Morgan, if you think I was being deceptive, but my actions were all out of love." Vic wrapped his arms around her and held her tight. "I'd do anything for my little sister."

Morgan laughed. "Well, lay low for a while because I've had about all I can handle of your interference."

Vic laughed and pulled back. "I promise to control myself from here on out, but I'm not sorry I helped you two along. I'm going to be an uncle and spoil this baby."

"I might have already placed a substantial order for baby clothes." Chelsea cringed and shrugged. "I'm not even sorry about it."

"I don't even know if I'm having a boy or a girl." Morgan chuckled.

"Oh, don't worry," Layla assured her. "She ordered plenty of both."

Morgan groaned. She couldn't even imagine the love and gifts that would be poured upon her child. Her family loved big and no doubt they would not hold back here.

"I'm surprised you haven't planned the baby shower," Morgan joked.

"We've booked the TCC already for April and said we were having a girls' night out party so nobody was suspicious. Hope that works for you and Ryan."

Morgan rubbed her head and Vic simply patted her shoulder.

"I'm done intervening, but maybe you were talking to the wrong siblings."

Morgan didn't care if her sisters wanted to throw a lavish baby shower. Her siblings wanted nothing but the best. She understood that even if she didn't like Vic's course of action.

Ryan wanted nothing but the best for her, too. She only wished her heart wasn't getting involved.

Fourteen

Ryan didn't know if this plan was going to backfire or win him more points, but he hadn't gotten this far in life without taking risks.

His staff was all too thrilled he'd dismissed them for the day when there was still daylight. But Ryan wanted his land to be all about him and Morgan for the day. He wasn't sure when his feelings shifted from wanting to fulfill a legacy to wanting to share all of this with Morgan. No matter when the slow fade happened, Ryan knew without a doubt this was where Morgan belonged. And for her to understand and see that as well, she needed to know about his life and what led him to this point.

There was nothing Ryan was more proud of than Yellow Rose Ranch. He didn't think that made him shallow or egotistical at all. He'd worked damn hard from his inheritance and wise investments, coupled with smart business sense, and he wanted to show off what he had created.

"What are we doing in the stables?"

Ryan turned as Morgan stepped inside. Her polished look never failed to impress and amaze him. She was everything he wasn't, and she didn't seem to mind that he lived in the same style of clothes every single day. She, on the other hand, never wore the same thing twice.

Today she had on a long black dress, cowgirl boots, and a fitted denim jacket. She could go from the girl next door to the elegant partygoer to the bedroom vixen in a blink and he was quickly discovering just how much he enjoyed each of Morgan's personalities.

"I thought I'd show you around," he told her.

She stopped at the stall that just so happened to house his stallion. Morgan smiled and reached her hand in. Midnight's nose came out enough for Ryan to see. Morgan's gentle touch and kind smile hit him in the gut and all he could think of was how she belonged here. This is where he would raise his family, and his wife would make this ranch her own.

"He's gorgeous." Morgan's hand rested on the side of Max's face as she glanced Ryan's way. "So gentle and sweet."

"He can ride faster than lightning," Ryan added. "He's my best buddy here and I wouldn't get anything done without him."

She dropped her hand and started moving toward him once again. Those eyes were fixed on his and he still couldn't figure out how she held such a strong power over him. She was absolutely mesmerizing in the most intriguing way.

"And is that why you brought me here?" she asked.

"To introduce me to your horse? That's a big step in a relationship."

Ryan couldn't help but laugh. "That's part of the reason. I want to show you around the ranch and since riding a horse is out because of the baby, I thought we'd start here and then we can ride around in the Jeep to look through the acreage."

Morgan reached him and crossed her arms over her chest. "I grew up on a ranch, Ryan. I'm well aware of what they look like and how they work."

"You don't know about Yellow Rose," he corrected her as he turned and held out his elbow. "Walk with me and I'll figure out where to start."

Her eyes darted from his face to his arm and she slid her hand into the crook of his elbow.

"Why don't you start with the name," she suggested. "Yellow Rose Ranch is beautiful, but I do wonder where it came from."

Ryan laid his free hand over hers as they headed toward the other end of the stables. He couldn't recall a time he wanted anything more than to have Morgan agree to marry him. They could live like this together, raise their child and any future children right here. Growing up on a ranch would instill values they wouldn't learn anywhere else.

That was just another area he and Morgan had in common. Even though she'd turned from the lifestyle, she still knew the ins and outs because she, too, had grown up on a large ranch. This step toward marriage was the right one and the only solution that made any sense. He had to make her see that she wasn't settling, she wasn't losing. In the long run, they'd both be happy.

"My mother's favorite flower was the yellow rose. She

always had them in the house and apparently everyone knew because they were all over at her graveside service."

Ryan could finally talk about his mother and remember the good instead of that instant feeling of pain and loss. Those emotions were still present—they would never go away, but at least he had learned to compartmentalize and he could smile when he thought of her.

"She was always happy, always wanting to make sure everyone around her was in a good mood," he continued. "It's just appropriate that her favorite color was yellow."

"She sounds like an amazing woman."

Ryan nodded as he led Morgan to the Jeep parked behind the stable. "She was, and she would love knowing she'd be a grandmother. No doubt she would have already had a nursery painted and fully stocked. She was all in with everything and loved her family."

"Family is important to both of us."

Morgan started to reach for the handle of the Jeep, but he beat her to it and opened the door. When he gestured her in, she gave him a side-eye and took a seat.

"You know, I'm still moving out at the end of the month, right?" she told him.

Ryan shrugged. "Of course."

He closed the door and rounded the vehicle to climb in behind the wheel. He started up the engine and turned the heat on because even though they were still in Texas, there was a chill in the air in December.

"I own just over twelve thousand acres," he started. "Definitely not the biggest ranch, but I'm proud of it and we're profitable and productive."

Morgan reached over and laid her hand on his on the console. Her soft touch stirred something inside him, something that wasn't arousal...but more pure and innocent. There was almost a comfort and understanding to her gesture.

"This isn't a job interview," she informed him. "Don't sell me this place, Ryan. Why don't you tell me why you love ranch life so much?"

Thoughts instantly swirled around in his head of all the reasons he felt alive on this property. From sunup until sundown, there was so much packed into a day. Not to mention the nostalgia surrounding him at any given time.

"Even on the hardest days, there's nothing else in the world I'd rather be doing."

Morgan squeezed his hand before releasing him. "That's how you know you're in the right profession. Nothing is perfect and it's not always easy, but if you still love your job in those down times, you're blessed."

"It's not just all that I've accomplished here," he added. "I have women and men who work for me that have become like family. This industry forms such strong, tight-knit bonds. Unless you're part of it, the concept is difficult to grasp."

Morgan pointed out her window as he drove along the edge of the pasture.

"What's that peak over there?" she asked.

"That's where we're headed first."

"I'm intrigued." She turned her attention toward him. "I thought we were just coming out here to look at your livestock."

"They're already in another pasture," he informed her. "There's something I wanted you to see other than animals."

Silence settled in the small space as he headed toward the surprise that he hoped didn't backfire. He wanted Morgan to see his life, really see it. She'd turned away from ranching before and here he was trying to pull her back in, to accept this and a marriage that was more like a business arrangement than anything else.

Could he fault her for turning him down?

Even she admitted that she didn't believe in love, so why wouldn't she just give in already?

"I spoke to Vic this morning before the shop opened."

Her statement pulled him from his own thoughts. He already felt sorry for Vic because he knew how angry Morgan had been last night when she'd figured out what had happened.

"How did that go?" he asked.

"I'm still irritated, but I truly think he had good intentions. Even if his methods were ridiculous, he really just wants to see me happy."

"And are you?"

He wanted her to be happy. He hadn't realized how much so, but if she couldn't see herself here or find contentment, then they both lost.

"Morgan—"

"My happiness is the least of my worries."

He reached over and took her hand in his. "Your happiness is equally as important as our child."

"No, it's not."

Ryan maneuvered around the bend as the old structure came into view. Just like every other time he rounded that fence line, memories came flooding back. He hoped they always did because that kept those moments, those people, alive inside him.

"I don't have you at my house just to convince you to marry me," he told her. "I'm trying to do what is best here and I want you to see that you can be happy, *we* can be happy, and that's what will make a good environment for our family. So your happiness is at the top of my priorities."

"How do you do that?" she asked.

"Do what?"

"You make me think and feel and...want."

Her last word came out on a whisper and damn it, he had a burst of hope. Having her come to the decision to stay had been his initial goal. He didn't want to force her to marry him or trick her into this union. Morgan was a strong woman and that was who he wanted by his side raising their child.

Ryan thought it best to say nothing and just let her deal with that statement and her thoughts on her own. His actions would more than show her why he wanted her here.

He pulled up to the old stone house and shut off the engine. He glanced toward Morgan to see her face and gauge her reaction.

"This is an adorable cottage," she stated. "I didn't know this was back here."

"This is where I grew up."

She jerked her attention to him, her eyes wide.

"There was all of this land surrounding the house," he told her. "Some was used for a farm, but it was all owned by different people. I knew I wanted this land, all of it, when I grew up. I wanted to prove I'd made it and that I could do anything I wanted."

Ryan reached up and cupped the side her face. "I know the ranch life isn't for you," he said, stroking his thumb over her bottom lip. "But all I've ever wanted was to be a cowboy, and that little boy's dream came true. I'm not trying to change you into someone you're not, and I'm not asking you to settle or rearrange your life. I'm asking you to be a part of this legacy and just marry me."

Tears filled her eyes and he didn't know if that was

the pregnancy hormones or if his words were finally getting to her. All he could offer was his little piece of the world, but never his heart.

"I have another surprise for you after this."

Morgan laughed as a tear slid down her cheek. "Do you sit around and think of ways to keep me guessing what's next?"

Ryan shrugged, swiping away the moisture from her silky skin. "Never thought of it that way. I'm just making sure you know that I'd take care of you and we don't need to get into the fact you're capable of taking care of yourself. I'm well aware. I just want you to know that you'd have a good life here and so would our baby."

He moved his hand to settle over her still flat stomach, all the while keeping his gaze locked on hers.

"I know we would," she admitted as she rested her hand over his. "But everything moved so fast and there hasn't been time to process all the changes so it's impossible to fully grasp another life change."

She closed her eyes and blew out a sigh before meeting his stare once again.

"I see my siblings all falling in love and getting married," she told him. "Part of me wants to believe love is real and if it's real, shouldn't I hold out for that? Shouldn't we both? We deserve to have that person in our lives who will be forever. Because you and I both know that if there hadn't been a pregnancy, then we wouldn't be here right now. There's no love between us, Ryan."

While he did hear what she was saying, and firmly believed that she meant each word, Ryan also knew he was wearing her down. She still had a few more weeks here and he wasn't giving up on his family.

"Not every marriage is a fairy tale." He turned his

hand to lace their fingers together. "But we can make our own happy ending."

When she opened her mouth, no doubt to turn him down again, Ryan held up his hand.

"Keep thinking about it," he told her. "Don't turn me down this second. My ego can't take all of the negative answers."

Morgan smiled and that was exactly what he wanted. He didn't want every moment between them to be so intense and serious. He didn't want to fight anymore when they got along so well in too many other areas. The only thing he wanted her to fight for was them. He wouldn't back down, not when he knew Morgan valued family and they had the same ideals.

But he still needed to show her where he came from so she could appreciate what he had now. He loved riding back here and getting the reminder that he'd started from humble beginnings.

Some had questioned why he never tore this place down since it was in the middle of his acreage, but that would be like trying to erase his childhood and those were memories he never wanted to lose.

"I have a few more areas on the ranch I want to show you before head back to the house." He eased away and started the engine back up. "The next surprise is even better than this one."

Morgan chuckled. "Can't wait."

Fifteen

At first, Morgan thought Ryan was just being overly ambitious to get her to marry him, but little by little she realized that beneath their squabbling and butting heads, there was merit. He was a hard worker, something she could appreciate, and he'd done nothing but put her first. Yes, he clearly wanted to cement his legacy, but he'd been working on that all while making sure her needs were not only being met but exceeded.

His old home had been simple and charming, a testament to the humble beginning he'd started with. Each moment she spent with him she realized there were so many layers to this intriguing man. More than she ever thought and she wondered if she'd ever stop discovering more about him.

"Keep your eyes closed."

Morgan stood in the hallway just down from her bedroom with her eyes firmly shut. After she'd seen where

Ryan had grown up, he'd taken her to the pond and talked about how he'd teach their child fishing. Then he took her the long way back to the barn and showed her a stall that would house their child's horse when the day came. He had everything all laid out for the future, but right now, he had planned something special.

"They're closed," she insisted. "But I can't stand it. What is the surprise?"

The click of a door echoed in the wide hall, and then Ryan curled his fingers around her arm and started guiding her forward.

"Just walk straight," he advised her. "Almost there and you won't run into anything."

She held out her free hand anyway because she had trust issues. "You're making me nervous."

Ryan's rich laughter filled the space. "Open."

Morgan blinked against the lights as her eyes traveled around the room. She gasped at everything presented before her.

"What have you done?" she asked as she started moving around. She really didn't know what to look at first.

"I hired a designer to come up with some model plans for the nursery," he explained. "I had to keep you out of the house for a bit longer when you got home, so I decided to show you around the ranch."

Morgan turned from the various model displays set up on tables to face Ryan.

"So was that cottage really the house you grew up in?" she asked.

Ryan nodded. "All of that was true and I wanted to show you anyway, so that was the best excuse."

Morgan walked around the model displays, each on their own stand, and was absolutely amazed at what he'd done for her. Never in her life had anyone surprised her to the point she was nearly speechless.

"I don't know what you've thought of for a nursery," he went on. "And whether you live here or not, I still want a place for the baby and I want you to decide what the room looks like. You would have more sense than me about this stuff."

Morgan listened to Ryan as she went back and closely studied the first display. Her heart felt so full, so happy. She really didn't know what to say right now because she was still absorbing the fact Ryan had thought to do all of this on his own. He'd wanted to make a special place for their child and he'd called someone to come up with such intricate plans.

Considering he hadn't known about the baby for too long, he likely had to pay quite a bit for this rush job. But each and every design was so stunning and utterly amazing.

She trailed her finger over the tiny crib, then the model-sized rocker. This was really happening and she bounced from being terrified to being excited. There was no in between.

"I told the designer different styles I thought you liked or information I've taken from your store and the way you dress. You seem to go toward classy with a bit mix of trendy…or that's what the designer said when I described you."

Morgan glanced over her shoulder and smiled. "I can tell you told her something about me. I love them all."

Ryan held his hands out. "Listen, I might wear the same things over and over and I might not know terms or fashion lingo, but that doesn't mean I don't pay attention."

One design had a crisp, clean look to the space with white furniture and pops of green and gold. Very classy.

Another design seemed a little more catered to the ranch with the dark woods, deep gray motif. There were a couple for each gender that were clearly for a boy or a girl as well, and Morgan honestly couldn't decide.

"How soon do we need to let her know?" Morgan asked.

Ryan moved to the opposite side of the room where a chaise sat in front of the floor-to-ceiling window overlooking the pond. He rested his hand on the slope of the high back and shrugged.

"I just told her I would be in touch," he replied. "So take your time or make notes about changes you want. She said she could add or remove anything and even combine various aspects from each one. I didn't know if you were thinking something neutral or if you decided to wait to find out the sex. I'm good no matter what, so that's your call."

That familiar, annoying burn started in her throat as her eyes started to fill. Morgan couldn't help but put her head in her hands. She was so tired of these roller-coaster emotions and riding this pregnancy wave. Her thoughts were all over the place from happy to sad to scared to excited. She didn't even know how to feel anymore...not that she could control it anyway.

Ryan was immediately there, pulling her into his warmth and strength.

"Damn it, I knew I overstepped," he murmured. "I'll have her come take everything back and you can design whatever you want. I thought this would be a good thing for you and you might like it, but..."

Morgan shook her head and eased back just enough to rest her hands on his chest and look him in the eye.

"No, this is... Well, this is the greatest surprise I've ever had. You mentioned the sex of the baby and everything just hit me, I guess. I was so shocked when I found out I was expecting and worried about what you would think, what the town would think. I'm fully embracing the reality that our baby is actually coming and we aren't just fodder for the gossip mill."

Ryan smoothed her hair from her face and held her head firmly in his hands as he leaned closer.

"This baby isn't a mistake or gossip," he told her. "We're going to raise her together and she'll have the strength and determination from both of us to do anything she wants in life."

Morgan smiled. "She? You want a girl?"

"I don't care what we have, but I just see you holding a little red-haired beauty. I've had dreams of it, actually."

"Is that so?"

He'd dreamed of their child? He'd dreamed of their baby looking like her, and Morgan couldn't help but wonder if his feelings were going deeper than he cared to admit.

"Are you worried?" she asked.

Ryan slid his hands into her hair and tipped her head back. "Not at all. You and I are going to be great parents."

At least one of them was confident. She used to find his arrogance annoying, but now she found that side of him to be a reassuring quality.

She needed more strength during this time in her life and she found herself drawing from him. Though the ease with which she could lean on him more and more terrified her, if she could keep this relationship physical and superficial, then she could hold on to her heart and not fall for a man who wouldn't love her in return.

Morgan took a step back and pulled her dress over her head. She dropped it to the floor and stood before him wearing only her undergarments and boots.

"You know that very large tub I kept trying to share with you?"

Ryan's mouth quirked as his eyes raked over her body. "I remember."

"Maybe you'll join me?"

She didn't wait for his reply as she walked out of the room. She knew Ryan would follow, and when she heard his boots echoing on that hardwood floor behind her, Morgan smirked all the way into her bathroom.

For now, everything in her world was right...but she'd set the boundaries and all of this was temporary. In just a couple weeks, she'd be back in her home and these passionate nights would just be a memory.

Jonas Shaw, the investigator, had called another important meeting. Morgan had asked Ryan to come with her for support, which really surprised him, but at the same time warmed him. They still weren't ready to come forward with...

What? The baby? Their unsettled living arrangement?

He didn't even know what to call their situation. Likely word had already spread about him being at her shop and the two of them not griping at each other anymore. He wanted to be here for her, in whatever capacity she needed.

The Grandins and the Lattimores all gathered at the Lattimore estate per the private investigator's orders. Jonas only called in both families when he had pertinent information, so Ryan couldn't help but wonder what new development had taken place.

Morgan caught his gaze from across the spacious formal living area. She'd wanted to stand with her siblings and he didn't want to intrude so he settled in near Jayden.

Yet just that one look she sent him had his heart racing. How did she do that? In a short time, they'd pivoted from verbal sparring to driving each other wild in the bedroom. But there was more...so much more going on between them. Now wasn't time or the place to try to figure out his feelings.

"You have any clue what this would be about?" Ryan whispered to Jayden.

"None," his buddy replied. "But it's got to be major for all of us to be here."

Jonas moved through the room and came to stand in front of the large floor-to-ceiling windows. The tall, slender man had become an ominous staple in Royal since the start of this investigation. He'd been trying to get to the bottom of Heath's claims. Why Cynthia had owned papers saying she'd been gifted untapped oil from Augustus Lattimore and Victor Grandin had remained a mystery.

"I'm glad you all could make it on such short notice," Jonas began as he tapped a folder against his thigh. "As you know, I've conducted several interviews, including ones with Augustus's former secretary, Sylvia Stewart, and the original surveyor, Henry Lawrence. I've also gone through every piece of paper Alexa could find. I now can share my conclusions."

Ryan crossed his arms and waited for the announcement as he glanced around the room to the members of both families, who had been friends for generations. The intermingling of their lives had woven so tightly, Ryan knew no bond could break them. They were all in this together.

"We know Cynthia had a brief relationship with Daniel Grandin," Jonas stated. "Without DNA, it took some time to get proof, but he was indeed Ashley's father."

"It seems that when Victor Sr. discovered the pregnancy, he didn't tell Daniel. He went to his best friend,

Augustus. They came up with a plan to offer Cynthia the oil beneath the Grandin estate as a bribe to remain silent. Victor didn't want his son caught up in a scandal. To sweeten the deal, Augustus Lattimore included his land. He couldn't let his best friend's last name be dishonored by his son's meaningless affair."

The gasps around the room seemed to echo, and Nolan reached for Chelsea's hand as her eyes went wide at the revelation.

"So the oil rights weren't an inheritance for Ashley," Nolan chimed in. "They were a payoff to get our mother to keep a dirty secret."

Jonas nodded. "It looks that way. I'm assuming the men figured she wouldn't have the resources to actually claim the oil, so that's when she later married Ladd Thurston. And you all know the rest of that story."

Cynthia had gone on to have the twins, Heath and Nolan.

"So once Heath finds out the rights were meant as a cover-up and not an inheritance, what will he do?" Jonathan Lattimore asked.

All eyes turned to Heath's brother, and Nolan merely shook his head and sighed. "I have no idea, to be honest. He wanted this for our mother, for Ashley. His heart is in the right place. I know not everyone believes that, but he just wants what he thinks belonged to our family."

"I don't even know what to say," Alexa Lattimore finally stated. "This is quite a bit to take in. So, does this end the investigation?"

"Unless I'm needed for more, I believe my part is done," Jonas claimed.

Silence settled over the room and Ryan tried to study each face. The members of these two families might actually have some closure right now, but again, everything hinged on Heath's next move.

"I'm sure this will be all the talk at the Christmas party tomorrow," Zanai whispered to Jayden. "I'll bet Heath doesn't show."

"He doesn't seem like the type of man who would back down or shy away from scandal," Jayden replied.

The Christmas party would certainly be all abuzz with gossip but Ryan had his own worries to deal with...like the fact he was getting deeper with Morgan. Morgan was still hell-bent on leaving his house at the end of the month, but he was just as hell-bent on keeping her there and building a life. He'd been robbed of that before and vowed never again. He needed Morgan to stay.

Because he knew if she walked away from the ranch, she'd never come back.

Sixteen

"You think we can make it out of the house with you looking like that?"

Morgan glanced in the mirror at the reflection of Ryan standing over her shoulder in his bedroom. His eyes held hers and Morgan spun around to take in the full view.

"This is just a white dress." She laughed as she gripped his lapels. "But you in a suit…that's pretty hot."

He started to reach for her, but dropped his hands.

"I don't even know where to touch you without messing anything up."

Morgan took his hands and settled them on her waist. "Never be afraid to touch me," she told him, then tipped her head to the side. "This is the first time I've ever seen you not in jeans and a T-shirt or naked."

Ryan's rich bark of laughter sent a shiver through her.

"Well, I've seen you in all aspects, and this dress is

making me want to skip the party completely and see what you have on beneath."

The bundle of nerves that started weeks ago swelled inside her. She had worries, fears and too many unknowns to remain calm.

"I'm wearing your favorite outfit under here."

His lips curved into a sultry grin. "My favorite outfit is nothing."

"Exactly." She patted the side of his face. "There's an excellent liner so you can't see a thing."

Ryan groaned and dug his fingers into her hips as he jerked her even closer. Their hips aligned and there was no mistaking his arousal.

"You're killing me," he growled. "I hate that we're not going together so I can walk in with you on my arm."

"Are you upset that I asked to arrive separately?" she asked, worried she'd put him in an uncomfortable position.

Ryan slid his hands up her arms and held on to her shoulders. "Not at all. I understand we have to find our footing here between us. That doesn't mean I don't want you by my side, but that can wait."

Guilt niggled at her because her feelings were growing and she had no idea what they were developing into or how to handle all of these sudden life changes. He wanted a marriage based solely on the baby and she couldn't help but feel like something much more was going on between them.

"I never want you to wonder if I think you and this baby are a dirty little secret," she explained. "With my sister's wedding and now this news about Heath and the oil, I don't want to add to all the chatter."

"I get it," he reassured her. "Believe me. After Chelsea and Nolan's wedding, we can figure out the best way to handle everything. People are going to find out about the baby, but maybe they'll also learn there's another wedding happening soon."

Morgan knew he still wanted marriage, now more than ever, and the temptation was so strong. But at the end of the day, she still had to do what she felt was right.

A week ago she was so adamant about saying no and now…well, now her heart told her to go for it, but her head told her to take a step back, evaluate the situation and calm down. Had they moved too fast? Could she trust her emotions at this stage? With so much confusion, she couldn't answer him right now. This wasn't something to rush into or take lightly.

The fact she waffled between her head and her heart really proved the strength of this pull toward Ryan.

"I'm going to head on out," she told him as she took a step back. "But feel free to peel me out of this when we get back."

The muscle in his jaw clenched as his eyes raked over her once again.

"That's a promise," he assured her. "Now get on out of here before I decide I don't want to wait and I don't care if I mess up your hair and makeup."

Morgan smiled as she grabbed her beaded gold clutch and headed out of her bedroom. The way he looked at her, the things he said to her, the way he treated her…how could she not be falling in love with the man?

Ryan Carter had more power over her than she ever wanted to admit. Love still terrified her, but at the same time, she wasn't sure if that was what she was feeling. All Morgan knew was that she didn't want to settle. That would never change. She only wished she knew more of what Ryan was thinking, of what he was feeling. Did he see her as more than the mother of his child and a bedmate? What held him back from opening up? Fear? Stubborn pride?

There were so many questions that she wouldn't get answered tonight, so she headed to the Cattleman's Club and decided to just have a good time...and she was already anticipating the after-party.

Seeing Ryan across the room proved to be more difficult than Morgan had figured. Actually, she hadn't thought about this part at all. She'd assumed they would arrive separately, be cordial, and maybe even share a dance. But Ryan had barely looked her way and she wasn't quite sure what to think about that.

She also hadn't thought about how odd it would be to walk around without a champagne flute in her hand like everyone else just to blend in. Perhaps she should have some sparkling water.

"You are stunning."

Morgan turned to see Chelsea and Nolan. The two held hands and were both beaming—apparently that was what love did to people. Could she be in love? Was that what had been happening to her over these past few weeks with Ryan? The idea thrilled and terrified her. She didn't know if she could rely on her mixed emotions and land on something so solid and monumental.

"Thank you," Morgan replied. "I see you went with the pale blue dress. Good choice."

Chelsea did a mock curtsey. "It was a toss-up when you ordered me three gorgeous gowns. This was Nolan's favorite, so the choice was obvious."

"Before we start mingling and dancing," Nolan chimed in, "I want to address the proverbial elephant that will be in the room tonight."

Morgan turned her attention to Nolan and the poor

guy's smile had faltered. Clearly he was embarrassed or uncomfortable at the latest findings, but there was no need to be. Heath was responsible for his own decisions.

"My brother—"

"I already know," Morgan assured him. "There are no hard feelings from me. Heath wanted to hold on to anything that was your mother's and I can understand that."

Chelsea wrapped an arm around Nolan's waist. The bond these two had was undeniable. They had overcome so many obstacles to be together and Morgan wondered just how they managed to be so strong.

"I feel I should apologize for his actions," Nolan added. "But that's not my place."

"No, it's not," Morgan agreed. "Is he coming tonight?"

Nolan shrugged. "I doubt it. He's pretty angry and frustrated and likely trying to plan his next steps. He wouldn't be in the mood for a party."

Morgan also imagined he wouldn't want to be in a room surrounded by Grandins and Lattimores. Yes, Heath wanted to honor his late mother and sister. It was hard to *completely* fault a guy for defending his mother. Still, he'd angered several people.

But Morgan had her own issues and Heath wasn't one of them right now.

"Nolan, would you care if I stole my sister for just a moment?" she asked. "I promise I won't keep her long."

"Of course."

Nolan kissed Chelsea on the cheek and stepped away, leaving them somewhat alone...save for the other guests mingling. Morgan motioned for Chelsea to follow and led her toward a corner of the room where they could have a little privacy.

"Something wrong?" Chelsea asked. "The baby?"

"No, no. Everything is fine. Well, with the baby. I just… I'm so confused."

Chelsea's brows drew together as she reached for Morgan's hand. "Is it Ryan?"

Morgan chewed the inside of her cheek and nodded. She would not get emotional here. Not only did her makeup look amazing for tonight, she really didn't want to have a meltdown in the middle of a festive holiday party.

"How did you know when you were in love?" Morgan whispered. She was glad she finally had a close relationship with her older sister to be able to ask this.

Chelsea's brows rose and a wide grin spread across her face. "The fact that you're even asking me that gives me so much hope. I love you and Ryan together."

Morgan glanced around to make sure no partygoers were within earshot. From the looks of things, the Royal elite had turned up. Most of the ladies wore dresses that she had ordered through her shop. From golds, to reds, to silvers…there was such a fun variety and they all looked so stunning among the twinkle lights, garlands and rustic lanterns suspended from the ceiling. The entire ballroom had been transformed into a winter wonderland.

"Has he said he loves you?" Chelsea asked.

Morgan shifted her attention back to her sister. "Oh, no. I'm just… I've got these feelings that are all over the place and I can't tell if I just have pregnancy hormones or if there's something more going on. But he opened up about his childhood, drove me around the ranch. He decorated my bedroom with a Christmas tree, and even put up lights and wreaths on his house so I'd feel at home during the holidays."

Chelsea sighed and squeezed Morgan's hands. "Honey, that man has fallen for you. Maybe he's too stubborn to admit it or maybe he hasn't figured it out himself, but that's love. Putting someone else's needs ahead of yours to make sure they are happy is the very definition. Relationships aren't fifty-fifty. They're one hundred-one hundred. Both parties have to put in their full effort for it to work. So if you're having feelings for him, tell him."

The thought of revealing her heart and exposing such a vulnerable piece of herself seemed much more intimate than sex. What if she told him and he didn't feel the same? He still wanted marriage, so what then? She'd still be trapped in a loveless marriage. No, this scenario would be much worse. A one-sided marriage would be a disaster.

"I don't know if I can do it," Morgan admitted.

Her sister released her hands and took a step back. "What? The Morgan I know isn't afraid of anything. You started an upscale boutique in the middle of a town full of ranchers and you've made it one of the most profitable businesses in the area. You're tackling this pregnancy like a champ and you're no-nonsense. So why are you letting your emotions control you?"

Morgan wrinkled her nose. "Because I don't like failing and I don't like rejection. What can I say? I'm human."

Chelsea's brows rose. "From the way Ryan has been staring this way, I think you might be surprised at his reply when you tell him the truth."

She'd be more surprised if he reciprocated her feelings. Before she said anything, though, she had to make one hundred percent sure she could trust her emotions. She had to be certain because not only did she not want to be hurt, she also didn't want to play with Ryan's heart. He might claim he wasn't looking for love, but what if...

"Thanks," Morgan told her sister. "I don't know what

I'm going to do, but I feel better. Now, let's concentrate on your big day. I'm glad it's soon because my boobs are already swelling and I don't know how much longer my dress will fit."

Chelsea rolled her eyes. "You have such problems. You will look gorgeous and if you need the dress adjusted any, I have my seamstress on hand."

Hopefully it wouldn't come to that because Morgan didn't want to have to explain the sudden weight gain.

Her sister gestured with her champagne flute as her focus shifted over Morgan's shoulder. "Looks like your guy is coming this way."

"He's not my guy."

Chelsea merely smirked. Okay, maybe right now Ryan was her guy. She just really wished she knew an actual label to put on this type of unique relationship they had.

"Ladies, you both look beautiful."

Chelsea smiled at Ryan, then glanced to Morgan.

"I appreciate that, though I have a feeling you had already seen my sister before you arrived."

Ryan's naughty grin gave him away and Morgan found her nerves unsettling. How could he do that? A simple smile and the way he could tip his head to one side as if to silently proclaim his innocence took a special skill...and Ryan appeared to have them all. He held so much power over her and he likely had no clue, which was just another reason that exposing her heart could be damaging.

And where would that leave them? They were bound together by a child forever and the last thing Morgan wanted was tension or animosity.

"I'll leave you two alone," Chelsea told them. "I need to find my fiancé."

Once she was gone, Ryan turned toward Morgan.

"Everything okay?" he asked, still keeping his distance.

Morgan forced herself to perk up and be cheerful. She definitely didn't want to start rumors or detract from her sister's big day coming up. Chelsea and Nolan had been through so much to make it to this point and Morgan wanted the entire experience to be absolutely perfect.

"Everything is great," she replied. Then movement just behind Ryan caught her attention. "Oh, there's Vic and Aubrey. I hadn't seen them yet."

"I want a dance with you before the night is over," he told her.

Morgan started to open her mouth, but he held up a hand.

"Nobody will think anything of it after the way we were kissing at the Masquerade Ball. We'll just dance, though. Nothing more, but it will be damn hard to keep my hands in an appropriate position."

There he went again with those sexy words that put instant images inside her mind. She'd only just arrived, but she was already counting down to when they would be back home alone.

Home.

Ryan's place felt like home, but for how long?

Damn it. She was in real trouble here.

Seventeen

Ryan knew Morgan and Chelsea were discussing something serious, likely something to do with him, from the way Chelsea kept glancing his way. He'd love to know what Morgan shared with her sister, but on the other hand, maybe it was best he didn't.

"Aubrey, you look stunning." Morgan reached for her soon-to-be sister-in-law and gave her a hug. "Of course, you always do, but that gold is perfect on you."

"Thank you." Aubrey beamed. "That white with your red hair is drop-dead gorgeous."

Ryan didn't know about color matching and what looked good with skin or hair or any accessories, but he could definitely agree on the drop-dead gorgeous. Morgan was always a stunner no matter how she dressed, but tonight she absolutely shone.

"What are you getting Chels and Nolan for a wedding present?" Vic asked.

Morgan shrugged. "I don't know. Want to go in on something together?"

"Yeah. Let's talk tomorrow." Vic replied as he wrapped his arm around Aubrey's waist and pulled her in to his side.

Jealousy speared through him. Ryan wanted to touch Morgan, to show her some affection, but they couldn't do that in public without raising more suspicions. They didn't need anyone knowing what was going on...not yet anyway. He still held out hope they would be announcing their engagement by Christmas. The ring was ready, *he* was ready. He just needed Morgan to be ready.

How could he protect his legacy if the relationship remained one-sided?

"I hope Heath stays away tonight," Ryan added. "He's caused enough of a scandal and folks just want to focus on having a good time and looking ahead to the holidays."

Vic nodded. "He'll be at the wedding next weekend. He's Nolan's best man."

"As long as Chelsea and Nolan's day isn't ruined, that's all that matters," Morgan told them.

Vic took a sip from his drink of choice and glanced around the spacious ballroom. "Jayden's here. I need to talk to him."

Morgan's brother slid his hand into Aubrey's as he eased her away. "If you both will excuse us."

Ryan nodded and once he was alone again with Morgan, he still kept his distance. Playing this part was ridiculous, but necessary. He wanted to get them over that hump and to the other side where they could be free and didn't have to hide any aspect of their relationship or the child they'd created.

"Is this just as awkward and difficult for you as it is for me?" she asked on a sigh, clearly frustrated.

Ryan slid his hands into his pockets. "These clothes are damn uncomfortable, but yes. In the past week, I haven't kept this much distance between us and I'm starting to get cranky."

Morgan stepped forward and motioned toward the dance floor. "Then let's have that dance now," she suggested. "Even friends dance together, right?"

He moved to close the distance between them, still not touching her, but close enough to see those bright blue eyes and the navy flecks. Her familiar floral perfume enveloped him, pulling him in even deeper. He'd grown so accustomed to everything about Morgan that he couldn't imagine trying to build a life with anyone else. This just made sense on so many levels.

"Is that where we are?" Ryan purposely dropped his gaze to her painted red lips, then back up. "Friends?"

"I don't know what label to put on us, honestly," she confessed on a whisper. "I know that I want to dance with you and then I want to go back home and let you fulfill that promise of peeling this dress off me."

"I like that you refer to the ranch as home."

He hadn't heard her say that before, and he wondered how long she'd thought of Yellow Rose as hers. Or maybe that was just a slip of the tongue. Regardless, he could tell she'd gotten comfortable at the ranch and he could easily see her there long-term with their child…and maybe more.

One step at a time, though. He had to win her over first.

When he'd built that house and started his life there, he had designed everything around his future and the family he would ultimately have.

Morgan didn't say a word. She just offered a sweet smile as she turned and headed for the dance floor.

They could talk about her thoughts of calling the ranch her home later. Right now, he wanted to dance with the woman he planned on spending his life with. Ryan followed those swaying hips at a distance and hoped he didn't appear too eager.

"I'm not sure I could've pulled this off without you by my side. Thank you."

Morgan stared down at the spread of food and bit her lip.

"You did it. I just supervised," Nelson assured her. "Ryan is a simple man. He likes meat and potatoes. You couldn't go wrong."

Morgan snorted. "Oh, I can go very wrong in the kitchen," she assured him. "But having your guidance gave me confidence."

Nelson patted her shoulder. "Ryan has never brought a woman to the ranch to stay, and just the fact you want to help and learn about his favorite meals really says a great deal about this relationship. Dare I hope this is serious?"

Having a man's baby was pretty serious, but even beyond that, Morgan had fallen for the man when she swore she wouldn't get more involved. Yet here she was, learning tips from Ryan's chef and waiting for him to come in from the pastures.

Morgan had called Nelson and asked him to come in on his day off. With her shop in good hands with Kylie, this was the perfect day for a surprise because Ryan never took days off from Yellow Rose. She couldn't wait to see the look on his face if she actually managed to pull this off.

"I'm not sure where we are right now," she answered Nelson honestly. "But I do love it here."

She wanted the conversation off the relationship and onto anything else.

Morgan faced the elderly man and smiled. "I really do appreciate you coming in on a Sunday. I'm sure you had other things to do like spend time with your family."

"My wife is likely at home quilting and enjoying some movie." His own grin had the wrinkles around his eyes creasing deeper. "I promise, she doesn't mind one bit. After nearly fifty years of marriage, you realize what really matters. She has her hobbies and I have mine. Cooking never feels like work and I love that you wanted to surprise Ryan."

Fifty years of marriage. Morgan couldn't even fathom fifty days, let alone years. That had to be one of the strongest bonds Morgan had ever heard of and she suddenly found herself wanting that deep connection. But how? A one-night stand hardly seemed the firm foundation for a lifelong commitment. Although they had moved beyond all the bickering they used to do. Maybe they'd made some substantial progress. Maybe she could start trusting the evolution of this relationship.

The alarm from the back door chimed through the house and the familiar sound of cowboy boots echoing off the hardwoods filtered into the open kitchen and living area. Morgan didn't know if she was more nervous or excited to show Ryan what she'd done. Well, what she and Nelson had done.

When Ryan rounded the corner, he stopped just on the other side of the island and stared at Morgan, then Nelson.

"Aren't you off today?" Ryan asked. Then his attention went to the various dishes on the counter. "Damn. I knew something smelled amazing when I walked in."

"Miss Morgan wanted to surprise you with your favorites," Nelson explained. "So she called me and I came to give her a quick lesson in the kitchen."

Ryan removed his hat as his eyes landed on her. "Is that right?" he asked with a grin.

There went those silly, naive jitters racing through her simply because the man smiled at her. She was carrying his child, they'd been intimate multiple times, and they were temporarily living together, yet the sweetest gesture somehow stirred up her emotions.

"If you don't need me anymore, I'll head out and let you two enjoy your dinner," Nelson told them.

Morgan couldn't help herself. She reached out and gave the elderly man a hug.

"You are the best," she told him, then eased back. "I can't thank you enough."

"No thanks necessary. I love what I do."

Nelson untied his apron and started to head toward the back door, but stopped and turned to face Ryan.

"You've got something special in that one," he stated, nodding toward Morgan.

Without another word, he left. Once again, the chime echoed as the door opened and closed. Morgan rested her hands on the top of the island and stared across at Ryan. He still had that silly grin and she couldn't help but smile back.

"I have no idea what made you want to do this, but it all looks amazing."

Morgan shrugged. "You've done so much for me and you're so busy. I don't know, I just wanted to do something to show you that I appreciate how much you've made me feel at home here."

Ryan started to circle the island, his gaze never wavering from hers. Morgan shifted to face him and when he kept advancing, she backed up until she hit the edge of the counter. Ryan leaned in, and his hands came to rest on either side of her hips.

"You smell like the barn." She laid her hands against his chest and laughed.

Ryan leaned in even closer. "You don't care," he murmured against her lips. "You might be prissy with your specialty clothes, but deep down, you're still a rancher at heart."

"I'm not," she argued.

"You love it here," he countered. "You told me so multiple times. I think you just needed a ranch where you could put your stamp on it."

Those bright blue eyes held her in place and had her heart quickening and breath caught in her throat.

"I haven't put my stamp here."

Ryan's low laugh sent a warmth spreading through her. "I assure you I wouldn't have put Christmas decorations up on my house or extra trees inside. I wouldn't have cleared out an extra stall for you to have a horse of your own if you want, and I never would have come in so early from working today had you not been here. Your stamp is everywhere."

She supposed that might be true, but she hadn't thought of things in that way before. She hadn't realized just how deeply she'd fallen into the ranch because she'd been too consumed with falling into the man.

Morgan slid her hands on up to his shoulders. "Your food is getting cold and I worked too hard for you to not enjoy it fresh."

Ryan nipped at her lips. "I'd rather enjoy other things right now."

Oh, this man knew exactly what to say to distract her and make her mind believe that this temporary setup could be something long-term.

But he'd never said anything about loving her or wanting something beyond building his legacy and raising the next generation of Carters.

"Let's eat first," she told him. "Then you can enjoy me however you want."

Ryan groaned and dropped his head, then took a step back.

"I really can't believe you called in Nelson for a cooking lesson."

Morgan crossed her arms and pulled in a deep breath, trying to focus after that promise of the extracurricular activities coming soon.

"I really didn't know what else to do for you and I'm not the best cook, so I thought I'd try. Who knows, maybe I'll like cooking and can whip up something on Nelson's days off. Don't count on that, but if we can go from fighting like crazy, then maybe I'll like cooking for us."

Ryan's brows rose as his eyes widened. "You're staying here?"

Morgan chewed her bottom lip and weighed her next words carefully. "I haven't made up my mind, but I'm not in a hurry to go just yet."

The way he smiled, like he knew something she didn't, had Morgan shaking her head.

"Don't get so cocky, now," she warned. "I didn't agree to anything. I just said I was staying awhile and thinking about this. The baby has to eat, too."

Ryan glanced to the mashed potatoes, baked steak, rolls, asparagus wrapped in bacon, and a chocolate cake and then back to her.

He quirked brow. "Interesting that all of this is my favorite."

"Yeah, well, I started with your favorites as a way to

say thank you for all you've done," she told him. "But that doesn't mean I'm staying, so stop looking at me that way."

"If you want to get naked, I can look at you a different way," he retorted.

Morgan smacked his chest. "Go sit down and I'll get us some plates."

He snaked an arm around her waist and pulled her close. "You go sit. You made the meal, the least I could do is serve you."

"Serve me? I do like the sound of that."

His lips feathered lightly over hers as his hand slid down to her backside. "I'll be serving you later, too."

A thrill shot through Morgan and she wondered if she would always have this feeling of excitement where Ryan was concerned. Was it just the fast-paced new scenario she'd found that made her so giddy? Or was there something much deeper that she should try to hold on to?

Her month was quickly coming to an end and she might just stick around a little longer to see where this all would lead.

Eighteen

Ryan didn't know why he was so nervous. This wasn't his wedding day, but since Morgan mentioned staying longer, that was all his mind could process.

Their conversation almost a week ago had him in knots. He wanted her to stay. He wanted to put that ring on her finger so they could start their life with the family they'd created.

And that was why he couldn't concentrate on anything else. He was giving Morgan this important day with her sister and then he would present her the ring to let her know just how serious he was. He knew she was starting to think about long-term and he couldn't let this opportunity pass. The entire future of Yellow Rose was on the line.

Ryan waited in the line of people entering the Texas Cattleman's Club. The doorways and railings had garlands and flowers draped and wrapped all over. As soon as he stepped inside, he felt as if he'd been transformed into something from a magazine with all the white and lights with touches of gold. The clubhouse had even more Christmas decor than it had last weekend for the Christmas party...and he hadn't even thought that was possible.

Evergreen trees lit up in groupings were all around the perimeter. The white cloth-covered chairs sat in neat little rows facing the stage in the main ballroom. The place was likely Chelsea's dream wedding come true.

Ryan wondered what type of wedding Morgan would want. Did she want something over-the-top and flashy, or would she be more low-key and want something on her family ranch? Or his ranch?

A wedding at Yellow Rose would be ideal for him, but he had to take this all one step at a time. Morgan wasn't even wearing his ring yet.

He wished they could have arrived together, but she had been with her sisters and the rest of the bridal party getting their hair and makeup done. He hadn't seen her dress or how she looked. He'd left her sleeping in bed this morning and had gone to the stable to check on his mare that was still recovering from a stillbirth. Morgan had been gone when he'd returned hours later.

When he wasn't with her, there was always a sliver of anticipation as to when he would again. What would she look like? Would she meet his gaze and offer a sultry smile? Why did he have these school-aged emotions and excitement each time he thought of Morgan?

Ryan found a seat toward the middle, but closer to the aisle. He wanted to see Morgan coming down. He wanted to catch her attention. He wanted her to constantly be thinking of him the way he was her.

As Ryan glanced around and nodded to a few people he knew, he couldn't help but wonder how many of these folks would be in attendance at his and Morgan's wedding. Because there was no way in hell he could let her go now.

Morgan knew Ryan was staring at her. Anytime she stole a glance in the direction of the guests, there he sat with those bright blue eyes locked onto her.

Although, knowing Ryan, he was likely staring at her chest because Morgan had a serious fear that one good inhale and she'd bust this zipper. Her breasts were so swollen even though her belly still showed no signs of the pregnancy. She actually couldn't wait and every day when she woke up, she stared in the mirror and turned to the side hoping to see something.

Morgan focused on her sister's vows and then Nolan's. The two were so perfect for each other as they stared into each other's eyes with their hands joined. Chelsea had been so excited to get down the aisle, she had been beaming all morning and afternoon. She was finally getting to marry the man of her dreams and live the life she'd always wanted. She couldn't believe both her sisters were married.

A heavy dose of remorse and sadness swept through her as she stood at her sister's side. This was everything Morgan didn't know she wanted. Not just the gorgeous flowing gown and the perfect bouquet and decor. But the love, the adoration they showed each other, the solidarity that could only come from such an unbreakable bond.

Morgan wanted that and she wanted it all with Ryan.

She glanced his way once again and he offered her a crooked grin that melted her heart. She'd never experienced these feelings with anyone else and she had no idea how he would respond to her truth. But she had to tell him. Ryan deserved to know and Morgan deserved this chance at happiness.

She wanted to say yes to his proposal, but she couldn't go that far without telling him she loved him first.

This would be the riskiest move she ever made and his response would change the course on her path of life. If he rejected her, she would move back to the Grandin ranch and they would have to coparent, but if he accepted her love and offered his in return, she knew they would have a beautiful life together at Yellow Rose. But she couldn't marry him if the love only existed on her side. An unbalanced relationship would surely crumble and that was a risk she couldn't take.

When the minister proclaimed Chelsea and Nolan were husband and wife, everyone in attendance clapped as the newlyweds shared their first kiss. Tears pricked Morgan's eyes. She smiled as Layla handed Chelsea's heavy bouquet back to her.

This is exactly what Morgan could have if she went after it…and she had every intention of going after Ryan Carter.

After the pictures outside the clubhouse and a few inside, Morgan looped her arm through Heath's as they made their way back into the ballroom with the rest of the wedding party. She wanted a quick word before the party began.

"I hope we can bury all of this between our families and focus on your brother and my sister," she told him. "I know that there has been so much animosity and anger, but it's time to move on."

Heath scoffed. "I will do whatever it takes to honor my mother's and Ashley's memory. Surely you can understand my position and that I have no hard feelings toward you, but I have to do something to make things right."

Well, that made her wonder about his next move, but Morgan refused to get into it with him at the reception. There would be a time and a place to tackle Heath Thurston, and maybe now that Nolan was married into the Grandin family, he could talk his twin into giving up this vendetta.

Heath guided her to the reception table with the rest of the party. "Family is everything to me," he added in a low tone as he inched toward her. "I'm sure even the Grandins can appreciate that."

Morgan leaned away from him. Now that Heath knew the truth about his mother being paid off with those rights, he seemed even angrier, which could be dangerous. What did he have planned now?

Morgan hoped more than anything that Chelsea and Nolan could have a fresh start without this black cloud of scandal hovering over them.

Morgan took a seat and immediately searched for where Ryan would be. She nearly laughed when she spotted him at the bar holding his tumbler of bourbon and Sylvia standing right beside him with her hands moving all around as she chattered, no doubt about some town gossip.

The poor guy stared back at her and looked like he wanted to be rescued. Considering she was his *friend*, Morgan would do just that.

She scooted her chair back and gathered her emerald-green skirt in one hand. The entire back part of the ballroom had been set up for the reception and was even more breathtaking than Morgan had imagined. There was something magical and almost hopeful about a Christmas wedding.

The soft music filled the room and the twinkling lights, the suspended lanterns, the tall adorned trees surrounding the perimeter all had such a romantic ambiance. Maybe she should ask Ryan to dance and tell him. She didn't want to wait to open her heart to him. So many emotions had been building inside her, and she hadn't realized until today just how much love she had for him.

And all this time, she'd never believed in such a commitment. She'd thought that was only for fairy tales, but there were too many of her family members and friends in this town falling in love, and Morgan had to believe that type of commitment truly did exist when you found the right person.

And she had found her person.

"Sylvia, you do look amazing just like I knew you would."

Sylvia turned to face Morgan and propped a hand on her rounded hip. "Well, thank you. I absolutely love this gown you chose for me. And, honey, you are radiant in that green dress."

Morgan shot a look to Ryan, and his smile and locked stare silently said he agreed. She loved the way he looked at her. It made her feel both sexy and beautiful. He had a way of doing things to her emotions and desires and he didn't even have to say a word.

"Thank you," Morgan replied.

"I was just going to get a champagne," Sylvia stated. "Can I get you one, dear?"

Morgan's breath caught in her throat and before she could reply, Ryan chimed in.

"The wedding party already has champagne at their table."

Yes. That was actually true, but she'd been so stunned that she hadn't thought of the logical reply. Clearly Morgan's nerves and thoughts were all over the place.

"Thank you anyway," she told Sylvia.

When Sylvia turned toward the bartender to order, Morgan gave a slight nod for Ryan to follow her. She had to stop herself from reaching for his hand and remember they were in a very public venue.

She hoped soon they would be able to go public with their love and their news of the baby. She hoped the folks of the town would embrace all that had happened in a positive way.

Chelsea stepped into view and Morgan startled as she reached for her sister's arm.

"Sorry," Chelsea stated. "I just wanted to catch you real quick. We're going to do the toast in about ten minutes. So that will be the speeches from Layla and Heath. Make sure you're back at the table."

Morgan had helped Layla rehearse her speech over and over all day. She truly wanted this day to be everything Chelsea had envisioned and dreamed of. Layla would do a great job.

"I'll be there," she assured her sister.

Chelsea's eyes shifted over Morgan's shoulder, and Chelsea merely smiled before she moved on to mingle with other guests. The DJ continued to play a nice mix of popular hits and slow love songs, perfect for the reception and dancing.

When she turned to talk to Ryan, she noticed his sights were not on her, but on Heath over near the entrance talking to Nolan.

"What did he tell you?" Ryan asked without taking his focus off Heath.

"Oh, just talking about taking what belonged to his mother and how he would do anything for his family. Don't worry about it. We'll deal with him another day."

Ryan's gaze darted her direction. "I don't trust him and I don't want him near you or our child."

"He won't hurt me," she assured him. "I think he's just upset by the fact that even his own surveyor hasn't been successful. He's lashing out and right now everyone is his target."

"Not you. Never you."

Ryan turned away and before Morgan realized what he was doing, he was across the room and standing before Heath. Morgan couldn't run after him or she'd look like the concerned girlfriend, but she did casually make her way over in time to hear Ryan deliver a threat.

"Morgan Grandin is off-limits to whatever new game you're playing."

Heath sneered. "And who are you to Morgan?"

"A friend," Ryan fired back. "Just keep your distance from her."

Heath raised a brow and glanced directly to her. "I'm not after anyone. I'm only here to take what was promised to my mother."

Nolan stepped between them and placed a hand on his brother's chest. "Let's all relax and save this argument for another day."

Ryan took a step back. "There's nothing more to discuss. Heath will keep his distance from Morgan."

"Again, why the hell do you care so much?" Heath volleyed back. "Unless you and Morgan are more than friends."

"Just friends," Ryan ground out. "I protect those I care about, as you can appreciate given your stance."

Ryan spun on his heel and Morgan had to step aside as he marched away. She didn't know whether to be mortified at the scene that had been made at her sister's wedding or let that blossom of hope bloom at the fact Ryan said he cared for her.

Morgan offered Nolan a soft smile before she walked

away, as well. In an attempt to keep up the friend persona for the public, she had to give Ryan a bit of space, but not too much. She wanted nothing more than to go to him, but she needed to give him time.

The next slow song that came on, she'd approach him and ask for a dance. They needed to calm down, to decompress and remember nothing else mattered right now but them and their baby.

If she could get him in an intimate embrace, they would have a few minutes to talk. She needed to see where he was in his head and tell him how much she'd fallen for him to see if there was any chance at all at their own happily-ever-after.

Nineteen

Ryan wished like hell he hadn't gotten so set off, but the mere idea of Heath Thurston talking to Morgan had not only made him jealous, Ryan wondered if he was still a threat to her family. He didn't like Heath's body language as they spoke. Ryan wanted to guard and keep Morgan safe from any more emotional upheaval.

Regardless of the encounter, Ryan didn't like it. He'd never been a jealous man, but seeing Heath arm in arm with Morgan walking back into the clubhouse after the photos had already put him in a bad mood. Maybe his protective streak intertwined with the jealousy, but either way, he wanted to keep Morgan in a bubble.

When she told him that Heath still mentioned getting what belonged to his mother, that was all Ryan needed to snap and step in to make sure she knew she didn't have to face anything alone.

"Dance with me."

The slow ballad filled the ballroom, and Ryan turned to see Morgan standing before him. That emerald-green strapless gown hugged her every curve and enhanced her bust in a way that made Ryan want to say to hell with what people thought. He wanted to grab her and dance the way he craved, with her body pressed firmly against his. He didn't want to have to worry about hand placement or if he grazed his lips over hers.

Did he want too much? Were these feelings more than he could handle right now? He liked to think he could take on anything, but even this avenue was new to him. He'd thought he'd been in love before...but look where that got him.

The moment they hit the floor, Ryan took Morgan's hand and pulled her into a dance. That long red hair curled down over one shoulder and those expressive blue eyes met his. She was the most striking woman he'd ever seen in his life and she was his—temporarily.

"Forget about Heath."

Morgan's words penetrated his thoughts and he shook his head. "I was actually thinking about how hot you looked in this dress, but he's still on my mind. I don't like that bastard."

"I didn't ask you to make friends with him, I asked you to forget about him," she stated with a firm tone.

Ryan nodded. "I get it, but I didn't like..."

Damn it. He sounded like a fool for admitting what he'd been thinking or how he'd felt earlier.

"You didn't like what?" she prodded.

He spun her around and dodged other dancing couples and tried to keep his voice low.

"I didn't like seeing you walking together, all right?"

A slow smile spread across Morgan's face. "You're jealous?"

"Go ahead, laugh about it."

"Oh, I'm not laughing," she corrected him as her hand tightened in his when he spun her once again. "I'm letting that nugget of information sink in."

The way she kept grinning at him like she had some special secret had him both worried and turned on. Nothing lit up a space more than Morgan's smile, but there was a little smirk there that didn't sit well with him.

"You've got something on your mind," he murmured. "What are you thinking that has you so happy?"

"I just never thought you'd love me the way I love you," she told him, her hands coming to rest on his shoulders. "I thought I'd have to tell you first and you'd run in the other direction."

Ryan stilled and brought them to a stop.

"What did you say?" he asked.

"I love you." Her smile got even wider and her eyes filled with unshed tears. "I never knew how liberating that would be to say. I never knew how right those words would feel. But knowing you love me back…"

Ryan's heart clenched as he tried to find his words and absorb the bomb she'd just dropped into his world.

"I never said I loved you," he corrected her. "That's not where I am, Morgan."

That smile faltered slowly until it completely vanished. Her hands slid down his chest and dropped to her sides.

"What do you mean?" she asked. "You just said that you didn't like seeing me walking with another man. You're jealous and the way you've been going all out at the house… How can you say that's not love?"

"Because it's not."

He refused to allow his mind to even go there. He'd tried that years ago and had been left standing with nothing. No family, no emotions. He'd vowed to never allow his heart to go there ever again.

"Then what is it?" she asked, her lips thinned as a lone tear slid down her cheek.

Ryan tried to reach for her, but she held her hands up and took a step back. He didn't want to make a scene, but right now all that mattered was Morgan and her emotions.

"I don't want to hurt you," he added. "I just have to be honest."

She let out a humorless laugh and swiped at the moisture on her face. "I guess you were honest all along. You told me from the beginning you only wanted to marry me for the baby."

Ryan cringed at that last word that came out just as one slow song ended and another began. The ill-timed statement drew the attention of everyone around them.

As if Morgan just realized what she'd said, she glanced around them. Ryan spotted Vic and Aubrey, Nolan and Chelsea, Jayden and Zanai, Sylvia and a whole host of other guests.

Ryan wished like hell he could turn back time and slip out the side door to talk to Morgan. But he'd had no clue whatsoever that she would reveal her love for him. When she'd mentioned staying with him, he assumed it was for the family, nothing more.

After a moment of awkward silence and tension swirling around them, Chelsea stepped forward and touched Morgan's elbow.

"Why don't you two take this to one of the other rooms?" she suggested.

Morgan turned her attention to her sister. "Chels, my word, I'm so sorry. I didn't mean—"

"I know. It's a tough time, but you need privacy."

Morgan nodded and gathered the skirt of her dress and headed out the ballroom.

Chelsea glanced to Ryan. "If you're not going to love her like she deserves, then let her go."

She turned from him and went back to her new husband, who was also glaring at Ryan.

Somehow being honest had gotten him in trouble, but he didn't have the time, nor did he care what anyone else thought. He'd hurt Morgan and that was all that mattered at this point. He would never intentionally harm her, so now he had to make sure she knew exactly where he stood.

Ryan headed out the ballroom and found her down the hall near the women's rec center. She stood with her back to him and as he approached, he had no idea if his touch would be welcome or if she'd jerk away.

Ryan reached for her anyway and laid a hand on her shoulder.

"Look at me."

She turned, and the soft glow from all the Christmas lights and the wall sconces illuminated the dampness on her cheeks. But there was more than just the tears. There was a pain and vulnerability in her eyes he'd never seen before.

"You don't need to say a word," she told him. "You never promised me anything and you said more than once that you only wanted to raise a family with me for the sake of your legacy. You made it perfectly clear that the baby was the reason for the marriage."

"I had no idea that you had stronger feelings," he explained. "You had told me you didn't believe in love."

"I didn't. Until you."

Guilt weighed heavy on his heart because Morgan was the last person he would ever want to break.

"Morgan—"

"No." She held up a hand and pasted on a smile he knew had to be tearing her apart. "We both know where we stand now and I don't want to ruin any more of my sister's day. I need to get back inside and listen to Layla's speech."

Ryan blinked. "You're going back in after everyone just found out about our baby?"

Morgan shrugged. "Why hide now? The secret is out, and just because my life is falling apart doesn't mean my sister's should. She's counting on me."

Morgan started to move around him, but he reached for her. His fingers curled just inside her arm and her gaze met his.

"We can talk back at the house."

Morgan closed her eyes and blew out a sigh before meeting his gaze once again. "We're done talking, Ryan. We're just...done."

And then she was gone, leaving Ryan standing in the hallway with a broken heart. He had no clue how the hell that had happened when he didn't even know his heart had been involved.

From the beginning, he'd vowed to win this challenge, to have her marry him. Now he realized the most important component had been Morgan all along. Not winning or losing.

And discovering that truth after the fact was how he'd lost everything.

Twenty

Morgan hadn't been back to the ranch in three days. She'd ignored Ryan's calls and texts, and thankfully he hadn't stopped in to her store. She had needed time to process everything that had happened, not that she thought she'd get over him in a few days. But she'd needed space to gather her thoughts before she approached him again.

She'd gone back to living at the family ranch and working all day at her business and realized just how empty her life was without Ryan. No shared dinners or fun flirting followed by a night of passion. There was no deep conversations that made her heart feel so alive. Even with her parents' support, the nights were still quiet. The silence seemed to mock her decision to tell Ryan her true feelings. Had she said nothing and just agreed to marry him, she'd still have him.

That wouldn't have been fair to either of them, though. She had never settled for anything in life, and refused to let her marriage be the first. Clearly, Ryan was still hell-bent on having his nuptials mean little more than a business deal.

This new chapter was something she was just going to have to get used to and deal with the best way she knew how. Living without Ryan would be her new normal. Even though she had only been at the ranch three weeks, that had been long enough to get her hopes up and make her want a real life with Ryan and not something out of obligation.

Unfortunately, she had to go back to the ranch to get her things. There was no way around it and she couldn't avoid Ryan forever. They were having a child and they'd just have to figure out how to get along.

And that was how she found herself sitting in her car, staring up at the Christmas lights dotting all the peaks and porches of Ryan's home. She'd been so happy and surprised the day he'd done that. The joy from that memory was now overshadowed by the pain of the loss.

She just wanted to get this all over with and go back to her house.

Morgan stepped from her car and pulled her jacket tighter around her. Supposedly there was a storm moving in…snow, of all things. That was just absurd in this area of Texas, but at this point, a freak snowstorm was the least of her worries.

The frigid wind cut right through her as she headed toward the front door and rang the bell. How silly was that? Just days ago this had been her home, a place where she'd envisioned living the rest of her life, yet now she stood outside ringing the bell because she was just a guest.

The foyer light flicked on and a moment later, Ryan opened the door. He didn't appear surprised to see her. If anything, he looked miserable.

"There's no need to ring the damn bell," he grumbled. "Come in."

Morgan stepped inside and took notice of his appearance. Messy hair, wrinkled tee, jeans, no shoes. He was still typical Ryan, but this version seemed sadder and frustrated. Well, welcome to the club.

"I just need to gather my things. I have quite a bit, so I can get a load now and come back tomorrow and finish," she informed him. "I don't want to be in your way."

She would not ask for his help. She didn't want him in her bedroom touching her stuff and packing like she was just going on a trip. She was leaving...for good.

"In my way?" he scoffed. "You've been in my way for months. You're in my head, in my space, you're everywhere in my damn house even when you aren't physically here."

Morgan blinked at his harsh tone, but remained still. Clearly, he was irritated, but right now she couldn't tell if it was at her or himself.

"Don't move out."

She jerked, knowing she'd heard him wrong because they'd already been over this. She'd told him she loved him and he didn't reciprocate the feelings. Sticking around now would only prolong the pain and the inevitable.

"Give this more time," he told her. "Give *us* more time."

"For what?" she countered. "We are at opposite ends of the emotional spectrum and the gap is too large to meet in the middle. Neither of us should settle for something we don't want."

When he stood there staring, the silence became too much, and Morgan shifted around him to head up the stairs. There was no point in dragging this out any longer than necessary. The pain wouldn't be erased in a day and they both just needed time.

The most important thing now would be to put the baby's foundation first. Morgan's broken heart and whatever Ryan was dealing with would just have to take a step back.

Morgan reached the bedroom she'd started out in before moving to Ryan's. Her clothes and personal belongings were still in the spare room.

As soon as she opened the door, there stood that damn tree. Why did every memory here have to be so amazing and wonderful? Why did he have to leave such an impression on her heart? Because she knew deep down that he'd ruined her for absolutely everyone else.

The sooner she got her things, the sooner she could leave. Staying here and traveling down memory lane would only hurt her further.

She stared at all of her makeup and brushes on the vanity and pulled in a deep breath.

"I don't want to meet in the middle."

Morgan glanced to the doorway, where Ryan seemed to fill up the entire space.

"What?" she asked.

"You said the gap was too large for us to meet in the middle," he clarified. "I don't want to be in the middle. I want to be on the other side…with you."

Tired and more than frustrated, Morgan sank down onto her plush vanity stool. She rested her elbow on the counter and rubbed her head as she tried to gather her thoughts and make sense of how they got here.

"I don't even know what you're trying to say," she told him. "How can you be with me when you don't love me? I told you I wouldn't settle and I meant it."

Ryan stepped forward and bent down to look her in

the eye, resting his hands on her thighs. His gaze held hers and she'd never seen such raw emotion staring back at her as she did right now.

"I don't want you to settle," he explained. "It wasn't fair for me to ask you to or just assume you would."

What was he trying to say? She didn't want to get her hopes up, not again, but there was that spark of hope igniting inside her. She didn't want to say anything. She needed to let him guide this conversation.

"These past few days have been hell," he went on. "Do you know how damn lonely this house was without you? All of these Christmas decorations seemed so cheerful and all I could think of was how much you loved them. You loved from the beginning with your whole heart and I never saw it. I'm not sure you saw it either until recently. But that's who you are, Morgan. You just shine with love and you showed me that it's okay to open my heart again."

Tears pricked her eyes as her throat clogged with emotions.

"What are you saying?" she whispered.

He shifted onto one knee and pulled something from his pocket. A box.

Her heart clenched as she gasped.

"Marry me," he said as he lifted the lid to reveal a stunning diamond with smaller stones along the band. "I've had this since the day after you told me about the baby, but the timing was never right. Now is the time."

Why did life have to be so cruel? This hurt more than walking away. To know she could have it all right now if she said yes, but she wouldn't really have it all…would she?

"I'm still not settling," she reminded him. "We're obviously both miserable, but that doesn't change the fact I fell in love with you, Ryan."

"I fell in love with you, too."

Morgan stilled. "What?"

Tears gathered in his eyes as well, and her heart flipped over in her chest. This was truly happening for her—for them.

"I fell in love with you," he repeated. "Maybe that first night we were together, maybe when you told me about the baby, or maybe when I hung those damn lights on the house. I don't know when it happened because I was too afraid to admit it to myself, let alone you. But being here without you was a hell of a lot worse than exposing my vulnerability and taking this risk."

He took the ring from the box and lifted her hand. His eyes met hers once again.

"I'm asking you to marry me now for all the right reasons." He slid the ring on, and held her hand and sniffled, obviously trying to hold back his own emotions. "I'm asking you because we love each other, because we have a child who deserves the best home, and because I want to build something bigger here with you than either of us ever imagined. I know you might find my words difficult to believe, but I wouldn't fight so hard if I didn't love you so damn much."

Morgan laughed as tears slid down her cheeks. She glanced to the ring that fit so perfectly and looked exactly like something she would choose.

"Yes," she told him. "I want to build everything with you from here on out."

Ryan let out a sigh and reached for her, wrapping his arms around her and resting his forehead against hers.

"I thought I had ruined everything," he whispered. "I can't handle the thought of you not with me forever. It scared the hell out of me."

Yeah, this man definitely loved her and three days of misery was worth the lesson they'd both learned.

Morgan framed his face with her hands and eased back to stare him in the eyes. "I guess we have more to announce to the town than just our baby."

Ryan smiled, then covered her lips with his for a brief kiss.

"What do you say we make our announcement at the New Year's Eve ball?" he suggested. "Since we're known for our public statements."

Morgan couldn't help but laugh. "I love that idea and I love you."

He nipped her lips once again. "Love you more. We might be stubborn and butt heads, but there's nobody else I'd want to do that with than you."

Morgan knew deep in her heart this was just the beginning of that grand dynasty Ryan wanted for his family. Day one of the rest of their lives had a beautiful ring to it.

* * * * *

MOST ELIGIBLE COWBOY

STACEY KENNEDY

For Dad,
who bravely battled against Parkinson's.

I miss you every single day.

One

"Hey, sugar."

Sitting atop a wooden bar stool, Colter Ward internally groaned at the cloying perfume infusing the air and itching his nose. Before he arrived at the Black Horse, the legendary cowboy bar in Devil's Bluffs, Texas, he'd figured the dirt and grime under his fingernails from a long day working on a cattle ranch, his unwashed hair and filthy clothes reeking of sweat and God knows what else, would keep any sane woman away tonight.

Irritated he was wrong, he chugged back his ice-cold beer to ease the tight muscles across his shoulders, hearing the liquid's glug in the bottle. The crisp, bitter taste rushed down his throat as he met seductive brown eyes belonging to a woman who on any other night would've spiked his attention. "Not interested." He coldly turned his gaze back to the television screen above the wall of liquor bottles, highlighting the latest Professional Bull Riding championship.

Lust simmered in her raspy voice. "Then I'll give you a few minutes to rethink why you should be interested," she said before heading back to her table on the other side of the bar, where her friend waited.

Colter had come to the bar like he did every Friday after work to unwind, not to find a woman to warm his bed. The place was pure country. Wooden stools butted up against a brass foot rail at a higher counter. Photographs of famous country singers, actors and athletes who'd passed through the small town over the years covered the wood paneling on the walls heading down a dingy hallway to restrooms at the end. Peanut shells littered the floors, and bowls of pretzels were scattered on the round tabletops.

"The ladies after you again?" Riggs Evans, the Black Horse's owner, and Colter's lifelong buddy, asked from behind the bar.

One look into Riggs's amused green eyes, and Colter snorted. "They're worse than a heifer protecting her calf from vaccinations." And he had a dozen scars to attest to a cow's viciousness where it came to keeping her calf safe.

Wiping up the condensation Colter's beer left on the counter, Riggs threw his head back and laughed, bouncing the messy jet-black curls atop his head. "I've never known you not to enjoy the ladies' interest."

"These aren't ladies, they're sharks."

Nearly a month ago, Colter's life had been a disaster after his divorce, but at least it was a quiet disaster. Everything changed when an article came out in a gossip blog out of New York City. In their fifty-state bachelor roundup piece, they named him Texas's sexiest bachelor of the year, after a photograph of him saving a calf from a rapid went viral. Ever since then, not only local women were hounding him, but women had started showing up from out of town chasing after Colter—and his family's millions—looking for some cowboy love.

The attention grated on Carter's last nerve. After his divorce, he'd put his focus on his family's ranch to ensure the Ward legacy continued.

For six generations, the Ward family had worked cattle and bred American quarter horses. Since they were old money, many had wanted to marry into the family over the years, but these past few weeks the women had been relentless. They stalked Colter. In public. At home. Even in his dreams. All he wanted was a cold beer and some quiet after a long, hard week. Not hungry women who wanted his dead heart.

He needed to get this story buried. And these women off his back. For good.

"Ah, dammit," Riggs suddenly snapped.

Down the other end of the bar, Willie, more often inebriated than not, was swearing at another patron, who looked ready to throw the old man against the wall.

Riggs sighed at Colter. "Let me know if you need anything else."

"Sure will." Colter picked at the slippery beer label on his bottle as country beats played through the speakers above the bar. Riggs had become a cop after high school, and a detective after that, but he'd retired after working a difficult case. He didn't need Colter's help. Riggs settled the matter quickly, serving both men a free drink and ensuring they sat apart.

Colter took another sip of his beer as a sweet voice next to him said, "I'll take whatever's on tap."

"Coming up," said Riggs, now back at his post, with a smile Colter had seen a thousand times over.

Her voice sounded familiar, but Colter refused to acknowledge her. He was so damn tired of turning down women. He wanted the spotlight put on the ranch, his family, not on himself. He kept his focus on the television screen.

"Colter Ward, right?"

Could he get twenty minutes to himself? Ready to feed her the same line he'd been using for weeks, he faced the woman with the soft voice, ready to unleash his frustration—but he stopped short.

Long waves of strawberry blond hair curtained a round face. Freckles dusted a small nose, and pouty lips had never looked so pink and inviting. Given that she was wearing a thin blouse and long skirt, nothing was left to his imagination. She had a body made for a man's hands—all the right curves in all the right places. Damn. He'd bet she smelled like a lavender field mixed with sunshine. He began rethinking why he didn't want to take a warm, lush woman to his bed tonight.

"Or am I mistaken?" she asked with a smile that snuffed out his thoughts.

Until he remembered she—and any woman—was currently the enemy. "Listen, I'm sure you're a wonderful woman, but let me make this unboundedly clear to you: I'm not looking for a relationship. I'm recently divorced and paying alimony to my ex-wife, and I've got enough emotional baggage to fill a barn. Believe me, I might have millions, but the hell I'll put you through ain't worth the money."

She lifted a single eyebrow, sliding onto the stool next to him. "Wow. After that gleaming introduction, I can assure you that I'm most definitely not applying for the job." She stuck out her hand. "I'm Adeline Harlow."

Unable to ignore the manners his parents had raised him with, Colter closed his callused hand around her delicate fingers, returning the handshake. "Colter Ward."

She laughed softly. "Yes, I've already told you that I know who you are. Do you not remember me?"

He gave her another look over, reassessing. "I'm afraid I don't. Should I?"

She pulled her hand away, leaving his skin tingling. "I should think so. I babysat your little brother for an entire summer."

He fought back through his hazy memories, and her name came to him. So did two pigtails, crooked teeth, a chubby face and baggy clothes. "Not the Adeline who'd sit on my parents' couch and write in those journals?"

"That's the one." She smiled.

He could hardly believe his eyes. He'd seen many pretty women, but Adeline was something entirely different. Something...*tempting*. "Jesus, you've left me a little speechless here."

She hit him with a smile full of sass. "Guess that's not a bad way to leave the unshakable Colter Ward."

He laughed dryly. "Believe me, Adeline, I'm shakable." Hating how darkly pathetic he sounded, he took another gulp of his beer.

"So, you're actually human after all, hmm?"

Glancing sideways, he held her playful stare. Though behind the mischievousness, he saw what he needed to know. Back in high school, he'd hung with the popular crowd, and Adeline had not. She thought he had it all. She was dead wrong. "Whatever gave you the impression that I wasn't human?"

Her grin widened. "You are Texas's sexiest bachelor, after all."

Damn that article. "Where did you move again?"

"New York City," she answered and then thanked Riggs as he delivered her beer.

As she took a sip, he asked, "I'm still news in New York City? That article came out weeks ago."

She set her beer down on the paper coaster. "What can I say? People love a hot, heroic cowboy."

He liked—probably more than he should have—that she thought he was hot. To shift the subject off himself, he asked, "Have you moved back to town?" From what he remembered, her mother had moved them away after that summer she babysat his brother, Beau, to be closer to family.

"No, I'm just visiting." Her spine bowed before she straightened her back and smiled again. "How's your family?"

"Beau and my mother are great."

"And your dad?"

Coldness sank into Colter's bones. "Five years ago, he was diagnosed with Parkinson's disease. It's progressing fast." Something Colter would never forgive himself for. He should have been there to help his father when he grew weak. Instead, he'd only focused on his crumbling marriage. He refused to fail his family again.

"Oh, I'm so sorry to hear that." Her hand came to his forearm, her warm gaze offering an alluring comfort.

"Thank you. It's been hardest on my mother." The heat from her fingers on his arm chipped away at the ice in his veins. "My dad's been in a wheelchair for a few months now. He's at a nursing home now but comes home often with the help of a nurse."

"Aw, that's hard." She slowly withdrew her hand,

reaching for her beer mug again. "Your parents were always so in love, so it's nice that he can come home sometimes."

Yeah, his parents were madly in love. He'd once wanted a love like that for himself. Until he realized that kind of love didn't happen for everyone.

She watched him closely, awareness reaching her kind, honey-colored eyes. "I saw that your family donated to the Parkinson's Federation this year."

The donation had been the largest his family had made yet—$300,000 in his father's name. "Whatever we can do to further research to help cure this cruel disease, we'll do."

She smiled softly. "Your family has always been so generous to our community."

He caught himself staring into her eyes, feeling an odd sense of nostalgia. Adeline had known the young man he'd once been, before his heart was ripped out. She didn't look at him like he was broken, the way his family did. Hell, even the way Riggs did sometimes. "So, Adeline, if you haven't moved back to town, why are you here?"

"To see you."

"Me?"

She hesitated. Then she hit him with, "I'm actually a journalist. I work for the blog that named you Texas's sexiest bachelor."

He lifted an eyebrow. "You wrote that article about me?"

"No," she said. "But my editor wants a follow-up story, because you've been such a hit with our readers."

"I see," he said, feeling the walls around him slam up. Wanting nothing to do with anyone involved in the blog that had turned his life into a circus, he polished off his beer. "It was good to see you, but I better get going."

"Wait," she said, clamping onto his forearm again.

He looked at that touch burning his arm, then into her widening eyes, which he almost felt like he could get lost in. Never in his life had he wanted to leave and stay in the same place all at once.

"One interview, that's all I'm asking for," she said with big, pleading eyes. "Then you can go back to your life, and I'll go back to mine."

"That article has turned my life into a spectacle. Why would I let you write another one about me?"

She gave him a beaming smile. "Because I'm utterly charming?"

He felt a crack splinter his wall against her. "No."

Her smile widened. "Because I'm a friend of the family?"

"No."

The playfulness faded from her face, replaced by something fierce that wrapped around Colter and yanked him forward. "Because what stands between me and the promotion I've worked my butt off for for years is an exclusive interview with you. Nothing—and I mean *nothing*—will stop me from getting my interview and earning that promotion. So, either you agree now and make this easy, or we spend the next few days playing a game that neither of us wants to play. But in the end, you will give me the interview."

A chemistry he had not felt in a very long time, if ever, burned between them, tasting rich, raw and tangible. "Why do you think you'd win a game we played?"

Her grin sparkled. "Because I never lose."

Colter could forget his own damn name under that smile. "Is that so?" He closed the distance, leaning near, pulled by something that felt warm, familiar and yet brand-new, too. The local women in Devil's Bluffs kept their distance from a man who'd already failed at marriage and clearly was not on the market. For weeks, he'd been running from women from out of town, all to keep his mind focused on the ranch and off the numb ache in his chest, and none had stopped him in his tracks.

Until *her.*

None had him wondering what she'd do if he acted on the heat burning in his gut and dropped his mouth to hers, declaring a challenge of his own.

Until *her.*

What kind of power did this woman possess?

"Yeah, that's so," she responded, heat flooding her gaze. "I know you're used to getting your own way." *Being a Ward son* echoed in the air between them. "But I'm up for a promotion, along with three of my coworkers. All I need to do is prove myself with an article that blows my competition out of the water. I *need* that exclusive, and you're going to give it to me."

Colter chuckled, both at the gall of her and how much he liked it, right as Riggs cleared his throat and said, "Was asked to deliver this to you."

He set the beer down in front of Colter, but Colter never looked away from Adeline's pinkish cheeks. Damn, he wanted to make those cheeks burn darker. "Send it back," Colter said, and Riggs took the beer away.

All the answers Colter had been looking for suddenly landed in his lap. No one was going to leave him alone. Not these women. Not Adeline. Not the gossip blog. Suddenly, things became clear, and he knew the path to regaining control of his life. "You want your story? I want these women off my back. Stay in town and pretend to be my girlfriend until this story dies down, and I'll give you the exclusive you want."

Her eyes widened. "You're serious?"

"Deadly serious," he confirmed. "I want my life back so I can focus on our ranch. You need a promotion. This is a win-win for both of us."

She gave a cute wiggle on her stool, her skin flushing. "I think you're giving me far too much credit. Why would women care if I'm your girlfriend?"

"I don't think you're giving yourself *enough* credit." He stared at her parted lips, her shining eyes, her slowly building smile, and closed the distance between them, waiting for her to back away. When she didn't and even leaned in closer, he said, "Trust me, they'd care." He captured her mouth, cupping her warm face, telling himself the whole damn time this was a terrible idea.

And yet…*and yet*, at the feel of her sweet, soft lips, he came undone. She tasted like the past, of easier times, happier times, and of uncontrolled passion. While he'd thought earlier she'd smell like lavender and sunshine, he was pleasantly surprised to find she smelled like sugar and spice. Heat flooded his groin as his scruffy cheek caught on the soft strands of her hair. He had no intention of stopping, but when she moaned eagerly, he remembered they weren't alone. He slowly broke the kiss and reveled in the heat simmering in her half-lidded eyes.

"And how will *that* make them care?" she purred.

"Look for yourself." He gestured to the woman who'd sent him the drink. And as she headed for the door, scowling the entire way, with her friend in tow, he added, "Like I said, they'll care."

Adeline watched the door shut behind the women before addressing him again. "No emotion. No intimacy, except for mandatory kissing to keep up the show. And tell the truth only to people you trust."

He inclined his head. "I can handle those rules. Can you?"

"Believe me, I won't get attached," she said.

He wondered why the promotion was so important to her, that she'd agree to such an insane idea, but he didn't feel it his place to ask. "Do we have a deal, then?"

The side of her mouth curved ever so slightly as she firmly pulled him into her and said against his mouth, "Yeah, cowboy, we've got a deal. You get a girlfriend. I get the exclusive." Her lips met his, and she owned his mouth, obviously proving a point that she could to both of them. Then she was gone, heading for the door.

"I thought you weren't interested in the ladies," Riggs mused.

Colter stared at the door as it shut behind Adeline, trying to catch up on what in the hell had just happened. He'd never done anything this spontaneous in his life, but he was done doing things the usual way and getting nowhere. He wanted the spotlight off him. For good. "I wasn't."

"Ah, so, she's not a shark, then?" Riggs asked with a laugh.

"No. She's...something else entirely."

Two

The tailpipe of an old Ford backfired as Adeline made it out onto Main Street, fighting the fluttery feeling in her belly. Her high heels clicked against the cracked sidewalks, her knees wobbling.

What in the hell was that?

Back when they were in high school, Colter had been the tough, out-of-her-league guy, while she'd been the quiet, shy girl, lost in her journals. He'd also been her biggest crush.

The day the photograph of Colter had landed on her desk and then went viral, she'd known why he'd become an instant hit with women all over the country. Colter was every woman's fantasy of a real-life cowboy. In the photograph, he'd been shirtless, his body stacked with hard muscle and his face devastatingly handsome. His chiseled jawline with its slight scruff, his full, kissable

lips, messy chocolate brown hair and his deep, penet
ing blue eyes made women swoon.

Her included. Since she was twelve years old.

Passing by a bakery, she caught a whiff of the yeasty
bread browning in the ovens, and she shook out her
hands, releasing the tension that was bubbling up. He'd
kissed her, and, the most shocking bit of all, she'd kissed
him back. She'd chalk it up to insanity, but she knew her
teenager's heart was currently bursting with joy.

Still.

What in the hell was *that?*

Feeling well on her way to having an out-of-body experience, she sucked in the fresh air that smelled of wildflowers and continued down the two-lane road. When
her mother had swiftly moved Adeline away from Devil's Bluffs, they'd traded one wealthy lifestyle for another. While Devil's Bluffs didn't have a Fifth Avenue,
it had the Promenade, a historic block in town. Above
the lightly trafficked road, lights twinkled over the entire
block of trendy local boutiques and art galleries, along
with designer shops, chef-driven restaurants, lively bars
and wellness and beauty stores. The pedestrians walking down the streets might have worn cowboy boots and
hats, but their jeans and shirts came from top designers.

Desperate to get her head back in the game and off
that kiss, she tucked herself into the corner of two shops.
She dug her cell phone out of her purse and on FaceTime
dialed her best friend, Nora Keller.

The moment Nora's sunny hazel eyes appeared on
the screen, Adeline felt her world come together again.
Blond-haired and beautiful, Nora was the type of pretty
that came from within. Her soul was kind and loving,
and that brightness shined through her oval face. Adeline wasn't as calm as Nora, and instead of finding the

right words, she blurted out, "I kissed Colter. Or, to be more specific, he kissed me and then I kissed him back."

Nora squealed, dropped the phone, sending it crashing to the ground. When Nora's face appeared again, she gaped, incredulous. "How? What? Why?"

"I'm not even sure what happened," Adeline admitted.

Nora blinked rapidly until her surprise faded to a sly smile. "That is not normally how you interview someone."

Adeline barked a laugh, unable to help it. She'd loved Nora since the day she met her, on her first day of tenth grade at her new school in New York City. She'd never felt alone after she had Nora in her life. "No, it's not protocol that I make out with the people I'm interviewing. But it happened. Oh, man, did it happen."

Nora squeezed her eyes shut tight, shook her head and then reopened her shining eyes, her hand on her chest. "Sorry, I'm absorbing this. I need a minute."

"Oh, is this shocking or something?" Adeline mused. "Wonder why that would be. Maybe because just one week ago I broke off my engagement to the man who I thought was my soul mate and now I'm kissing someone else?"

Nora snorted. "Yeah, *that*."

Adeline tipped her head back against the cement wall behind her and heaved a long sigh, expelling the confusion clouding her thoughts. "I don't even know what happened. It's like one minute I was reminding him I used to babysit his younger brother, and the next I was telling him there's nothing I won't do to get this story. Then he said he'd give me the story if I'll be his fake girlfriend to get all the women in town off his back. Then he kissed me to prove that being his girlfriend would benefit him."

"Well, did it?"

"Did it, what?"

"Did it benefit him?"

"It made a woman hitting on him walk away, so I'd say yes."

Nora blinked. Twice.

"Oh my God, say something, Nora," Adeline gasped.

"I don't even know what to say. This is shocking. And so not like you that I'm still processing." She nibbled her lip and then gave a tight smile. "I mean, Colter is absolutely gorgeous, so kissing him couldn't have been bad."

"It wasn't," Adeline said quickly. "It was..."

Nora leaned in until her face filled up the whole screen. "It was *what*?"

"My God, Nora, it was out-of-this-world incredible," Adeline said on a sigh. "I have never, ever had a kiss like that before, not even with Brock." Who, up until one week ago, had been the love of her life, the man she'd given five years to, the one she'd planned on marrying only a month from now—and the man who was cheating with his secretary, Stephanie.

When her boss had offered her a way out of the city for a little break to interview Colter for an exclusive, she'd jumped on the chance. Brock had texted and called, first every hour, now three times a day, but she hadn't answered a single call or text and powered off her phone unless she was using it. She didn't even know what to say—or where her heart sat in all this mess.

"Honestly, it's like I just lived the very thing my teenage self would have died for. I have no idea what to make of that."

Nora's mouth curved. "Maybe you shouldn't make anything out of it. Maybe this mini vacation won't only be about giving your heart a well-deserved healing moment—and getting the promotion you've worked so hard for—maybe it might be the best rebound vacation ever."

Salacious images of Colter kissing her so passionately in other places of her body stole into her mind. She shivered, still feeling him against her tingling lips. "I'm pretty sure my therapist would tell me doing anything like that is a terrible idea."

"Then she's a terrible therapist and should be fired immediately," Nora said seriously. "Incredible sex with a hot cowboy, who also was your biggest crush, sounds like the best way to heal a broken heart to me."

Adeline laughed. Nora had always been the braver, bolder one.

"All right, so tell me, what does being his fake girlfriend entail?" Nora asked, settling back into a chair. The watercolor painting of the New York City skyline behind her indicated she was in her home office, where she worked as a freelance researcher. "And why does he even need you to do that for him?"

Adeline waited for a pedestrian to walk by before she answered, "I guess the article has brought him unwanted attention from money-hungry women, but to be honest, it almost seemed like more than that."

"Oh, yeah, how?"

"He got divorced a year ago." She learned that tidbit from the article that went viral. "It sounded painful. I think maybe he wants to be left alone." She paused to shrug. "I get the feeling there's more going on there, but I'll keep digging until I have those answers."

Nora gave a lopsided grin. "Well, he wanted to be left alone—until he kissed you."

"Not a real kiss, though," Adeline corrected. Though she couldn't imagine what a real kiss would feel like if that one was for show. "I realize this is an insane idea,

but I want his story. Dammit, I'm owed this promotion."
Years of hard work and long hours had led to this step-up
and pay increase. The day Brock broke her heart, she'd
made a promise to herself: no longer would she lean on
anyone but herself financially. Her life would not change
because she'd thrown Brock out of it. She needed that
money now more than ever to cover all the expenses she
and Brock used to share.

Nora gave a curt nod. "Just get your story and get back
to me here, okay?"

"Believe me, I want that just as much as you do. I'll
be home before you know."

"Good," Nora said, pushing her shoulders back. "Text
me any updates on Colter. Especially the sexy ones."

"If there is any sexy anything to tell you, you will be
the first one I call, believe me." Two pedestrians were
coming closer. "I'll call you later, okay?"

"Sure. Love you."

"Love you, too. 'Bye."

Feeling more grounded than when she left the bar,
Adeline returned her cell phone to her purse. She straightened her shoulders, lifting her head, ready to face Devil's Bluffs again. The Dove Hill Inn was only two blocks
away, where she was booked in for a two-week stay.

Ready to soak her feet in a hot bath and write some
notes on the one and only Colter Ward, she only got two
steps forward before she froze, rooted to the spot on the
sidewalk, her heartbeat thundering in her ears. She took
in the old, worn plaid jacket, the jeans with the oil stains
and the weathered face of the man coming out of Jackson's Hardware. His dark hair was covered by a faded
tan-colored Stetson, and his head was bowed, hiding from
the world, his shoulders curled with his hands stuffed in

his pockets. For a tall man—over six feet—she'd never seen anyone look so small.

The weakest part of her heart could never forget him. *Her father.* Eric Lowe. A perfect stranger.

She'd only learned his name from her mother when she turned sixteen. Nora had helped find a photograph of him online. One picture of him smiling on the website of the mechanic shop he owned in town.

Adeline clutched her arms to her chest, holding in the warmth trying to seep out of her. A million times she'd told herself what she'd do if she saw him again. She'd confront him, demand answers for why he'd refused to acknowledge he had a child.

Now, in the moment, she did the exact opposite. She dived behind the closest bush, eating dirt and cedar needles, watching as he got into his truck.

"Looking for worms?"

At the low, smooth voice, she shot back to her feet with a gasp and met Colter's amused eyes. "I fell," she lied breezily.

His mouth twitched. "Mmm-hmm." His gaze roamed her from head to toe, bringing heat to places that shouldn't be heated by any man so soon after she'd ended her engagement.

Then again, Colter wasn't any man. Now wearing his black cowboy hat, he was the man of her teenage dreams.

For as long as she could remember, she'd watched him from afar at school, swooning over everything he did. Her journals back then were full of entries about him, and she was sure she had scribbled "Adeline Ward" all over them.

When he met her eyes again, he said, "You don't look injured."

"I'm fine." She blushed, brushing dirt off her knees. "Sorry, did you need something?"

He offered her a card. "I realized on my way back to my truck that I hadn't given you my number. I took a guess you were staying at the inn and was on my way there."

"Good guess." She accepted the card. "Thanks. I'll be in touch tomorrow."

A slow-building grin spread across his face as he winked. "I look forward to it, New York."

And as he turned, heading in the opposite direction, her teenage heart combusted.

The wind feathered through the wild grass and crops as Colter rolled up to the stop sign at the all-way stop. Hardy wildflowers hugged the sunbaked two-lane country road deep in the heart of Ward land. Five hundred and sixty thousand acres of prime Texas countryside were home to six lakes, ten thousand Hereford and Angus cattle, and hundreds of American quarter horses. They sold some of the horses after weaning and shipped them throughout North America. Beau trained those with talent for reining before selling or shipping them off to a professional reiner to increase their value. The stallions at Devil's Bluffs Ranch produced talented, stunning horses, and the price tags for an offspring weren't cheap.

He pressed against the gas, the engine a loud rumble as he drove past the edge of the twenty-five thousand acres of the property that were used for the cattle to graze and to raise crops for internal use. The ranch, established in 1854, was now a well-oiled machine, and Colter felt proud of the legacy of the Ward name.

Ten minutes down the road, he passed the driveway leading to his rustic, ranch-style limestone house with distressed wood accents. The home sat atop a hill overlooking the largest lake on Ward land. He carried on down the road, and soon he passed through the wrought iron gates of his brother's two-story sandstone house, with double cherrywood front doors. On the left side of the property was a twenty-horse barn with a black roof.

When Colter parked his white Ford 150 next to Beau's blue Dodge Ram, he spotted Beau working a horse in the round pen. Austin, Beau's five-year-old son, stood on the fence planks with the heels of his cowboy boots hanging off, barely able to see over the railing. His Stetson looked too big for his slender body, but he refused to wear anything smaller. Austin had a strong personality, just like his dad.

As Colter's boot sent a pebble skipping along the driveway, Austin glanced back over his shoulder. He looked nothing like the mother he'd lost. Annie had died suddenly when Austin was only a few months old—a brain aneurysm, the medical examiner had reported. Austin was all Ward, a near-spitting imagine of his father with wise blue eyes, slightly curly brown hair and a mischievous smile.

"Uncle Colter," his nephew exclaimed, soaring off the fence. His cowboy boots kicked up dirt as he charged forward.

Colter caught the kid as he leaped into his arms. "Having a good day, I take it?"

Arms locked around Colter's neck, Austin beamed. "Dad let me ride Big Joe today."

"Big Joe? Wow, buddy, that's a huge horse to ride." Big Joe was also the oldest, laziest, fattest horse on the farm, but all Austin cared about was being upgraded from a pony.

"I rode him like a champ," Austin stated, wiggling out of Colter's arms and returning to his place on the fence.

Another thing Austin got from his dad—a hefty amount of confidence.

Colter chuckled to himself, watching Beau slap a rope against his leg as the chestnut mare trotted around the pen. When Colter returned to Devil's Bluffs after his divorce, he'd took over the cattle side of the business, as his father could no longer work, but Beau had taken to horses from a young age. There was no greater horseman than his brother.

Beau stepped out in front of the mare, raising his arm. The mare turned the opposite direction and carried on in a trot. Colter had always been proud of his younger brother, but never as much as when he gave up on his competitive dreams as a professional reiner to raise his son after Annie passed away.

Life hadn't been easy for Beau. But for Colter, the best part about coming back to Devil's Bluffs was being more involved in his nephew's life.

Colter reached the fence a moment later, where Beau had already latched the lead rope to the horse's halter and called over a farmhand. "Give her a good walk out before hosing her off," he said, handing off the horse.

The farmhand led the horse away, and Beau took off his cowboy hat, wiping at the sweat on his forehead, and approaching the fence. "Beer?" he asked Colter.

"That'll do."

Beau's gaze fell to his son. "Go help Lee with Pumpkin. Listen to what he tells you."

"Okaaaaay," Austin wheezed, taking off running after the farmhand, who then reprimanded the boy for running up behind the mare.

Colter raised his eyebrows. "Pumpkin?"

"Austin named her," Beau explained, heading toward the house.

Colter fell into stride next to his brother, smiling at his nephew, who now walked slowly and carefully. He couldn't think of a better place to raise a son. It sure beat the big city.

When they reached the porch, Colter took a seat in the closest cedar chair, while Beau headed inside.

He returned a moment later, offering him a cold beer. Beau placed a third beer on the top of the porch steps before sitting next to Colter. "What's up?"

A Friday-night beer had been a long-standing tradition of the Ward men after an exhausting workweek. "You'll never believe who I ran into at the Black Horse just now."

"A woman lusting over you." Beau grinned.

"Hilarious." Colter snorted, stretching out his legs. "No, your old babysitter, Adeline Harlow."

"Adeline," Beau said, mulling over her name. Until awareness filled his eyes. "Pigtails. Overalls. That Adeline?"

Colter nodded. "That's the one. She works for that gossip blog that ran the story about me."

Beau gave a low whistle. "I bet that conversation went well."

"It went terrible. Until I realized we could both get what we wanted. I get a fake girlfriend to appear taken and get these women out of town. She gets the story about me to earn a promotion she's after."

Beau raised his eyebrows. "Care to explain all that in greater detail, since not a lick of it made any sense?"

Colter recapped what had happened since he'd looked up and found himself trapped in Adeline's pretty eyes.

Beau finished his sip of beer and then asked, "Should I be worried about you?"

Colter chuckled against the rim of his beer. "Not that I know of. Why?"

"You're single. You're not dead yet. Why are you so against the idea of women wanting to date you that you're arranging a fake relationship—which, by the way, is insane?" His brother leaned back in his chair, crossing his ankles. "Why not have a little fun? You deserve that."

Colter hung his head, guilt weighing him heavily down into his seat. Had he not focused so much on his own pain with his failing marriage, he would have come home sooner. Maybe his father wouldn't have become so frail so fast if he hadn't had to work so hard. "I've got the ranch on my shoulders. I don't have the time or energy for a woman." And he'd already failed at one marriage.

"Now, that's just a damn shame," Beau muttered. He took another long draw of his beer before he continued, "You said Adeline's pretty now?"

Colter nodded. "Gorgeous."

"Hot in a big-city way?"

Colter pondered the question, remembering just how she'd looked in her high heels, but then shrugged. "Fancy, yeah, but there's some small town there, too." He paused, following his brother's gaze as Austin now climbed on a round bale. "But we both know a pretty face can hide a whole lot of ugly."

"Ain't that the truth, brother," Beau agreed, then gestured out to the driveway. "Might want to tell Mom and Dad about this arrangement before news hits the gossip train."

Colter caught sight of the white wheelchair-accessible van stirring up dust on its drive toward the house. They'd purchased the vehicle for his parents a few months ago when his father was struggling to get around and needed to use a wheelchair. Not long after that, they'd hired a full-time nurse to help his mother at home. As each day passed, things became harder for Dad. He couldn't use the bathroom, shower or eat without help now. That's when they knew he had to move to the nursing home for full-time care.

When the van came to a stop near the porch, Colter fought his instinct to go and help the driver, along with the nurse, assist his father out of the van. His father, Grant Ward, did not like the help, so Colter left it up to the nurse, who knew how to deal with headstrong men.

As the nurse wheeled Dad up to the house, Mom's clear blue eyes met Colter's, her shiny gray curls bouncing with her steps. His mother, Beverly, was a beautiful woman, with a smile that could brighten the coldest of days. He rose and trotted down the porch steps, meeting her halfway. He kissed her cheek. "Hi, Mom."

"Hi, boys." She leaned in for Beau's kiss, and then she reached into her purse, taking out a tall cup with a straw.

She cracked the beer and poured it into the cup as Austin came running over. "Grammy," he exclaimed, launching himself at her.

She awkwardly caught him with a laugh. "Hello, my baby. I'm happy to see you, too." In a classic mom move, she kissed the top of his head. "Come on, let's go in and we can watch a movie. I brought cookies."

Austin charged forward up the steps, and his mother handed Colter the cup with the beer inside and followed Austin into the house.

Colter took a seat on the top porch step, with Beau taking the spot on the bottom. No matter how long it took his mother, the driver and the nurse to get Dad here for their Friday-night beer, he always came. Colter was grateful for that. For these little moments he knew would eventually come to an end.

With shaky arms, Dad held out his hand and took the

cup. The nurse gave a smile before returning to the driver, giving them privacy.

"Hey, old man," Colter said.

"Who are you calling old?" Dad joked, the straw rattling in the cup as he managed to get it to his lips.

Colter fought against helping, forcing himself to be still.

Loud music erupted from the living room inside from whatever movie his mother had put on as Dad finished his sip. "Update me on the ranch," he said once he released the straw.

"Nothing much to report on my end," Beau replied. "It's been a good, quiet week—lots of great training. We've got a couple of fancy fillies coming up."

Dad gave a firm nod, slowly placing his cup on the side table attached to his wheelchair. His gaze shifted to Colter. "You?"

He nearly told his father about his arrangement with Adeline, intended to quiet his life that had become a circus, until he looked at the haunting darkness in his father's eyes. His father had his own weight to carry now. Nothing mattered above that. Everything else could wait. "Nothing new here, either," he said, as Beau lifted his brows.

"Cattle's all good, then?" Dad asked.

Colter cupped his father's shoulder, and for the first time in his life, he lied to his father. "Yeah, Dad. I'm all good, and so is the cattle."

Three

The next morning, Adeline woke up early and hit the ground sprinting. She'd done her best not to think of Colter or her father, who probably wouldn't even know she was his daughter if he saw her on the street. Instead, she left the inn for the cozy local coffee shop a block away that roasted its beans in-house. They also had a killer caramelized brown sugar and dulce de leche latte. And one of the best cinnamon rolls Adeline had ever tasted.

Sitting in a corner booth, with her earbuds playing soft rock, she'd spent her morning and early afternoon catching up on emails and scouring the internet for what she could find on Colter. Turned out, it wasn't much. He'd received an award from the city of Seattle for an emergency landing he'd done after the helicopter he was flying lost power. He had saved the life of the governor of Washington, who'd been on board. It didn't come as much of a surprise that Colter had become a pilot of some kind.

She recalled he'd taken flying lessons for as long as she'd known the Ward family.

By the time she finished her lunch of chicken, quinoa and Tuscan kale salad, she'd learned all she could without talking to the source directly to fill in the pieces. Determined to write a strong piece—not only for the promotion, but to do the Ward family justice, as she'd always been fond of them—she texted Colter, using the phone number on his business card. Hi. It's Adeline. Can I interview you today?

His response came a few minutes later. Dinner tonight at 6, Longhorn Grill?

She'd never heard of the restaurant and guessed it was new. She responded, I'll be there. See you tonight!

Looking forward to it, New York.

Her belly somersaulted at his obvious nickname for her now. Dear Lord, it was like a man had never called her something other than her name before. Didn't help that she could hear the drawl in Colter's low voice, setting off shivers that desperately wanted to become trembles and moans.

Putting a stop to that nonsense, she slammed her laptop shut and headed back to the inn to finish her work for the day. She curled her hair and added some makeup before swapping out her comfortable clothing for a flowy white frock with a ruffled trim and strappy heels more suitable for dinner.

Once she was back on the town, when dinner was still an hour away, she realized the restaurant was across town near the local newspaper's office and decided to make a quick stop before meeting Colter.

The nineteenth-century building housing the *Devil's*

Bluffs Chronicle had received a makeover since Adeline had been there last, with fresh paint and new windows. Though, when she opened the door and it creaked in greeting, the sound was wonderfully familiar. Even the dusty smell hadn't changed. Waylon sat behind his desk, deeper wrinkles on his face than she'd remembered, his hair all silver now.

"Oh my goodness, is that Adeline?" His bright blue eyes were just as Adeline remembered—kind.

"Hi, Waylon," she said, shutting the door behind her. "It's so good to see you."

He rose, moving around his desk with a limp that hadn't been there years ago, to wrap Adeline in his warm embrace. She sank into him, holding tight. Waylon was the reason she didn't hate men altogether. He'd showed her what a good man truly was.

When he leaned away, he asked, "Please tell me you've moved back."

"Sorry, but no," she said before releasing him. "I'm only here for a couple weeks."

Waylon cocked his head. "On a job? I follow your articles all the time."

Of course he did. No one had supported her love of writing more than Waylon. She'd done her high school co-op at the newspaper, and she'd loved every minute of her time there. Leaving Waylon had been the hardest part about moving to the big city, but they'd stayed in contact over email throughout the years.

"I'm actually here to interview Colter Ward," she explained. Waylon's posture perked up, and Adeline smiled, knowing she'd come to the right place. Waylon was a great researcher as well as editor. He gathered secrets like he gathered stories—bountifully. "I wondered if you could tell me a bit about what Colter's been doing since I've left town."

"Not much to tell," Waylon said, limping back to his seat. "He married his high school sweetheart, Julia. Left for Seattle, but, like everyone from Devil's Bluffs, he came back." A pause. "Wasn't quite the same guy, though."

Adeline leaned against the desk. "How was he different?"

Waylon paused to consider, tapping a finger against the armrest. "He's quieter now. Like the city broke him. But if you ask me, it was Julia that had a hand in that."

Adeline studied Waylon's pinched expression. Her mentor loved everyone. "You didn't like his ex-wife?" she asked, surprised.

"Not that I didn't like her, but they were different... not meant to be, I'd say." Then his expression shifted, bringing warmth back into his features. "But the big city looks good on you. It didn't break you at all. Look how grown-up you are. You sparkle, Adeline."

"Thanks," she managed. She didn't feel good inside. After the breakup with Brock, she'd felt crushed, confused and, if she were being honest with herself, lost. On top of that, she didn't feel like she belonged in the big city anymore, as much as she didn't feel like she belonged in Devil's Bluffs.

Just as the room began to close in on her, she hastily shoved thoughts of her life away, staying focused on Colter. "You haven't heard anything more about him from any of the gossip in town?" Small towns, even wealthy towns, always had a long line of gossipers. "Nothing that I might use in my story?"

"Colter is good stuff. Both those Ward boys are. They

do a lot for the town and take good care of their parents. If you write anything, write about that."

Adeline took some mental notes, but she knew Colter being a good man wouldn't give her the enticing piece she needed to earn her the promotion. She needed to dig deep, find Colter's truth, his weaknesses, his successes—which would only make him more attractive to the blog's readers.

Waylon's watch beeped, drawing his gaze. "And that's a day." He rose, powered off his computer and gently escorted Adeline out before locking up. She'd always respected Waylon's balance between home and family life. He made time for his wife of forty years and his children. Always.

"It really is so great to see you," Adeline said. "Say hi to Marjorie for me."

"I sure will."

Adeline hugged him once more and said her goodbyes with the promise to come back soon. Though she was getting tidbits of Colter's story, she knew all the good details would come from dinner tonight.

The Longhorn Grill was only a two-minute walk down the moderately busy street, and when she arrived at the chic, modern restaurant with bright white walls and warm wooden accents, a hostess seated her quickly.

Then the front door opened, and Colter entered, speaking to the hostess. Adeline swallowed. Deeply. *I am in way over my head.*

Yesterday, Colter had looked rough, like a cowboy who'd spent his day working hard on the ranch. He'd smelled of sweat, of man and of things that shouldn't arouse a woman, but somehow had only made him more masculine. She exhaled against the quickening of her breath at his crisp black button-up tucked into light jeans that hugged his thick thighs. She'd never felt jealous of clothes before, but she'd give her last year's salary to mold herself to Colter the way the fabric did. Warmth flooded her when his stare caught hers and held as he began walking to the table, the side of his mouth curving. Dear Lord, *that* man was far too handsome for his own good, oozing testosterone and charm, nearly melting her into a puddle on the hardwood floors.

Two women had followed him into the restaurant, but as they saw him headed Adeline's way, they frowned and turned their attention to the two cowboys sitting at the bar. Gosh, the women really were relentless.

When Colter reached the table, he leaned near, and her nerve endings stirred as his lips met hers. The kiss was polite, a show for their audience in the restaurant. Her body forgot that memo, and as he pulled away, she moved with him, reaching for *more*. Light-headed, she inhaled his spicy, woodsy scent and wanted to forget that she'd *just* broken off her engagement and her heart was still raw and bleeding.

Before she crawled up his strong body, she yanked herself back and relaxed her posture, like his kiss didn't send her body into overdrive. "Hi," she said in a voice that sounded too controlled even to her ears. "I see the ladies are still following you?"

"Hey." He took a seat across from her, removing his cowboy hat and placing it on the chair next to him. "Not as many as there have been, so I'd say our arrangement is working. Have a good day?"

She pretended not to notice the way his arm bulged when he carved a hand through his hair. She failed miserably. Godness, he was *hot*. "Quiet day," she told him. "I spent most of it at the coffee shop researching you."

He lifted an eyebrow. "Find out anything interesting?"

"Not really."

"Good. I'd much rather you hear about me from the source."

You and me both. She smiled instead of saying that aloud and was glad for the interruption when the waitress arrived at their table. Once she took their orders, she returned quickly with Colter's beer in a tall, frosty glass and Adeline's glass of pinot grigio.

"All right," Adeline said after taking a long sip of her wine. She savored the dry, crisp taste before taking her journal from her purse. "About that interview—"

"Nah, not just yet."

She blinked. "Not just yet?"

"We've got time to interview me later," he said, returning his glass to the table. "Tell me about you."

"Why?" she asked, baffled.

"I'd like to know about the girl who left Devil's Bluffs—" his heated gaze roamed over her "—and the *woman* who came back."

She shifted against her chair, wishing the restaurant had turned the air-conditioning on higher, but at his dancing eyes, she straightened. Women must drop to their knees for this man, and it was embarrassing how all that charm and killer smile made her want to do the same. "It's really not that interesting. We moved to New York City when my mom decided she'd had enough of small-town living."

"Your dad didn't care that you left?"

She swallowed the sudden emotion clenching her throat with another long sip of wine before answering him. "I've never met my dad."

"Ever?"

She shook her head. "After I was born, he didn't want to be involved, and my mother respected his choice."

"Brave woman."

"No one is better than my mother," she agreed. "She was everything I needed, so having an absent father wasn't really a big deal." At least that's what she'd keep telling herself until she believed it. "I think my mom only told me about him because I eventually asked."

"You don't want to meet him?"

"Not particularly," she answered honestly.

Obviously sensing she had nothing more to say on the matter, he shifted the subject. "You like it in the big city?" he asked.

"I love New York City," she said, playing with the stem of her wineglass and noticing her fingers drew his attention. "I can't imagine living anywhere else on the planet."

His eyes lifted and head cocked. "It's not too loud?"

"Oh, it's loud, and a little bit smelly, too." She laughed. "It took a very long time to get used to being in a city. Devil's Bluffs has, what…ten thousand people?"

He nodded. "About that."

"So, yeah, it took a bit to settle into a city with so many people, but not only did I get used to it, it's weird now when things are too quiet."

"Must be an adjustment being back here, then."

She stared into the face of the guy who'd starred in all her teenage fantasies. "It sure is something."

His slow-building smile stirred her nerve endings. Keeping that heated stare on her, he took another long draft of his beer before asking, "Why is the promotion so important to you?"

The questions were moving closer to what she didn't want to talk about, but she couldn't withhold the truth. One thing she'd learned about interviewing anyone over the years was to stay honest about her life. How could she expect the same from anyone if she didn't reciprocate? But, oddly, what was normally uncomfortable to admit wasn't with Colter.

"It's important because my job is legit all I have left in my life." His eyebrows began to squish together, but she pushed on. "A week ago, I found out that my fiancé, who I'd been with for five years, Brock, was cheating on me with his secretary. Yes, it devastated me. Yes, I'm still heartbroken. And yes, I have no idea what I'm going to do when I get back home."

"Understandable," he said gently.

"But what I do know is that all my dreams, all my plans, were gone in a blink of an eye. So, now all I have left is my job, and instead of crying on the floor like the pile of dirty clothes that I feel like, I'm fighting for a promotion to make sure that when I go home I have at least one thing that I can look into the mirror at myself and feel proud about."

His face locked down tight halfway through her speech, his expression revealing nothing. Until he said, "Do you have a cell phone?"

"Yes. Why?"

"Grab it and come here."

She hesitated, watching him closely for any hint of what he was up to and repeated, "Why?"

A low chuckle escaped him as he waved her forward. "Just come here, will you? I won't bite."

She cursed her thoughts when she wondered, *But what if I ask you to?* She hesitantly reached for her cell in her purse and rose, sidling next to him. He had her on his lap a second later, and sitting on his lap felt good...*really good...too good...devastatingly good.*

"Unlock your phone," he murmured into her ear. "Take a photo of us."

She laughed nervously. "For real?"

"Indulge me," he said.

Her skin felt alive with sensation as she did as he asked.

When she set her camera to selfie mode and lifted the phone, his heated gaze engulfed her. Though it was her own eyes—and the raging lust in them—that stunned her more. She'd done love with Brock. He'd taken her virginity, and their sex life had been good. Lust, however—she'd never tasted this rich, needy desire that Colter evoked in her.

He licked his lips before brushing his mouth across her ear. She shivered, shutting her eyes against the yearning filling her, as he murmured, "Take the picture, Adeline."

She managed to reopen her eyes, finding his intense stare locked onto hers as she snapped the picture.

He leaned away, grinning. "Yeah, New York, post *that* on Instagram."

None of this is real. She repeated the words again and again in her head, reminding herself this was all for show, as she returned to her seat on shaky legs. Back in her chair, she didn't even recognize herself in the photograph. Her pupils were so dilated, nearly all the honey color of the irises was gone. Her cheeks were flushed deep red, and her lips were parted, begging for his kiss. "You do realize the mess this will create for me," she told him.

He grinned salaciously. "Trust me, if anything is going to piss off that prick who hurt you, it's going to be that picture."

The huge, gaping hole in her heart wanted Brock to hurt. Badly. Not thinking too much on it, she posted the picture, along with the caption "Nothin' beats dinner with a cowboy!"

When she set her cell down next to the silverware,

Colter raised an eyebrow. "Must feel good to show him what he's missing, right?"

"It does," she admitted, "but it feels better to feel like I'm something worth missing." Until the words left her mouth, she hadn't realized how Brock's cheating had made her feel. Worthless. She didn't feel worthless tonight with Colter.

"He's a fool if he's not missing you, Adeline." Colter's eye contact firmed as he leaned forward, closing the distance.

Rational—she'd always been proud of having that trait. Logical—she never swayed from doing the right thing. But her body wasn't screaming levelheadedness at her as she squeezed her legs together, desperate for friction against the ache between her thighs, yearning for his touch.

"The porterhouse?"

She jerked back at the waitress's squeaky voice, broken from the wild spell he'd woven around her. A spell leaving her drenched, trembling, breathing heavily.

"That'd be me," said Colter, his voice husky.

Blushing, Adeline kept her focus on the squash risotto placed on the table in front of her.

"Do you need anything else?" the waitress asked.

Colter gave a low, throaty chuckle. "A couple of cold glasses of water, please."

Adeline caught his devilish grin and laughed softly. "Yes, *ice*-cold, please."

When they left the restaurant and began walking along the lit-up Promenade, Colter's stomach was stuffed full, warm and satisfied. Truth was, he felt more comfortable than he had in a long time. So comfortable that when Adeline twined her fingers with his, he didn't even flinch.

One look at the women sitting on the bench and watching them approach with hungry eyes indicated why she'd made the move. But he'd begun to enjoy the woman herself, beyond this deal they'd made. She shared her life's ups and downs easily, no matter how painful it was. He didn't possess that skill. And yet, *and yet*—he wanted her to know him.

Every word she'd said during dinner surprised him. She was funny, cute and fascinating—nothing like he remembered the awkward, shy kid who'd barely acknowledged the world around her. He gave her a quick look, finding her focused on the women they passed, wondering if her situation made her more appealing. She was leaving in two weeks. She'd *just* broken off her engagement. If there was any woman safe enough for him to enjoy some skin-to-skin pleasures with, Adeline was a safe bet. By the way she was squirming in her seat tonight, he'd also bet she was feeling the same way about him.

Her sweet laugh suddenly drew him out of his thoughts. "I have never had so many women give me dirty looks in my life," she said.

"I find that hard to believe," he admitted. He could barely keep his eyes off her and his thoughts PG-rated.

"Why is that so hard to believe?"

He took his time roaming over her face and didn't deprive himself of a glimpse at her spectacular cleavage. "You're beautiful, Adeline. Women get envious of that."

She blushed, quickly looking back ahead of her, paying attention to where she was walking. "It wasn't... I wasn't always like this, as you know. I was a late bloomer, and honestly, without my best friend, Nora, I'm sure I'd still be in a pair of overalls, lost in my journals."

An image of her, naked but for a pair of overalls,

flashed in his mind, making his cock twitch. "You won't hear me object to overalls." He'd bet she'd fill them out in all the right places. "They can be sexy when worn right."

Adeline released his hand to nudge her elbow into him. "Nora would gut you if she heard you say that. She takes pride in the fact that she helped me find my sense of style."

"She's a good friend to you?"

"The very best of friends," she replied. "My life is better because she's in it. We're very, *very* close. Are you and Beau still like that?"

"We are," he said. "But I also have Riggs, the bartender at the Black Horse. He's my closest and oldest friend."

"Nice. I thought I recognized him last night. He went to the same high school as us?"

"He did, but he enlisted in the military after high school and then became a cop. He only opened the bar this last year."

Ahead, a German shepherd walking with its owner began barking at the border collie across the street. She waited until they passed and the dogs quieted before she said, "Okay, enough about me and my life. You promised me a story."

"You're right, I did." He gestured to the cobblestone pathway, hugged by big, mature trees, that headed into the park. "Ask away."

"From what I've learned, you lived in Seattle for a time. Is that true?"

He nodded, shoving his hands into the pockets of his jeans. "After I got married to Julia, we moved to Seattle. Did you ever meet her?"

Adeline snorted a laugh, pointing to herself. "Pigtails

and overalls, remember? We weren't exactly hanging in the same circle of friends."

"Right." He paused, and then after thinking about it, he added, "You probably wouldn't recognize her now, anyway." Adeline watched him closely, and he knew he was revealing too much, but it felt wrong to withhold parts of himself, no matter the risk there. "Off the record?"

She inclined her head. "You've got my word."

He waited until they passed a couple picnicking in the gazebo before he began. "After we got married, Julia was hired by a big event-planning company out in Seattle. I had obtained my helicopter pilot's license for the ranch to oversee our cattle and land, but when we moved to Seattle, I was hired on by a company in the private sector that provides private helicopter and plane flights."

"I saw the award you got."

He smiled remembering that day and the pride he'd felt for a job well done. "I enjoyed my job there. I worked mainly with politicians and celebrities."

"Neat," she said. "You were happy out there?"

He shook his head. "I hated the big city, but we never planned on staying. The plan had always been for Julia to get a few years of experience, and then we'd come home."

"What were your goals?"

"Either to continue flying for a private company back here in Devil's Bluffs or work for medevac."

"You didn't want to open your own company?"

"I wanted to fly, not run a business."

"All right," she said after a moment of processing. "So, then, what changed?"

"Julia changed," he admitted, his cowboy boots clicking against the stones on the pathway. "The country girl I fell in love with vanished, replaced by a woman focused on high society and living a lavish lifestyle. She turned into a woman I didn't even recognize. A woman I had nothing in common with."

Adeline nodded in understanding. "Is that why you're not together anymore?"

"That's part of the reason." He gestured to a bench beneath a big shade tree and waited for Adeline to take a seat before he joined her. "It wasn't a single reason that ended the marriage. It was the accumulation of a few things."

"Do you mind sharing them?"

He probably shouldn't have, but, lost in the comfort of her kind eyes, he couldn't stop himself. "I want kids. She did, too, until suddenly that wasn't something she cared about. It was the bigger celebrity she met, the more expensive party, the dress that no one else had. And then, one day, she told me that she no longer wanted to have children."

"That ended it, then?"

Colter looked past the trees back to the road, transfixed by the twinkling lights glistening against the street. "I received a call one night from my mother, telling me that my father's Parkinson's had taken a turn for the worse and she couldn't look after him anymore." When he met Adeline's tender gaze, he liked how she listened, intent and tuned-in. "She begged me to come home. My father couldn't run the ranch anymore, and she needed me." A sour taste filled his mouth as he said, "When I asked Julia to come home, she said she wanted to stay in the city. Before I left for home, she asked for a divorce."

"Ouch, that's hard," Adeline said, her hand on her heart.

A nod. "That information I would prefer to keep out of the article, but what you can put in it is that I came home after my divorce and stepped into my father's role as CEO of Devil's Bluffs Ranch."

Adeline pulled her cell phone from her purse. "Sorry, is it all right if I take notes?"

"It's fine." He leaned back, placing an arm behind her on the bench, fighting against wanting to drag his finger over her soft shoulder.

"It must be hard for your dad not to be working. I always remember him being such a hard worker."

"I imagine all of what he's going through is hard," Colter admitted.

She agreed with a nod and made a few notes on her phone. "Are you happy to be back home, stepping into his big boots?"

"Yes."

Their gazes held for a beat. Of course, she called him out. "Liar," she said.

"That obvious, huh?" he asked with a snort.

"Yeah, pretty much."

He slowly drew in a big, deep breath before blowing it out his mouth. "It's not that I'm not happy to be heading up the ranch and taking over my father's role. I'm proud to be leading the Ward legacy, but it's that for the last handful of years, nothing in my life has been picked by me. My hand has always been played for me, and I don't like that." By the tenderness sweeping across her face, he knew he'd said too much. "Of course, that's off the record."

She gave a gentle smile. "How about we just say the emotional stuff stays off the record, so you don't have to keep saying that. All right?"

"Deal."

She hesitated as an elderly couple walked by, hand in hand, strolling into the still evening as the sun began to set, before glancing his way again. "When it comes to stepping into your father's role and becoming CEO of Devil's Bluffs Ranch, what do you want people to know?"

"That I'll take care of the land, give back to the community and honor the hard work my father has done."

She hesitated, her eyes searching his. "You know, if you ask me, Julia made a huge mistake letting you go."

He parted his lips to respond but found his voice gone. His body was screaming *yes*. His mind was screaming, *Don't repeat your mistakes. She's a big-city girl, and you already failed at love once with someone who'd prefer skyscrapers to cowboy boots.*

But the breeze carried floral scents as something passed in the air between them. Something real and raw, and so foreign that he wanted to wrap himself around the wonderful feeling—when her phone slipped from her hands.

"Oops." She laughed nervously.

"I got it." He went down on one knee and reached for her phone.

When he offered it to her, their fingers brushed. That sudden touch simply became a tease. His mind wasn't leading him as he lifted his hand and stroked her cheek—it was only a response to how she looked at him. Gentle, and yearning for his touch, she was the most beautiful thing he'd ever seen.

Just like that, his body won over his mind.

Even though he knew she was a city slicker who hated his town and who was leaving after she had her story, he leaned into her. Her lips parted, a soft breath escaping, in the moment before his lips pressed to hers. She melted into his kiss, rising to the demand when she parted her mouth to let his tongue slip inside.

He kissed her. For a good long while. Until he broke

away when he heard the chattering women behind him, gasping and giggling. He found Adeline smiling.

"You always kiss that good or is it because you're being watched?" she asked.

She thought he'd kissed her because of their audience, but she was dead wrong. He chuckled, brushing his thumb against her bottom lip, puffy from his kiss. "Can't blame a guy for wanting to put on a good show." He rose, slipping her hand into his. "Come on, I'll walk you back to the inn." Before he did something he did not want others watching.

Four

The next morning, Adeline woke up in the too-soft queen-size bed at the inn, surrounded by a wall of pillows. The morning sun gleamed through the window, revealing a room far too French country for her tastes. From the toile wallpaper to the frilly curtains and the floral patchwork quilt, everything about this space felt too...*happy.*

Suddenly reminded what she'd posted last night, and only now realizing that her boss might not approve of her getting so close to the subject of her story, she immediately checked Instagram. The photograph of her and Colter had earned a few hundred likes. Not enough for her editor to notice. Even this morning she could still see the heat brimming between them.

She hoped Brock saw the picture and choked on it.

With a sudden burst of happiness, she closed Instagram, realizing she'd missed ten calls this morning. Two from Nora. The rest from her mother. And a dozen more text messages urging Adeline to call them immediately.

She leaped out of bed, calling home first. Her mom, Lorraine, answered on the first ring. "What's wrong?" Adeline exclaimed.

"Adeline Marie, do you have anything that you want to tell me?"

Adeline spun, heading for the window to look outside, wondering if the world had blown up. When a quiet street greeted her, she sighed inwardly. She was proud her mother had gone back to school after they moved to New York City to become a therapist, but sometimes—like *now*—her knowledge as a therapist got mixed with a mother's intuition, and the invasion into Adeline's life was a bit much to stomach. "It's not what you think, and it's really complicated, but Colter was goading Brock with that photograph I posted on Instagram."

"What photograph on Instagram?" Mom paused. "I have not seen a photograph on Instagram. The photograph I'm talking about is the one of Colter proposing to you."

"What?" Adeline yelled before reeling in her voice. "Wait...*what*?"

"Go to Facebook, my dear. You've been tagged," Mom said dryly.

Adeline scooped up her laptop and jumped back onto the bed. She logged in and opened her Facebook account, finding thousands of notifications, but then she saw the post.

She recognized the woman's profile picture—she was one of the women from last night who'd been laughing with her friend after Colter had kissed Adeline. The woman's angle prevented her from seeing the cell phone

Colter was handing her, and… "Oh my goodness, it looks like he is proposing to me."

"Yes, it certainly does," Mom agreed. "It's everywhere on your social media. All these strangers talking about you. Congratulating you, for heaven's sake."

Adeline blinked at her phone, wishing the room would swallow her up. "Okay, first, I'm not engaged to Colter."

"I should hope not."

"Second, it's not what it looks like. He was handing me my cell phone back. You just can't tell from the picture."

"Ah, I see," her mother mused. "That makes perfect sense, because don't you know that everyone kisses each other when handing over a cell phone?"

Adeline cringed. She nearly made up an excuse but knew she needed to do one better for her mother. "Okay, so I kissed him a couple times."

The silence on the other end of the phone was deafening. "Honey, be honest with me. Are you okay? If this is some rebound fling that you need, fine."

Adeline shuddered. "Mom, I know you're a therapist, but I don't want to talk about this with you."

Her mother ignored Adeline like she hadn't spoken and went on. "But if this is because of your broken heart and you are about to make a huge mistake that you will regret, come home."

Knowing that her mother would hop on a plane and arrive in Devil's Bluffs if she thought Adeline was having a breakdown—and loving her for caring that much—Adeline said, "It's neither of those things, actually." She caught her mother up on her arrangement with Colter.

Lorraine paused for a long time once Adeline finished. "Kissing him is part of this arrangement?" she asked.

"It makes our fake relationship more believable to all the women who are hounding him," she said, but then she knew her mother would read right through her lie. "I might not be hating that part, though."

More silence followed, and Adeline held her breath as the long seconds ticked by. Until her mother's sweet, comforting voice filled the phone line. "Just remember, my love, that Devil's Bluffs is not an easy place for you to visit. Your emotions will be rocky there. Brock *just* broke your heart, and you are still reeling from that. Please keep your well-being your top priority."

Yeah, well, what if kissing a smokin'-hot cowboy is good for my well-being? Adeline gave her head a hard shake. *Not part of the agreement.* "I hear you loud and clear," she responded instead, "but honestly, I'm okay. I think coming here was good for me. It's like coming home, in a weird way. I think I needed to remember who I was before Brock, if that makes any sense."

"It does make perfect sense, and I support you," Mom said.

The one positive of having a therapist for a mother was no matter how much she got into Adeline's emotional status, she was encouraging all the way with her decisions. "Thank you. I love you."

"Love you, too, honey."

They said their goodbyes, with Adeline's promise to keep in touch.

Sudden footsteps sounded outside the door before they faded away. Sitting on the end of the bed and staring at her phone, fighting to understand how to deal with this shit show, she started when her cell began to ring.

Nora. She answered the FaceTime call and said, "I can explain everything."

Nora's eyes were bulging out of her head, her mouth open, no words escaping.

"It's not what it looks like," Adeline said.

Nora blinked.

Adeline sighed heavily, rubbing at the throbbing in her temple. "Last night, Colter and I went out for dinner…" She relayed everything that had happened. The good, the shocking, the sweetness and the sexiness, finishing with the moment when Colter got down onto one knee to give her the fallen cell phone. "I'm obviously not engaged."

Nora choked out a laugh. "Okay, good, because for a minute there, I thought you'd up and lost your mind."

Adeline plopped back against the pillows on the bed. "I can't believe this is happening."

"It's crazy how real it looks," Nora said, sitting behind her desk at work. "And hot—like, really, really *hot*. Especially the picture on Instagram."

"I know," Adeline breathed, still feeling the butterflies fluttering in her belly.

Nora's eyes searched Adeline's for a moment before she grinned. "Okay, so maybe all this isn't so bad?"

"Except it's turning my entire world upside down," Adeline pointed out. "How does this make me look? One week ago, I was engaged to Brock. Everyone at home knows he cheated." Because she'd emailed all their guests to explain the wedding was off. She hadn't sugarcoated that email. It probably wasn't her finest moment, but she'd figured simple wording—The wedding is off. Brock cheated on me—summed it up the best. "Even my mom is worried I'm hanging on by a thread."

"Who cares what anyone thinks?" Nora countered, waving her hand. "Just do you, girl, and do what makes you happy right now."

If only life was ever that simple.

A sudden hard knock sounded on her door. Suspecting the innkeeper was delivering her morning coffee, the way she had yesterday morning, Adeline jumped off the bed and whisked the door open. Colter's heated gaze roamed her from head to toe, reminding her she wore a nightie and nothing else.

"Nora, I have to go," she said.

"Is that a good idea?" Nora asked, her eyes dancing. "Next thing you know, you'll be pregnant."

Colter chuckled, looking out-of-this-world handsome in a light gray T-shirt and worn jeans, paired with a dark tan–colored Stetson.

Nora's eyes widened. "Oh, is that *him*?"

Adeline flipped the phone around. "Nora, meet Colter. Colter, meet Nora."

"Hi, Nora," Colter said with his charming smile.

"Okay, I see what all the fuss is about," Nora said, her voice chipper. "It's nice to meet you, too, Colter."

"All right, babe," Adeline said, turning the screen back to her.

Nora mouthed, *He is so friggin' hot.*

Adeline restrained her laughter, nodding in agreement. "I love you, but I need to go and deal with this."

"Good luck," Nora said. "Let me know if I need to get a maid of honor dress."

"That is not funny at all." Adeline groaned. She ended the call to Nora's rolling laughter.

Colter leaned in the doorway, filling up the space, arms crossed against his wide chest. "Hi, wifey."

"That isn't funny, either." With a huff, she tossed her cell onto the bed. She took out a pair of cutoff denim shorts, a bra, panties and a black shirt before slipping into the en suite and changing quickly.

When she came out and slipped into her black flats, Colter was sitting on the end of the bed. "Ah, come on," he said. "It's a little funny."

She snorted, hanging her nightgown on the hook on

the back of the door. "I can't imagine any of this being funny to my ex-fiancé and his family, who are really lovely people even though their son is an asshole."

"I'm sorry about his family," Colter said. His mouth twitched. "But I'd pay cash to see that prick's face right now."

"Actually, so would I," she admitted, her broken heart squeezing in agreement. She pressed herself against the door, folding her arms. "So."

"So." He smiled, cool and collected.

Again, she huffed, tossing up her arms. "I have no idea how you can be so calm about all this. What a mess we made!" The ringing of her cell had her stepping toward the bed. One look at the screen, and her stomach sank. "Oh, God, please, no." She promptly answered her phone. "Claire, let me explain."

"You are brilliant, Adeline, just brilliant," her editor exclaimed. "You don't need to explain anything. You wouldn't believe the attention this is getting. Keep sending pictures—draw this out for as long as you can. It's only going to push your article further."

Adeline gasped, "No, wait."

Oblivious to Adeline, Claire continued, "Keep it up, girl. Keep it up." The phone line went dead.

"Why. Is. This. Happening?" Adeline groaned, sliding to the ground, dropping her head into her hands. "My editor is thrilled. *Thrilled!*"

"Oh, come on," Colter drawled. "It's not that bad being engaged to me, is it?"

She peeked through her fingers. "Honestly, how are you handling this so well?"

He rose, his presence a wall of strength as he approached, offering his hand. "Because I have been in a bad situation. This isn't bad, so what is left to do but laugh about it?" She slid her hand into his, and he helped her to her feet. "For one, this only benefits me. Now I'm not maybe taken, I'm off the market. Two, once you go back to New York City, all this will die down. I'll tell everyone we broke up, and you can tell everyone that it was a big misunderstanding, and that's that."

She blew out a long breath. "I guess you're right. What is fretting about all this going to do?"

"See, I'm even making sense. Not too bad for a fiancé, right?"

She laughed, relishing the way the tension faded from her chest. "Definitely better than the one I had."

His fingers dragged against hers when he released her hand, and the move seemed deliberate. Her nipples puckered in response. "All right, New York, pack your things. Let's get you to your new home."

A cold wave hit her, any heat tingling in her limbs evaporating. "Pardon?"

One eyebrow slowly lifted. "You do plan on keeping your end of the bargain, don't you?"

"Ah, yeah, but where am I going?"

He leaned against the desk, folding his arms, giving her a knowing look. "No one in town will believe we're engaged if you're not living with me."

One second…

Another…

Then another…

"Oh, shit," she breathed.

Five

Twenty minutes later, Colter cursed when he drove up the laneway to his house. His mother and Beau were walking back to the truck parked at the porch steps. "The cavalry has arrived."

"Please tell me you have already talked to them," Adeline muttered. At his silence, she frowned. "Why aren't you saying anything?"

"Because, in this case, I think silence might work better to my advantage than saying the wrong thing."

She snorted a laugh.

Grinning at her, he parked his truck behind Beau's and turned off the ignition. By the time he was outside, walking around the hood, Adeline was already greeting his family.

"I never would have believed it if I hadn't seen it with my own eyes," his mother said, opening her arms to Adeline. "Sweetheart, how are you?"

Adeline walked right into Beverly's arms. "I'm doing well," she said before stepping away from the woman who Colter knew for certain gave the best hugs. "Before you ask, no, I'm not engaged to your son. I'm really sorry about all this, Beverly."

"Don't be sorry, honey." His mother smiled fondly at Adeline. Colter remembered that his mother had always thought the world of Adeline and gave Beau trouble often whenever he gave Adeline any grief. "How about you just explain what's going on?"

Colter shoved his hands into his pockets and got a smirk from Beau before he turned his attention to Adeline as she filled his family in on the happenings as of late. He watched, impressed she didn't look to him for help once. Christ, he'd never seen a sexier woman in his life.

"So," said Adeline, wrapping up a story he never would have believed himself. "Is this all crazy? Yes. But it's actually working out for both of us."

Mom shook her head slowly, obviously taking the time to absorb all this insanity. "Well," she eventually said, "if you're not hurting anyone, and you're both getting something out of this, I guess that's good."

"The engagement part was not part of the plan," Colter explained to his mother. "I'm sorry if this causes you any trouble with your friends."

"It won't," she said with her warm, comforting smile. "I'll let the ones that matter know about the situation. The others who don't… Well, they don't matter."

"Thanks, Beverly," Adeline said. "I really appreciate it."

Mom took Adeline's hand. "Not a problem, honey. Whatever we can do to help you get your promotion, we'll do."

When Adeline finally acknowledged Beau, his brother

gave Adeline a slow, inappropriate once-over. Colter shoved him on the arm, and Beau chortled, glancing back into her face. "Adeline." He took her into his arms, the hug lasting longer than necessary. "It's good to see you."

"It's good to see you, too," she said, stepping back. "You're much taller than the last time I saw you."

Beau grinned. "You're much more…"

This time, Colter punched him on the arm, and Beau burst out laughing.

Mom watched furtively before giving Adeline a knowing look. "As you can see, things haven't changed too much around here."

"That's a good thing." Adeline smiled, but then her smile fell. "Though I am so sorry to hear that Grant's been unwell."

"Thank you, honey," Mom said, her voice breaking. "It's been a hard journey for all of us."

Adeline reached out, placing a comforting hand on Mom's shoulder. "If it's all right, I'd love to come by and visit both of you while I'm here in town."

"Of course." Mom beamed. "Come by the house whenever you'd like."

"Wonderful," Adeline said, slowly dragging her hand away.

Beau cleared his throat, drawing all the attention, and threw an arm around Colter's neck. "Well, since you two aren't engaged, congratulations aren't due." He grinned at Adeline. "Which means you can come by my place, too, anytime you want."

Colter elbowed him, and as Beau let out an *oof*, Colter growled, "Shouldn't you be getting back to work?"

"Beau, stop digging at them," Mom snapped in a stern voice.

Beau tipped his hat at Adeline. "Jokes aside, it is really good to see you. You're looking great."

She smiled. "Thanks. You, too."

Colter scowled at the back of his brother's head the entire time he headed for the truck. Before driving off, Beau threw him a grin. Ensuring his mother couldn't see, Colter gave him a rude gesture. His brother laughed as he drove off, a trail of dust following his truck down the laneway.

"You two really haven't changed, have you?"

Turning to Adeline, Colter said, "No, he's still as annoying as ever."

"Your relationship is cute," she said.

"Cute? Not sure I'd call it that," Colter countered. "He'll always be the annoying younger brother, but he's a good father to his son, Austin."

She stared after the truck heading off into the distance. "I wish my mom and I could've come for Beau's wife's funeral. It seemed so wrong to only send flowers, but I couldn't convince my mom to come back."

"Don't feel bad. I've got no doubt Beau appreciated knowing you were thinking of him." Leaving her at the porch, he returned to the truck, took out her bags from the back and then gestured her inside. "Come on, let's get you settled."

Once he unlocked the door, she followed him inside and he led her through the house to the right side, where the bedrooms were located. The master was on the left, and the two guest rooms were on the right. He entered the bigger of the two, which had an amazing view of the sunrise.

As she approached the queen-size bed with the cream-colored duvet and accent pillows that a designer had brought in after he built the place, Colter set her bags down. If the house had been his decorating style, it would have no style at all, but he had purchased the artwork on the walls at the gallery downtown to support local artists.

He stayed by the door, unable to take his eyes off her as she surveyed the room. He felt oddly comfortable having her there in his space. Damn, maybe he was lonelier than he thought. "You'll be okay here?" he asked, breaking the silence.

"More than okay." She turned to him with a smile that warmed something icy in his veins. "You've got a gorgeous home. When did you build it?"

"The year before Julia and I married." Leaning against the door frame, he folded his arms. "My dad's deal had always been that once Beau and I saved up enough for a down payment for a construction mortgage, we could pick a spot and build."

"So like your dad to always help you, but at the same time make you work hard to earn it."

Colter agreed with a nod. "Yeah, that's him pretty much summed up." He glanced around the room he rarely came into anymore. "I built this home thinking I'd start a family here." He'd imagined this space being a nursery. "Now, of course, it's a lot bigger than I need. But if I've learned anything from my divorce, it's to always expect the unexpected. Life rarely works out as planned."

"Truer words have never been spoken."

His smile felt more honest than it had in a long time. He jerked his chin toward the hallway. "Want a tour of the rest of the house?"

"Yes, please."

He showed her the other guest room, the large master bedroom, with the king bed and dark gray leather headboard and sleek black furniture, and where her bathroom was, and then he set out some towels for her.

When they ended up back in the open kitchen that overlooked the rustic dining room and living room, where a black leather couch rested in front of a big stone fireplace, with a flat-screen television in the corner, she said, "You know, this might actually be the best thing that could have happened."

He wasn't so sure of that. How was he going to stick to the rules and not make things intimate between them? His thoughts were indecent enough already without her sugary aroma constantly invading his senses. But they were in this *together*, apparently, and today was the first morning he'd gotten out of his truck downtown and a woman wasn't waiting there for him. The plan had worked. "Why is that?"

Her sassy grin pooled heat in his groin. "It's not often I get to live in the house of the person I'm writing about."

"Best be on my best behavior, then." Something he needed to constantly remind himself of with her around. He glanced at the clock above the gas stove. "I need to get to work, but I can call you later if you want to discuss meals for the week."

"Don't worry about that," she said, her eyes gleaming at the chef's kitchen. "I actually love cooking, so dinners will be mine."

"All right, that works," he said. "Since I suspect I'm up before you, I'll handle breakfast."

"What time do you wake up?"

"Five."

Her eyes widened. "In the morning?"

"Yeah, sometimes earlier."

She shuddered. "You're right, you're up first. Breakfast is yours. I'll head out later today to grab us some food. Just text me anything you need."

"Sounds good." He headed to a drawer and reached in,

grabbing a set of keys. "Here's the spare set for the house and my truck. Use it like it's yours. Company pays for gas." He took out a fifty-dollar bill from his wallet and set it on the counter. "That's for my share of the meals. Maybe next week we can hit the grocery store together?"

"Sure, sounds like a plan."

He intended to leave her then and get his day started, but he hesitated and realized he owed her a story that included his day-to-day life now. "Got anything pressing to do right now?"

"Nothing urgent, just boring emails to get to. Why?"

"I missed doing my usual flight around the ranch to check in on the cattle and horses. Before you get to those emails, want to—"

"Yes," she blurted out.

He chuckled at her all but bouncing as she followed him out the back door to the helicopter pad resting next to the hangar. He nearly purred at his sleek six-seater Airbus helicopter. Once he reached the chopper, he checked the weather to ensure clear skies before doing his preflight inspection. He finished, confirming the gas cap was secure, and then helped Adeline into her seat, assisting her with fastening her seat belt, pretending he wasn't enjoying every stroke of his fingers against her.

After securing her, he offered her the aviation headset. "Last part, so we can talk."

She settled it onto her head and beamed. "Ready!"

Again, he chuckled, not sure if he'd ever seen anyone so excited to fly with him. He finished his final walk-around inspection before getting into his seat, buckling up and sliding his headgear into place, adjusting the microphone over his mouth.

"Still ready?" he asked.

"Hell yes." Her voice sounded muffled through the headset, but her dancing eyes flooded his chest with warmth.

Focusing on his job—to keep them both safe—he confirmed the flight controls were in the correct position before he powered up the helicopter and lifted off, the ground moving farther away as the seconds drew on. Her loud squeal brushed across him, and he felt a rush of adrenaline storm through him.

"Okay, I can totally see why you love doing this," she said, staring out her window.

"I've always loved to fly," he admitted. "There's a freedom I find in it that I don't feel doing anything else. But the views also don't hurt. In Seattle, while busy, the skyline was quite beautiful."

"But not as beautiful as this," she breathed, awe in her voice. "I forgot how stunning it is out here."

He glanced out her window, finding the rolling hills of Ward land, grassy meadows as far as the eyes could see. The lake stretched along the west side, the cattle grazing next to it as expected. He circled them at a distance, not wanting to stir up trouble.

"What exactly are you looking for?" she asked.

"Calves, injured or sick heifers—anything that would need us to ride up to tend to them."

She glanced at him, sidelong. Damn near the sexiest thing he'd ever seen in that seat next to him. "If there was any of that, you'd send cowboys to this area?" she asked.

"Exactly," he agreed. "Smaller ranches would just ride out daily to check on their herd, but luckily for me, I have an excuse to fly out every morning when the weather cooperates." He gave the cattle one final look, not sensing or seeing any problems, before he turned east. "We'll check in on the horses now."

"Is Beau involved in that end of the company?"

He nodded, holding the yoke steady. "He was working toward becoming a champion reiner and riding for the USA team professionally when Annie passed away, so we hire riders now to show our horses for bragging and breeding rights."

"What does Beau do, then?"

"Handles all the sales and trains the horses before they begin to show. It's not quite what he dreamed of, but I know he enjoys his work."

She glanced out the front window, nibbling her lip before addressing him again. "And what about you? Do you enjoy your work?"

He smiled. "I get to do this every day. I feel fortunate for that."

She snorted a laugh. "You just avoided my question. You know that, right?"

"It's not avoidance, it's the truth," he admitted. Probably a little to himself, too. "I might not be doing what I love all the time, but my family needed me. Nothing comes before them."

"And that's why having all these women trying to hit on you was a distraction you didn't want?"

He nodded. "You got it, New York."

She watched him a moment and then gave him the sweetest smile he'd ever seen. "You know, you're making it very easy to write about you."

"Why is that?"

She glanced back out her window. "Because you're an incredibly good man."

Later that afternoon, when Adeline was sitting in a booth at the coffee shop, coins clinked into the tip jar at the counter from a paying customer as she recalled what she'd seen of Colter's house. When she began typing on her keyboard, the aromatic scent of espresso infused the air.

For all the money the Ward family is worth, the simplicity of Colter Ward stands out. The art decorating the walls of his house wasn't created by famous artists, but local artists who painted the beauty of Devil's Bluffs, a town he clearly loves.

"Is that the one?"

A sharp voice cut through the murmur of voices, past the radio playing in the background. Adeline took a long sip of her milky latte drizzled with caramel, tuned in to the women sitting at the table across from her.

An airy slurp of an empty cup. "Yeah, that's her. I don't see what's so special about her."

The old version of Adeline would have kept staring at her laptop, pretending she didn't hear them. But she wasn't that same shy teenager who was too afraid to speak up. She turned toward the catty women and cleared her throat. When they met her gaze, she said sharply, "What's special about me is that I'm really—like out of this world—incredible in bed." She might have laughed at their bulging eyes if she wasn't annoyed on both her own and Colter's behalf.

Staring them down, she could only smile as both women rose and quickly left the coffee shop. She began to understand why Colter had been desperate enough to make the arrangement with her in the first place. She'd never had so many women glare at her in her life and make snide comments. These women chasing him were like sharks.

With a sigh, she looked out the giant glass window

with a view of the street, watching as cars and trucks drove by. She was returning her thoughts to her article when her cell phone dinged.

A quick look at the screen, and her mood soured further.

Brock had texted, Adeline, please, please call me.

She heaved another long sigh. For over a week, she'd ignored him, and that had been working, but she didn't reach her phone and dial his number for Brock's sake. She called for his parents, who had likely seen the photo, too, and whom she had grown close to over the years she and Brock dated. Deep down, she knew the breakup of their relationship wouldn't only tear apart her and Brock's lives, but it would affect those who loved Brock and had to look him in the eye after the terrible thing he'd done.

Brock answered on the first ring. "Adeline?"

"Hi, Brock," she said, leaning back against the leather booth.

"Thank you for calling," he breathed.

Hearing his tight voice was adding salt to an open wound, and it burned, reminding her she was still hurting. Deeply. "I take it you saw the article."

"I did. Is it true?"

A dry laugh escaped her. "No, of course not. It was a misunderstanding."

"That kiss didn't look like a misunderstanding."

She ground her teeth. "My life is not your business anymore." Her gaze fell to the barista behind the long counter stacked with chrome espresso and frothing machines. "I called so you could let your parents know what's going on. I'm sure this is all very confusing for them."

A pause, the thick whir of the frothing machine filling the silence. "They miss you," he said eventually.

She shut her eyes and breathed past the squeezing of her throat. "I miss them, too. Please let your mom know that I do plan on reaching out and I'll call her when I'm back in New York City."

A beat.

Then his voice blistered, "Adeline, please let's talk about this. I hate that everything happened like it did. I hate that I hurt you."

"I didn't call to talk about this," she snapped before reminding herself the conversation was pointless. But she hated the part of her heart that wanted so desperately to say *let's fix this somehow*. The part that still loved him, that believed they'd stay together forever, regardless of how he'd hurt her. "Please tell your mother what I said." She ended the call before he could say anything else.

Knowing she'd never get anything else done, she packed up her laptop and did what she always did when feeling down—she hit the grocery store. She bought all the ingredients for homemade cookies and spaghetti and meatballs, avoiding making eye contact with the women glaring her way for taking the gorgeous Colter Ward off the market.

Once back behind the wheel of Colter's massive truck, she ducked her head, hoping no one recognized her while she attempted to maneuver out of the parking spot. In New York City, she depended on public transportation, walking and the odd Lyft. She hadn't driven a vehicle in a long time—certainly not a truck that took up the entire road.

When she arrived back at Colter's, she found the house empty. Perfect. Standing in Colter's kitchen, she opened her Spotify account and played her pop songs playlist. As Lady Gaga's voice filled the kitchen, she shut out the world, her bleeding heart and all the confusion, and she did what always made her feel better—she began cooking.

It wasn't until the meatballs were simmering in the spaghetti sauce on the stove and someone cleared their throat that she realized she wasn't alone anymore.

She turned around on a gasp, holding the spoon in her hand like a knife that would never protect her.

Colter leaned a shoulder against the wooden beam separating the kitchen and living room, crossing his arms over his strong chest. "Sorry to interrupt your dance party."

She blushed all the way up to her eyeballs, hurrying to turn the Michael Jackson song down. "How much did you see?"

"All of it," he said, grinning devilishly. "Liked it, too."

She blushed for an entirely different reason now, suddenly becoming aware of the dirt smudging his face and hands, the outdoorsy scent clinging to him. And that they were very much *alone*.

"What's all this for?" he asked, gesturing to the snickerdoodle cookies cooling on the counter. Plus, the dirty pots and pans in the sink for the spaghetti dinner.

"I talked to Brock today," she explained, cringing at the mess she'd left. "When I'm upset, I cook."

He studied her. Then he smiled. "Let me take a quick shower, then I'll help you clean up."

Him. In. The. Shower. "Okay, yeah, sounds great. Spaghetti will be ready in a half an hour."

"Excellent."

While he headed off down the hallway, instead of imagining what Colter looked like soaking wet, with water beads trailing down his six-pack, she began cleaning up the mess.

By the time he returned from his shower, wearing

gray jogging pants—that should be illegal for hot men to wear for the way they accentuated every masculine thing about him—and a black T-shirt with the ranch's logo on the front, she had washed up most of the messy kitchen.

Though he still grabbed the drying cloth and sidled next to her, beginning to dry and put away the dishes. "Heard you had some driving issues today," he said with a smirk.

"You did not," she gasped, splashing water into the sink.

He nodded, chuckling. "I got some complaints today about a slow driver holding up traffic."

"For real?" she countered, aghast. "Do people have nothing better to do than call you and complain?"

His mouth twitched. "I assume they thought you worked for me."

"Still, driving slowly isn't a terrible thing."

"Except for the people needing to get somewhere on time."

She flicked water at him, and he laughed easily, in a way that she never would have dreamed she could've made him laugh. Which got her thinking… "Can I ask you a personal question?"

He took a pan from the sink and began drying it. "Sure."

"You divorced a year ago. You're unattached, free to do whatever you want, so why, when I saw you in the bar that first night, were you so against the idea of a woman's attention? Most men in your situation would take full advantage of ladies chasing after them."

"Most men haven't stepped into a multimillion-dollar ranch they need to head up."

She scrubbed at a crusty spot on the saucepan. "So, you're not looking to date because you're too busy?"

He hesitated, giving her a long look. "Is the journalist asking me or the woman?"

"The woman," she said immediately. Before she realized she was edging the line of breaking their fake relationship's rules.

Regardless, he answered, "I'm not against the idea of dating again. I still want to grow old with someone and look back on my life knowing I did things right. Family has always mattered to me, and that hasn't changed."

"I sense a *but* in there."

Another hesitation. This time, the silence dragged on until he finally bowed his head to the pan he was drying. "But I'm not good at love."

Hoping he saw she understood, she agreed, "I'm not very good at it, either."

"I'm not so sure about that," he countered, opening a big drawer and placing the pan inside. "In your case, it seems you were blindsided by an insecure asshole who mishandled your heart."

"Yeah, well, I could say that in your case, it seems that you gave all of your heart to someone, and even that was not enough."

He snorted a laugh, flipping the towel onto his shoulder. "I suppose you could say that, but I'm sure I have fault in there somewhere, too."

She returned the smile. "And I'm sure I'm at some fault in my situation, too."

He leaned a hip against the counter, folding his arms. "How could you possibly be at fault for someone cheating on you?"

"I still haven't figured that out," she admitted, "but honestly, I haven't really figured out anything. I just packed for this trip and left all of that stuff back home."

She handed him the saucepan, and as he began drying it, he asked, "Did you suspect Brock was cheating?"

"No, and I think that was the hardest part. I had no idea anything was wrong. I'd been planning our wedding, so blind to everything."

"How did you find out?"

"His secretary, the woman he was cheating with, called me." It had been the hardest phone call she'd ever received in her life. Her soul had left her body that day, and only now was it beginning to feel like it was coming back. "I guess he'd been telling her that he was leaving me, but then she saw the wedding invitation and realized he'd been lying to her, too."

"He lost both of you, then?"

"Seems like it," she said with a nod. "Today on the phone, he was all apologies and wanting forgiveness, but he's probably saying the same thing to her. And you can't fix cheating."

"Once trust is gone, it's gone," he agreed.

"Yeah." She reached for the cookie sheet and began scrubbing at the burned cookie spots. "Did you suspect anything was going wrong with Julia?"

"Yes and no," he said, drying a big wooden spoon. "I knew she'd changed. She became more about fancy things than quality time. It was like the wealth in Seattle swallowed her up and she couldn't see a small-town life anymore. The woman I married changed until I didn't even recognize her anymore."

"So, what didn't you expect, then?"

A pause. "We had a miscarriage, and what I hadn't expected was her reaction to it."

"I'm really sorry for your loss. That must have been hard."

"It was," he said, "but to be honest, what I won't ever

forget was the look on her face when we had the ultrasound, and it was confirmed we lost the baby."

"What did she look like?"

"She was relieved."

Adeline's hands stilled on the pan. "There's something seriously wrong with her if that was her reaction."

He gave a slight shrug. "Or she felt trapped and suddenly she realized she had an out."

Her heart reached for his as her soapy fingers touched his arm, fully aware of the flexing bicep beneath her fingers. "I'm so sorry, Colter. I can't even begin to imagine how difficult all of that must have been for you."

"It was the worst time in my life," he said gently. "But life does go on. I moved back here. She moved on with her life in Seattle."

"You haven't heard from her since?"

He shook his head. "Truthfully, I doubt we'd have anything to say to each other. We are two different people now."

"Was it hard coming back here without her?"

"At first, yeah, but then my focus became about my family and the ranch, where it should have been all along."

She slowly released his arm, although she struggled against keeping her hand against his warm strength. "Does that mean you feel bad that you moved to Seattle?"

"Bad? No," he clarified. "I made a choice, and I live with that choice, but I know I let my family down when I moved away." He bowed his head, his voice rough. "I let my dad down not taking over the ranch then. And I can't help…"

"Can't help what?"

He glanced sidelong, emotion burning in his eyes. "I

can't help but wonder, if I'd stayed and let my dad retire, if he'd be better off than he is now."

She grasped his forearm again, pleading for him to hear her. "You cannot blame yourself for his Parkinson's. That's not on you, and the Grant Ward I know would never have retired unless he was forced."

"Maybe." He watched her closely...intently. Until heat, and nameless things, simmered in the air between them.

She quickly turned back to the sink, but not before Colter captured her chin, bringing her attention back to his emotion-packed gaze. "I'm sorry for you, too, Adeline."

"Thank you," she breathed, narrowing her focus on his slightly parted, totally kissable lips.

What had felt a little sad now felt red-hot and needy. His eye contact firmed, erasing the room around her. She became all too aware of the racing of her heartbeat. But as the timer on the stove beeped, indicating dinner was ready, she took a step back, distancing herself from what her body craved.

Him. Naked. Now.

Not part of the fake relationship!

Blowing out a slow breath, she quickly moved to the stove and turned off the dial but dared to take one quick look over her shoulder at him. Hard in every place that mattered, he gripped the counter tight and watched her with hungry eyes.

"Come on," she said, keeping things firmly in the "not intimate" category. "Get it while it's hot."

He tossed the towel back onto the counter and grinned. "Is that an invitation?"

Her mouth dropped open as she blushed up to her hairline.

His laugh filled the kitchen as he grabbed a plate and began scooping up noodles.

But as she filled her plate, she couldn't help but wonder... *What if it was?*

Six

Six days later, Colter dipped the helicopter to the right, following the cattle stirring up dust below. On the ground, the Devil's Bluffs Ranch cowboys were running the cattle to another pasture to prevent overgrazing. He was their eyes from above. A calmness settled over him as the sun glistened high in the sky over the meadow. He took solace when they rotated the cattle's and horses' pastures. It gave him more time in the air.

Below, a calf suddenly bolted left, breaking free from the herd. Colter stayed on the black calf. He said into the mouthpiece linked to an earpiece in the ear of Shane, a longtime cowboy on the ranch, "Lost calf on your ten o'clock."

Shane spun his horse and galloped toward the calf, until he guided him back toward the heifer frantically searching for her baby.

Colter circled back, staying atop the herd, following

the cattle as ten of the best cowboys Colter knew, along with four Texas heelers, moved the cattle from one lake to another, where the grass had grown high.

Long minutes went by on the cattle drive. Colter embraced every single one where he wasn't stuck in a stuffy office, enduring long meetings and going over fiscal reports. This part of his job he loved, along with when he got his hands dirty, dealing with the cattle. His past was full of wonderful memories of the summers he spent on the ground with the cowboys. Those easy days were long gone. He missed fixing fence boards and simpler times.

When they eventually made it to the new pasture, the cattle settling into their new spot next to the lake, Shane looked up at the helicopter, giving a thumbs-up. Colter returned the gesture, then turned the helicopter to the left, returning home to a stack of paperwork and a couple meetings later this afternoon. His heart felt like it was shrinking as he spotted his house off in the distance. Just then, his phone rang through the interface in his headset. He hit the answer button. "Colter."

His mother's sweet voice filled his ears. "Hello, my dear, it's your mother, wondering if you'd like to come for lunch."

Lunch always meant *we need to talk*, but he'd never turn down one of his mother's home-cooked meals. "I can get there within an hour."

"Lunch will be ready," she said.

He ended the call and returned to his house, where he completed the postflight inspection, disappointed his flight was over. He missed the days when he flew for most of his day.

Within forty minutes, and after responding to several important emails, he was on the road. Another fifteen minutes later, he was arriving at his childhood home.

The old, two-story stone farmhouse rested next to the largest barn on Ward land, where sick cattle were tended and recovered. A bunkhouse was to the west of the barn for any cowboys who preferred to live on the property, but his father paid his cowboys well and most had families living off property. The cowboys who stayed were younger men and women who preferred the cheap rent and board, since Dad never gave a cowboy a free ride.

Colter parked near his mother's car and entered the house. The smell of spices overwhelmed him. There wasn't a day he'd come home when his mother wasn't cooking or baking something for her family. He left his boots at the door and his cowboy hat on the hook, and he found his mother in the kitchen they'd renovated a few years back to brighten up the small space. "Smells delicious." He met her at the stove, dropping a kiss on her cheek.

"Hi, my sweet boy." She wore a yellow dress he'd seen many times. "You just missed Adeline."

Like he'd done a thousand times before now, he took a seat at the big island in the kitchen and waited for his mother to bring in a hot meal. "She was here?"

"Oh, yes." Mom stirred the homemade soup on the stove. "She's been stopping in for the last few days."

"To talk about me?"

His mother glanced over her shoulder with a stern look, pointing her wooden spoon at him. "Colter James Ward, we did not raise you to think that highly of yourself."

"It's not arrogance, it's confusion," he corrected. "If she's not talking about the story she's writing on me, what's she doing here?"

"She's come by to help with your father," Mom said, warmth in her voice, returning to stirring the soup.

He leaned his arms against the quartz countertop. "That's kind of Adeline to help you."

"She's good stuff, that woman. Always has been."

He'd known Adeline was different the second he set eyes on her in the Black Horse, but he hadn't known then what made her stand out. Adeline had a heart of gold. And that sweetness was changing him—he could feel it down to his bones.

It didn't take much for him to know this fake relationship was beginning to feel all too real. He knew the dangers, knew he'd never move back to the big city, but he couldn't help feel what he felt around her.

In the days he'd spent with her, he'd laughed more than he had in the last year, and every moment with her made the weight of the responsibilities piled onto his shoulders lessen. He began to forget all the things he'd lost when he moved home.

"There is a reason I called you over here," Mom said, interrupting his thoughts. She scooped some soup into a bowl. When she set it in front of him, she continued, "I received a call today about Elenora Davis's charity dinner in Dallas that we always go to." The charity benefited the children's hospital. A cause Elenora, a dear friend of his mother's, had always believed in. "I…forgot…"

He reached for the spoon she offered. "You're going through a lot, Mom. Cut yourself a break if you can't keep everything straight in your schedule."

She gave him a smile, but the warmth never reached her eyes. "I know you hate these kinds of fancy events, but—"

"It's fine. I'll go in your place."

Mom leaned against the counter. Her stare was pained. "I know you are sacrificing a lot for your father and me. We want you to know that we see all your sacrifices and appreciate everything you are doing for your family and the ranch."

"I'm not sacrificing anything," he lied breezily.

Her brows shot up, her look becoming all-knowing. "I am your mother. Have you forgotten you cannot lie to me?"

A rough laugh escaped him. "I'll never forget. You won't let me."

"That's right, I won't," she said, turning back to the stove. She fixed herself a bowl and then joined Colter at the island. "Why don't you ask Adeline to go to the gala with you?"

"Not a bad idea," he said, scooping up the beef soup. "It'd be a good way for her to see all the charity work that we do as a family. It'd be nice to see that in her article."

At the thick silence, he glanced sidelong at his mother. She smirked. "Is that really why you'd invite her?"

Now it was Colter's turn to stick his spoon out at his mother. "Don't be nosy."

"I'm not nosy," she said, her eyes twinkling. "Just curious. You haven't really been seeing anyone, and you two seem to be getting cozy."

"Forced coziness, don't forget."

Mom dismissed him with a wave. "Just because two people are forced to stay together doesn't mean feelings can be forced."

Shaking his head, he scooped up another spoonful of soup. "See, just can't help yourself getting nosy."

"Of course I can't. I'm your mother," she said.

Pondering whether to talk to his mother or not, he ate a spoonful of his soup. And another. And another.

Until he realized he wanted his mom's advice.

"It's a sticky situation," he admitted, his spoon clanging against the bowl. "She broke off her engagement just two weeks ago."

"Oh?"

"Her fiancé cheated."

Mom's hand flew to her chest. "Poor thing. That's just terrible. Who would do that to her?"

"An idiot," Colter said.

"Indeed." Mom nodded. "But I do see what you're saying. Wrong time. Wrong place."

"Wrong *everything*," he offered. "She's leaving to go back to New York City in a little over a week. Even if there is something there—and I'm not saying there is—starting anything between us seems...pointless."

"Happiness, no matter how short an experience it is, is never pointless." Mom paused to place a comforting hand on his arm. "You were dealt a hard blow with Julia. It's been a year since I've seen you smile like you do with Adeline. Any time you smile like that, it can't be pointless."

He stared down at his soup, considering her words. Before he glanced at her. "Enjoy the experience is what you're saying."

"Exactly." She removed her hand to reach for her spoon again. "Life is made of a thousand experiences. Some experiences are short. Some may be longer. But in this big, messy thing we call life, always look for the happy moments, the good people, and cling to them with all your might."

He knew his mother spoke from experience of what she was currently going through with his father's declining health. While this year had been hard, she had more than forty years of happiness to look back on. In the comfort of the woman who loved him unconditionally, he opened his heart. "Trying again is..."

"Terrifying?" his mother offered.

A nod. "Maybe even more so when there are obvious obstacles in the way."

She smiled gently and patted his cheek. "My boy, there is something worse than having nothing. It's having everything you could ever want but being too afraid to chase after it."

He absorbed her words, then wrapped his arm around her. "You are one helluva smart woman."

"Yes, son, I know." She smiled, patting his arm.

Seated behind his desk at the newspaper early in the afternoon, Waylon asked, "What can I do to convince you to come work for me?"

Adeline looked up from her laptop after adding another thousand words to her article. She always wrote long and refined her piece during edits. In this case, especially so, since the words came easily. The Ward family donated to the library and high school and supported the Devil's Bluffs community. What had started as a fluff piece about a hunky cowboy was becoming so much more. She knew why—she was seeing Colter differently. He was no longer a teenager crush but a *man*.

Realizing she had yet to answer and her old mentor's soft gaze was fixed on her, she admitted, "I do miss it here." She shifted against the rock-hard wooden chair. "I miss the simplicity of a small town. The quiet. And yes, I miss *you*."

He chuckled. "Good."

Where she sat at the desk next to him, the space was the same size as her editor's corner office in New York City. Newspaper articles were pinned on the four walls, along with historic pictures of Devil's Bluffs' past. "Every memory from my co-op here is a good one," she told him.

"See, if that isn't a good enough reason to move back, I don't know what is." Waylon winked. He took a sip from his mug that read, Of Course I'm Awesome. I'm an Editor. A gift that likely came from one of his two adult children.

Adeline envied how Waylon made his marriage work. How he loved his children. She wanted all those things. Now... She shook her head, not allowing herself to fall into a deep hole she would never crawl out of. "If only it was that easy to just snap your fingers and change your life," she said. "I miss writing the stories I did here."

A sparkle hit Waylon's eyes as he opened a drawer and took out a folder. "These ones, you mean?"

"You did not keep them," she said, quickly moving to his desk and accepting the file folder.

His smile shined. "Just have a look."

Moving back to her desk, she opened the folder, heat radiating through her chest. "Oh my goodness. I can't believe you kept them."

"Of course I did," Waylon countered. "You were so proud of all the stories you did. I didn't have the heart to throw them out."

She began fingering through the old articles. The very first time her writing ever made it into a publication. From the Christmas musical at the elementary school to the elderly-animal adoption at the animal shelter to the pumpkin-carving competition at the fall festival. She'd covered all the town's events, telling the stories of the people who passionately supported the community and brought people together. "This is amazing," she said, but then she stopped breathing when she reached one article.

Daddy & Daughter Dance Raises $20,000 for Kids' Cancer Foundation.

Adeline's eyelids suddenly felt gummy as she read over the words she'd written so long ago. Words she remembered were the hardest she'd ever wrote, drawing on something cold and hurting deep from her soul, reminding her, *Your dad did not want you.*

"I remember that article being difficult for you," Waylon said.

She started, not having realized he'd come to stand by her.

Swallowing back her emotions at the dreaded memory of having to attend the event without her father, she managed, "It was very hard."

Father's Day, bring your kid to work, sports games—all those times when a father was necessary had always been hard growing up, but none had been quite like the dance, when she'd been forced to watch happy daughters dance with their proud dads. "But it got easier, because luckily for me, I had a really great stand-in father to make that night one to remember."

"Still one of my favorite nights," Waylon said, squaring his shoulders. "Even got you out on the dance floor."

"Plus, you bought me the prettiest corsage."

"You were the prettiest girl there."

She felt breathless watching him. This man from her past who gave her so much without ever asking for anything in return. "You know, it's odd, but I thought coming back home was going to be so hard."

He leaned back against his desk, folding his arms over his faded button-up. "It hasn't been?"

She shook her head. "It's been the exact opposite. Maybe it's because what happened with Brock was so terrible." She'd caught Waylon up on her recent breakup this morning over coffee and warm croissants from the bakery. "So now anything else that happens doesn't seem as bad. But being back here has been like walking down a wonderful memory lane. I think I forgot how delightful everyone is here."

"Revisiting the past can be a good thing," Waylon agreed with a gentle smile. He returned to behind his desk. "Even the hard parts. Sometimes with a new perspective, everything can look different."

"I think that's very much true," she agreed, returning the smile.

Turning her attention back onto the folder, she began skimming through her articles when her cell phone beeped. One look at the screen, spotting Colter's text message, and her heart leaped up into her throat.

Got any plans tonight?

Gathering herself, she blew out a long breath and then texted back, Not that I know of. Why?

There's a charity gala in Dallas I need to attend on my parents' behalf. Interested in tagging along?

She gawked at the text and reread what he'd written a couple times over. Was this a real date or a fake one? It sounded like a real date. Should she be dating? This was too soon.

"Whatever you're overthinking, stop it," Waylon interrupted, not bothering to look up from his desk.

Adeline snorted, shaking her head at him. Most times she hated having such a readable face. Then she decided to take Waylon's advice, texting back, Sure. Besides, she was writing an article about Colter's life. Of course he'd want to show her these charity events.

Though the little voice in her head screamed at her, *This is a date.*

She finished texting, I'll need to grab a dress. What time are we leaving?

I'll fly us there. Leaving at 5. If you're up for it, I'll book us at the Rosewood Mansion for the night and we can fly home in the morning.

I'm up for it. Hell, suddenly she was feeling up to anything, everything and whatever came in between. And *that* was confusing.

She watched the three little dots, waiting for his text. His response came a few seconds later. Good. Tell the dress store to send the bill to the ranch.

She began responding that she'd feel terrible if he paid and she'd buy the dress herself, when his response popped up.

The ranch pays for my suits, too. Don't feel bad and obligated to buy the dress yourself.

Well, she did feel obligated. She'd always felt weird when men bought her anything. Her therapist had indicated it came from her never wanting to depend on a man, since her father had failed her, but she didn't want to make a big deal out of this, either. She began typing, Okay, then, I won't. Can I donate the dress after to someone needing a prom dress? She remembered the program from when she was in high school.

That's a great idea. We'll donate one of my suits, too.

Awesome. See you by the helicopter at 5.

Looking forward to it.

"Let me guess—you took my advice and that's what got you smiling?"

She laughed, catching Waylon's smirk. "Of course I took your amazing advice. That was Colter. He invited me to attend a charity event in Dallas tonight."

Waylon's brows rose. "Oh?"

"Don't look at me like that," she said sheepishly. "We're going as friends."

His brows rose higher. "In my experience, a woman only smiles like *that* when she's got something to smile about."

She tried to hide her blush, rising from her seat. "A reason to buy a new dress is always something to smile about." She gathered up her things. "Do you mind if I come back in a couple days and work here again? It's been nice."

"Adeline, you are always most welcome," he said. "You're even welcome to come back and take over when I retire."

She froze midway to shoving her cell phone in her purse. "You're retiring?"

He leaned back in his chair, watching her closely. "Well, it's about time. I'm pushing sixty-five."

It seemed impossible to even imagine the newspaper without Waylon. "What will you do then?"

"Marjorie wants to travel. We're talking about selling the house and downsizing. Then we'll set off to see some of the world."

"You deserve that," she said, and she meant it. "How absolutely wonderful for you and Marjorie. Do you have someone who is stepping in for you as editor?"

"Oh, I'll find someone suitable," he said, "but that's why I asked if you'd come back. I'd rather it be you that takes over my beloved newspaper."

She closed the distance and threw her arms around him, feeling like the world for this second seemed so full of love. "Your trust in me is appreciated, but New York City is my home now."

"Then I'm happy for you," he said softly.

When she leaned away, the reality of a cruel, cold world rushing back in, he flicked his hand, dismissing her. "Now go. Be wild and free. Make terrible decisions."

She slid her laptop bag's strap over her shoulder. "You never would have said that to me before."

"You're right, I wouldn't have told a sixteen-year-old girl that," he said with a sly grin. "But you're not that young girl anymore, are you?"

"No, I certainly am not."

Seven

Seven

Even after the forty-minute helicopter flight to Dallas, Colter still couldn't take his eyes off Adeline. Ever since she came out of the guest room and left him speechless. Dark makeup surrounded her eyes, making the honey color warmer. The sexiness of the long, slinky black dress she wore had him wiping his mouth. Her bright red–painted lips brought...*hunger*. A desperate ravenousness that was becoming harder to ignore.

Once they arrived at the Hotel Crescent Court in the art-centric part of Dallas, Adeline exited the Escalade the hired driver had picked them up in, and Colter's fingers twitched to reach for the back of her dress that was cut low and stroke the soft skin. Her hair was up, revealing the long line of her neck, tempting him to slide his tongue right *there*. But even as lust battered his senses, he knew more was going on between them than lust alone. And he wasn't sure what to make of that.

"Would you like me to bring your bags to the Rose-wood Mansion, sir?" the driver asked Colter.

"Yes. Thank you," Colter said, shaking the driver's hand. "I'll reach out when we're done here."

"Excellent. Enjoy your evening."

As the driver returned to the Escalade, Colter narrowed his attention on the stunning woman gazing up at the trellises on the exterior of the grand hotel.

"Good heavens," Adeline gasped, "this place could rival any upscale hotel in New York City."

"It is stunning," he said, "but nowhere near as stunning as you in that dress."

"Thank you." She looked him over the way a lioness studies its prey before she pounces. "You're not looking too bad yourself, cowboy."

"I'm glad you approve," he said, heat flooding him.

How tempted he was to call the driver back and take them to the hotel instead. But, like a cold bucket of ice water pouring down on his shoulders, he remembered he had a role to play tonight. Best he play it.

"Before we go in," he told her, reaching inside his suit's inner pocket and offering her the ring he'd put there for safekeeping, "I thought it made sense for you to have this."

Her eyes widened before her brows lifted. "Are you sure this isn't a bit early in our relationship?"

He barked a laugh. "Probably, but life is better when you take some risks."

"Touché." She echoed his laughter and offered her hand. "I guess it does make sense to have a ring if we're meant to be engaged."

"Mmm-hmm," he agreed. He slid the ring onto her slender finger. "This ring belonged to my grandmother.

She would've gotten a real hoot out of this arrangement we've made. She had an amazing sense of humor."

"I wish I'd gotten to know her better," she said sweetly. "Gosh, her ring is gorgeous."

"A near-perfect fit, too." He had no doubt his grandmother would have gotten a hoot out of that, too. He offered his arm. "All right, the future Mrs. Ward, ready to go enjoy ourselves?"

She linked her arm with his. "You do know all of this is incredibly weird, right?"

"Weird, yes." He led her through the main doors of the hotel, walking past the doorman holding the door open. "But as far as I'm considered, weird doesn't feel all that bad."

A pause. Then her dazzling smile hit him straight in the chest. "You're right, it doesn't."

He passed people he recognized from other charity events. The rich and famous of Texas who all came together to support a cause.

"Colter," a banker Colter had met before called the moment they reached the hallway leading to the ballroom. "Wasn't expecting to see you tonight."

Colter shook the man's hand. "I would not have missed it." He turned to Adeline. "Let me introduce Adeline Harlow, a journalist out of New York City."

The man's eyes gleamed at Adeline. "Very nice to meet you, Ms. Harlow."

"You as well."

It took another ten introductions before they finally made it inside the ballroom. Vaulted ceilings topped high walls with crown molding and glossy hardwood floors. Waitstaff circulated the crowd to offer canapés and switch out empty champagne flutes for full ones. Colter arrowed for the bar, needing a hard drink more than ever. After greeting the white-gloved bartender, Adeline ordered a glass of wine, and he a scotch on the rocks.

After the bartender delivered their drinks, Adeline asked, "This isn't your type of thing, is it?"

"No," he said, placing a hand on her lower back, guiding her off to the side of the bar. "I've never been much of a schmoozer."

"Oh, I find that hard to believe," she said with a laugh. "You were all charm back in high school. I remember some of the teachers eating out of the palm of your hand."

"She's not wrong there."

Colter's muscles went rigid in a heartbeat. The soft music playing around them dulled in his ears. His focus narrowed on Adeline's gaze shifting over his shoulder. Her lips tightened.

Not particularly wanting to, but feeling obligated, he turned around and expected to see his ex-wife. Instead, he found a stranger. Everything about Julia had changed since the last time he'd seen her. Her blond hair was now a lighter shade. Somehow her eyebrows were darker and thicker. The lashes on her brown eyes were not hers. Her cheekbones, lips, face shape—even the large amount of cleavage popping out of her red dress—did not belong to the woman he remembered. "Hello, Julia," he said cordially.

She smiled, though her face hardly moved. "Hello, Colter." Her cold eyes shifted to Adeline. "I'm sorry, you look so familiar. Do we know each other?"

"We do, actually," Adeline said. "Adeline Harlow. We went to high school together."

"Adeline," Julia said, mulling over the name. "Your face is familiar. I'm not sure I can place your name."

Colter nearly took Adeline's hand and drew her back, wanting to keep her far away from this part of his past, but Adeline said in an easy tone, "That's not very surprising. We didn't exactly run in the same circles."

"Ah, that must be it," Julia quipped. To Colter, she asked, "Where's your parents? I thought they always attended this event."

"My dad is not well enough to do these events anymore," Colter said.

Julia's hand pressed against her chest, her voice sounding sincere. "I'm so very sorry to hear that."

Colter inclined his head in thanks. "What brings you to the event?"

"Oh, my boyfriend is on the board of the children's charity," Julia said, bringing her hand to her diamond necklace, fingering the delicate band. "We arrived in Dallas a couple days ago but don't plan on staying long."

The murmur of many voices filled the air as Adeline said, "The hospital does such amazing things for little ones and their families. What an amazing charity to be a part of."

"Yes, it is," Julia agreed. "My Bronson gives so much of himself and his time to many charities."

Colter had never felt the urge to roll his eyes. Until now. Though when he caught the well-dressed dark-haired man approaching them, he figured a fight at a charity dinner was not how the night should go.

"Bronson, come," Julia called, waving her hand at him.

Colter knew the man. They'd met the tech billionaire through a friend Julia had made. "Bronson," Colter said when the man reached them, offering his hand as a sign of peace. "It's good to see you." Oddly enough, he felt no jealousy, no anger, *nothing* at the thought of this man being with Julia. Though he did wonder if Bronson knew the income Julia received wasn't from her failing company but came from Colter's own pocket.

"Nice to see you, too," Bronson said, returning the firm handshake. His dark eyes shifted to Adeline. "Bronson Bailey."

"Adeline Harlow," she said and shook Bronson's outreached hand before pressing herself against Colter, bringing a wallop of heat. Suddenly feeling a whole lot better, he wrapped his arm around her as her eyes twinkled. "I'm Colter's fiancée."

"Fiancée?" Julia repeated, giving Adeline a harder look now, reassessing, before she pulled back her surprise and put on a smile. "Oh, that's nice. I hadn't heard the news."

Colter locked his hold around the warm, spectacular woman in his arms, aware of the game Adeline played. "We haven't officially announced the news."

"We like our privacy," Adeline told Julia. She angled her head, pressing her hand against his chest. "Don't we, babe?"

Damn if he didn't like her calling him *babe. Probably a little too much.* "Yeah, that's right, we do." Leaning down, he pressed his mouth to hers, momentarily wishing they were anywhere but there. And it wasn't until he felt her melt against him did he know for certain he was kissing her not for the show, but all for himself.

He'd broken the single rule of their fake relationship, and he didn't feel the least bit bad about it.

When he broke away, her dilated pupils greeted him. Rosy-cheeked, she gave him a breathless smile when a bell began ringing, indicating everyone should take their seats for dinner. Acknowledging Julia and Bronson again, she said, "We should really get ourselves settled at our table. We hope you enjoy yourselves tonight."

"You as well," Bronson said.

Colter had begun leading Adeline away when Julia gasped, "Your grandmother's ring."

He spotted the ire in Julia's eyes, only now remembering that Julia had wanted the ring when he proposed. "It turned out my mother could let the ring go after all." At the reddening of Julia's face, Colter said to Bronson, "Enjoy your evening."

Guiding Adeline toward the circular dining tables covered in white linens and gold-edged china place settings, he wondered if the very reason his mother had given him the ring—which she'd said she could never part with—tonight was because she knew Julia had planned to attend.

He couldn't fight his smile.

Feeling slightly warm from the two glasses of wine she'd drunk during the salmon dinner, Adeline gladly followed Colter onto the dance floor. He settled them into an open space between dozens of dancing couples, the musical instruments harmonizing, as he spun her once before bringing her tight against him. She noted he'd lost his coat before dinner, rolling up his sleeves. Somehow, he looked even more handsome.

The slide of his hand low on her back, matched with the smell of his woodsy cologne, made her dizzy. She still couldn't quite believe how nicely he filled out his black-and-white suit with a thin tie. Add his black cowboy hat, and Colter had never suited the most-eligible-cowboy definition more.

The live band played Etta James's "At Last," and Colter easily guided her through the dance like he'd done this a thousand times before. "How, and when, did a small-town cowboy learn to dance this good?" she asked.

He dipped his chin, hitting her with warm eyes. "Julia made me take lessons before we got married."

"They most certainly paid off."

His smile was made of naughty things that made women's panties disappear. "I'm glad you think so."

My God, he felt good. Smelled so good. Heat spiraled through her in no way she'd ever experienced with any man. *Why don't I want to take this any further, again?*

Desperate to find any sense of her sane mind, she focused on the band, lost in the song they were playing, and she exhaled slowly. Talking. That had to cool the jets. "Seeing Julia must have thrown you off tonight," she asked, distracting herself from his hot, *hard* body.

"Actually—" he pulled her in closer, sprawling his hand just above her bottom "—it didn't throw me off at all."

She swallowed, suddenly aware of every spectacular line of him. "That must be unexpected."

"Unexpected, yes, but good," he agreed. "It lets me know I've healed what needed to be healed from that relationship."

"You should feel proud of that. I wish I could even begin the healing part."

His eyes searched hers, his hand pressing tighter, bringing her even closer, an odd sense of safety swelling. "It's been a year since Julia and I ended things. You can't compare our relationships."

"I guess you're right," she said, "but at least you can face Julia. I haven't done that yet. I've only talked to Brock once, and that was to make sure his parents were okay after the news of our fake engagement broke."

"You'll talk to him when you're ready," Colter said with a slight curve to his mouth. His thumb stroked slowly across her back. "Though I, for one, don't think you owe that man a damn thing or a second more of your time."

She instantly regretted the open-back dress for the access it gave him. "Thanks." Desperately trying to ignore the building heat seeping into her from his touch, she pressed on, "Why did seeing your grandmother's ring ruffle Julia's feathers so much?"

"After my grandmother passed away, Julia said she wanted the ring. I asked my mother if I could have it when I planned to propose to Julia, but my mom said no."

"Why?"

He shrugged. "My grandparents were married seventy-two years. I think, for my mom, the ring is a symbol of our family. I'm sure it's hard to part with."

Adeline agreed with a nod. "I'm pretty sentimental about stuff like that, so I totally understand. But no wonder that dug at Julia a bit. I should have flashed it around more, like she was flashing around that necklace."

He chuckled. "Noticed that, too, did you?"

"Of course I noticed," Adeline said with a huff. "It's impossible not to notice how much she's changed. She doesn't even look like herself anymore."

"No, she doesn't," he agreed. Then his voice dipped lower, becoming throatier. "However, I'm not looking at her tonight." He pressed himself into her, leaving no space between them. "I'm looking at you."

Fake relationship. Fake relationship. Fake relationship.

Heat spiraled low in her belly, and soon, all she knew was his hefty erection pressed against her. The other couples dancing all faded away—even the music seemed to stop as he brought his mouth near. She asked in a rush, "If your mother had your grandmother's ring, how did you get it for tonight?"

"I asked her for it." His eyes searched hers before lingering on her mouth. "Perhaps it's not so hard giving something away when you know the engagement isn't real."

Yes, see, a fake relationship. "I imagine that's very much true."

His attention slowly lifted to her eyes again, and his smile nearly melted her bones. "Are you truly interested in this or are you trying to distract yourself?"

She cursed the blush rushing to her face. *Get it under control, girl!* She considered what to tell him and what to keep private, but she decided she wanted him to know her, considering all that he'd shared with her. "The truth is, being here with you, dancing like this—" *feeling your massive erection* "—would make my teenage self die from happiness."

His brows drew together. "What do you mean?"

"I had a big crush on you all through school," she said quickly before she chickened out.

His thumb stopped its dance on her back. "Did you really?"

"Yes, big-time," she admitted with a laugh. "I was such a cliché. The girl staring at the guy from afar, daydreaming you'd come over and notice me."

"I had no idea," he said, his thumb resuming its slow dance along her skin.

"It's for the best, really. I had big daddy issues and I probably would've ended up in a bad place if any guy noticed me back then."

"You don't have those issues now?"

She shook her head. "Years of therapy helped with that, and growing up, too, realizing that life isn't perfect. People aren't perfect. And whatever happened with my father is on him, not me."

"That's a good realization."

She swayed her hips, following where he guided her. "It is, but it also doesn't stop me from wondering about him. Who he is now. What he's like."

"I think that's natural," he said. "But I also think he doesn't deserve you, either."

She couldn't fight her smile. "See, you are totally crushworthy."

His voice lowered, even deeper this time. "Does that mean you still have a crush on me?"

"Aren't all the girls crushing on Colter Ward right now?" she teased, and he chuckled.

Beneath her dress, her nipples puckered, an all-consuming need filling her with every slide of that thumb across her flesh. "But it's different now," she continued, "because back then you were the hot guy I couldn't stop looking at. You barely said a word to me. I made you into this perfect guy in my mind. But the thing is, you've grown into this incredible man. I think that actually makes you hotter."

He stopped dancing then. Intensity flashed across his expression. "I wish I saw you then like I see you now. I'm sorry I didn't."

Promises were in his eyes. Heated promises. Sweet promises.

Promises that at any other point in her life would have been the greatest thing to ever happen to her.

The room began to squeeze her as this fake relationship suddenly became all too real, the air becoming thin and impossible to inhale. Turning away, she booked it for the French doors with thick velvet drapes on either side.

Once outside on the balcony, she was surrounded by lush greenery and flowers of all colors, with gas-powered lanterns casting a warm glow into the night. She made it swiftly to the wrought iron railing and gulped at the air, feeling like her skin was on fire.

"Did I upset you?"

At Colter's low, regretful voice, she turned to face him, gripping the railing tight. "You didn't upset me." Holding his stare, she knew the moment he realized what was wrong by the way his expression became taut...*penetrating*.

He took a step toward her.

She held up her hand. "I need a minute."

"Do you?" he murmured. "Or do you need something else?"

A whimper escaped her, her knees weakening with every step he took.

Closer.

And closer.

Until he stood directly in front of her.

She fought to slow the racing of her heart, which was beating faster and faster. "What are we doing here, Colter?"

His hands came next to hers on the railing, the strength of his body encasing her. "Seems pretty self-explanatory to me."

Her head was screaming *no*. Her body was screaming, *Kiss me. Now!* "This is supposed to be a fake relationship, remember? We made rules that we are breaking. This is a terrible idea."

"Actually, I don't think it is." His lips met hers then, hot and wicked, and as his tongue slipped into her mouth, her hesitation evaporated.

She realized with his sizzling kiss that she was fooling herself. She'd wanted this to happen from the second she saw him again. And while her battered heart refused to jump into this game, she could do what Waylon had suggested: *Be wild and free. Make terrible decisions.*

Tonight!

When his hands braced her face as he angled her head, deepening the kiss, she felt her body rise to his challenge. The need flooding her to not think, to just...*indulge.*

"You have a past," he said, trailing scorching kisses down her neck. "I have a past. None of that matters now, don't you feel that?" He slid a hand down over her bottom, thrusting her against him. "Don't you feel this? *This* is all that matters now. I want you, Adeline." He nipped at her jawline before looking her in the eye again. "Do you want me, too?"

Safety. Comfort. Strength. Colter was all those things. But he was something more, something *tempting*. Something special that made her decision all too easy. "Yes, I want you." She grasped the front of his shirt, and before she met his challenging kiss with one of her own, she purred, "Preferably right now."

Eight

Colter kissed *her*. Roughly. Passionately. On the ballroom's balcony. Outside in front of the Hotel Crescent Court while they waited for the driver. In the back of the SUV on the drive to the Rosewood Mansion. In the elevator on the way up to their room. Urgency had nearly had him paying for a room near the ballroom, but he never stayed at the same place as an event—keeping business and personal separate always worked for him. But instead of taking her then and there, he hesitated for one important reason.

He didn't want Adeline to regret him.

So, he gave her time.

Time to change her mind.

The moment he shut the hotel room's door and turned back to the lavish room with king-size canopy bed and antique furnishings, he realized his worry was without reason. She stared at him hungrily, obviously feeling the same all-consuming need he couldn't ignore. Not anymore.

Breathless, he pressed his back against the door as she tucked a finger under the thin strap of her dress, slowly pulling it down. Until the fabric slid down along one bare breast. Colter's cock hardened to steel so swiftly he groaned as she revealed one taut, rosy nipple.

"Adeline," he murmured.

"You want to see more?" she rasped.

"Definitely more." He groaned.

Nibbling her lip, her cheeks flushed bright red, she repeated the move on the other strap of her dress. The fabric slowly slid down until her dress pooled at her feet.

Colter took in the view...*stunned* by what he saw as she toed the dress off to the side. Her curves were perfect. The gentle lines of her body were perfect. She was perfect. Bare on top, the only fabric she had on were black lace panties. He'd seen women naked. He'd even seen beautiful women painted in pictures. Movie stars on the big screen. No one came close to Adeline.

"You're so damn beautiful," he told her.

Her chest rose and fell with her heavy breaths when she reached up to remove her panties.

He tsked. "Those are mine to take off."

"Oh?" she asked playfully. "Then why don't you get over here and take them off?"

He locked the door behind him and then approached, allowing himself the time to look his fill at her. Her breath hitched when he reached her, taking her chin in his grip. "I might have been your crush, Adeline, but believe me, right now, you are mine." He saw the effect of his words, the way she softened. Her hands tangled into his shirt, and he helped her with the buttons.

Needing more of her, he sealed his mouth across hers

as she brushed the fabric over his shoulders. When she reached for his pants, he let her unbuckle his belt, but he assisted her in shoving them down. He never stopped kissing her. Not when she explored each part of his body, like he was a prize she'd been waiting to claim. Not when she broke the kiss to look at his hardened length, discover the size of him. Not even when she gripped his cock and stroked him gently. He groaned and kissed her chin, her neck, her breasts, nipping at her nipples, unable to get enough of her.

Only when her hands slid back up his arms did he stop and drop to a knee in front of her. Her cheeks were flushed bright with color, her eyes wide as he tucked his fingers in her panties and gingerly dragged them down. His attention went to the soft curls as he slid the fabric off her foot, tossing them aside.

"Damn, New York, look at you." He pressed a kiss to her belly…her inner thigh…moving closer and closer to where her trembling told him she wanted him to go.

She threaded her fingers into his hair. "Please," she whispered.

Ravenous need stormed over him at her plea. But there was something more that he wanted. More than his own need. *Her taste.* Desperate to have all of this surprising woman who was changing him as a man, he glided his tongue against her. Her soft moan was the only sound he heard as he brought her to pleasure.

Over.

And over again.

Slowly. Carefully. Intently.

Until her breathing began hitching, her body shaking with the force of his tongue caressing her. But it wasn't enough. Not nearly enough. He added one finger into his affection. Then another.

Giving her more…taking her higher…and soon she broke apart around him, a beautiful mess of satisfaction, shuddering against his mouth.

He only backed away when her soft whimper brushed across him. She released the tight hold on his hair, so he pressed a final kiss to her thigh and rose. Her half-lidded eyes held his as he gathered her in his arms and laid her out on the bed. Her legs were parted, cheeks and chest flushed beautifully, an invitation he wouldn't refuse.

Hastily, he retrieved his wallet from his pants, and as he reached for a condom, she took his hardened length into her hands.

"You're not the only one who wants to play," she rasped.

He grunted at the feel of her tight hand against him, tossing his head back before he forced himself to watch her have her fun. A rumbly growl rose from his chest at the playfulness in her eyes. He'd never known a woman who was bold, brave, sweet and shy all at once. The combination was devastatingly perfect. His perfect woman, one he never knew he wanted or needed.

She was wreaking havoc on his control.

His legs began trembling, pleasure rushing through his veins with the frantic beat of his heart. When tension rushed up his spine, he stepped free, breaking her hold. Throbbing and on the brink of losing it, he growled, "The only way we end tonight is with me inside you."

"Then get over here," she said, grinning, sliding farther back on the bed.

Eager to feel her, he sheathed himself in a condom and then joined her on the soft mattress that bounced under his weight. He blanketed his body over her, pulling one of her thighs back as he went. A beauty beneath him, he sealed his mouth across hers and primed himself at her entrance.

Then he pushed forward, entering her halfway. Though he was nearly seeing stars at the pleasure skyrocketing through him, her tight kiss told him to wait.

She gasped against his lips, "Colter."

"Yeah, New York, you're going to take all of me." He sealed his mouth across hers again, deepening the kiss. He slowly pumped his hips, relishing her wet warmth and hold. He broke away, kissing her jawline. "I've wanted this from the moment I saw you."

"Me, too." She moaned as he thrust forward slightly, moving in deeper.

Again.

And again.

Until he groaned against her neck, seated all the way to the hilt. He nipped at her neck, and her eager moan lifted his attention. She panted with urgency, so he lowered his mouth to hers and kissed her. Deeper. Harder. Until she whimpered, wiggling beneath him, meeting him thrust for thrust.

Right there, taken by pleasure alongside her, he began moving gently, slowly.

Her moans traveled like wildfire across his flesh as he kissed all the exposed parts of her. She arched her back when he latched onto a nipple, so he sucked harder. Nibbled the hard peak until her moans turned raspy. Desperate.

She grabbed his bottom, locking her ankles around his thighs, and he let go of his restraint. Giving them what they both wanted, he rode her hard, fast, each thrust building until their minds were stolen and overwhelmed by pleasure.

Skin slapped against skin. The smell of their sex infus-

ing the air. She became too much. All of her. The great-
ness of her. The feel of her. He broke the kiss, needing to
watch her fall apart in his arms. Though nothing prepared
him for the emotions battering his chest when he looked
deep into her eyes. Her guard was down, her soul right
there for the taking, and damn, did he want to claim her.

Any control he might have had was currently stripped
away. His movements became frantic as her screams
begged him to finish her.

He stared into her beautiful pleasure until the very
last moment. Only then did he dare shut his eyes and lose
himself to sensation, hearing her final scream of satisfaction as she followed him over the edge.

"Oh, hell, yes, girl. *Get it*," Nora said through the
phone line as Adeline sank down on the closed toilet seat.

In the white marble bathroom, with gold accents on
just about everything and rich floral scents from the pot-
pourri infusing the air, Adeline pressed her cell phone
to her ear, keeping the conversation private. "This isn't
a huge mistake?" she asked.

Nora scoffed. "Um, no, sleeping with that hella sexy
cowboy is the best decision you've ever made. Why are
you even questioning this?"

"Because I feel like somehow in all this, our fake relationship, fake engagement, whatever you want to call
it, nothing is fake anymore."

"Would that be such a bad thing?"

"I don't know," Adeline answered honestly, staring
at the all-glass shower across the bathroom. "It's just
messed up. I mean, who breaks off her engagement and
then suddenly gets with someone else?"

"Lots of people," Nora said. "Besides, Brock cheated
on you. It's not like you don't have a good reason to move

on with your life. You've had a crush on Colter for forever. You deserve to have a little fun."

Adeline nearly didn't respond but knew that would get her nowhere. "Yeah, but that's what you don't get, Nora. Colter isn't a guy you just have fun with. He's incredible. He's so good to his family, his community—even to me."

Nora hesitated, a long, obvious pause. "You're catching feelings?"

"Catching them?" Adeline laughed. "I've had feelings for him since high school. And now he's this grown man who's—" she stared at the closed bathroom door—to Colter on the other side "—just perfect in every way. God, Nora, he's my dream guy. In bed and out of it."

"I'm not really seeing the problem here," Nora mused.

Adeline huffed, rising and moving in front of the mirror. She wore a white hotel robe. Her makeup was smudged beneath her eyes, her hair messy, satisfaction glistening in her glossy eyes. "It's just confusing, because none of this was supposed to happen. I came here to write a story, and now everything is all over the place and I'm wondering what in the hell I'm doing here."

"What do you mean, *everything*?"

Adeline moved to the large soaker tub and sat on the edge. "My dad...this town...it's getting in my head."

"Have you seen your dad again?"

"No," Adeline said, pressing her toes against the cool marble floors. "It's just weird. I'm around Colter's family all the time and they are just so close, it's making me feel like something is missing in life, even though I have you and my mom, which has always been enough."

"I think you're forgetting your father is not like Colter's family. He wasn't there for you at all."

"I haven't forgotten," Adeline confirmed. Then she

gave her head a good hard shake. "Like I said, everything is just…getting confusing."

"Well, I don't really know what to say about your dad but to say be careful. He's not going to care about your heart, so protect yourself."

"Yeah, probably best."

Nora paused again, obviously considering what Adeline had told her. "Here's what I do know. Two men in your life have been utter disappointments. It sucks. The only thing you can do is control how you respond to them. And I say, when you finally meet a guy who is everything you have ever wanted and then some, you'd be insane not to act on it."

"Even if he lives in a small town that I'd never move back to."

"Even if," Nora said. "Maybe this is your shot at true, lasting love. When it's that kind of love, it'll work out. It always does."

"So don't shut this down is what you're saying?"

"Yes. Let things go where they want to go. Either something will come of it or you'll come home with an amazing story of how you had two hot weeks with your biggest crush."

Adeline smiled, a sudden weight lifting off her shoulders. "That is quite the story."

"It is. Now get back out there and enjoy that cowboy."

"Yes, ma'am," Adeline said before adding, "I love you, Nora. Thanks for listening."

"You'd do the same for me. Love you, babe. Talk soon."

The phone line went dead, and Adeline left her cell phone by the sink, hearing a knock on the hotel room's door. She waited for the door to open, and when she came out of the bathroom, she found Colter shutting the door, a tray in his hand, wearing a robe matching hers.

"Snacks," he said, pulling off the silver lid, revealing fruit and almond butter.

"Yum." She joined him on the king bed with its white duvet and wall of pillows, sitting cross-legged. He placed the tray down in front of her and then slid on his side as she remarked, "You do realize we broke our own rules."

"Yup, and I don't give a shit," Colter replied, tossing a piece of apple into his mouth.

"Until you do give a shit," she said, reaching for an apple and dipping it into the almond butter.

He froze midway to picking up another apple and arched an eyebrow. "Explain what that means."

"I just mean, isn't this exactly what you didn't want? We fake dated so that you could get women away from you."

"That's different," he said.

"How?"

He winked. "Because I like you."

Her insides turned to mush, but she didn't get the chance to reply as he dipped the apple in the almond butter and then lifted it to her mouth.

His voice lowered as she took a bite. "I knew there was something special about you the moment you walked into the bar."

"Oh?" she asked. "Special how?"

He dragged the apple across her lips. "I liked the way you looked at me. Not like a prize. Like a man." He hesitated, eating the remainder of the apple. She licked the sweet flavor off her lips as he continued, "More than that—you didn't look at me like I was broken."

She lifted her brows. "People think *you're* broken?"

He grinned, tapping her nose. "See, that surprises you. I like that."

"No, seriously, though, who would think that?" she countered, snagging another apple and dipping it in the butter before taking a nibble. "You honestly seem like the most put-together guy I know."

"If you'd come here six months ago, you would have thought very different."

"Because of the divorce?"

He nodded. "At the time, I felt like I'd failed my family for leaving them in the first place. I felt like I failed to hold my marriage together. I felt like, in every aspect of my life, I failed. I didn't come home in a good place."

"You were heartbroken," she said gently.

"Terribly. I drank too much, refused to talk to anyone and worked too damn hard. I was pretty miserable to be around."

Laughter and footsteps sounded outside their door before fading away. "What changed all that?"

He hesitated and visibly swallowed, pain evident in his voice and on his face. "My dad came to the house one night. He wasn't in a wheelchair then, but he knew his body was failing him. He gave me an out on running the ranch. He told me I could return to flying, because he'd hired a CEO to fill his role."

She took his hand, hoping somehow that eased the obvious hurt he felt at the memory, as he continued, "He looked me in the eye, man to man, and in the darkest days of his life, probably hating to even ask, he thought of me and of my happiness."

"So, then you thought of him and got better?" she guessed.

He ran his thumb over the back of her hand, his attention remaining there. "Exactly." When his head lifted again, his gaze was filled with warmth. "It made me see that I needed to get over myself, because what I was going through was nothing in comparison to him. I promised him that day that I'd shape up."

"And you did?"

He nodded, proud. "I did."

Gosh, to just *change* for the better. She envied his ability to do that so easily.

He ran a finger along her jawline, drawing her out of her thoughts. "What's that look all about?"

"I wish I could do what you did," she admitted. "Hell, I'm still wondering how I nearly married someone who was cheating on me."

"Cruel people are very good actors."

She shrugged. "I guess, but I honestly just don't know how to pick up and move on like you did. I know that, soon, I'll have to go home and face Brock and his family, and I'm not sure how I'll do that."

"Finding strength in heartbreak didn't happen overnight," he said, adamant. "It took me six months of punishing myself to get there."

"Oh, great. Is that what I have to look forward to?"

He suddenly moved the tray out of the way and grabbed her leg, pulling her toward him. She let out a squeal as he hovered over her. "You'll never go to that dark place, because your sweet, sunny heart simply couldn't." He pulled the tie on her robe until it fell open, then kissed her neck, her breast, her stomach.

She threaded her hands through his hair as his kisses continued lower, setting her on fire. "I thought you said you were hungry."

"I am," he said, pressing a kiss to her inner thigh before moving closer to where she wanted him. "But I'm just hungry for something else now."

"Oh, yeah, what's that?" she rasped playfully.

"You." His tongue met her heated flesh.

As she arched off the mattress falling into the pleasure, she realized Nora was right—this was the best decision she'd ever made.

Nine

Four days later, Adeline was living on an orgasmic high. Every minute of every day she'd spent with Colter had seemed better than the one before it. She'd spent her mornings shadowing him at work for her story and the afternoons writing what she'd learned about Colter with Waylon.

She'd finished her article two days ago, but the article was the furthest thing from her mind. First, she didn't feel like writing about Colter anymore—she felt like experiencing him for real. Second, in just two short days, she'd leave Colter and Devil's Bluffs behind.

The thought seemed nearly impossible. She'd never felt such hunger for any man. Such desire, like she never could get enough of him. No matter how many times she and Colter had fallen apart in each other's arms—in the morning, afternoon, at night, whenever they could—she wanted *more*.

But her bigger problem? Her heart was reaching for things with Colter that complicated everything. Because she knew if Colter lived in New York City, she'd keep dating him without question, without hesitation, regardless that she was fresh off a breakup. Things with Colter were good...*too good.*

A thought she desperately tried to push away as she slid into cowboy boots she'd borrowed from Colter's mother. They pinched at the ankles, but sore feet were the least of her worries.

Horseshoes clicking against the driveway drew her gaze up. Colter approached with two horses, tacked up and ready to ride, and she gulped. *Yup, terrible idea.*

"Regretting saying yes to a ride?" Colter asked, smirking.

"A little," she admitted.

"You've really never ridden before?" Beverly asked, swinging back and forth in the rocking chair on the farmhouse's porch.

"Never in my life," she answered.

"You're a Texan," Colter rebuked, stopping at the porch and shaking his head in disapproval. "That's a travesty."

Adeline slid the borrowed tan-colored cowboy hat onto her head and rose. "A Texan who lived near town and who only set foot on a farm when I babysat Beau."

"We should have had the boys take you," Beverly stated. "Shame on us. Isn't that right, Grant?" She patted her husband's hand.

Where he sat in his wheelchair, Grant's eyes were glazed over today. He stared off at the barn, mumbling words no one could decipher.

Adeline wasn't sure whom to feel worse for—Grant, since the last few days had not been easy on him. She could hardly believe how much frailer he looked in such a short time. Or Beverly, Colter and Beau, who all suffered right alongside him. She'd never seen Parkinson's up close and personal before. She'd had no idea how cruel the disease was, or that dementia came into play with Parkinson's and how fast it stole someone away.

When Grant didn't acknowledge them, still staring off at the barn, mumbling, Beverly patted his hand. "Exactly. We did Adeline wrong." To Adeline, she added, "It's good Colter's rectifying this."

"Let's hope so," Adeline muttered, trotting down the porch steps. "I may actually die in the process."

"I'd never let that happen," Colter said, tapping the rim of her cowboy hat.

She felt marginally better.

In quick work, Colter gave her a leg up and she was hoisted atop the white horse. He adjusted her stirrups and then mounted his black horse as easily as she climbed a set of stairs.

"Enjoy yourselves," Beverly said as they rode off.

"Thanks," Adeline called before studying the way Colter held his reins in one hand. She did the same and asked, "What do I need to know here?"

"Squeeze your legs to go faster. Give a little tug on the reins to stop and say *whoa*. Not much more than that. Just go nice and easy." He gestured to the horse. "Pearl will take good care of you. Just relax into the saddle and enjoy the ride."

"Okay," she said hesitantly. Pearl was massive and powerful, but Colter looked relaxed, so she followed his advice.

They passed the barn, where cowboys were busy working. Pearl followed Colter's horse up the small hill along a dirt trail until they entered a flat pasture. Her horse seemed to know what she was doing, so Adeline rested one hand on her leg, the other holding the reins on the horn of the saddle.

As they headed deeper into the meadow, surrounded by lush vegetation and rolling hills, she studied the cowboy next to her. Colter's relaxed shoulders. His lax expression. He looked the same when he flew—at home and most comfortable.

She was beginning to feel the same way, too.

The days she'd spent back in Devil's Bluffs had left her breathless. The sex had been the greatest of her life. Each day that passed only seemed to sizzle more. She couldn't fool herself—she was happy. Probably the happiest she'd been in a very long time. She wished more than ever that this relationship wouldn't end in two days. She was not only spending more time with Colter than she ever had with Brock, and she was happy to do so, but she wondered if this was what a healthy relationship looked like.

Quiet. Comfortable. Easy.

"My dad was looking rough, huh?" asked Colter, breaking the silence.

She noted the tension in his eyes. "A little, yeah. It's very sad."

He gave a slow nod, then set his troubled gaze back on the view ahead of him. "My mom was telling me this morning that it's the recommendation of the nursing home that he doesn't leave the property anymore. It's too much for him."

"I'm sorry, Colter," she said, wishing she could reach for him. "I can't imagine how hard that must be for all of you."

"I'm most sorry for my mother" was all he said.

Her heart broke for Beverly, too. Pearl grabbed a mouthful of grass before quickening her walk to catch up to Colter's horse. "Is that why you left a job you loved and came home? For your mother?"

He glanced at her sidelong, heaviness in his stare. "Family stands above all. They needed me. It wasn't even a question if I'd come home."

"Even if it meant giving up your dream job?"

"Even if."

Pearl suddenly tripped a little before she righted herself. Once Adeline knew she wasn't about to hit the dirt, she added, "You're a good man, you know, giving up your dreams and desires to make sure your family is happy. Not everyone would do that."

He watched her closely. Then heaved a sigh. "If I learned anything from what's happening with my father, it's that at the end of your life, it's not money with you or a dream job—it's your memories and your loved ones."

She smiled but couldn't take her eyes off him. Behind his tough, cool-guy persona was a man with strong morals, a family man, and one who selflessly put his own wishes and dreams aside to do right by his family.

Dear God, he was her dream come true.

"I envy the relationship you have with your family," she admitted, the morning sun beating down on her. "The way you guys are there for each other. I can only imagine what your Christmases must be like. Is it as magical as I think it would be?"

"It's pretty magical," Colter agreed with a laugh. "My mom really goes all out. You didn't have that with your mom?"

"Oh, I did," she countered. "My mom is amazing and always did what she could to make every day magical for me, but I just mean, having family. Brothers…a dad… that kind of thing."

A long pause followed. Then, "Have you really not wanted to meet your dad?"

She hesitated now, touching on that sore spot to see if she could talk about it. She was relieved to find it didn't hurt like it used to. "My mom only told me his name when I turned sixteen, and I think she only told me that because she never expected me to come back here."

"Was she protecting you?"

"I think so." She nodded. "My dad never wanted children. When my mother told him she was pregnant, he was clear about his views on becoming a father. My mom said he was a big drinker. She decided it'd be better for me not to be involved with him, and he thought it better, too."

He cocked his head. "What do you think of that?"

"You mean, do I think it was honorable he stayed out of my life, knowing he'd be a bad father?"

Colter nodded, resting his hand on the horn of his saddle.

She looked away to give Pearl's neck a stroke, her mane gorgeously long and flowing. "It took me a long time to see the good in what he'd done—" she glanced his way again "—but yes, I do think it's honorable that he stayed away if he knew he'd be a terrible father. But I guess it kind of makes me sad, too."

"Why sad?"

"It makes me wonder what happened to him that he wouldn't choose more love in his life."

A sweet smile crossed Colter's face as an eagle shrieked above, soaring through the air. "You've got a big heart, Adeline."

"Probably a bad thing, really."

"How can *that* be a bad thing?"

The wind rustled the long grass as Pearl snatched another mouthful. "Because it puts you in situations where you get hurt. Trust me, I've got the bruises to show for it."

A long pause followed as Colter frowned. He finally asked, "Does your father still live in town?"

"He does, yes," she explained. "I actually saw him when I first arrived. Remember when you found me on the ground?"

His mouth twitched. "When you fell, right?"

She snorted. "Fell into a bush to avoid my dad seeing me."

Awareness touched Colter's face. "Ah, that makes more sense. Do you think he saw you?"

She shrugged. "Honestly, I doubt he'd even recognize me. Why would he? I'm a perfect stranger to him."

"I cannot understand how a man could do that to his daughter," Colter said gruffly. Though his voice softened when he asked, "Can I ask who your father is?"

She hesitated but then realized she shouldn't have. She wanted Colter to know her. "He's Eric Lowe."

Colter's brows shot up. "From Lowe's Mechanics?"

"That'd be the one," she said, shifting her hips with Pearl's rhythm.

"Jesus," Colter snapped. "He works on all our trucks for us."

"Whatever you do, please don't change that," she countered. "I don't want it to be weird for him or anything." When she saw the vein protruding in the middle of Colter's forehead, she hastily added, "Really, Colter, I didn't tell you to make a fuss. Just being honest."

He tore his gaze away, his glare burning up the tree line ahead of him. "All right," he eventually said calmly. "I won't make a fuss. Do you plan on going to see him while you're here?"

"See him?" She pondered the thought. "No, I've got nothing to say to him. What would I even ask?"

His glare returned and burned. "Not a damn thing, but you could show him how amazing you are and that his failures didn't break you."

Her heart squeezed in all the right ways. "Thank you for saying that."

"I'm only saying what's true," he said gently. Then he rubbed the scruff on his chin. "I never would have guessed he's a drunk."

"Maybe he's just good at hiding it."

"Maybe," Colter agreed.

A comfortable quiet settled in, and Adeline didn't feel the need to fill it. There was a certain peace to riding a horse in nature. She made a mental note to add this experience to her article—to discuss how both the Ward sons were very easygoing and laid-back people—when suddenly Colter stopped his horse. Adeline's automatically stopped, too.

He met her with a soft expression. "There are three things I know for certain. One, your father made the biggest mistake by not having you in his life. Two, if you change your mind and you want to meet him, I'll be there with you, by your side."

Her heart skipped at the idea of meeting Eric Lowe. She'd never considered it. Didn't see the point of it, but now, after being around the Wards, she couldn't help but wonder if perhaps she was missing out. Maybe her father did regret not knowing her... "And three?" she asked, curious.

He grinned from ear to ear. "I've got a killer right hook that I'd be glad to introduce him to, if that suits you."

She barked an unexpected laugh. "Thanks. I'll certainly keep that in mind."

Later that night, in Beau's rustic kitchen with its oak cabinets and dark quartz countertops, Colter nudged a wood block carefully out of the Jenga tower, which began to wobble before the blocks crashed to the live edge table.

Sitting across from him, Austin screamed in joy, jumping up. He high-fived Adeline. "We got him," his nephew exclaimed.

"We sure did," she said with a laugh.

Austin bounced in his chair. "Can we play again?"

"Sorry, buddy, it's bedtime." Colter rose, pushing his chair under the table. "You're already up later than you should be."

"But…but…"

"Your dad will have my hide," Colter reminded his nephew. He wasn't sure what time Beau would get home after his date with a woman Riggs had introduced him to at the Black Horse, but he wasn't taking chances with his brother giving him grief. "Neither of us wants to deal with that."

Austin's shoulders slumped, but he eventually perked up again, remembered his manners. Beaming at Adeline, he said, "Thanks for babysitting me."

"I had so much fun," she told him, restacking the blocks until the tower was built again. "Next time, we'll kick Uncle Colter's butt playing Monopoly."

Colter's jaw clenched against the awareness that hit her expression the second her mouth shut. There would not be a next time. Soon, she'd be back in New York City and returning to her life there.

Austin didn't know that. "Oh, yeah, totally kick his butt," Austin said, smiling, before taking off down the hall.

"You shouldn't encourage him," Colter told her with a smile.

She held up her hands in surrender. "But you make it so easy."

"Ha-ha," he said with a snort, following Austin down the hallway and into his bedroom. "Pj's on and brush your teeth, buddy."

"On it," said Austin, and in a flurry, he grabbed pajamas from the drawer, spun on his heels and headed off to the bathroom.

By the time Colter pulled the patchwork quilt back on the bed and turned off the bedroom's light, the night-light giving off slight, warm light, Austin was jumping into bed. "All set?" Colter asked, tucking him in.

"Yup." Austin turned onto his side, snuggling into the pillow.

Colter missed reading a book to Austin at bedtime but had been firmly told by his nephew that he was too old for that now. "Sleep well, little man." Colter tousled his nephew's hair.

When he went to turn away, Austin asked, "Can Adeline come over tomorrow to play Monopoly?"

"Sorry, bud, but I think she's busy."

Austin pouted. "When can she come, then?"

Colter hesitated, the question suddenly seeming daunting. He took a seat on the side of the bed and explained gently, "I don't think she can. She's heading back home to New York City soon, where she lives."

"Can't she move here?"

Such an innocent question, from an innocent kid. "That's a hard thing for adults to do sometimes."

"Doesn't seem so hard," Austin muttered. "Just pack her stuff in boxes and bring it here."

Colter tousled his nephew's hair again. He wished that was the case. Every day that passed seemed to get better than the one before it. Things with Adeline were easy, hot and spectacular. Were she not leaving, he'd believe he was in the beginning of an incredible relationship that was only getting better as the days passed. "Believe me, if I could have her move here, I would."

"Then ask her," Austin said.

Feeling like the kid was smarter than he was, Colter rose and moved to the door. "I'll think about it. It's time for sleep. 'Night, buddy."

"'Night."

Colter headed out the door, leaving it open a crack just as Austin liked it. He heard Adeline's laugh followed by Beau's on his way back to the kitchen.

When he reentered the kitchen, he found Beau leaning against the kitchen counter while Adeline still sat at the table. She'd packed the game back into the box. "You're home early," he said to his brother.

Beau looked at his watch before arching an eyebrow. "A little late for bed, don't you think?"

Colter shrugged. "Better late than never."

Beau snorted a laugh, folding his arms. "As for being home early, I'm not sure I could have taken more." He sighed. "I spent an hour learning about everything her ex-husband did wrong."

"That good, huh?" Colter snorted, sidling up to Adeline, wrapping his hands around the back of the chair.

"Worse than you could even imagine," his brother grumbled. To Adeline, he asked, "Can you make a photograph of me go viral? I could use the help in finding a woman."

"I wish, but sorry, I'm not that good," Adeline said, grinning, rising from the table. "Austin and I did kick Colter's butt a few times playing Jenga, so at least the night wasn't a total waste."

"At least there is that." Beau winked.

Colter huffed, moving to the door and picking up his Stetson from the hook. "We better get on our way before you two team up on me and somehow I end up losing more tonight."

"What a chicken," Beau called after him.

Adeline laughed, and Colter gathered her close in his arms. "You think that's funny, huh?"

Her eyes twinkled as she melted beautifully against him. "Extremely."

He'd never yearned to keep anything, but he wanted to keep Adeline. Close. Just like this. For as long as she'd let him. It'd been a year since he'd dated anyone. What started out as fake was certainly not that now. Days of happiness had erased that line, but questions kept echoing in his mind. Why did he have to meet her now? Why couldn't he have seen her back in high school? Why did she have to live in the damn city?

His body vibrated with his need to keep her with him. But he wasn't sure if he could convince her to stay. He knew why he'd asked about her father, why he'd pressed the matter—he was desperate to remove her obstacles so she could see Devil's Bluffs as home again.

Gently, he pressed a kiss to her forehead. "You're both traitors." He opened the door to their continued laughter. Then said to his brother, "Sorry about the date."

Beau shrugged, moving toward them. "A night out is a night out. Thanks for entertaining Austin."

"He's a real cutie," Adeline said, stepping outside.

Out of sight of Adeline, Beau mouthed, *She's a keeper.*

Colter nodded agreement and then joined Adeline outside. They said a quick goodbye to Beau and hit the road a few minutes later. The beams of Colter's headlights lit up the dark, windy road as he drove in the opposite direction from his house. Adeline didn't seem to notice they weren't going home until he left Ward land behind and slowed down in front of the high school.

When he turned into the driveway, she asked, "What are we doing here?"

Colter parked the truck. "Fulfilling a fantasy."

"What are you talking about?" she said with a laugh, following him outside.

He met her at the hood and took her hand, leading her toward the football field. Memories flooded him. Good ones. When life was easy and fun and he'd thought happiness was a right given to anyone. Now, of course, he knew better and knew that happiness came from hard work. Both in relationships and out of them.

Once they reached the football field, a quiet, dark, still night around him, he moved to the bleachers, not seeing anyone that would interrupt his plans for the evening.

She slowly moved closer to him, giving a sexy smile. "You can't be serious."

"Oh, I'm very serious," he said, tugging her into him. "Tell me what you thought about when you saw me at school and were crushing hard." He slid his hand down to cup her bottom, bringing her up against him. "Did you think about me doing this to you? Bringing you closer?"

"Yes," she rasped.

He dragged his nose against hers. "Did you think about my mouth?"

"Yes."

He sealed his mouth over hers and kissed her passionately. "Like this? This is what you wanted?"

"Yes, I wanted you to kiss me." She hesitated before rasping, "But there was something else I always wanted to do to you."

"What was that?"

Her smile tightened his groin. He went hard as steel as she lowered to her knees and reached for his belt.

He arched an eyebrow at her. "*That* is what you thought about doing to me?"

She nodded slowly, nibbling her lip. "Touching you. Tasting you. Yes, it's all I thought about." She got his belt open and began unzipping his fly. "And all I'm thinking about now."

A rough laugh escaped him. "You and I would have gotten along very well back then, New York."

Her eyes shined as she opened the front of his pants and slid them down enough that his cock sprang free. "Really? So, you would have liked this?" She licked up the length of him.

He threw his head back and groaned as she took him deep into her mouth, her hand following behind. "Christ. Yes."

He couldn't think, focus, do anything at all but feel every bit of her silky tongue and wet mouth as she brought his soul into her hands. Every move was skilled, like she had the playbook on how to drive him wild.

Until he felt the tremors rock him, the heat shooting up his spine. One look down at her head bobbing on him and he was a near goner.

He reached for her before she could finish him. He spun her around until she was pressed against the bleachers. "Stay there for me, New York." He took a condom from his wallet and hastily sheathed himself.

He couldn't take his eyes off her as he reached around, unbuttoning her jeans and shoving them just down past her bottom. The need to claim her—and to keep her right there with him and give this thing between them a real shot—overtook him as he stepped in close behind her. He slid his hand between her thighs, finding her ready, and he didn't need more of an invitation.

Her heady moans echoed around him as he positioned

himself at her entrance. With a growl, he gripped her hip and entered her in one swift stroke.

Her shout of ecstasy brushed across his senses. That was all it took to drive him wild and eliminate any sense of control.

This time, he didn't go slow and easy.

This time, he held her hips, pinned her against the bleachers and rode her hard, commanding her body. Their moans blended, their jagged breathing uniting in the roughness of the pleasure.

Until her inner walls squeezed him tight, her scream of release satisfying something primal deep inside him. Only then—when she was screaming his name—did he follow her, roaring, bucking and jerking against her, wishing every single day for the rest of his life could be this good.

Ten

"How's engaged life?" Riggs asked the following day in the Black Horse.

Sitting across from him in a booth, Colter replied against the rim of his beer bottle, wet with condensation, "Hilarious." He'd had a busy morning at the ranch with a couple of sick cattle but made time for lunch with Riggs. He swallowed the beer, the taste of hops and spices lingering on his tongue, and then set the bottle down on the table. A little too firmly, judging from Riggs's raised brows.

"That good, huh?" Riggs asked.

"Actually, it's too good," Colter admitted to his childhood friend. "It's so good that it's easy to forget all this happened because of a fake relationship."

Riggs shook his head slowly. "What a situation to be in."

Colter agreed with a nod. "It's been...*interesting*."

He felt all his guards fall in the comfort of his friend's presence. Riggs had been there for him when he'd come home after his divorce, broken. Whenever Colter needed an ear, Riggs listened. "Listen, I'm sorry I haven't been around much."

"Ah, don't be sorry," Riggs countered, straightening the cardboard menu stand on the table. "She's making you happy. Nothing beats that. How much longer is Adeline here?"

The bartender behind the bar—must be a new employee, since Colter hadn't met him—filled an order from a chatty patron sitting on the stool. The very stool Colter had been sitting on the day Adeline uprooted his life for the better. "She's set to fly home tomorrow morning."

Riggs frowned. "That soon, huh?"

"Too soon." Two weeks was all he had with her. But those weeks had been the best he'd had in a very long time. Fourteen days with her was not enough time.

Riggs sipped his malt scotch, the ice clanging in his glass. "Have you seen the article she's written about you?"

"Not yet." Colter hesitated. "Not sure I want to. If it's finished, it'll mean she's going back to New York City."

"Obviously not something you want."

Riggs knew Colter. Truly. He'd been his friend the longest. His greatest ally. "She is the greatest thing to happen to me. Is it insane of me to hope she doesn't write the article? That she decides she wants to live the story with me instead of heading back to the city?"

"No, it isn't insane," Riggs said after a moment of consideration. "But it's a big ask."

"Yeah, it is," Colter agreed, picking at the label on his beer. "Doesn't mean I don't want to ask it. The very last thing I want right now is for her to go home. Things are good. Better than they've been in so damn long."

Riggs cocked his head. "Have you asked her if she feels the same way?"

Colter snorted. "Not sure I want to know her answer." She liked him, that he knew. She was happy...and *satisfied*, that he also knew. He had finally found a woman he could see himself getting serious with again. But the obstacles stopping them from being together were there, and there was nothing Colter could do to remove them. She was heartbroken. Devil's Bluffs was not her home.

Frustration cut through him as he carved a hand through his hair. "She's *just* coming off a heartbreak. A big one—that I know for certain she has not dealt with."

"Maybe she doesn't need to deal with it," Riggs offered. "Not everyone deals with things the same way. If you ask me, you should man up and ask her to stay. You deserve happiness. Choose that."

Cheering from a table across from them grabbed Colter's attention. On the flat-screen television on the wall, a Professional Bull Riding event had just gotten underway. That explained why, even at midday, the bar was packed. He smiled at Riggs. "Thanks. Appreciate that. How are things with you?"

"Can't complain," Riggs said with a slight shrug. "Bar's doing well. Nightmares are staying away—" Colter knew Riggs's sleep was often disturbed by PTSD "—and the ladies are coming in plenty."

"Literally?" Colter asked.

Riggs barked a laugh. "Of course, man, of course." He took another sip of his drink before adding, "We should get a poker night going."

Damn, it'd been weeks since they had one. They usually got together at least weekly. "I'll get a call into the ranch to see who wants to join," Colter said. Beau would want in, as he usually did, and a few of the cowboys always joined, too.

He went to grab his beer when his phone beeped in his pocket. One look at the screen, and he smiled. *Adeline.*

Her text read, Can I see you?

He fired off a text back. Sure, I'm at the Black Horse. Meet me here.

Her response popped up a moment later. I'm just at the coffee shop. Be there in a few.

"What's up?" Riggs asked.

"Adeline's coming by in a couple minutes." He tucked his phone back into his pocket. "I'm glad we could do this."

"Me, too." Riggs slapped a hand on the table. "And it's good to see a woman making you smile from a text alone. She must be some woman."

Colter smiled. "She is."

True to her word, Adeline arrived at the bar a few minutes later, after Colter had already settled his bill. She strode past the patrons, garnering looks from the men there. Colter leaned back against the booth, taking his fill of her as she approached.

Damn.

Her silky blouse clung against all her incredible curves. The tight black pants and heels were just begging to hit his bedroom floor. But more than the lust alone driving him, his chest warmed whenever she came near.

Her eyes twinkled with heat, as if she could read his thoughts. "Hi," she said when she sidled up to the table. She stuck her hand out. "Riggs, right?"

Riggs gave her his charming smile that all the ladies loved. He took her hand and shook it gently. "That'd be me, and you must be Adeline."

"You got it. It's really nice to meet you." She studied the empty plates, with only chicken wing sauce and bones, on the table. "Sorry, am I interrupting?"

"Not at all," Riggs said, sliding out of the booth. "We're all done here, and I gotta head back to work anyway." He gathered up all the plates, as well as Colter's empty beer bottle and his glass. "Can I grab you a drink, food, anything?"

"No, thanks, I'm okay," she replied.

Colter gestured her into Riggs's seat, and she took his spot as Colter said to Riggs, "I'll be in touch about that poker game."

"Sounds good to me," Riggs said before setting that charming smile back onto Adeline. "Again, nice to meet you, Adeline."

"You, too. Hope to see you soon."

Colter gritted his teeth, beginning to hate that line. Because she wouldn't see him again. She was leaving tomorrow morning. Unless he could think of a way to convince her that staying with him would be the best decision of her life.

Riggs turned away but not before waggling his eyebrows in obvious approval over Adeline. Colter couldn't agree more.

He focused back on Adeline, taking note of her wringing hands. A jolt shot through his limbs at the unease on her face. "Everything okay?" he asked, hoping she was changing her mind about leaving.

"Sort of," she said. "I mean, kind of."

He arched a single eyebrow at her.

She laughed nervously. "Okay, I guess that makes no sense at all. You see, this morning I was talking to Nora about everything that has happened, and how I'm feeling about stuff...and..."

Colter hung on bated breath, waiting for her next words to make him a very happy man. But she surprised him.

"I actually have a big favor to ask," she said.

"Of course. Whatever you need. What's going on?"

She rubbed the back of her neck, visibly swallowing. "Can I still take you up on your offer to come with me to meet my dad?"

Of all the things he'd been expecting her to ask, that wasn't it. He reached for her shaky hands, taking them in his. "Are you sure you want to do that?" He wasn't sure he wanted her to meet the bastard who had turned his back on his own child.

She pondered for a moment. Then nodded firmly. "I keep going back and forth, to be honest. Do I want this? Do I not? But in the end, after talking to Nora, and after our talk about him, I feel like this is my one and only chance to meet him. To find out what happened from his side of things. To understand what went so wrong with him that he could turn his back on a child."

She hesitated and drew in a deep breath. "I want him to see me. See that I'm doing well. And, if I'm honest, maybe I'm hoping a little that I can alleviate any guilt he has for being absent in my life. Maybe it could help his alcoholism."

Christ, this woman amazed him. He paused to consider what he'd heard. He couldn't help but hope that maybe—just maybe—she was trying to make her life better in Devil's Bluffs for herself. That she was also thinking of the future and how she could make things good here. Or at least doable so she didn't have to leave at all. Maybe, just maybe, they could somehow make this work.

Feeling desperate to keep her there, and safe, he held

her hands tight. "If you need answers, then let's get them."

Cheers erupted again from the other table as she smiled. "Thank you. I'm not sure I could do this alone."

"You could do this alone," he said, brushing his thumbs against her soft skin. "But I'm glad you asked me." He hesitated, thinking of her father. From what he knew of the man, he was decent enough. Although Colter didn't know Eric's history. "What if he disappoints you today?" he asked, throwing that out there.

"I've considered that," she said. "And, to be honest, I'm not sure how I'll feel about it all. I just know that I don't want another day to pass without at least seeing him face-to-face." She hesitated. Then her voice strengthened. "I don't want to be the person hiding behind bushes to avoid him. I want to face him."

"Then we go," Colter said immediately.

She inhaled sharply, then slid out of the booth. "It's probably best if we go now, so I don't realize this is a huge mistake and I change my mind."

"You *can* change your mind, you know," he told her.

"No—" she lifted her chin "—I really can't. I need these answers."

The drive across town to Lowe's Mechanics took fifteen minutes, though it felt like a thousand had gone by. Sitting next to Colter in his truck, Adeline fidgeted the whole way while he took the roads easy. She wanted this. She *needed* this to look herself in the mirror every day. She refused to be that shy girl who was too afraid to speak up again. But her nerves didn't get that memo.

They drove past gorgeous mansions that sat high on hills. Farms' brands were on every metal gate leading up to million-dollar houses. Old money lived here in this part of Texas. Since she'd been there last, new mansions had seemed to pop up everywhere. The land belonging to the state now housed neighborhoods. Money was sprinkled everywhere on the land now.

Until they reached the small auto body shop on the corner of the road that had yet to have a millionaire take it over to knock it down. Her insides twisted. Eric's shop looked better than she had expected. The white paint was fresh, the garden cute, with big hostas filling up most of the space and brightly colored wildflowers occupying the rest.

Colter pulled into one of the parking spots in front of the shop and cut the ignition. He shifted in his seat, looking at her straight on. "You don't have to do this, you know." He placed a big, comforting hand on her thigh. "If you want to leave, we leave, no questions asked."

She studied the shop's sign, which likely glowed at night. Eric might not make millions, but his shop was well cared for, not quite the place she'd expected an alcoholic to own. Which only made her even more curious about the man. "Actually, I do need to do this," she said, tapping into a well of strength she hadn't known was there. "The other day when we talked about my dad, all I kept thinking was, maybe he's the reason I ended up with someone who eventually cheated on me. Maybe it isn't Brock I need to find peace with, it's my dad." Desperate to not change her mind, she opened the passenger door and got out. "It's time I find out what really happened from his side of things."

Colter removed the keys from the ignition and hopped out, joining her at the passenger side of his truck. "Want me to come with you?" he asked, his brow wrinkled.

Warmth flooded her as he took her hands, squeezing tight. "Thanks, but I need to do this alone."

"All right." He tugged her into him, wrapping his arms around her tight. His kiss gave her just the right amount of reassurance she needed. "You've got this," he said against her lips. "I'm here if you need me."

Oddly, she believed him on both fronts. It registered in her mind how much she trusted Colter. How, even after Brock cheating, she believed every word this man said. Always. She liked his steadiness most. "Thank you. I appreciate that."

She gave his hands a final squeeze before releasing him. Digging deep into her well of strength, she left Colter behind and approached her father's shop. Both bays were open, with vehicles on lifts and ramps. Music played on the radio, barely audible over the sound of an electric drill.

"Excuse me," she called to the man working beneath the car. "I'm looking for Eric Lowe. Is he here?"

"Yeah, sorry, one moment," the man replied, moving out from beneath the car. When he began approaching, he wiped his hands on his oil-stained coveralls. His fingernails were rimmed with black grease. Her mind stuttered, taking in his brown hair with silver at the sides, round brown eyes and height, of over six feet.

"I'm Eric Lowe," her father said, frowning at something over her shoulder. "What can I do for you?"

Adeline followed his gaze, glancing over her shoulder. Colter leaned imposingly against his truck, glaring daggers at Eric. Her heart swelled with affection. Having someone in her corner felt good. *Real good.* Drawing in a deep breath to find her bravery, she faced her father. "I… I am—"

"Adeline," Eric wheezed, the color draining from his face. He took a wobbly step forward. "You're my daughter, aren't you?"

The ground rocked beneath her feet. "How did you know?" she managed.

Eric's gaze roamed her face. His voice shook. "You look just like your mother."

The unexpected softness in his eyes rocked her back on her heels. Tears welled in her eyes, and she cursed every single one. She dug her nails into her palms, letting the pain help her hide her emotions. She studied the hard lines of his face, every wrinkle, his dark eyes. "I certainly don't look anything like you."

"Not much like me, no, but your hair—" he visibly gulped, statue-still "—it's my mother's color." He glanced over her shoulder, scanning the area. "Is your mother here, too?"

"It's just me," Adeline answered. "I thought maybe I should come and meet you."

His eyes, full of dark shadows, widened. "That was brave of you. I'm glad you did. There's...things to say...things to explain."

She stared at this perfect stranger, not sure what she'd expected to find. But this soft-spoken, obviously hard-working man was not it. "I—"

"Daddy," a high-pitched voice squealed.

Adeline spun on her heels, spotting a young brown-haired girl, probably around ten years old, charging toward them.

The girl waved a paper in her hands. "I drew a painting!"

Behind her, a woman a bit younger than Adeline's mother's age strode toward them, holding hands with a little boy, who looked around seven years old.

"Oh, wow, look at that," Eric said, studying the picture of a cat sitting on top of a mushroom. "Just incredible, Sissy. You are quite the little artist."

"I am terribly sorry for interrupting," the woman, who must be Eric's wife, said to Adeline before guiding her daughter toward the shop. "Our daughter forgets that not everyone is as excited about her art as we are."

Adeline wanted to speak. She tried to, but nothing came out of her parted lips. A sour taste hit the back of her throat as she watched the woman plant a tender kiss on Eric's mouth, followed with Eric kissing the top of his son's head.

Adeline's world stopped turning, ice chilling her veins as the family chatted for a moment.

When they vanished into the office off the bay, Adeline barely managed, "You have a family?"

"I do, yes," Eric said, shoving his hands into his pockets. "A loving wife and two incredible kids."

Stepsiblings? *Family.* The air seemed to thin as Adeline fought to inhale. She gripped her stomach as it churned. "But how? You're an alcoholic. Not a family man."

Eric's shoulders hunched as he bowed his head, not meeting her gaze. "That is true," he said in a small voice. "I was an alcoholic for a long time. An ugly one. Even a terrible person, too." His head finally lifted, a flush creeping across his cheeks. "But I got help. I got better. And I changed my life."

No. No. No.

Her mind was scrambling to find a logical excuse for his actions. None of this made any sense. "If you changed for the better, why didn't you try and find me?" A telephone rang off in the distance, but the sound seemed so far away as the realization dawned on her. "You didn't want me," she whispered.

He took a step forward, stare pained. "It's not like that."

She retreated a step. Of all the reasons she'd thought she didn't know her father, it had never occurred to her that he'd have a perfect family. One that she had dreamed of her entire life. A mom. A dad. Siblings.

She took another step back, an ache burning in the back of her throat. "This was a mistake. I shouldn't have come here."

"No, wait…" Eric reached out to her, his eyes wet. "Adeline, please…"

Even the wind seemed to go still as the pain of his betrayal ripped her apart. Turning, she ran toward Colter, who was already charging her way.

"Wait," Eric called.

Colter caught her in his arms and snarled, "Don't."

She heard her father skid to a halt behind her at the single powerful word growled from Colter's throat.

Her stomach rolled as Colter led her to the truck. She trembled as he opened the passenger-side door and she leaped inside. Everything went quiet; her heartbeat thundering in her ears no longer made a noise. She felt oddly sluggish. A hum filled the heavy silence, an emptiness invading all the warm spots inside.

Until she heard her father say, "Colter. Please. Just wait."

"I said, *don't*, Eric," Colter said through gritted teeth.

Vaguely, she suddenly became aware they were driving again, but she couldn't recall Colter joining her in the truck or driving away from the shop. All she knew was Colter's strong, comforting hand on her thigh and that his strength was a pulsating force next to her. She stared out her window at a hawk soaring over the crops, wishing she could be that bird, that she could fly far, *far* away from here.

Eleven

A couple hours had gone by since they'd arrived home, and Adeline still hadn't come out of the guest room. Not that Colter blamed her—he'd been fighting against driving back to Eric's to take out his frustration on her father's face. He'd finished responding to the couple emails he'd needed to handle before he ended up in the kitchen and began cooking dinner.

Still, Adeline never came out of the room.

Goddamn you, Eric.

Colter never should have let the meeting happen. Because now the truth stared at him hard. Adeline wouldn't just want to leave Devil's Bluffs—she'd want to run and get on the first flight out of there.

Expelling a sigh to cut through the tension along his shoulders, he turned down the stove, letting the beef stroganoff simmer. He cleaned up the used dishes, setting the pot back onto the hanging rack above the island.

Time seemed to stand still when he knew she was in that room, crying. His house had never seemed emptier, quieter. The only sound came from the bubbling of the sauce on the stove, and his skin began to crawl.

Unable to stand the distance between them any longer, he moved down the hallway and stopped outside the guest room. He cocked his head, listening, but couldn't hear a single sound. Earlier when he'd walked by, he'd heard her on the phone—he figured to her mom or Nora.

He knocked once. "I've made dinner. Please come out. You must be hungry."

A long pause.

Again, he knocked. "Adeline?"

"I'll be out in a few minutes," she said, her voice sounding scratchy.

His fists clenched at the obvious tears she'd been crying. Yet again, he felt helpless to assist someone in his life. "I'll be in the kitchen," he told her before heading that way.

When he reached the stove again, picking up the wooden spoon off the banged-up cutting board, his cell phone rang on the countertop. He snatched it up, discovering his lawyer was calling. "Daniel," he said into the phone. "What's up?"

"Hi, Colter, sorry to call so close to dinner," he said in his gravelly voice. "I received a call from Julia's lawyer a few minutes ago. They're requesting a meeting."

"A meeting." He set the wooden spoon back down. "Did they say what they want?"

"To be honest, I'm not exactly sure," Daniel answered. "Which is the reason I'm calling. Has anything transpired between you two that I should know about?"

Colter moved to the big window in his living room, staring out at the trees dancing in the breeze. "Nothing that would warrant a meeting. I recently saw Julia at a charity event in Dallas. We were amicable."

"All right," Daniel said, and he paused, perhaps taking a note down. "Nothing happened between you two there that would upset her at all?"

"Nothing that would warrant a meeting." Colter did not feel the need to tell his lawyer about his fake engagement. "Besides, what more could she possibly want? Is she entitled to something else I'm not aware of?"

"No, she's not," Daniel said with a sigh. "I can refuse the meeting, but I suggest we have it. Meeting face-to-face is always better than over a phone call."

"All right." Colter bit the inside of his cheek to stop himself from saying things he shouldn't. "I'll be there. Send me the date and time when you've got it."

"Will do. Enjoy your night."

Colter ended the call with a curse, tossing his cell onto the counter.

"That couldn't have been a good call."

His gaze snapped up. He discovered Adeline standing in the kitchen, her arms folded over her chest. His chest squeezed at her red-rimmed eyes. "It wasn't," he said, moving to her in an instant. He opened his arms, and she walked right into them. "Julia has requested a meeting."

"Why?" she asked, wrapping her arms around his waist.

Colter pressed a kiss against her forehead, liking how she fit so perfectly in his hold. "Your guess is as good as mine."

She gave him a good squeeze, then stepped out of his arms. "When's the meeting?"

"I don't know yet," he said. Done talking about Julia, and not wanting the focus to drift from Adeline tonight, he moved to the cabinet next to the sink and took out two plates. "Beef stroganoff okay?"

"Yes, sounds amazing," she said with a small smile, following him. "Thanks for making me dinner."

He began adding egg noodles from the strainer in the sink to her plate. "I'd ask if you were all right, but I know that's a stupid question."

She took out forks from the drawer. "It's not a stupid question, and I am all right."

"Do you want to talk about it?" he asked, scooping the sauce onto the noodles.

"If you have wine, then yes, along with a giant glass."

"That I can do," he said, handing her the plate.

He quickly fixed his own dinner, setting the plate on the kitchen table, and then grabbed a bottle of red wine from the wine rack. He poured them both a glass while she took a seat at the table. When he set a glass in front of her, he said, "So. Today was a day."

She gave a dry laugh. "It was, for certain, a day."

He joined her at the table and waited while she stared down at her meal. "I really wasn't expecting him to have a family."

"I'm sorry I never told you," he said, hating himself for it. He had figured she simply hadn't wanted to discuss Eric's family, and he hadn't wanted to add another dagger to her already-bruised heart. "I didn't realize you hadn't heard that when you learned about him."

She lifted her head, her eyes haunted, wounded. "You have nothing to apologize for," she said softly. "How could you know what I know and what I don't?" He took her hand in his, drawn into the pain seeping from her. She visibly swallowed before continuing. "From what I knew of Eric, he was an alcoholic. A terrible person. But today, that's not who I saw. I saw a family man. A father who was beloved by his family. Did you see how they looked at him? They adored him."

Colter squeezed her hand and nodded. "From what I've seen of him since I moved home, he's good to his family. It's why I was surprised when you said he was an alcoholic. That's not the man I know."

Her breath hitched and her chin trembled. "Then, if he is this great guy, why wouldn't he have tried to find me?"

Her weepy eyes felt equal to a dagger in his chest. He grabbed her chair, yanking her closer to him, cupping her face. "Whatever Eric did or did not do is on him. Not on you. You are a beautiful, brilliant, strong woman, and I have no doubt that Eric saw that today and regrets whatever terrible choices he's made along the way."

"Maybe," she said quietly, hanging her head. A tear dripped onto her bare leg. "Maybe not. But it doesn't change the fact that he should have been there in my life. For all the important moments. Even for the unimportant ones." Her voice got smaller, shoulders curling. "I wanted him there."

Colter tucked a finger under her chin, lifting her gaze, needing to read those eyes. He wiped the tears from her face. "I'm sorry he wasn't there for you. He should have been."

"I think…" Her voice broke. "I'm honestly just sick of men disappointing me. It's like I keep trying. I keep thinking that somehow I won't be disappointed, and yet, every time I am."

"A man should never disappoint you," Colter said, adamant. "If they don't fix where they've gone wrong, they are not a man."

She heaved a long sigh that seemed to lessen the load on her shoulders. "I just keep thinking to myself, at what point should you stop caring? At what point do you say, enough is enough?"

"When someone hurts you deeply," he said immediately, cupping the side of her face. "That's when enough is enough. Neither Brock nor Eric deserved you. Don't forget that."

She leaned into his touch, her voice trembling. "But what if it is not about them? What if it's me?"

"It's not you," he stated firmly. "All this shit, Adeline, it's all on them."

Another tear slid down her rosy cheek. "How do you know?"

"Because I would rather take a knife to the heart than hurt you," he said. "That's how I know it's not you." He spread his legs and pulled her chair even closer. Holding her beautiful face in his hands, he continued, "Listen to me very carefully. Brock is a fool. Eric is a fool. Don't let their mistakes become your heartbreak."

Sweetness softened the pain in her expression. She placed her hands over the top of his and laughed through the tears. "Has anyone told you lately how absolutely wonderful you are?"

He cleared more wetness away with his thumbs. "You just did, and that's all that matters."

"Thank you for being you. For being here. For everything, really."

He stared into her warm, honey-colored eyes, and had no idea how he was going to let her go. Life never did seem quite fair. He had regrets in his life, and he knew at this moment that not noticing her back in high school was up there with his greatest.

Somehow he needed to convince her that staying here with him was the best thing for her. And he knew now was the time to lay his heart on the line.

Leaning in near, her sugary-spicy scent engulfed him, desperate, hot need overwhelming his senses. Before his mouth met hers, he replied, "Thank *you* for being you. For being here. For everything, really."

His mouth met hers, and as he gathered her in his arms, pushing aside their plates and laying her out on the kitchen table, the last thing on his mind was their untouched meals.

An hour after they reheated their dinners in the microwave and finally ate, Adeline held her breath and sank beneath the hot bathwater in the claw-foot tub. The sounds from the house were muted, a silence she needed now more than ever. Nothing made sense. She'd talked to Nora earlier, but the only truth that remained was that she never should have visited her father. Because now she had simply added another time in her life where a man had failed her. Her happiness, her trust, her well-being all felt unhinged, ready to break in a heartbeat.

She broke the water's edge with a gasp, drawing in a breath of the warm air. She took in the bathroom with subway tiles on the walls and black shutters on the small window, the flickering candle smelling of vanilla on the vanity, desperate to relax her mind, when her cell phone rang. A quick look over the edge of the bathtub revealed her mother was calling.

She sighed and quickly dried her hands on the towel she'd left on the floor next to the tub. "Hi, Mom," she said into the phone, steeling herself for the conversation ahead.

"Hi, sweetie," Lorraine replied. "I got your message. Is everything okay?"

Her soft voice instantly made Adeline feel marginally better. "Sorry, I know it probably wasn't the best message for you to hear." Her mother had been the first one Adeline had called after she got into bed and hid under the sheets earlier. She didn't even remember what she'd said on the message, but she knew she'd been sobbing.

"The message was just fine," Mom said gently. "You sound better now."

"I ate and talked with Nora and Colter," Adeline explained. "I feel better. Raw. But better."

Mom paused. Then, "What prompted you to go see your father in the first place?"

Apparently, she hadn't explained a lot on the message. "I don't even know," she admitted, running her hand through the smooth water. "Actually, no, that's not true. I think it's because being back here has just brought a lot up. I kept thinking that maybe if I met him, I'd understand more of myself. That I'd see he was this terrible drunk, and I could finally accept that he's just a bad guy. That Brock is a bad guy. And then I could move on with my life, knowing there are bad people out there, but I don't have to change because of them."

"So, you thought meeting him would solve all your problems?"

"Yes," she admitted. Before her mother could comment, she added, "And I know that's dumb."

"It's not dumb, Adeline," her mother rebuked. "But life is rarely that easy or black-and-white." Mom hesitated again. Longer this time. When she spoke again, her voice was filled with curiosity. "Does any of this have to do with Colter?"

Of course, her mother missed nothing. "Yes. No. Maybe."

A soft laugh filled the phone line. "That sure, are you?"

Adeline lifted her hand, watching the water droplets

fall from her fingers. "I'm not sure about anything, if I'm being honest. I don't even know what I'm doing. Why am I still here? Why did I play along with this fake engagement? Why did I go see my dad?" Now it was Adeline's turn to pause. The same thought that had battered her mind earlier resurfaced. "Tell me, honestly, if I was one of your patients, would you think I was losing it?"

"Absolutely not," her mother said instantly.

"Then what would you tell me?"

Her mother paused to consider. Then, "You *are* my daughter and could never be my patient, but I'll say this to you. You've been hurt, and cruelly so. What Brock did to you assaulted your trust and happiness. You must deal with that. Until you do, you'll never see things clearly. Your heart will always be tainted."

Every single word rang true in Adeline's heart.

Mom continued, "I can tell you like Colter, and that what started out as something not real has become very much real, but it would be unfair to bring anyone else into your life knowing that you're incapable of giving them all of yourself. Right now, you simply can't offer that. You can't forget the past. You can only heal after the blow you've been dealt. But pain is pain, my sweet girl. Ignore it long enough and it'll come chasing after you."

Adeline absorbed her mother's advice. "I've made all this very complicated, then?"

"What do you think?"

"Ugh." Adeline sat up, sending the water splashing in the tub. "I think I just want you to tell me what to do."

Her mother chuckled quietly. "My darling, you would never listen to me even if I did."

Knowing her mother was right on all counts, and feeling better, she said her goodbyes and ended the call with a promise to call again tomorrow before her flight.

Done with pitying herself, well aware it would get her nowhere but hiding back under the bedsheets, she got out of the tub. She quickly dried off and put on cotton pajamas before heading out of the bathroom.

She stopped short. Colter sat on her bed, her laptop in front of him. She'd done some work on the article after talking with Nora to get her mind off her unruly emotions. The tightness of his eyes told her he was reading her article. "You don't like it?" she asked, her bare feet feeling stuck to the hardwood floor.

"I like it a lot." He met her gaze. "It's good."

She winced. "Normally when someone likes something, they don't look like they've eaten a sour lemon."

He snorted a laugh, patting the spot next to him on the bed. When she sat, the mattress bouncing beneath her, he continued, "No, really, I do like it. The article is excellent. You've put my family in a good light, mentioned what the Wards stand for and made us appear to be real, hardworking people, instead of something silly, like 'Texas's sexiest bachelor.' I appreciate that."

She nibbled her lip, hating the nerves fluttering in her belly. "You sure?"

"Yes, I'm sure," he said, shutting the laptop, placing it behind him on the bed. "Truly. I liked what I read." When he rose, her breath hitched as he drew closer. "But it also reminds me that your job here is done and you're leaving tomorrow morning."

Her heart felt like it was shrinking. She wasn't ready for this conversation. "You forgot?"

"I didn't forget, but I suppose I had held out hope." He gathered her in his arms until she straddled his lap, holding her close. Pressing a kiss to the top of her head, he said, "I think somewhere in my thick head, I thought you'd stay with me rather than writing a story about me."

A swell of safety and comfort surrounded her, but a cold slice cut through, reminding her of her mother's advice. She had yet to deal with Brock and, now, the recent blow of her father. With Colter, this was all her teenage dream, a fantasy that couldn't possibly last, no matter how much she wanted it to. "But—"

"Your job. Your promotion," he offered grimly.

"Exactly," she admitted, sliding off his lap and rising, suddenly needing distance. Her heart wanted to stay in his arms, but her head, her worries and concerns, knew that to offer Colter more was unfair. She wouldn't hurt anyone like she'd been hurt. "This is...*complicated*."

"I know," he muttered, shoving his hands into the pockets of his jeans.

Emotion clogged up her throat as she fiddled with her fingers, ignoring her hands that so desperately wanted to touch him. "Besides, New York City is my home. It's my safe place. Nora is there. My mom, too."

He gave a slow nod. "I know that, too."

And yet, *and yet*, the look on his face wasn't satisfied. "Colter, asking me to stay here is like asking you to move to the city. You have your life here. With your family. It's an impossible want."

"I also know that, too." He hesitated. Rare, heady emotion swelled in his gaze. "I also know that somewhere along the way, this fake relationship has become very real to me. I know that everything in that article is written from an angle because I care deeply for you, and I know that you care about me, too."

"I do care about you," she said. And with a soft laugh, she added, "Remember, I was the one with the crush."

"Somehow we can make this work. I know I want to. Don't you?"

She never got the chance to reply before his cell phone rang. He pulled his phone from his pocket and said into it, "Beau, what's up?"

A long pause followed. Colter's gaze locked onto Adeline's. His skin turned ashen. "When did this happen?" Another pause. "What's his condition?" And another long, horrible pause. "All right, yes, I'm on my way." He ended the call, shoving his phone into his pocket. "My dad's in the hospital."

"What?" Adeline exclaimed, rushing to his side, gripping his arm tight. "What happened?"

Colter looked shell-shocked, unmoving, unblinking. "I don't know much other than he's had a stroke."

"Oh my goodness, is he okay?" she asked, pressing a hand to his chest, feeling the thundering of his heartbeat.

Slowly, Colter shook his head. His jaw muscles clenched once. "No, no, he's not. He'd stopped breathing before the ambulance arrived at the nursing home. The medics resuscitated him, but he hasn't recovered. He's on a ventilator."

"Oh, no, Colter," Adeline gasped, coldness sinking into her bones, holding her tight. "Please. What can I do to help you?"

"Come with me," he said, his voice slow, detached. "I need you to come with me."

She took his trembling hand in his. "Yes, of course, I'm with you." She wrapped her arms around his waist, holding him close.

"Thank you," he whispered into her neck, enveloping her in his arms.

The warm, affectionate man she'd grown to know

over the past couple weeks, the man who held her now, was not the same man as he stepped back, releasing her. Fierce-eyed and jaw set, she recognized this man from the day she first saw him again in the Black Horse. She knew, as they raced to his truck, she was looking at the eldest Ward son with a legacy resting on his shoulders.

Twelve

With every step from the parking lot toward the hospital, located in a larger neighboring city to the west, Colter felt like the world was moving in slow motion around him. Adeline held his hand tight as he led her inside the hospital, the automatic doors closing behind them with a whoosh.

At the end of the hall, he spotted Beau and his mother talking to a doctor in a long white coat. As they passed by the waiting room, he saw Austin sitting in one of the chairs, playing on his iPad.

Squinting against the bright light overhead, his chest tingled as he hurried his steps. They passed a busy nursing station, followed by another corridor to the right that led to another wing of the hospital. The closer he got to his family, the more the dark-haired doctor's voice became clear.

"I'll give you time to discuss this as a family. I'll be

back shortly," the fortysomething doctor said before he walked off in the opposite direction.

"Mom," Colter said.

His mother turned, burst into tears and walked straight into his open arms. He released Adeline's hand and locked his arms around his mother as she broke apart in his arms. Vaguely, he sensed Adeline and Beau were embracing, but he stayed focused on his mom. Heard every one of her cries. Felt every shake of her body. He didn't count the minutes while the strongest woman he knew sobbed in his arms. He only held her until her cries quieted, her trembling lessened and she had the strength to back away.

Keeping his arm around her, he asked gently, "What happened?"

Mom's hands shook as she wiped at the tears on her cheeks. "Today, when I went to see Dad, he seemed off. He had a lot of confusion—more than usual," she answered. "Nothing he was saying really made any sense, so the nursing staff was keeping a close eye on him."

Beau added, "The situation was challenging, because some of Dad's behavior was usual for him with his dementia. But the behavior was also warning signs of a stroke."

Mom sniffed, reaching into her purse and taking out a tissue, wiping at her nose. "The nursing staff didn't realize he was having a stroke until it was too late."

Adeline asked, "Once they realized, they rushed him here?"

"Yeah," Beau told her, his voice cracking. "But it was too late. He's unresponsive."

Colter cocked his head, that word not registering. "What do you mean, unresponsive?"

"When the paramedics arrived at the nursing home,

they had to intubate him," Beau explained, shoving his hands into his pockets. "Dad's not breathing on his own right now."

Colter's knees weakened, the pale walls seemingly moving closer and closer, squeezing him tight. "There must be tests they can do—"

"He's suffered severe brain damage from the lack of oxygen," Mom said, her voice blistering. "There is no test that can fix this. The machine..."

Beau stepped forward and wrapped an arm around her and explained, "The machine is what's keeping him alive."

"Oh, Beverly," said Adeline, throwing her arms around his mother, tears in her eyes. She whispered sweet, soft comforting words.

Colter felt numb, as if he was standing there in the cold, empty hallway but also floating away. He'd been worried about himself and losing Adeline when his father had been going through this? His stomach rolled, threatening to expel his dinner all over the shiny floor.

Beau placed a hand on Colter's shoulder, squeezing tight. "It's bad, brother."

Colter nearly shook Beau's comforting hand off, but he didn't want to upset his mother more. He was the older brother. The one responsible for his family. For weeks, he'd been lost in himself, thinking *only* of himself. He should have been there for his mother, so she wasn't alone when all this happened. He should have spent more time at the nursing home. He should have been there yesterday to say goodbye. He never should have left for Seattle, leaving his father to work harder than necessary at his age. He should have taken over the ranch earlier, not chased his dreams, and maybe, his father's health wouldn't have declined so fast. He should have done a million damn things differently. He couldn't even begin to imagine what his poor mother had gone through watching her husband get intubated. "What did the doctor say?" he asked no one in particular.

Beau took Mom's hand as Adeline returned to Colter's side and answered, "Just that we need to discuss as a family what to do."

He absorbed the words, fighting even to remember how to put one foot in front of the other.

Mom asked softly, "Do you want to see him?"

"Yeah, yeah," Colter said absentmindedly.

Thoughts evaded him as he followed his family, along with Adeline, down the hallway and into a cold room on the right. The moment he saw his father, he believed two things for certain.

One, his life would never be the same after this day.

Two, he'd lost his father.

The man lying in the hospital bed, covered in a white sheet, tubes everywhere and monitoring wires leading to machines, didn't resemble the mighty cowboy Colter loved. A heart monitor beeped, breaking through the heavy silence. A nurse stood next to his father's bed, reading Grant's vitals and writing them down in a chart. He saw all this with his eyes, and yet he still couldn't believe it. He was living in a nightmare.

The nurse finally turned to them after finishing her notes and said to his mother, "I'll give y'all a moment."

"Thank you," Beau said.

When she left the room, Colter nearly sank to his knees, his breath trapped in his throat.

Adeline didn't freeze up. She walked right up to the bed and placed her hand on his father's arm. It gutted him to watch as she bowed her head and he saw her lips moving, saying a silent prayer for the man so many loved.

His father...

Sounds became muffled as she returned to his side, taking his hand in hers, but his fingers felt cold, icy.

"Colter," Beau said firmly.

Colter jerked his gaze to his brother. Beau wrinkled his brow. Right. Colter needed to do...*something.*

For as long as walking up to the hospital had felt, the walk toward Grant's hospital bed felt ten times that. His dad's arms were pale, frail in a way Colter had never seen before, his hands ashen, weak. He stared down at the fragile body and couldn't see his father anywhere in this man. And yet, *and yet,* when he took his father's hand, he felt desperate for a simple squeeze in return.

But there was no twitch of his father's fingers.

Not a single sign of life.

Colter dropped to one knee, placing his forehead on his father's hand. He even smelled different...not of earthy crops and wilderness, but of nothingness seeping through the veil of antiseptic.

He shut his eyes and said a prayer to any angel that could hear him to carry his father's spirit, wherever it lingered, to where it needed to go. *I'll take care of Mom,* he whispered in his mind, hoping his father heard him. *You don't have to worry about her or the ranch. Your legacy will live on.* Tears welled beneath his closed eyes. *You set the bar of a great man, and if I am half the man you were when I have a family, I will consider myself lucky.* He squeezed his hand one last time. *I'm going to miss you, old man. I love you, Dad.* He rose on shaky legs.

"We need to discuss what to do next," Beau said, breaking the heavy, daunting silence in the room. "The doctor is coming back to get our answer."

Keeping his father's cold hand in his, Colter glanced over his shoulder, finding his family—Adeline included—in tears. "What does the doctor need to know?" he asked.

Mom dabbed at the fallen tears on her cheeks with her tissues. "The doctor has said we can keep him on the machines and see if there is any improvement."

"Improvement for what kind of life, though?" Colter countered. He turned to face his family fully. "Who are we keeping him alive for? Him? Us?" His words felt taken right from his father's mouth. "Even if he recovers a little, what life will he lead? His Parkinson's was only getting worse. It will only become harder for him."

Mom nodded, tears rolling down her cheeks. But he knew she could never say the words that needed to be said. Even Beau bowed his head, unable to face a decision no one wanted to make.

Adeline just cried, honest, sweet tears for his family rolling down her cheeks.

Colter itched to go to her, a desperation eating him alive, and yet...*and yet*, his father's hand... He should have been there with his father more. He should have come home sooner. He should have been there for his family. Always.

Mom's gaze roamed over her husband of forty-five years, her high school sweetheart, before she gave a long exhale. "Your father and I talked a lot about his wishes when his Parkinson's got worse, before the dementia set in. He was adamant that he did not want to be on life support."

For one last time, Colter squeezed his father's hand. He hoped his father knew that when Colter stepped into Grant's boots, he'd never step out of them. "Then we will honor his wishes," he told his family.

Adeline's eyes burned as she somberly followed Colter into the house a few hours later. Just past midnight, the house had never seemed emptier. The silence more daunting.

Grant Ward had passed away nearly immediately after the ventilator had been turned off. She had stayed next to Colter as he and Beau held their mother while they mourned the loss of such an incredible man. Adeline had waited until they began talking quietly, and then she took her leave, joining Austin out in the waiting room so he wasn't alone.

"Is Dad coming back soon?" Austin asked when she took a seat next to him.

"Yeah, buddy, soon," she replied, and he'd gone back to his game, not knowing that he'd lost his grandfather.

The family joined her not long after, and Beau had left with Austin to deliver the terrible news to his son. Adeline had remained in the waiting room while Colter assisted his mother in making arrangements with the funeral home.

Once Colter finished talking to his mother, and after they dropped her off at Beau's to stay the night with him, Colter had not said a word. Not when they arrived back at his house. Not when he got out of his truck and walked up the porch steps. Not even when they went inside.

He didn't take his boots off at the door, heading straight to his bedroom. Adeline shut the front door behind her and locked it with a sigh. She wasn't sure what she'd do if she lost her mother. Probably be a ghost, living in the world but feeling like she didn't belong. Floating through time and space, wondering exactly what she was meant to do and where she should go.

Doing the only thing that felt right at the moment, she headed for the liquor cabinet and poured him a shot of whiskey. Silence greeted her as she padded down the hallway. She found him sitting on his bed, his head bowed.

When her foot creaked against the floorboard, he glanced up. Haunted eyes met hers. "Come here," he said, patting his lap.

She closed the distance, sliding onto his lap. She offered him the drink.

"Thank you," he said, downing the shot a second later. He placed the glass on the floor next to his feet before he enveloped her in his arms, resting his face in the crook of her neck.

His muscles vibrated under her fingers. "Please tell me what I can do for you," she said.

"I'm not sure what anyone can do," he replied. "My dad is gone."

She fought her tears, wanting to stay strong for him. "I'm so sorry, Colter."

Leaning away, he heaved a long sigh. "I'm finding this hard to navigate, because the truth is, there is a small part of me that is grateful for the stroke. He is no longer suffering." He paused to tuck her hair behind her ear, following the movement with his gaze. "For years, we've watched him slowly die. Watched him fade away until I could barely recognize him. These last couple weeks only seemed to get even harder. It's been cruel."

She agreed with a slow nod. "Sometimes, death is a kindness, no matter how much it hurts."

"I think that's very much true," he said, sliding his strong hand onto her thigh. "I worry about my mother. She's been with him so long." He paused, cocking his head. "I actually don't think she's ever lived alone before. She moved right from her parents' house into our farmhouse with my dad. I'm not exactly sure what she'll do without him."

"Your mother has you, Beau and Austin. She's not alone. She'll lean on all of you."

A slow nod of agreement. Silently, he glanced down to their joined hands, and stillness fell between them. Before now, the silence had always felt comfortable, easy. But tonight the silence felt unsteady, filled with a hundred unknowns.

When his head eventually lifted, his brows were furrowed. "I never expected you. You walked into Riggs's bar that night and shook my entire world up."

She cupped his face, dragging her fingers against the rough scruff. In a moment of sadness and death, her heart opened, revealing truths she wanted him to know. "I never expected you, either. You were my crush. My heartthrob. But you've become so much more than that."

Warmth penetrated deep into her chest at his small smile. "I want you to know that you've made me happy these past weeks. Happier than I've ever been in my life."

Why did this sound like goodbye? She shifted off his lap, kneeling between his legs to see him better. His expression was unreadable, his emotions locked up tight. "Colter—"

He pressed a finger softly against her lip. "Please, let me talk. I need to get through this."

She closed her mouth, nodding him on.

His chin dipped, his hair hanging over his brow. "Earlier tonight, when we talked, I believed that maybe, just maybe, we could somehow make this work. I would have done anything to get you to stay. But tonight is only a reminder that we are playing a game we're going to lose."

She cringed, reeling from a reality she didn't want to face. Somehow, she'd convinced herself that her feelings were easily controlled. That she could, and would, walk away. But now, nothing seemed simple anymore. She wanted to say, "No, we can do this," because suddenly, it seemed impossible to believe she'd never see Colter or his family again. "Your family needs you," she said, reading between the lines.

"More now than ever."

"I know," she whispered.

One hand came to her nape while the other brushed across her cheek. "I know you care about me, Adeline. You don't have to tell me—I can see it."

"I do care about you," she said. "More than I think I've let myself believe."

"I'm glad for it." His gaze roamed her face, as if he were trying to memorize this moment for a lifetime. "But you have a good life in New York City. A life you've worked hard for. A promotion you deserve. You should have all your dreams come true."

"You should, too," she told him.

His eyes searched hers, his mouth pinching. "There is a truth here that I can't ignore any longer. Only pain lives here in Devil's Bluffs for you. It would be cruel of me to ask you to move here for me. Selfish in a way that I refuse to be. I will not be that type of man. Not now. Not ever."

Her breath hitched. "And I can't ask you to leave your family."

"No, you can't," he said in agreement. "And even if I wanted to, I can never leave them. Not after my father…"

Her hands ran up his thighs, the muscles beneath her touch rigid. "I'm not ready to say goodbye to you," she managed.

"I'm afraid that's exactly what you need to do."

"We don't have to do that yet," she implored, her heart leaping up in her throat. "I'll cancel my flight. I'll stay to help your mom and you. For the funeral."

All the warmth in his expression suddenly washed

away, replaced by coolness. "Your flight is tomorrow morning. You should be on it."

"My God, Colter, I can stay," she said, sitting back on her heels. "I want to stay. Let me be here for you through all this."

He adamantly shook his head. Then he rose. "To draw this out is only going to hurt us both worse. I need to be with my family now. I can't think of anyone else but them."

Of course, she understood, but… "I can be there for your mother. I can help you all."

"You have a life back in New York City you have to get back to." He headed for a closet. A moment later, he came out with a full duffel bag. "You can stay the night here. Call an Uber tomorrow morning to drive you to the airport and charge the ranch."

"Colter, please wait," she said, rising, taking a step closer.

He retreated by stepping backward toward the door. "I need to be with my family. I can't think of anything else but how to help my mother find her way."

"I can go with you. Please," she begged, tears welling in her eyes. "Don't do this. Let me be there for you."

He froze in the doorway, and his shoulders lifted and fell with his long sigh. When he glanced over his shoulder, his gaze was distant, so far away from seeing her. "There is nothing here for you. We both know that. Go home, Adeline."

She wanted this. She had told him as much earlier. This could never work between them—there were too many obstacles in their way.

That made sense.

But what didn't was how everything suddenly seemed wrong when she heard the front door shut behind him.

His grandmother's ring was a sudden heavy weight on her tingling finger. She slid the ring off, leaving it on his dresser. She'd removed a ring before—Brock's ring—but *this* was worse than heartbreak. This felt like a piercing dagger to her heart.

Thirteen

Three days had passed, painfully slowly. Three days of regretting every minute that went by since Adeline had gone home to New York City. Three days of staring at his grandmother's ring, which Adeline had left on his dresser. Three days of missing *her*. He missed her laugh. Her voice. Her lush body. Even as he sat in a comfortable chair around an oblong table, in the all-glass boardroom in his lawyer's office in Dallas, his gut twisted.

Why had he told her to go?

Why hadn't he kept her close?

Why had he pushed her away?

With regrets piling on top of regrets, he gazed out the floor-to-ceiling windows to a day that matched his mood—dark and gloomy. The passing days had seemed to grow heavier, longer. Dad had been buried in the local cemetery near his parents. The funeral had brought all the townsfolk, and many out-of-towners, a show of how loved his father truly was by those who knew him best.

"Colter."

He jerked his attention back onto his lawyer next to him, suddenly reminded he wasn't alone.

Sitting across from him were Julia and her lawyer. Besides the cloying weight of Julia's perfume, she looked like the Julia he'd once loved. Simply dressed, not much makeup on her face.

"Can I have a minute alone with Colter?" Julia suddenly asked her lawyer.

Dressed in a well-fitted four-piece suit, her lawyer frowned. "I wouldn't—"

"I'll only be a moment," Julia snapped.

Her lawyer finally nodded and rose, glancing at Daniel as he did.

Daniel lifted an eyebrow at Colter in question, and Colter nodded in approval. "It's fine."

Julia reached for the pitcher of water and poured herself a glass as the lawyers left the boardroom. The same room where she'd once refused a fair deal Daniel had drawn up, instead demanding far more than she was legally allowed. Against Daniel's advice, Colter had signed her lawyer's agreement. He had wanted peace, not years spent fighting over his money.

When Daniel shut the door behind him, Julia finished her sip of water and then said, "I heard the news about your father's passing. I'm so sorry, Colter. Grant was a wonderful man."

Colter inclined his head at her sympathy. Wanting to be anywhere but there, he pushed on, "You called this meeting, Julia. Why am I here?"

A flush crept across her face. "I wanted to say that I'm sorry for everything I've done to you."

He was so stunned by her apology that it took him a moment to process that she'd said it. Still, he hesitated, unsure of her motivation. "What are you sorry for, exactly?"

"All of it," she countered, her ears turning red. "For how I handled everything after the miscarriage. For how I just let you leave without really explaining. For how I handled the divorce. For how I took more from you than I should have. For...*everything*."

Colter leaned forward, lacing his fingers together atop the table. He gave her a level look. "Is this really why you called this meeting? Just to say you were sorry? You could have done that over the phone."

"I wanted to talk to you face-to-face," she explained gently, sounding like the woman he had once loved. "I knew you wouldn't have met me if I hadn't arranged a meeting between our lawyers. I thought about calling, but I doubted you would've answered."

"I wouldn't have," he told her honestly.

She winced, hands curving around her middle. "I deserve that."

He had trouble believing his eyes. This wasn't the cold woman he'd left in Seattle.

Through the glass boardroom door, his gaze turned to Beau, who sat in the waiting room near the receptionist. His brother was frowning at him.

Colter schooled his expression to neutral as Julia said, "When I saw you with Adeline at the charity dinner, I guess it shook me. That night I realized that we've both moved on, and yet, things are still hanging there between us."

"That was your choice," he countered. "My paying alimony was not my decision."

"I know that," she said in a small voice. "Which is

why I called this meeting." Her hand shook as she took another long sip of her water. She placed the glass back on the table. "When the lawyers come back in, you'll find out that I'm engaged to Bronson."

Colter lifted an eyebrow. "Do you want my congratulations?"

"No, of course not," she said, shaking her head slowly. "But I didn't want the alimony to stop because I'm getting remarried. I wanted it to stop because I, for once, actually did the right thing." Her breath hitched, chin quivering. "I've made mistakes. Big mistakes. But I want to start my life with Bronson doing things better." She paused to draw in a shaky breath. "I want you to be happy with Adeline."

He froze in his seat, the glass walls feeling like they were shattering around him. "You want me to be happy with Adeline?" he repeated.

She nodded. "I saw the way you two looked at each other and how in love you are, and, like I said, it shook me. It made me realize that I've become this person that even I don't like. It sickened me to think that you can't live your happiest life because I've got you chained to me. And I don't need you to be. When Bronson proposed, I felt…like it was time to finally move on. Time for us to let go of the past and be happy again."

Sighing dejectedly, he leaned back in his chair, seeing for the first time in a very long time the woman he'd thought he'd grow old with. "I think it's time for that, too," he told her.

"Good," she whispered. Then her voice broke. "I am sorry, Colter. For what I did to you. For how cruel I was."

Colter took in her wet eyes and inability to barely look at him. "You're fixing this now, Julia. You're doing the right thing, and that can only lead to something good."

She gave a small, sad smile before waving her lawyer back into the room.

It took a little over an hour to dissolve their original agreement. Colter kept wondering if his ex-wife would change her mind, but she never did, signing her name without a shake to her hand. He didn't hesitate in signing his.

When the meeting concluded, Julia rose, and Colter felt years of pain and shame vanish from his chest as he called, "Julia." She turned back to him, and he added, "Be happy."

She gave a genuine smile he hadn't seen in a long time. "You, too."

As they vanished down the hallway, passing by Beau, Daniel said, "That was unexpected."

Colter rose, pushing his chair back under the table. "It was." He offered his hand. "I can't thank you enough for being there for me through all this."

"We were glad to represent you and to know you," Daniel said, clasping Colter's hand and returning the handshake.

Colter said his final goodbyes to Daniel, and soon exited the boardroom, heading out to meet Beau.

His brother had refused to take no for an answer when he'd suggested he join Colter today. "Everything go okay?" he asked.

"It went better than okay," Colter explained, and then he gave his brother a rundown of the meeting and of Julia's change of heart.

When he finished, Beau's eyebrows were raised. "She wanted to renege on her settlement?" he asked in disbelief.

"Surprising, I know, but yes, she did," Colter answered, gesturing toward the elevator doors.

Beau followed him to the elevator. When Colter pressed the smooth button, Beau gave a low whistle. "Damn. Do you think your engagement to Adeline—"

"Yes," Colter with a laugh. "Yes, I think for some reason my moving on had Julia moving on, too."

The elevator dinged before the doors opened. Once inside, the doors shutting behind them, Beau said, "Well, I guess you owe Adeline a big thank-you."

Colter nodded, leaning against the wall as the elevator began to descend.

When the doors opened and they stepped out into the bustling main lobby of the high-rise, Beau said, "Speaking of Adeline, while I was waiting for you, scrolling through my phone, I came across something." He offered his cell phone.

Colter froze on the spot, adrenaline tingling through his body. He read the article's headline: Texas's Sexiest Bachelor Has a Brother. And He's Even Hotter!

Colter snorted at Beau. "I take offense to that headline."

His brother barked a laugh, cupping Colter's shoulder. "Sometimes the truth hurts, brother. Not much you can do about that."

Fighting against giving Beau a rude gesture, he kept reading. First noting Adeline's name at the top. The article was familiar. He'd read the same one sitting on his bed days ago on her laptop. Only this time, he wasn't the one mentioned in the article. "Did you know she was writing this article about you?" he asked his brother.

"Yeah, she called and asked my permission."

Colter jerked his head up, flabbergasted. "And you let her?"

"Of course I did," Beau said with a slight shrug. "Like I said, I could use a little viral attention."

"Trust me, you're not going to want it," Colter countered.

"I'll be fine," Beau said gently, throwing a warm smile his way. "If it means the pressure is off you, then I can handle it."

"Beau. I can't believe you did this for me."

Beau grinned. "I'm the best, I know."

Colter couldn't laugh like he normally would. He only stared at his brother, reeling from what Adeline had done. She'd kept their time together *theirs*, just like he had told her he wanted.

His head swam, confusion making his thoughts cloudy. He was unable to see a clear way forward. He looked to his brother. "What should I do?"

"Go after her, you idiot." Beau snorted. "Seems self-explanatory."

Colter carved his hand into his hair. "It's not that simple, Beau. There are huge obstacles between us. She'd have to give up a lot. Or I will. It's the only way it could work."

Beau cupped his shoulder again as people moved throughout the busy lobby and said, "This is very simple, Colter. Remove the obstacles."

New York had never looked bleaker as Adeline arrived at the cute two-story in Brooklyn after taking the subway. She stood beneath the streetlight, not even sure what had brought her to Brock's parents' house tonight. Only knowing she couldn't run anymore. Run from her pain. Run from her troubles. Run from how everything seemed entirely wrong since she'd left Devil's Bluffs. She missed Colter. His touch. His strength. His steadiness. She missed waking up with him every day. She missed cooking meals together and laughing over dinner. She missed every damn thing.

She even missed his grandmother's ring. Her finger feeling naked now.

Deal with Brock first, then see where you end up had been Nora's advice this morning after Adeline felt like the strands of her sanity were breaking away.

An older woman passed by her on the street, dragging a cart full of groceries, and gave a pleasant smile. Hoping the good mood continued, Adeline climbed the porch steps of the town house in the heart of Windsor Terrace, only a short walk from Prospect Park. When she reached the door with the lion's-head door knocker, she rapped briefly.

Loud footsteps moving closer sounded before the door whisked open.

Brock's light brown eyes widened. "Adeline," he exclaimed.

A stark contrast to Colter's ruggedness, Brock's brown hair was stylish, not a strand out of place. Clean-shaven, he wore dress pants and a white dress shirt rolled up at the sleeves, an expensive, flashy watch on his wrist. Brock embodied New York City.

"Hi, Brock," she said, the whoosh of a city bus speeding past the only movement. Until a pale-faced Brock glanced over his shoulder. When his gaze met hers again, he was stroking his dark eyebrow. "Stephanie is here, isn't she?"

Brock bounced from foot to foot. "I didn't know you were coming over."

"Actually, it's okay that she's here," Adeline said, a revelation to herself, too. It occurred to her then why she wasn't bothered—Brock no longer mattered. "Do you mind if I come in and talk to you?"

"Ah..." Brock didn't move an inch.

"I'm not about to lose my mind on both of you," Adeline said with a soft laugh, hoping to put him at ease. "I just want to talk to you, and Stephanie, too, if that's okay."

Suddenly, Stephanie popped her head into the hallway. She was the whole package, with her big brown eyes, designer clothes and long, straight brown hair. Adeline knew why Brock was drawn to her. Stephanie *was* stunningly beautiful. "Is it okay if we talk?" Adeline asked her.

"Um, yes," Stephanie said hesitantly. "Brock, let her in."

He stepped out of the way to let Adeline pass. She entered, leaving her shoes on as she followed Brock into the sitting room. A place she'd been so many times over the years, and where so many happy memories were made.

She stopped near the couch, not bothering to sit down. Once they sat next to each other, Brock taking Stephanie's hand, Adeline said, "I don't want to keep you long, but I think we both need closure."

Brock and Stephanie exchanged a long look. Then Brock said to her, "That's why I've been calling. To make all this better, for all of us."

She stared at their joined hands, searching for any pain from that. None came. *Colter...* "I couldn't have talked to you then, because there was a finality about it all that I wasn't ready to deal with," she admitted, laying everything she felt on the line. "But things are different now. Everything has changed. And I'm tired of running away from the things that hurt me." She paused to draw in a long breath and hastily continued, "The truth is, that cowboy I was photographed with, Colter, is someone I have grown incredibly close to, and a few days ago, his father passed away."

"I'm so sorry," Stephanie said, a hand on her chest.

The honest sympathy shining in her eyes only ce-
mented Adeline's next steps. "After all I've been through
lately, I've come to truly understand how short life is.
How I never truly appreciated that. How I never really
looked hard at our relationship and realized there was
obviously something wrong."

Brock remained motionless, though his shoulders
began hunching.

Before he could say anything, Adeline continued,
"You either cheated because you're lacking something
in yourself—"

Brock winced. "I—"

"Please let me finish," Adeline interjected. When he
closed his mouth, she went on. "Or you cheated because
you have something special with Stephanie. But you also
felt like you owed me something. Maybe, in your warped
way, you wanted to end things with me, but you felt bad
about hurting me."

She hesitated again, glancing to their hands, their
knuckles white, to collect her thoughts. Looking up into
both their blank faces, she added, "Seeing that you're
still together, I'm guessing that it's the latter reason you
cheated on me."

Brock released a low, slow breath. "I am sorry for
hurting you, Adeline."

She searched his eyes and found what she was look-
ing for. "I actually believe that you are, in your way. But
I didn't come here to give you forgiveness. You hurt me.
Deeply. That won't ever change."

"Then why did you come here?" Brock asked quietly.

"To tell you that if Stephanie truly is your one true
love, then I understand." Colter's kindness, his affection,
his strong character, all filled her mind. "Because if Col-

ter had come into the picture when we were together, I would have left you for him in a heartbeat."

Brock cringed, his eyes narrowing, before his expression went lax when Stephanie glanced sideways at him.

"So, I guess all that is left to say is…" She looked between Stephanie and then at Brock. "Life is too short to remain stuck in the past. I hope whatever you two were looking for, you found in each other."

Blank stares greeted her, and she smiled, her chest radiating with warmth. For the first time since she received Stephanie's call, she felt back on top of her life and free from her heartbreak. Turning on her heel, she headed for the front door.

Right when she opened it, she started, nearly walking into Brock's parents.

"Adeline," his mother exclaimed, her auburn curls bouncing atop her head. Her stumble only lasted a moment. She opened her arms in haste. "We weren't expecting you, dear."

"I made a surprise visit," Adeline explained, embracing the woman who held a special place in her heart.

Brock's father frowned beneath his thick mustache. He glanced over her shoulder at Brock and Stephanie, now entering the hallway, before addressing Adeline. "Is everything all right?"

Adeline gave a firm nod. "More than all right." She followed Brock's father's gaze, discovering Stephanie now in Brock's arms. "Brock and I got it wrong." To his mother, she added, "We did everything wrong, but somehow, it's okay that it all fell apart. We'll be happier for it in the long run." She took his teary-eyed mother back into her arms. "Just because we didn't work doesn't mean you can't keep in touch. Please do so."

His mother wiped her watery eyes. "I'd like that very much."

Feeling like a blanket of pain had suddenly been whisked off her, Adeline trotted down the porch steps, heading to the subway. Her steps felt lighter. The air felt easier to inhale.

The ping of the crosswalk sounded before Adeline hurried across the street. When she reached the curb, her cell phone rang in her purse. A quick look at the screen revealed an unknown number.

When she answered, a familiar voice she couldn't quite place asked, "Is this Adeline Harlow?"

"It is," she said, her heels clicking against the sidewalk.

A pause. "This is your father."

She froze in the middle of the sidewalk, rooted to the spot. "Eric?"

"Yes. Please don't hang up."

The air suddenly felt impossible to get into her lungs. On wobbling knees, she headed for a bench on the side of the street beneath the streetlamp. Horns honked off in the distance as she sank onto the hard wood. "I'm not hanging up" was all she could manage.

"I am so sorry for the way I handled things when you came to see me," Eric said, his voice rough. "I was taken by surprise." Another pause. Longer this time. "I'm also sorry for how I've handled everything. I made a real mess of things. But I needed you to know that when I finally got sober and got myself right, I did try to see you. By the time I went looking for you and your mother, you both had moved away. I thought, at the time, that was best. I thought you would hate me."

What he said made the world feel like it was slipping away from her. She couldn't even begin to process the meaning behind his words. But something tickled in the back of her mind. "How did you get my number?" she asked.

"Colter gave it to me," Eric explained. "Earlier today, he came by the shop... We had a chat."

"What did he say?" she asked, her heart thundering in her ears.

"He made it very clear to me that you weren't the one responsible for making this right between us. And he was right about that—this is all on me. I should have tried harder, but I was so terrified you'd hate me. I was a coward. The very worst kind." His voice blistered. "I want to make this better, Adeline. Whatever I must do— family therapy, whatever you want. I just want to get to know you. Please."

Colter's words began repeating in her mind: *There is nothing here for you. We both know that. Go home, Adeline.*

But there was something in Devil's Bluffs for her.

Colter.

His actions weren't of a man pushing her away. They were of a man protecting her. A man trying to make a safe home for her.

"Adeline. Are you there?" Eric asked.

She gulped at the air, trying to steady the ground beneath her. So much had happened in, what...an hour? Her mind raced, body heated, but somehow in all that her words came easy. "I'm here, and yes."

"Yes?"

Feeling for the first time in a very long time like her life wasn't already decided for her, but she owned her next steps. She said, "Yes, I want to get to know you, too."

Fourteen

"Thanks for getting someone to watch Austin," Colter said to Beau the following afternoon, sliding onto the chair at his kitchen table next to his mother.

Leaning against the counter, arms crossed over his chest, Beau said, "No problem. Austin was glad for the playdate with his buddy."

Colter inclined his head and then studied his mother. He noted the darkness under her eyes, but he saw the strength there, too. Beverly would live on, fiercely and happily, to honor the life she'd had with Grant. To enjoy the remainder of her days appreciating the wonderful life they'd built.

She was quite the woman.

A woman who reminded him of someone else. A woman Colter refused to miss any longer. A woman who, he'd realized, had his whole heart. If losing his father had taught him anything, it was he couldn't wait for happiness to find him—he needed to chase it.

Determined to fix where he'd gone so terribly wrong, he said, "I'm sure you are wondering why I've called you over here."

Mom set her spoon down on the saucer after stirring her tea. "We're curious, yes. What's going on?"

"I've decided to take your advice," Colter told his brother. "I'm going to remove those obstacles in my way."

"Oh?" Beau asked, eyebrows lifted. "How are you going to do that?"

Colter focused on his mother's gentle eyes and heaved a sigh, dreading what came next. "I know this comes at a terrible time." He took her hand. "But…"

"You're in love with Adeline," Mom stated casually.

Colter snorted a laugh. "I'm that obvious, huh?"

"To your mother, yes," she said, patting his arm in the way she always did to let him know everything was fine. "So, I take it, you've called us here because you've decided you need to leave home and head back to the city."

He should have known his mother would have already had this all figured out. He huffed another laugh. "Why don't we just skip the part where I talk and you just tell me what I should do next?"

Mom smiled sweetly in her motherly way. "Now, that I can't do. I can only tell what you were thinking so far."

Her love was nothing he took for granted. Her kindness made him want to do better. "I'm aware my leaving now comes at a bad time, and I'm sorry to spring this on you."

"Don't be sorry," his mother replied immediately. "Life happens. You can't hit the pause and start buttons on living your life. We lost your father, yes, but he would want us all to keep living and to be happy."

Colter agreed with a nod. "I kept thinking that I needed to be here, to do everything, to honor Dad, to do right by him. But I've come to the realization that Dad would be more disappointed if I let my chance at happiness go, to keep on in a role that is not fulfilling me and that is keeping me from Adeline."

"He would," Mom agreed.

Beau asked, "You're really thinking about moving back to the city?"

"It's the only way to have Adeline," Colter explained. He'd thought all this through. From every angle. "Her life is in New York City. It's a sacrifice I can make for her to be happy, and I will make it." At Beau's wrinkling brow, Colter pressed on, "I know taking on more work would be impossible for you. You have enough on your plate."

"It would be too much with Austin," Beau stated, carving a jerky hand through his hair.

"I know, and I wouldn't do that to you," Colter explained, running his thumb against the wood grain on the table. "Obviously, it will take more than this conversation to figure everything out, but first, I want to stay on as CEO for the ranch but lessen my workload."

Beau cocked his head. "How?"

"Hire a CFO. We'll take my salary and put it toward hiring some office staff. People to run day-to-day business on the cattle side of the ranch in my absence. And we can promote Shane to Farm Manager to run the farm, so I can return to doing what I love."

"Flying," Mom offered.

"Exactly. I miss spending more time in the air." Colter leaned back in his chair, stretching out his tight legs beneath the table. "I reached out to my old employer, and they've offered me a position with their New York City affiliate. They'll pay me well. I don't need the money I'd make here as CEO."

Mom paused to consider, taking another drink from her teacup, the floral scent infusing the air. "Okay, but what does this mean for the ranch, then?"

Colter took his mother's free hand in his, holding tight. "Like I said, I don't want to give up my position overseeing the ranch, but heading up the company was Dad's dream. He did it well. I want to honor that—keep it going in the Ward name—but it's not my dream. It's never been my dream."

Mom paused as she set her teacup back on the saucer. Then her voice cracked. "Your father didn't want either of you to give up your dreams to take over the ranch. He only wanted you to be happy. So, if moving back to the city and flying is what you want, Colter, then please, do that."

He noted her high chin but spotted the slight waver in her expression, too. He pressed his other hand atop their joined hands. "I will always be involved with the ranch, but ever since I stepped into Dad's role, I've been thinking I couldn't have it all. But I can. *We* can. We simply have to make some changes and hire the right people."

"You'll still oversee the cattle side of the ranch?" Beau asked.

"Yes," Colter replied. "If all goes as I think it will, I can fly home for any important meetings and be in control of the direction of the farm and any big decisions. But I suspect most of my business can be done remotely." He looked to his mother, taking in her falling expression. "I also thought, if I can somehow get Adeline to forget that she just ended a relationship and get her to love me, we could split our time between the city and here, coming back on weekends and any other time we can. Not paying Julia alimony anymore would make that doable now."

Mom smiled, teary-eyed. "That would make me very happy."

"Good," Colter said, squeezing her hand. "Please take what I'm saying to heart. I don't want to walk away from the ranch. I want our land and business to stay under Ward protection, but I need to make these choices for myself."

Mom held on to him just as tight. "You should make these choices. You've done so much for your father and for me. You deserve to be happy." She watched him closely, then patted his hand. "But you're right, this isn't something that will happen overnight."

Beau's gaze was distant, thoughtful, as he scraped a hand against his jawline. "I suppose we'll have to build office space if we're hiring staff."

"I thought perhaps near the main road, where that patch of land never seems to grow a damn thing," Colter offered.

"That could work," Mom said before releasing Colter's hands to sip her tea.

Beau gave a nod of approval. "I like this idea. I think it's good, and I think bringing in fresh eyes with new ideas could only help the ranch. I'll help wherever I can."

"Thank you," Colter said to his brother. "I know this is a big undertaking that will take some time to get resolved." To his mother, he added, "I'm still here. For you. For the ranch. No matter what."

"I know that," she said with an affectionate grin. Her gaze fell to the full duffel bag near the back door. "What's your plan now?"

"I'm flying to New York City tonight and will do my best to convince Adeline that she loves me, too."

"That girl loves you," Mom said. "We could all see it."

"Let's hope you're right" was Colter's only reply.

"Come on, then, Beau," said Mom, slowly rising from her seat. She placed her teacup in the dishwasher. "Let's get out of your brother's way."

Colter rose, and before his mother headed for the door, he embraced her. "You'd tell me the truth if this upset you, right?" he asked.

"I'm not upset, honey," she said, cupping his face, rubbing his cheeks like she had for as long as he could remember. "I adore Adeline. Nothing would make me happier than making her a part of our family." His arms tightened around her when her voice trembled. "The one thing I know that I got right in life was loving your father. When you have true love, a great love, life has meaning." She brought his face down and kissed both his cheeks. "Following your heart only leads to good things. I'm proud of you."

He hadn't thought he needed his mom's approval, but a heavy weight on his shoulders eased with her support. "Thank you."

Beau took Colter into a rough hug. Then he let go and said, "Just don't say something stupid and mess it all up."

"I'll try not to." Colter snorted, following them to the front door.

Outside on the porch, Beau trotted down the steps, waiting at the bottom to hold Mom's hand as she walked down, when Mom suddenly stopped.

"Oh, I forgot to mention," she said, glancing at Colter. "Do you still have your grandmother's ring?"

"Yeah, of course," Colter replied. "Want me to get it?"

"Hmm." Mom's smile slowly built. "I think it's best if you keep it."

Seated in the back seat of the Uber, Adeline said into her phone to Nora, "I think I'm going to puke." Ever since she got off the phone with her father last night, she'd been on autopilot.

She'd used a good chunk of her savings to take a private flight, using the same company that Colter had worked with before, to get to Dallas fast. Then an Uber got her the rest of the way, and she'd been on the phone with Nora ever since.

The Uber driver glanced in horror at her in the rearview mirror. She waved him off. "Don't worry, I won't puke in your car."

With a relieved look, he glanced back at the road.

"That poor driver," Nora said with a laugh. "And, dude, let's be real here. You have faced Brock and your father and have come out stronger and happier for it. Those things were both hard as hell. What you have with Colter is easy. This is good. You deserve this. Relax."

"I do deserve this, don't I?"

"Yes, you do. So stop almost puking, lift up your beautiful chin and go and get your cowboy."

Adeline smiled—a real smile that seemed to feel so honest now that she was back in Devil's Bluffs. New York had felt different when she'd gone back. Like nothing made sense there anymore. Here, everything seemed... *right*.

The Uber driver turned into the driveway, and Adeline spotted Beau's truck driving away from Colter's house and down the road. Her stomach fluttered with butterflies as she said, "We're here. I need to go."

"Call me after. Good luck," Nora said.

"I will. Love you."

"Love you, too."

Adeline ended the call and then asked the Uber driver, "Can you please go faster?"

The driver hit the gas, speeding up the driveway, and

she tapped her fingers against her twitchy leg. Until she saw Colter's truck in the driveway. He was there... and she was... Well, she hadn't quite figured that part out yet.

When they reached the porch, the car's tires skidded to a halt. "Thank you," Adeline said, taking her overnight bag with her as she exited the Uber.

"Enjoy your evening, miss," the driver said.

She slammed the door shut, and as he drove off down the driveway, she walked closer to the house. Until she stopped, pressing her hand against her chest, convinced she was having heart palpitations. Through the big front window, Colter was heading toward the back door, carrying a duffel bag.

"Are you...leaving..." She threw the strap of her bag over her shoulder and ran as fast as she could muster around the house, spotting him heading toward his helicopter.

Breathless, she yelled, "Where are you going?"

He stiffened. Then he glanced over his shoulder. Like he couldn't believe she was standing there, he dropped his bag and moved closer, but not as close as she wanted him. Not nearly close enough. The distance between them felt cold...empty.

"Where are you going?" she repeated.

"To the city," he said, statue-still. "To you."

"You hate the city."

"I love you more."

All the guards around her heart shattered. "You love me?"

"Madly." He took a step toward her, warming the air between them. "Deeply." And another step. Until he stood directly in front of her. "I am in love with you, Adeline, and I don't want to live without you."

Her breath hitched. Tears welled in her eyes. "I love you, too."

"Now *that* is exactly what I wanted to hear." He charged forward and gathered her in his arms as she wrapped her thighs around his legs.

The dry air brushed across her as his mouth met hers, and she gave everything she had to him. She wasn't thinking hesitation or lust—she was only thinking about the rightness of the moment. How it didn't matter if everything made sense between them. Somehow, someway, this was going to all work out, because they were meant to be together.

She vaguely felt him moving, but his sizzling kisses never broke away. Not until he reached the back door to open it and kicked it shut behind them. While he carried her to the bedroom, she placed butterfly kisses on his mouth, his jaw, his neck, where she nipped a little.

He groaned deep, then tossed her on the mattress. She laughed, bouncing against it, but stopped when he hovered over her. Intensity stared back at her. "How are you here?"

"Well, Eric called," she told him, cupping his handsome face, scraping her fingers against the scruff. "He told me what you said to him. I guess I realized that while it is scary for me to stay in Devil's Bluffs, and my life is very uncertain here, there is also nowhere else I'd rather be."

He slowly shook his head, pulling her up to sitting. He went down to one knee in front of her. "I've already talked to my family. We're hiring staff to handle the cattle portion of the farm. I'm moving to New York City."

"I mean, you are more than welcome to move there if you want," she said with a slight shrug. "But earlier today, my boss and I came to an arrangement that I would freelance for her. I also accepted the position as editor for the *Devil's Bluffs Chronicle*, since Waylon is retiring."

His eyes widened. "You're moving here?"

"No, I'm not moving here," she corrected. "I *moved* here. Tonight." Of course, then she realized she'd spoken too soon. "I'll need to go back to New York City to pack up all my stuff and ship it here. Then sell my condo. But my heart...it lives here, in Devil's Bluffs."

"With me?"

She cupped his face again. "With you."

"Adeline," Colter murmured, resting his forehead against hers. "I was ready to uproot my whole life, and here you are offering me everything. Changing everything. Like you did from the first night I saw you at the bar."

"Changing everything for the better," she said. "I know why my mom left here, why she needed to move away. But this is my home. It's always been my home. And I want to get to know Eric. I want to see where all this takes me."

"I'll be right at your side to do that, too."

"I know," she said, her chest swelling with possibilities. "I thought, maybe, we could go to New York City on the weekends sometimes to visit Nora and my mother."

"We can go as often as you want," he said, adamant. "Do whatever you want."

She laughed, stroking his face. "Better be careful. You're offering me the world, and I just might take you up on it."

"I will give you everything," he said. "And then I will give you even more. You made me believe in love again when I thought that was impossible."

She felt breathless, weightless and everything in between as she said, "You made me fall in love with you after the greatest betrayal. Though, to think on it, maybe I've always loved you."

Emotion-packed eyes held hers as his hand lowered to his pocket, and then he put his grandmother's ring on her knee. "I took too long to notice you, but I won't ever not see you again. This ring never should have come off your finger. What do you say, New York—will you marry me for real?"

Her finger tingled as he slid the ring back onto her hand. What had been missing was now whole again. "Yes, Colter, absolutely, yes. I'll marry you."

Intensity and happiness and so many other things she could never name flashed through his expression as he sealed his mouth across hers. He swept her away in a kiss that was more that affection, it was a promise, one she felt weave around her.

Frantically, he removed her clothing, piece by piece, and she removed his until there was nothing between them. Only skin against skin, and all the love between them. He backed away only once, to sheathe himself in a condom, before his kiss turned hot and wicked as he laid her out on the bed.

"Not tonight," she told him. "Tonight, I want to have you." She squirmed out from under him until he allowed her to push him onto his back. Staring down at the man who'd stolen her heart so early in her life, and then again when she wasn't looking for love at all, she straddled his waist and gazed upon him. His handsome face. His mouthwatering, muscular physique. "This might end badly for me, you know," she said, wiggling her hips to find the tip of him.

"How is that?" He groaned as she sank down on him, gripping her hips tight.

She brushed her puckered nipples against his chest. "I'm going to be the most hated woman in Devil's Bluffs." He moaned, his eyes shutting as she moved slowly, taking him in, inch by inch. "I have taken Texas's sexiest bachelor off the market...for real."

"Let them be jealous." He lifted his head off the bed, capturing her mouth. His hands roamed every inch of her until he cupped her breasts, massaging them.

She couldn't think as sensation overloaded her. Touched by him, filled by him, she couldn't talk anymore. Not as she pressed her hands on his chest and shifted against him, back and forth, overwhelmed by how amazingly he stretched her. How deep he was. How his hands claimed her. How his touch invaded deep into her heart.

Pleasure began blinding her as she tipped her head back, bouncing on him, his gripping hands helping her move faster, harder until she found a rhythm that brought the intensity they both needed. His groans followed the sound of skin slapping, mirrored by her own moans, the scent of their sex driving her higher.

She moved harder, faster yet, needing *more*.

Then she was staring into smoldering, half-lidded eyes as he fisted her hair, bringing her mouth down to his. He kissed her with a passion she hadn't known before. A statement no man had ever placed on her body.

She knew, with absolute certainty, that from this night on, he was hers and she was his.

Like he knew it, too, he growled against her mouth, an animalistic sound that spoke to every feminine bit of her soul. With his free hand, he grabbed a fistful of her bottom and thrust up from below.

Just like that, time stopped clicking.

And they hung, on the edge, staring into each other's souls, until their love blew their worlds apart.

Fifteen

Standing in the kitchen, listening to Blake Shelton on the radio, Adeline placed the drying towel back onto the stove's rack. One month had gone by since the night Colter slid his grandmother's ring back onto her finger. One night that had changed everything for the better. The first couple weeks had been a hectic mess and left Adeline busier than she had ever imagined possible. With the help of her mother and Nora, they'd packed up her condo in three days and shipped all her belongings to Devil's Bluffs.

Now Colter's house didn't feel like just his house anymore. Her stuff was all there, too. He'd gladly taken some of his things away so she could hang her favorite pieces of art and decorate the space to put her touches on things, too. Devil's Bluffs finally felt like home.

Her home.

She'd started the process of taking over for Waylon, but his retirement was a few months off, so she had time to get settled. And she had already written a few freelance pieces for the blog. But it wasn't only her life settling—Colter's was as well. Every day when he came home from flying the helicopter, he arrived with a big smile. The same smile that had been there ever since they'd hired a CFO and three other employees to run the business side of the Devil's Bluffs Ranch, plus promoted Shane.

Everything had somehow settled into place, and life was...*good*.

As Colter finished drying a pot, Adeline focused on the one part of her life that was the hardest. She smiled at Nora on FaceTime as her best friend complained about the current employer who contracted her. "She can't be that bad," Adeline said.

Nora gaped. "She is worse than you could probably imagine. I have never met a person so into herself in my life. It's unbelievable. Seriously, she can talk about herself for an hour straight. I timed it."

"An hour, for real?"

"Yes," Nora exclaimed. "An hour. Then, no matter what anyone is talking about, somehow we end up talking about her again. She's got all these conspiracy theories she believes. When someone tries to disagree, she is horrible to them. Honestly, I think she might be the devil."

Behind her, Colter chuckled. Which abruptly ended as the front door burst open.

Beau bolted inside, slamming the door shut. "You owe me," he growled. When he turned around to lean against the door, his face was bright red, his nostrils flaring from obvious exertion. "You owe me so bad."

Colter relaxed with a laugh, hanging the drying cloth next to Adeline's. "I told you that you never should have gone viral on purpose."

"I had no idea it would be this bad." Beau glared. "You *both* owe me. This is crazy."

Nora snorted a laugh.

Reminded that her best friend was still on FaceTime, Adeline said, "I'm actually really glad you're here, Beau," she told her future brother-in-law. "Since you're Colter's best man for the wedding—" they were in the planning stages of a small, personal ceremony "—and Nora's my maid of honor, you two should probably meet." She turned her phone around, and Beau's brows furrowed.

Eyes narrowed, he closed the distance and snatched the phone away. "What was that laugh about?" he asked Nora.

Adeline nibbled her lip, holding in her laughter now. If Beau thought Nora would back down when pressed, he was dead wrong.

As expected, Nora said, "My snort laugh, you mean?"

"Yeah, *that*." Beau's chest heaved.

Nora didn't hesitate for a single moment. "Because I find what you said hilarious. Seriously, you have available women chasing after you and you're unhappy about this. What is wrong with you?"

Beau lifted his brows. "What would you do if you were in my position?"

"I'd enjoy the ride," Nora said, and Adeline knew she meant that. Nora was wild and free and never settled down. Adeline couldn't imagine her ever being in a serious relationship. "Free dinners. Coffee dates. Fun nights out. Oh, what torture you must be enduring."

Beau's nostrils flared again. "Then you make a photograph of yourself go viral."

"I can't," Nora said dryly. "I'm not nearly as hot as you."

One eyebrow slowly lifted. A beat passed between them. As though, for the first time, Beau had actually gotten a good look at her. "The problem here is it's not only women hunting me down, it's reporters." He finally handed the cell phone to Adeline, and said to Colter, "I want to get out of town for a while."

"It's that bad?" Colter asked.

Beau nodded. "Can Austin stay with you two for a couple weeks? You'll have to take him to school and handle lunches and his baseball games, but I can't allow him to deal with this nonsense. He can't understand why there's people always following us."

Colter sidled next to Adeline, leaning against the island. "Yeah, of course he can stay. Where are you going?"

Beau gestured at Adeline's cell phone. "I'll let you know later."

Adeline withheld her laughter.

"Just being a voice of reason," Nora piped up. "But reporters never back down unless given a reason to."

"They won't have a choice," Beau spat. "I'm leaving tonight."

Nora was grinning. Adeline fought her smile. Her best friend was the worst kind of instigator.

"I wouldn't recommend that," Nora offered.

"Why is that?" Beau glared at the phone.

"Because they'll hunt you down wherever you go," Nora said dryly. Then she shrugged, "At least that's what I'd do." And being one of the best researchers Adeline knew, Nora would find him, too. She uncovered buried secrets no one else could find.

Beau closed the distance again and held out his hand for the phone. Once Adeline handed it to him, he said to Nora, "They will never find me."

Nora grinned. "They will, believe me. You should re-think your strategy."

He made a noise in the back of his throat.

"Are you always this grumpy?" she asked.

Beau frowned at the phone and harrumphed before he handed Adeline the device and left, slamming the front door behind him.

"That went well," Adeline said, lifting the phone back to her face. "I can tell already you two are going to be the best of friends."

"Men are silly," Nora said.

"Man here," Colter called.

"You're Adeline's man. That's different," Nora said with a sheepish smile. "I need to get going, but keep all the wedding plans coming. I'm loving everything you're sending me. Are you still planning on coming to New York City this weekend to see your mom?"

"That's the plan," Adeline answered.

"Great," Nora replied. "Then let's make sure we do something fun on the town. Colter needs to get some city nightlife into him."

"I'm not sure that sounds appealing," Colter muttered.

Nora either didn't hear him or wasn't paying atten-tion, since she added, "All right, you two, lots of love. Toodles."

"Love you back." Adeline sighed when the screen went black. "That was a disaster," she said to Colter.

"Not a total disaster," Colter said, tugging her close, wrapping her in the warmth of his hold. "Beau seemed to not mind Nora."

"You cannot be serious," she gasped. "I've never seen him be so snippy with anyone."

Colter pressed a kiss on her forehead before he shrugged. "He's obviously in a mood over being hounded by reporters and available women, but he also backed down. Beau never backs down. Trust me, I know, he's been the annoying younger brother most of my life."

Adeline considered and then shook her head slowly. "Nora's right—men are silly."

He tapped her nose, grinning. "Women make us that way." Holding her tight around the waist, he watched her a moment, his gaze narrowing on her mouth, and only then did she realize she was nibbling her lip. "What's wrong?" he asked.

"Maybe we should hold off on planning the wedding until Beau is back and everything has calmed down."

"That is a hard no from me," Colter countered, caging her between him and the kitchen counter with his arms braced on either side of her. "Plan away—" he dropped his mouth close to hers "—because I'm already growing impatient."

"Impatient for what?" she asked, running her hands up his strong arms, flexing beneath her touch.

He brushed his lips against hers. "For you to be my wife."

She slid her hands up his squared chest. "Is that all you want?" she rasped.

"Oh, I want much more than that." He grinned, weakening her knees in a way she hoped he'd always weaken them.

"Good—you are my crush, after all." She angled her head back, leaning up, offering herself.

"Not your crush," he corrected, brushing his lips across hers. "I am yours and only *yours*."

"And I am irrevocably yours." She smiled against his lips. "I love you, Colter."

"Love you back, New York."

* * * * *

COMING SOON!

We really hope you enjoyed reading this book. If you're looking for more romance, be sure to head to the shops when new books are available on

Thursday 8th December

Newport Community Learning & Libraries

MILLS & BOON

THE HEART OF ROMANCE

A ROMANCE FOR EVERY READER

ODERN
Prepare to be swept off your feet by sophisticated, sexy and seductive heroes, in some of the world's most glamourous and romantic locations, where power and passion collide.

STORICAL
Escape with historical heroes from time gone by. Whether your passion is for wicked Regency Rakes, muscled Vikings or rugged Highlanders, awaken the romance of the past.

EDICAL
Set your pulse racing with dedicated, delectable doctors in the high-pressure world of medicine, where emotions run high and passion, comfort and love are the best medicine.

ue Love
Celebrate true love with tender stories of heartfelt romance, from the rush of falling in love to the joy a new baby can bring, and a focus on the emotional heart of a relationship.

Desire
Indulge in secrets and scandal, intense drama and plenty of sizzling hot action with powerful and passionate heroes who have it all: wealth, status, good looks…everything but the right woman.

EROES
Experience all the excitement of a gripping thriller, with an intense romance at its heart. Resourceful, true-to-life women and strong, fearless men face danger and desire - a killer combination!

To see which titles are coming soon, please visit

millsandboon.co.uk/nextmonth

LET'S TALK
Romance

For exclusive extracts, competitions
and special offers, find us online:

 facebook.com/millsandboon

@MillsandBoon

 @MillsandBoonUK

Get in touch on 01413 063232

For all the latest titles coming soon, visit
millsandboon.co.uk/nextmonth

Also by Jules Bennett

The Rancher's Heirs
Twin Secrets
Claimed by the Rancher

Taming the Texan
A Texan for Christmas

Angel's Share
When the Lights Go Out...
Second Chance Vows
Snowed In Secrets

Discover more at millsandboon.co.uk

USA T... ...as ublished over sixty books and never tires of writing nappy endings. Writing strong heroines and alpha heroes is Jules's favourite way to spend her workdays. Jules hosts weekly competitions on her Facebook fan page and loves chatting with readers on Twitter, Facebook and via email through her website. Stay up-to-date by signing up for her newsletter at julesbennett.com

Stacey Kennedy is a *USA TODAY* bestselling author who writes romances full of heat, heart and happily-ever-afters. Stacey lives with her husband and two children in southwestern Ontario. Most days, you'll find her enjoying the outdoors or venturing into the forest with her horse. Stacey's just as happy curled up indoors, where she writes surrounded by her lazy dogs. She believes that sexy books about hot cowboys can fix any bad day. But wine and chocolate help too.

**The item should be returned or renewed
by the last date stamped below.**

Dylid dychwelyd neu adnewyddu'r eitem erbyn
y dyddiad olaf sydd wedi'i stampio isod.

BETTWS

1 9 DEC 2022

5   JAN 2023

1 2 APR 2023

To renew visit / Adnewyddwch ar
www.newport.gov.uk/libraries